A PHIL RODRIQUEZ NOVEL

A Murder Too Close

Penny Mickelbury

FIVE STAR
A part of Gale, Cengage Learning

Detroit • New York • San Francisco • New Haven, Conn • Waterville, Maine • London

Set in 11 pt. Plantin.
Printed on permanent paper.

LIBRARY OF CONGRESS CATALOGING-IN-PUBLICATION DATA

Mickelbury, Penny, 1948–
A murder too close : a Phil Rodriquez book / Penny Mickelbury. — 1st ed.
p. cm.
ISBN-13: 978-1-59414-712-8 (hardcover : alk. paper)
ISBN-10: 1-59414-712-4 (hardcover : alk. paper)
1. Private investigators—New York (State)—New York—Fiction. 2. Arson investigation—Fiction. 3. Arab Americans—Crimes against—Fiction. 4. September 11 Terrorist Attacks, 2001—Social aspects—New York (State)—New York—Fiction. 5. Lower East Side (New York, N.Y.)—Fiction. I. Title.
PS3563.I3517M87 2008
813′.54—dc22 2008031531

First Edition. First Printing: November 2008.
Published in 2008 in conjunction with Tekno Books and Ed Gorman.

Printed in the United States of America
1 2 3 4 5 6 7 12 11 10 09 08

For my friends Pat Cummings and Genie Cooper
and for all New Yorkers:
You're still standing.

Chapter One

I like to think of myself as a normal, regular guy, in the sense that I don't consider myself unusual or special in any way. I'm a second-generation New Yorican—a native New Yorker of Puerto Rican ancestry. I'm thirty-something, a shade under six feet, in excellent physical condition, have all my teeth and most of my hair, which I wear short in the summer and long in the winter. Simply put, I wouldn't stand out in a crowd. Not a New York City crowd. Maybe in Portland or in Des Moines, but we're not talking about those places. We're talking NYC, the Big Apple, where I earn my living, which may be the one area in which I stray from the norm: I'm a licensed private investigator. Not necessarily a big deal—there are thousands of us in New York State, most of that number in New York City—but a step, perhaps, removed from the run-of-the-mill kinda guy. Where I choose to practice my trade—Manhattan's Lower East Side—also may, in the estimation of some, mark me as unusual, but I wouldn't have it any other way. This is my home turf: The East Village, Alphabet City, Little Italy, the Bowery, Chinatown. I know and understand the people who live here, in the narrow buildings crowded and bunched together on the narrow, crooked streets, fanned by the breezes of the East River, and they know and understand me. It's a good match. Usually.

I looked across the desk at the man who was asking a favor of me. People know that I do favors on occasion. Not every job requires a contract and a retainer. A small favor, done out of kindness or respect, can generate a lot of goodwill, which can be more valuable than money in my business. Probably in a lot of different kinds of businesses. However, what Sam Epstein was asking me to do was not a favor, it was an act of professional suicide, and that's exactly what I told him.

"You're not asking for a favor, Sam. You're asking me to stick my nose where it definitely does not belong, and maybe damaging my reputation along the way."

"How does this damage your rep, Rodriquez? Tell me that!" Sam slapped the desk top with the palm of his hand and it made a sharp, cracking sound. He'd always been an emotional, excitable guy. I'd known him since junior high school, which is how and why I knew this about him. We weren't friends or pals back then, just what today, I suppose, people would call associates. He'd worked in his family's dry cleaning store and one of my jobs as a kid was to ferry my grandfathers' uniforms back and forth to the cleaners. Both *abuelitos* were doormen at high-rent West Side apartment buildings, and were expected to look as elegant as the people for whom they opened limousine and building doors and picked up and delivered packages. The Epstein Dry Cleaners and Laundry was a neighborhood mainstay, opened by his grandparents and now operated by Sam and a cousin. So, like I said, we weren't pals but I've known the guy for more than twenty years, so when he called and said he wanted a word, I didn't hesitate. I should have remembered, though, how he was and, given that, I should have known that the favor Sam Epstein would ask wouldn't be something simple and uncomplicated like getting a building inspector or a traffic warden to lighten up or look the other way.

"I know the kind of strain you're under, Sam . . ."

He cut me off. "Then help me out, here, Rodriquez. Please."

The helpless pleading in his voice almost got to me. Sam's older sister and only surviving sibling was killed in the attacks on the World Trade Center. She was a secretary, working for a temp agency, assigned that one day to an office near the top of the second tower. She left an eight-year-old daughter who now was fourteen and who became Sam's responsibility on that awful September day. He could have refused and sent the girl to Florida to live with his parents, her grandparents, who gladly would have taken her, but Sasha had visited Miami Shores and that wasn't the place for her; she was a New York City kid to the bone. So she and Sam shared the large rent-controlled apartment in Stuyvesant Town where the family had lived for more than forty years, and things had moved along smoothly—"under the circumstances"—Sam said, until last month, when Sasha began a friendship with the son of the owners of an Indian restaurant. It was this friendship that had Sam's already ruddy face looking like it burned with fever. It was this friendship that sparked Sam's call to me.

"Think back to when we were that age, Sam. How often did we fall in love? Not to mention out of love, for that matter."

"It's not the same thing!"

"Sure it is . . ."

He cut me off again. "Kids these days do stuff we didn't even know about when we were that age." He looked as if the thought made him want to throw up.

"You're right about that part. But you're not asking me to make sure they're not getting it on in her bedroom when you're at work. You want me to, I believe the word you used was 'discourage,' the boy from seeing Sasha. And the reason you want him 'discouraged' is because of his race. And that's racist and I won't do it, Sam. Not for you or anybody else. And since you asked, that's how it would hurt my reputation. If word got out that I sided with anybody against anybody else based on race or color, I'd be finished in this neighborhood!" I was getting a bit emotional myself at the thought.

"We're Jewish, Rodriquez!"

"No shit, Epstein," I said as dryly as I could, hoping the absurdity of it would lighten the moment, but the irony was wasted. Sam wasn't in the mood to be lightened. If his face got any redder he'd look like one of those cartoon characters with smoke coming out of his ears.

"Look what they did to our country, and now you want to let them destroy my family! Or what's left of it! Frankie, his name is supposed to be!" The way Sam said the name made it sound like a curse, or some other disgusting thing. "Those people, they don't have names like 'Frankie'! It's probably Farouk or Farsi or some damn thing like that!"

This had gone too far, way beyond excitable and emotional. This was getting close to Line In The Sand territory for me. I got up, walked around the desk, and sat on the chair next to Sam. I put my hand on his shoulder and squeezed. He looked at me and the hurt and fear and sadness and anger and loss in his eyes were more than one human being should have to bear. But the reality was that he wasn't the only one so burdened. I remembered other eyes: Jill Mason's and Carmine Aiello's and Arlene Edwards' and Bert Calle's and my own Yolanda Maria's. I had learned from those people that while hurt, fear, sadness, anger, and loss can really kick your ass and might even bring you to your knees, you don't have to bleed to death from the beating and that you can stand up straight again if you have the will to do so. "Sam, the boy and his family are, more than likely, Hindu, not Muslim. And believe me, his parents are as dismayed as you are by this thing."

He gave me the kind of look that called my intelligence into question, and when I realized why, I had to laugh. "Don't tell me, Sam: You can't imagine how some lowly Hindu people would have the nerve not to be happy to have their son dating Princess Sasha Heller." I stood up. It was time for Sam to leave.

Thankfully, he took the hint and got to his feet. "Tell you what, Sam. I'll check the boy out," I said, leading Sam to the door, "make certain he's not a pimp or a drug dealer or a religious fanatic. In the meantime, the smart thing to do, I'm telling you, is ignore the kids and let the thing run its course. You should be trying to get some free meat samosas and they should be trying to get some free dry cleaning out of this situation while it lasts."

"I'm just trying to do the right thing is all."

"I know you are, Sam." We were at the door but I didn't open it. "Speaking of doing the right thing, what about Sasha's father? I thought he was going to share some of the responsibility of taking care of her." I knew Jack Heller, too, from way back. His family had owned a deli on Avenue A that saved its old, spoiled meat and bread to sell to Puerto Ricans and Blacks. The deli went under before Old Man Heller realized that his neighborhood's hue was changing. By the time he'd caught on, it was too late—either to change his ways or for anybody to care whether he did or not.

Sam shrugged. "He's got a new family now. He wanted to concentrate on them, he said, but I think the new wife didn't want any reminders of his former life. Besides, Sasha doesn't really like him all that much. Never did . . . even before . . . you know."

I knew. I opened the door and let Sam out into the frosty early March night, withholding from him my thoughts about his former brother-in-law. The woman Jack Heller lived with wasn't his wife and her children weren't his children and what a useless piece of shit he was that he couldn't bother to travel fifteen or twenty blocks to see his own daughter whose mother had perished in the most horrible way. Truly he was his father's son. Then I thought that Sasha Heller probably had pretty good judgment for a fourteen-year-old if she didn't care for her father. And if she did like the Indian kid, Frankie, I didn't expect I'd find that he was a closet lowlife. Or a religious fanatic who, in my book, were a dangerous breed no matter what religion or god they were pushing.

I stood in the doorway watching the traffic and the people. Both street and sidewalk were clogged, but at least the people were moving. All the traffic could do was emit exhaust smoke and horn blares and wait for lights to change from green to yellow to red and back again. I shivered in the cold air and finally closed the door. I locked it, pulled down the shade, and turned off the front lights. Yolanda wouldn't return to the office tonight—she had taken her mother to a doctor's appointment—and we didn't get many walk-in clients. People who wanted to see us, like Sam Epstein, usually called first and arranged to come early in the morning or late in the evening because, like Sam, they wanted to guarantee a measure of privacy. People wanting or needing the services of a private investigator usually didn't want their friends and neighbors privy to that fact.

I stood in the middle of the floor and surveyed the large, spacious room that was the office of Phillip Rodriquez Investigations. It occupied the ground floor of the three-story, narrow tenement building that my partner, Yolanda Maria Aguierre, and I owned. It was an open space and felt more like a living room than an office. That had been Yo's idea—to make clients feel as relaxed and comfortable as possible since whatever had brought them to us in the first place most likely was anything but relaxing and comfortable. The floor was carpeted and there were a couple of sofas and easy chairs and side tables, along with the requisite desks and chairs. At the back of the room, behind a series of Shoji screens and newly installed sliding doors, were a fully equipped kitchen and full bathroom at one end, and Yolanda's computers at the other. She had three of them and a new laptop that went everywhere she went. I could safely and effectively operate one of them. The others scared me silly. But if a scrap of information existed about anyone or anything at any time or place, Yolanda could—and eventually would—find it on one of her computers.

I went to my desk, sat down, and turned on the gooseneck lamp. It cast a mellow glow on the darkened room and I felt as at home as if in my own living room. I took a notebook out of my desk drawer and wrote down, word for word, everything that Sam Epstein and I had said to each other, and included my thoughts and feelings about what he wanted me to do. Then I lowered all the window shades, turned down the heat, put on my coat, hat, scarf, and gloves, set the alarm, and headed out into the night. Traffic was still crawling along on both the crosstown and uptown-downtown streets and it still was cold. March for sure was the cruelest month. Temperatures had begun to moderate just enough so that the more optimistic among us would begin to anticipate the arrival of spring, but not enough so that anyone would be foolish enough to leave home without hat, scarf, and gloves. March was the month in which winter held on with both fists, determined not to let go. March was the month in which the wise among us had learned to expect a blizzard before flowers, green grass, and heat from the sun made it to town.

I started the trek home, the conversation with Sam still ping-ponging around in my head, my brain walls registering every bounce. What I was thinking and feeling—and wondering and worrying about—was what could have given Sam Epstein the notion that I would hurt a fifteen-year-old boy? For that, in truth, was what he wanted me to do. That's what "discourage" him really meant: Break something on the boy's body. And the more I thought about it, the madder I got. How could he think I'd do something like that? I'd never been a bully, as a kid or as a man. Sure, I could and did and would hold my own, and with my fists if it came to that, but I'd never in my life started a fight and I'd certainly never fought anybody smaller, weaker, or younger than myself. Grown men did not hurt children or women.

"You son of a bitch." I'd spoken the words out loud and space automatically cleared around me on the crowded sidewalk, but nobody stopped or gave me more than a passing glance. New Yorkers. You gotta love 'em. Or not. But the extra space on the sidewalk allowed me to change direction, intention, and plans. Instead of heading home and ordering dinner delivered from my favorite neighborhood deli, I would eat Indian tonight. There was no need for me to rush home. My romantic interest, Consuela deLeon, a social worker at Beth Israel Hospital, worked the late shift tonight—not off until eleven—after which she'd go home to the Bronx. So, I could go eyeball young Frankie, satisfy myself that Sam was being hysterical, and justify my anger. I didn't know the name of Frankie's family's restaurant, but I knew where it was. I'd never eaten there—meat samosas were the only thing I really liked at Indian restaurants and if not for Yolanda and now Connie, I'd never have occasion to enter one. But being a New Yorican, I could always eat rice, and Indian cuisine always came with a side of rice.

The wood smoke smell that permeated the Manhattan air in the winter was a comforting presence on my walk; it calmed me and helped dissipate the anger that had built inside me against Sam Epstein. I could imagine myself at home, sacked out on the couch, the TV on but muted, Latin jazz on the radio, the fire roaring, as I waited for Connie's call. She always called on her late nights, to let me know she'd arrived home safely. We'd talk while she unwound and released the stress of the day, and there was plenty of it since she counseled victims of various forms of sexual trauma and abuse, and when we hung up, I'd always drop immediately off to sleep. So warmed was I by my fantasy that I almost forgot to be damn near frozen from the fifteen-block walk to the Indian restaurant, so when the scream of sirens split the air close enough to hurt my ears, I was quickly slapped back into reality. Immediately I noticed that the smoke smell was heavier, denser, and more acrid, and that the energy on the sidewalk had shifted. People were on alert, on guard. There was a fire, and it was nearby. I allowed myself to be carried by the crowd's energy along the sidewalk toward whatever was happening, my gloved hands hard against my ears in a futile attempt to protect against the undulating wail of the sirens.

The crowd suddenly halted, and so did I, behind a police barricade. Thick black smoke rose rapidly. I looked where everybody else was looking and saw sky-bound flames, heard the fire roar and crackle like an angry living thing, and I knew that the arson investigators had a long night ahead of them. A quick break in the crowd provided me with a glimpse of the fire. It took a couple of seconds for what I'd glimpsed to register, and I pushed and shoved my way to the front. The Taste of India was, in fire department parlance, fully involved. Like most businesses in this part of town, stores and restaurants were ground level, with residences above. The flames from the Taste of India had penetrated the restaurant ceiling and invaded the apartment above. Ladders from two trucks were extended toward the upper floors even as the powerful streams of water were aimed at the equally powerful flames. I, like everybody in the crowd, was mesmerized by what was unfolding before us. I had been a New York City cop for four years before turning private, so I felt comfortable saying that cops could call themselves the City's Finest all they wanted. Firefighters truly were this city's—any city's—bravest. Most cops, myself included, would rather face a fool with a gun any day than rush head first—and deliberately—into a burning building. I could see them inside the restaurant now, and inside the upstairs apartments, resembling hulking movie monsters in their masks and protective gear. I said a silent prayer that no life would be lost tonight, especially not fifteen-year-old Frankie's, then I forced my way back through the crowd. I didn't want or need to watch further.

The crowd closed itself behind me, leaving me exposed to the night air. The combination of the heat from the fire and the heat from the crowd had protected me from the cold, and suddenly I was shivering, but I knew the temperature wasn't to blame. I didn't want to voice the thought but it hopscotched around my head anyway, and wouldn't be quiet: Sam Epstein had torched the Taste of India. I didn't want to think that or believe that, but I couldn't stop myself. Until an hour ago, if someone had said to me, "Hey, you know Sam Epstein from the dry cleaners? Well, he just torched a restaurant at the height of the dinner hour," I'd have said, "No way. I know Epstein. He might fly off the handle but he'd never do something like that." But an hour ago, that man had asked me to hurt a boy, and now that boy's family's restaurant was burning to the ground on a frigid March night. Maybe the people who'd been eating dinner were burning, too. Maybe the people who worked in the restaurant were burning, too. Maybe the people who lived in the apartments above the restaurant were burning, too. Maybe Sam Epstein and I needed to talk.

I don't know when I started, but I was running now, headed uptown on Second Avenue. The wrong direction from where I lived. I stopped. I was panting, heaving, my lungs too full of smoke from a burning building to support that kind of exertion in sub-freezing air. I bent over, my hand on my knees, my head dangling below them. Would Sam Epstein really kill people? I straightened up, coughed some of the crap out of my lungs, and shook my head to clear it. I was standing in front of a doughnut shop. I wanted more to eat than doughnuts, but right now, something was better than nothing. I went in, ordered coffee and a bagel and cream cheese at the counter, then took a seat at a back booth. I had my cell phone in my hand before I loosened my scarf or unbuttoned my coat. I got Sam's number from information and dialed. Sasha answered before the phone had completed its first ring.

"Hi, Sasha. My name is Phil Rodriquez. May I speak to Sam, please?"

Silence. Then, "Phil Rodriquez who saved Dr. Mason from a murderer?"

My turn for silence. How the hell did she know about that? "Ah, Sasha, can I speak to Sam, please?"

"Did you really cut off the guy's dick?"

Jesus, Mary, and Joseph. "No, Sasha, I didn't cut off anybody's anything. I helped Dr. Mason out of a bad situation, that's all. Now, can I please speak to Sam?"

"What do you want with my weird Uncle Sammy? And anyway, he's not home yet. He had a meeting after work. Although I don't know what kind of meeting he could have. But he should have been home by now. He said he would be. He's really late."

I ended the call as the waitress dropped my order on the table. Some of the coffee sloshed out of the cup. I touched the bagel. It was hot. I opened the cream cheese packet and spread some on the bagel and watched it melt, then spread strawberry jelly on top of that. Sam wasn't home, hadn't been home. His after work meeting was with me, and it had been over for more than an hour, and I was thinking that after he left me, he went and burned down a restaurant. But that wasn't the worst of it. Sam Epstein had thought that I'd do bodily harm to a teenaged boy and his fourteen-year-old niece thinks I castrated a man.

Chapter Two

I walked the eight blocks from home to work just like always the next morning, stopping at Willie One Eye's newsstand for the three papers I always buy, and at the tiny fruit and vegetable market old Mrs. Campos has operated since she was young, where I buy bottles of fresh orange and carrot juice. Willie, who sees more with his one eye than most people do with both, noticed immediately that I was out of sync, but being a man of the streets, he knew better than to ask the reason. He merely squinted at me and suggested that I take better care of myself. Mrs. Campos attributed my failure to flirt with her to my budding romance with Connie and graciously forgave me. This time.

My spirits lifted, as always, when I reached my building and let my eyes linger on the brass-plated buzzer box: Y.M. Aguierre at the top, Dharma Yoga Studio in the middle, and Phillip Rodriquez Investigations at the bottom. A small building, perhaps, but it housed big dreams that had come true for the three of us who spent most of our waking hours here. Inside, the lights and heat were on, one of the many advantages of having a partner who lived on the premises. Yo emerged from behind the screens when she heard me enter, her smile brighter than electricity and warmer than steam heat.

"Peace, Brother Man, and *buenos dias,*" she said, raising her hands to catch the bottle of carrot juice I tossed her. Our morning ritual, played out once again.

"Back at you, my Sister," I said, shedding hat, coat, and gloves.

"What's wrong?" she asked, and I told her.

"I saw that story on New York One this morning," she said. "People died."

I nodded. I'd seen it, too. "Any more about the identities of the fatalities?"

She shook her head, tossed the carrot juice back to me, and headed for the computers. If there was any new information about the fire, she'd find it. I hung up my coat and went into the kitchen. I poured our respective juices into glasses and headed into Yo's office. She didn't notice me, so busy was she at her computer keyboards. I cleared a space on the desk top for her juice, though I don't think she noticed, and headed back to the kitchen. By the time I had a bagel toasted and buttered she was standing in the doorway, glasses riding low on her nose, her brow furrowed. *"Nada,"* she said.

"Maybe they don't know yet," I said. What I was thinking was that as hot as that fire was burning, any remains would be charred beyond recognition.

"But if any of the victims belonged to the Patel family, they'd know."

"Is that their name, Patel?" Frankie Patel, I thought.

Yo was right there with me. "If that boy is dead, and it's because he was the wrong color to date Sam Epstein's niece, she'll never forgive him. He might have thought he was doing the right thing, but she'll hate him forever."

"If he killed that boy, I'll hate him forever." I finished my orange juice in one long gulp and wiped my mouth on the back of my hand.

"Are you going to confront him?"

I hesitated only briefly. "Yeah, I am, but I don't want to. I don't want any part of this, Yo. But I can't just ignore it and I can't not know . . ." I stopped mid-sentence as a thought came back to me. "And speaking of knowing stuff, how would Sam's niece know about Jill Mason?"

Dr. Jill Mason was a psychiatrist who'd moved her practice to the neighborhood a year ago following the deaths of her husband and daughters. Jill was a local girl made good—born Black and poor in our tenement neighborhood, but smart enough to scholarship out to college and med school and into an Upper East Side medical practice. She had married money and earned money and brought the riches and her talent back home following the automobile accident that had forever altered her life. Only somebody didn't want her back because he thought she remembered what he'd done to her many years before, when she was just a child. I was hired to keep Jill safe, while finding out who wanted to hurt her. I had done that, and I had made the lowlife bastard sorry he'd ever laid eyes on Jill Mason.

Yolanda gave me one of her looks. "Everybody knows about Jill Mason, Phil."

I gave her a look back. "This kid thinks I castrated Itchy Johnson! 'Cut off the guy's dick' is what she said!" That part of last night was just coming back to me and I was feeling its impact for the first time.

"You didn't really think those little hoodlums who worked for Itchy would keep quiet about his . . . disability, did you?"

"But I'm not the one who did it to him!"

Yo laughed. "But having it be you makes for a much better story. This is the stuff of urban legends, Phil."

I was about to protest when it hit me. Smacked me right in the face. Damn near broke my nose. This is why Sam Epstein thought he could ask me to "discourage" Frankie Patel. If I would cut off a guy's Johnson, surely I'd smack somebody around a little bit. What's a few bumps and bruises compared to castration? "This shit's not funny, Yo," I said in what I hoped was a nasty, snarling tone. She only laughed harder.

"You should go talk to Epstein, then go do the security assessment profile at that apartment building on Avenue B," she said, through unsuccessfully stifled laughter. "That property management company has a dozen buildings. If they like us, that job alone could carry us for a year." It was amazing how quickly she could return her focus to matters of business, even in the midst of a joke at my expense. Then again, she's the one who'd had a five-figure bank account when we were college juniors and I could barely afford beer and a burger at the same meal.

I finished my bagel, washed my plate and glass, and loaded my canvas carryall with the equipment I'd need at the Avenue B building. Thanks to good word of mouth from the Golson sisters who owned half a dozen buildings in the neighborhood, we had picked up the security work for other property owners and managers, but this would be, by far, the largest and most profitable. I strapped my gun on only because Yolanda was watching, grabbed a cell phone off the charger and dropped it into my pocket, donned the five pounds of winter outerwear, and headed for the door. "Keep an ear on the fire story," I said. I didn't wait for a reply. I knew I didn't need to.

The air stank of things burnt and burning—of things that never were meant to burn. This was not the scent of cozy fireplaces, but the stench of death and destruction. The police barricade still kept on-lookers at bay across the street from the gaping hole that once had been the Taste of India restaurant. The Fire Department's arson investigation van was parked on the sidewalk, and a Fire Marshall's sedan was at the curb. And so was an SUV with the seal of the Department of Homeland Security imprinted on the side. I knew the seal when I saw it because it had become a familiar sight in lower Manhattan in these years following the terrorist destruction of the World Trade Center towers. Every time there was a Level Orange alert, Homeland Security vehicles roamed the city, as if their very presence would thwart an enemy attack. But what were the Feds doing at a routine fire in a restaurant?

I got as close as I possibly could to the burn site, leaning in toward it as if I could determine from the sickening stink whether a kid had burned to death there, and whether someone I knew was responsible.

"Can I help you, sir?"

I turned around to see a Homeland Security guy standing much too close to me, giving me that hard look that Federal agents seemed to think made them formidable. That's how I knew he was Homeland Security, because he certainly didn't extend to me the courtesy of introducing himself. "Help me with what?" I answered his stupid question with one of my own and I saw his jaw tighten and the muscles work. He was maybe forty, my height but thinner, with blond hair, pale blue eyes, and crooked teeth. And he was getting mad, not that it took a lot these days to get a Fed riled up.

"You seem to be more than a little interested in events here."

"The place where I had planned to have dinner last night burned down, so yeah, I'm interested. Maybe you could define 'more than a little'?" This guy had pissed me off and I didn't mind letting him know it.

"Do you . . . did you eat here regularly?" the Fed asked.

"What difference does that make now?" I said, and walked away from him. I hadn't taken three steps when this guy was in front of me. It was either stop or knock him down. I chose the prudent course, and gave him back a version of his own hard look.

"I asked you a question."

"And I gave you an answer."

"But not a helpful one," the Fed said, trying, belatedly, to put something resembling nice in his tone of voice. "What would be helpful for us is if we could talk to people who frequented this establishment on a regular basis."

"Well, that wouldn't be me," I said.

"So, why were you planning to eat here last night?"

"Because this is still the United States of America and despite your best efforts to do away with them, we American citizens enjoy certain freedoms. And one of them is the freedom to decide where I want to eat dinner on any given night without having to secure the permission of the Federal government." I'd taken a step closer to him, crowding him the way he crowded me, and he clearly didn't like it. But he wouldn't back up, so there we were, literally toe to toe on the sidewalk across the street from the burned out and smoldering, stinking Taste of India. "It's none of your business why I chose to eat here last night, or where I choose to eat tonight. But I'll give you a hint: I just lost my taste for Indian food." When I walked away from him this time, he didn't stop me, for which I was grateful, because now I was less mad than worried. What the hell was going on that the Department of Homeland Security cared about a fire in a neighborhood restaurant?

I headed toward Epstein's Cleaners with a renewed sense of purpose. I now was confused as well as angry and worried, not a happy mix of emotions on the best of mornings, and definitely a bad mix on one spitting snow flurries in defiance of the morning's weather forecast. I couldn't take it out on the happy-faced meteorologist who reminded me, as if I needed reminding, that late winter snow storms were a New York staple, but Sam Epstein was fair game.

His cousin, whose name I couldn't remember, if I'd ever known it, was at the front counter. She was a plump, pleasant-faced woman, probably ten or twelve years older than Sam and me. I knew enough about the family to know that she and Sam were related on the Epstein side, and I thought maybe she was the daughter of Sam's father's sister—she had the same reddish coloring of the Epsteins. She looked up when the tinkling bell over the door signaled my arrival, and pushed reading glasses off her nose, up into her pretty red-blond hair. She'd been doing something with what looked like receipts, and she pushed them out of the way as I approached, probably to clear space on the counter for the dirty clothes I didn't have.

"My name is Phillip Rodriquez. I'd like to speak with Sam, please."

"Oh. Of course. How are you, Phil? Long time, no see." She gave me a wide, warm smile and I think she'd have hugged me had there not been that counter separating us. "Sammy said he was expecting you. He's in the back, if you want to go on through."

I was caught off guard again. This certainly couldn't become a habit. I'd come here expecting a tooth-pulling session, only to be greeted like a long-lost relation and to find that Sam was expecting me. "Thank you," I said, and turned sideways to squeeze behind the counter.

"You probably want to leave your coat up here," Sam's cousin said, still treating me like I was a cousin, too. "It's hot as hell back there." I quickly shed the coat, stuffed the hat and gloves into the sleeves, and gave it to her. "That was a good thing you did for Dr. Mason," she said.

"Does everybody in town know about that?"

"You know down here. It's still like a little village. At least it is with the people and families who've lived here for a couple generations."

I nodded. Yeah, I knew "down here." It's how I knew she was Epstein family and not just an employee. She was looking at me, waiting for me to say something. "I'm just glad things turned out all right for Dr. Mason," I said. "She's an important part of this community."

"She sure is. She's worked wonders with Sasha."

"Sasha?"

The cousin bobbed her red-gold head up and down emphatically. "You know, Sam's niece. She's been seeing Dr. Mason for a few months now. I wish she'd been seeing her, you know, right from the beginning."

I didn't know and I suppose confusion was written all over my face because the cousin hastened to explain that Jill Mason was treating perhaps half a dozen neighborhood children who had lost parents or other relatives in the World Trade Center disaster. When I met Jill, she was treating the young victims of a serial rapist. If this day took any more strange turns, I was thinking I'd call and make an appointment for myself: Confused PI in need of immediate therapy. "The woman's a saint," I said, and meant it.

"She sure is. You go on back, straight through, all the way. Anybody can tell you where to find Sam if you don't see him."

Not only was it hot as hell, it was cavernous and loud and steamy. The chemical smell couldn't be healthy, and I noticed that everybody but me had on a mask. As I made my way to the rear of the huge space, I recalled that one of the reasons my grandfathers had their uniforms cleaned at Epstein's was because, as their logo boasted, it had a plant on the premises. Epstein's is where all the small dry cleaning and laundry operations sent their work. This wasn't, I realized, just a job for Sam Epstein, it was a major business that employed, by my eyeball best guess, a couple dozen hearty souls.

Sam was at the very back of the room waving his arms at me, waving me forward. I picked up my pace. "This is some operation," I said when I reached him.

He nodded and beckoned for me to follow him up some narrow metal stairs to a glass-enclosed box that afforded a view of the entire floor. When he closed the door, it was like going momentarily deaf. The room was soundproofed. Sam removed his mask and a pair of ear plugs. When the mask came off, I could see the guilt and shame creeping across his face. "I didn't do it, Rodriquez. I swear to you, I didn't do it."

"Then who did, Sam? If it wasn't you, then who was it?" If I were keeping score, that would have been points for me. A sick look joined the guilt and shame on Sam's face. He shook his head back and forth but he didn't say anything. There was a clock on the wall and it showed me that I had exactly seventeen minutes to get to my Avenue B appointment on time, which meant that I had no time left to screw around with Sam. "If that boy is dead, I'm turning you over to Homeland Security."

Sam jumped, then squeaked, "Homeland Security! What're you talking about, Rodriquez? What do you know . . . what's Homeland Security got to do with anything?"

"They're crawling all over the fire scene, and you know how they do business: If they decide to take an interest in you, you might as well paint yourself in invisible ink, 'cause that's how fast you'll disappear." I'd wanted to scare him, and I'd succeeded. He started to sweat even though the box was cool as well as quiet, and he now looked just plain miserable. He backed up into the corner of box-room, and dropped his butt onto a stool that was there.

"The boy's not dead, that Frankie. He's fine."

"How do you know?" I couldn't keep the relief out of my voice.

"Sasha saw the story on the news this morning and called him on his cell phone. Every kid in America has a cell phone these days, you know? They were up all night. His family. Frankie's. The person who got killed was a delivery boy . . ."

"So you managed to kill a kid anyway," I said, nasty replacing relief in my voice.

"It just all got out of hand . . ."

I looked at the clock again. "I've got to go, Sam, but we'll talk again. This evening. Same time, same place. And I want answers." I opened the door and the sound hit me like a sledge hammer and the heat enveloped me like a wool sweater in August. I all but danced down the narrow staircase, and all but ran the length of the long room back to the front of the store.

"Is Sam all right?" the cousin asked me as she gave me my coat.

I bit back the residual nastiness. This woman didn't deserve that from me. "I'm sorry but I don't know your name," I said instead.

She smiled. It was a nice smile. "Eleanor Stillman. Everybody calls me Ellie."

"I'm sorry I had to ask, Ellie. I've seen you around for years, knew you were related to Sam, but I guess we never had occasion to talk."

"You and Sam are closer in age," she said, helping me into my coat. "Is Sam all right?" she asked again.

I thought before I answered. "Sam's got some problems that he's trying to work out," I finally said, pleased with myself that I had avoided the truth and a lie with the same sentence.

"Are you helping him?" Ellie asked.

"I'm trying to," I said. Less of the truth in that one.

She smiled her nice smile again. "Then it'll be okay," she said.

The four-story walk-up on Avenue B was a dump, pure and simple. I could tell from half a block away that a security prevention evaluation would be a waste of my time. I only kept walking because the management company had a dozen other buildings all over town and the law of averages dictated—and I hoped—that they all wouldn't be as sorry as this one. The upside to the situation was that I could probably do the entire evaluation in less than an hour. Starting with the building entrance, problem number one: I walked right in, followed by two other men. I stood aside to let them pass, knowing better than to allow two strangers to stand behind me in a strange environment. They brushed past me as if I didn't exist and headed for the stairs. Problem number two: Anybody walking up a semi-dark staircase is either a potential victim or a potential criminal. Problem number three: The semi-darkness was due to burned out and/or non-existent light fixtures. Problem number four: The lights that existed were exposed instead of mesh covered, and were barely sixty watts. Did I say waste of time? Try waste of effort.

"Mr. Rodriquez?" I turned to find a man built like a heavy-duty trash compactor coming through the building's front door. Mike Kallen from the management company, I guessed. I gave him my hand, got a quick, firm shake, and a rueful look. "So, what do you think? We've got our work cut out for us, huh?" He managed a tight laugh as he said it, and I picked up the faintest hint of an accent, too faint to determine its origin, though not Latin; I was sure of that.

Since he was being honest, I decided to follow suit. "How serious are you, Mr. Kallen, about securing this building?"

"We've got to make the effort." He looked up and down and all around. "We're the new management group and I've got this part of town. They told me this was the worst of the lot, so I thought this was the best place to start. It's got to get easier from here, don't you think?"

"I think I'm glad you like a challenge, Mr. Kallen," I said, and told him my first impressions. Then I asked what the units rented for and when he told me, I told him that in addition to security, he should make some decorating changes, too. I didn't know why anybody would pay that kind of rent to live in a building with walls the color of baby shit and floor tiles that started cracking in the middle of the last century and I told him so.

"I'm glad to see you've got a sense of humor, Mr. Rodriquez." But he wasn't laughing when he said it. Neither was I.

"I'm not laughing, either," Yolanda said when I related the story to her and she, as usual, proceeded immediately and directly to the bottom line. "Did you find out where the other buildings are? And are we getting the job?"

I reached inside my carryall and extracted a sheaf of papers. Most of it was the evaluation of the Avenue B building, but three pages of it were the contract with the KLM Management Group. Kallen had the signed contract in his pocket. He had just wanted to meet me, he said, to do his own evaluation. Yo turned to the back page to check the signatures, then looked at me over the tops of her glasses. I took the check from my pocket and gave it to her. She scanned it and nodded her satisfaction.

"So, what's he like, our new client?"

I told her how he looked like he'd been born in a gym and was doing squats before he could walk, and about the accent that I couldn't get a handle on, and about the weird questions he asked, though they hadn't seemed weird until I'd left him; at the time he was asking, they'd only seemed annoying and picky, like the guy was going to micromanage the job. "It's only now that it seems weird," I said, thinking back and recalling the details of the conversation.

"Give me an example," Yo demanded, wrinkling her nose.

"Well, he wanted to know who got copies of the prospective employee background checks and the prospective tenant background checks. I told him KLM Management got all that and nobody else. Then he wanted to know if we retained copies and when I told him yes, he wanted to know why. So I told him—that it was to protect ourselves in the event of a lawsuit. Then he wanted to know whether we told the cops if any of the background checks came back dirty. So I told him that we worked for him, not the cops, and that our reports were confidential." The more I played the conversation with Kallen over in my head, the weirder it felt to me.

"You said he had an accent, right? So, maybe he comes from one of those countries where there's no such thing as privacy and confidentiality."

"Yeah," I said darkly, "like the New and Not Improved United States of America," and related my encounter with the Homeland Security agent. Instead of amazed or amused, though, Yo looked angry, which pissed me off all over again. "Oh, I suppose you're going to tell me I shouldn't have expressed my true feelings to the agent."

"Why do you do that thing with cops?"

"What thing, Yo?" Now I was well and truly pissed.

"That macho, I-can-kick-your-ass-if-I-really-want-to thing. That my-dick-is-bigger-than-your-dick thing. That my-balls-hang-down-to-my-knees thing. You do it with cops all the time and it's dangerous, Phil."

I looked at her while formulating an appropriate response. Then I realized that she wasn't angry, she was frightened. Really and truly scared. I raised my hands, palms out, in surrender. "Nothing's going to happen to me, Yo. I promise."

"You can't promise that, Phil! You said it yourself: 'The New and Not Improved United States of America.' Things are different now. They can tap your phones and search your home and open your mail any time they want and they don't need a reason or a warrant. And they can 'detain' you. Scoop you up off the street, take you to a secret lock-up, and nobody will know where

Chapter Three

"Have you seen Sam? Do you know where he is?" Ellie Stillman, her voice seeming to rise an octave with each word she spoke, ignored the three customers in line at the counter, addressing me over their heads the moment I entered the dry cleaners a few moments after eight the following morning.

"He's not here?"

"Hey, lady! Do you mind? I'm gonna be late for work," the man at the head of the line complained. Ellie looked at me and I signaled that she should take care of her customers and that I would wait. I could use the time to organize my thoughts. None of the things I was thinking about Sam Epstein when I walked in the door of the cleaners had him on the run, and despite the fact that he thought I'd stoop low enough to hurt a kid, I still was giving him the benefit of a whole bag full of doubts. If people thought—believed—that I had developed a violent, sadistic streak, well, maybe I could understand that, given the nature of my work. But one thing nobody would ever think or believe was that I would abandon my business, my life's work; and no matter how silly Sam Epstein behaved, he wouldn't, either. I knew he'd never walk away from three generations of his family's sweat equity. Wouldn't, couldn't.

"Phil!" I looked toward where I heard my name called and saw a middle-aged Black woman take Ellie's place at the counter, and Ellie was beckoning for me to come around, the way I had the day before. I immediately removed my coat; I knew we were headed for the steamy back room. I didn't try to talk. I just followed Ellie through the building, up the stairs, and into the box. As soon as the door closed and quiet permitted, she started talking. "He didn't go home last night. Sasha called me at about three this morning. She'd gotten up to go to the bathroom and discovered that Sam wasn't home. I rushed over there—I live way up in Yonkers, Phil! And Sam never came home, I called his cell phone every ten or fifteen minutes . . ." She was talking so fast and breathing so hard that I stopped her.

"Ellie, slow down. Calm down. Catch your breath." I took her shoulders and squeezed a little bit and gave her a little shake and she immediately got control of herself, nodding her head up and down to let me know that she was under control. "I take it Sam's never done this kind of thing before?"

"Not even when he was a kid. Sam is the most responsible person I've ever met. Maybe even too responsible, you know? Almost obsessive about some things, Sasha being one of them. And he certainly wouldn't leave her alone all night. You'd think he was that child's father, the way he dotes on her." Now she was shaking her head back and forth and her chest was heaving again.

I couldn't think of anything to say that would be soothing or comforting, and I knew that's what Ellie Stillman wanted and needed to hear: that Sam was fine, that there was some acceptable explanation for his absence. "When did you last see him?" I asked.

"Last night. We closed at six, just like always. Then the night crew came in—you know we run a major part of our operation from six until one a.m.?" I hadn't known that and Ellie explained that much of the actual cleaning and laundering was done at night so that the top windows in the back room could be opened. "Otherwise, it would be too unbearably hot."

I thought it already was too unbearably hot, but didn't say so. "These night crew people, you know them? All of them?"

Ellie nodded emphatically and spoke the same way. "They've worked here for more years than I can remember, every one of them. In fact, once we leave, the night supervisor, Alfred Miller, is in charge and he's the one who locks up at two in the morning. I actually called him at home at a little before three to ask him what time Sam left." Then, as if she realized what she'd said, added, "I only did that because I knew he'd just gotten home and hadn't had time to go to bed."

"And what time did Sam leave, Ellie?"

Tears filled her eyes, as if she finally gave in and allowed some horrible thought to take hold. "Just before seven. I left at six-thirty and Freddie—that's what everybody calls Alfred—he said Sam left just after I did."

"And he never went home? Sasha never saw him last night?" She shook her head and the tears leaked from her eyes and dropped onto her face and slid down her cheeks. "Cell phone messages still going directly into voice mail?" This time she nodded her head. "Who are Sam's friends, Ellie? What does he do on weekends, for fun, recreation? I know he takes good care of Sasha, but he has to have a life of his own." I had watched Ellie's face and by the time I finished speaking, she had undergone a major transformation: From scared and sorrowful to lip-curling, teeth-gnashing mad.

"Tim McQueen, Patrick Casey, and Joey Mottola. Three of the sorriest pieces of shit on this planet." She pushed the words out of her mouth as if they were the rancid meat Jack Heller's people used to sell to their undesirable clientele.

I didn't try to hide my surprise. "When did he start hanging with those guys?" I knew all three of them and her assessment of them was dead on. And they'd no more have been running buddies with a Jew than they would have with my Spic self. In fact, if memory served correctly, both Sam and I had had to outrun Timmy and Pat more than once to get home in one piece. And their terrorism didn't stop until I enlisted the help of some of my cousins from East Harlem, who enlisted the help of some of their friends from Black Harlem, to put a hurting on them. Of course, nobody fucked with Joey Mottola because his back-up put people in the cemetery. And now Sammy Epstein was buddies with them?

"After . . . after what happened." Lots of New Yorkers, especially those directly impacted and affected by the World Trade Center destruction, couldn't bring themselves to call it anything, and certainly not the nine-one-one that seemed to be the rest of the country's favorite descriptive term. As far as we're concerned, that's a telephone number. "They're cousins, you know, Timmy and Pat, and their grandpa was some kind of maintenance man or custodian down there and he died. And that just seemed to, I don't know, put more meanness and mad inside them. And Joey—he's the one started this campaign of hate against anybody that wasn't white—and it didn't take much for Timmy and Pat to fall in line behind him. And Sammy was hurting so bad it didn't take much for him, either."

"Hell, Ellie, those guys hated anybody who wasn't as white as they were when they were in elementary school! And that meant anybody who wasn't Irish or Italian. In fact, half the time they even hated each other."

She nodded. "I know. What I mean is especially people like . . . like . . . anybody who dresses in their native clothes, like Muslims and Arabs and . . ."

"And Hindus," I said softly. And the pieces started clicking into place. I could hear Sam saying, "It just all got out of hand." I could hear Yolanda saying, "I think he meant the hatred."

Ellie watched me for a moment, then said, "I called Uncle Dave, Sam's father. I hated to do that but I didn't have a choice.

I can't keep this place running by myself, and I can't take care of Sasha. She's already refused to come home with me to Yonkers and I certainly can't leave her in that apartment alone." She started to cry again. "What is happening, Phil? What's going on? What's this all about? You said you were helping Sam with a problem? What is it? You have to tell me!"

I had really stepped in it this time. I struggled with what to tell her, knowing that I did, in fact, owe her some kind of explanation. Sam wasn't officially and technically a client, so confidentiality wasn't an issue. But I sure as hell wasn't going to tell what he'd asked me to do, especially in light of what I'd just learned. I took a deep breath. "He was all worked up about some boy that Sasha's dating . . ."

"Frankie Patel? He bothered you with that?"

"I told him I thought he was overreacting, that kids today fell in and out of infatuation just like we did, and I thought I'd gotten him calmed down," I lied but it didn't work. Ellie's face changed again, horror this time taking center stage.

"That fire last night at the restaurant. Sammy did that?"

"I don't know, Ellie. Please don't jump to that conclusion. I don't know and until there's something solid to go on . . ."

"Ellie, come to the front, please. Ellie, to the front."

I was saved by a voice from the intercom. Ellie glanced at the clock, swore, then turned and ran from the box. I followed her down the stairs and through the noise and the heat and the steam and the chemical smells, to the front of the store, being as amazed as the first time I did it how it could manage to be so much cooler and quieter out here. There were at least ten people in line in front of the counter; I could see why the harried woman behind the counter had called for help. I squeezed my way from behind the counter, got my coat, and squeezed my way out of the front door. I got into my coat and hat, then waited while three people exited the dry cleaning store, and three more entered, before I could stick my head in and tell Ellie that I'd call her later. And before I could leave, there was more entering and exiting Epstein's establishment. I walked away thinking there's no way Sam Epstein could or would walk away from this. I also almost convinced myself that for the same reason, there was no way he could have torched the Patel family's means of livelihood.

And it would be quite a while later in the day before I again had time to think about the Epsteins and the Patels because when I got to the office, Yolanda and Mike Kallen were waiting for me. Kallen, surprisingly, looked a little nervous. Yo looked ready to chew nails. "I would say good morning," I said, "but it hasn't been so far, and you two don't look likely to change my luck for me. So, I'll just say, Mr. Kallen, what brings you here so early in the morning?"

To his credit, the man managed to look a combination of sheepish, guilty, and apologetic. He was holding a coffee cup that he put down on the table nearest him, as much for something to do as he collected himself as to get rid of it. "I, ah, that is we, ah, my partners, changed our minds. We don't want to go forward with the contract."

To my credit, I neither laughed in his face or threw him out on his ass. To my credit, I did as I'd been trained by my partner to do and kept my mouth shut where matters of money were concerned and looked over at Yolanda. "Ms. Aguierre?"

"As I have explained to Mr. Kallen, we have a signed contract. Of course, we don't want to force—" and she hit the word force with lots of it—"our services on anyone, but it would be a bad business practice to merely void a signed contract. So, as I also have explained, we'll gladly terminate your contract in exchange for fifteen percent of the value of said contract, plus retention of the retainer."

"But that's not fair! You haven't done any work!"

"I spent three hours of my time and shared a considerable amount of my knowledge with you yesterday, Mr. Kallen. But beyond that, nobody forced you into signing a contract, and please remember that you called us. We didn't solicit your business." I looked at my watch. "And now you're wasting more of our time. So what's it gonna be, Mr. Kallen?"

He looked for a moment like he wanted to turn ugly but he got his face under control. Or most of it; his eyes remained narrow slits and ice blue glinted at me through them. "Don't you even want to know why, Mr. Rodriquez?"

I shook my head. I was halfway across the room, heading for the kitchen and my own cup of coffee. I turned back to face him. "I don't care why, Mr. Kallen. And it's none of my business, really. You made a decision and then you changed your mind about it. I do it all the time, and I don't owe anybody an explanation when it happens. But I do realize that there often are consequences attached to a change of mind. So should you." I was now officially sick and tired of Kallen and I shot Yolanda the look that told her if she wanted this thing to end on a polite note, she'd better handle it.

"Well, you can humor me, Mr. Kallen," Yo said, "and tell me why you don't want to go forward. Did somebody give us a bad review?"

"No. I'm . . . we're just not comfortable with anybody but us having access to the background information on potential employees and tenants. Mr. Rodriquez said that your company keeps a copy for your own protection but I really don't understand why you would need protecting."

"Suppose, Mr. Kallen, that you refuse to rent one of your units to a person because we report to you a bad credit history for that person. And suppose that person sues you for defamation. Or suppose you fire a building maintenance man because our background check reveals an arrest for theft. And suppose that person sues you for wrongful termination. And suppose in both cases your defense is that we supplied you with faulty information. And suppose that we don't have any documentation to support our findings because you're not comfortable with anybody but you having access to that information." Yolanda was practically snarling by the time she finished all her suppositions. "I suppose you realize where that would leave us, don't you? But then, you wouldn't care."

Kallen didn't have anything to say to that. Nor did I, for that matter. Yo had done a much better job of telling the man to go fuck himself than I would have. "I hope you have a better understanding now, Mr. Kallen, of why we retain certain records," she said so sweetly it gave me a toothache.

He didn't say anything for a moment. He stood there, looking from one to the other of us. Yolanda made and kept eye contact with him; I didn't. I hung up my coat and poured a long overdue cup of coffee. The caffeine was starting to work when Kallen said, "Okay."

That's all he said and now I did look at him. Then I looked at Yolanda, but she was looking at Kallen, too.

"Okay what?" I said, borrowing a little piece of Yo's snarl.

"Okay you're right. I didn't understand before but I understand now everything." In an instant our cold, calculating, savvy Manhattan wheeler-dealer property manager had become a walking advertisement for the need of all those profitable ESL businesses all over town. Kallen must have heard himself because he quickly reverted to type. "I can see this situation from your perspective and you're quite right not to leave yourselves vulnerable."

Now he sounded like an American actor trying to sound British in a 1940s-era movie, and I remembered hearing or reading that once upon a time, English as a second language classes relied on British films to teach diction. But that was in my grandparents' day. "It's nice to know you don't think we're being unreasonable," I said, and could hear in my memory a friend of my grandmother's, a Black woman, saying, "That's mighty white of you." I must have smirked a bit at the thought because Kallen gave us a smile and a little shrug, and raised his palms in a so-sue-me gesture.

"When can you start?" he asked.

"We can get you a written evaluation of the Avenue B property, complete with recommendations, in the next few days, and we'll begin scheduling site visits for the other properties immediately," I said, and told him we'd start background checks on prospective employees and tenants as soon as we had names. "And please make sure all the names include as much information as possible, Mr. Kallen—social security numbers, date and place of birth, current address—anything to prevent us from confusing one person with another and creating the kind of problem Yolanda mentioned." And so we don't waste time and money spinning our wheels I thought, but didn't say.

He said that he'd have that information delivered by messenger immediately then nodded as if our commitment to get started immediately was what he'd come to get, wished us a pleasant day, and left, closing the door just a little harder than necessary.

"If we've just signed on to do business with the Russian Mafia—no, demanded the right and the opportunity to do so—I'll shoot myself," Yolanda said.

"I'll shoot you and save you the trouble," I said. "But of course you know better since you checked them out before we offered them a contract," I added, making it a statement of fact and leaving no room for a question, because I knew that Yolanda ran checks on everybody and everything that was potential business for us. She hurried over to her desk and was back in a second with one of the brown accordion folders she uses for active cases. Sometimes these files got so thick and heavy she had to wheel them around on an office chair. This one was practically empty. Yolanda opened it and gave me several sheets of paper, then told me what was on them before I could even begin reading.

"KLM is a very respectable property management company with twenty years . . ."

I cut her off. "Is Kallen the K and are they Russians? That's all I want to know."

She shook her head. "The K is, or was, Richard King, Senior, who died a few years back, and nobody in those three letter's a Russian. Richard King Jr. is the boss these days and Kallen's an employee, been with the company about three years, place of birth listed as Brooklyn, New York."

We looked at each other, not needing to speak the obvious, but I said it anyway: "He's from Brooklyn like I'm from Beijing."

"He lied," Yo said.

"That song and dance about the contract was a lie, too," I said, though I didn't have the documentation to back it up.

"Let's do this job and be done with it, Phil. Take the money and run."

I wanted to be out from under whatever it was Kallen was peddling in the worst way, but I needed to know what "it" was; you couldn't dodge the ball if you didn't see it coming. We did security evaluations and background checks for several institutions, public and private, and thanks to our discovery of a serial rapist employed as a weekend porter in a neighborhood apartment building, we'd been hired by other building management companies to vet their employees and tenants, too. At the time we got the business from the Golson sisters, I'd felt bad for the company we replaced, at least until I realized that their failure to discover a discrepancy in the rapist's employment application gave him access to a building and a neighborhood full of vulnerable little girls. So, I wasn't worried about being able to do the work for Kallen, and try as I might, I couldn't see a crooked angle ready to be played in this scenario: We tell KLM Management how to improve the security of their apartment buildings; we tell where they're specifically in violation of any laws or building codes; we run background checks on the names they supply us and supply information without prejudice. We don't say to KLM Management, don't rent an apartment to Mary Doe because she's got bad credit, or don't hire John Doe as maintenance man because he said he was a high school graduate and he's not. That's not our job. It's our job to gather and supply the information. But like we told Kallen, if we provide information that a prospective employee or tenant did time for rape, and KLM hires or rents to that person, and that person commits a rape, that's going to be KLM's problem, not ours.

That's why I'd first thought that Kallen didn't want us to retain copies of the background reports, but that didn't make sense. And he backed off that demand too quickly for that to be a reason, and I couldn't find a reason or rationale for his bizarre behavior. So, we'd do what Yo suggested: Get in, get out, and cash the check before Kallen had a chance to change his mind again.

We spent the remainder of the morning finishing up the paperwork on two very lucrative jobs, and the paperwork on two others that had barely paid for themselves. But that was why we did business on the Lower East Side. We knew that the people in this part of Manhattan—the lower part, east of Fifth Avenue, south of 14th Street, and north of the Brooklyn Bridge—lived interesting and complex and challenging lives, they just lived them on smaller budgets in smaller spaces than the people on television and in the movies who hire private investigators and don't flinch at the retainer and the daily rate. I'd known I wanted to be a private cop since reading my first

Spenser and Hawk book when I was about thirteen. But I didn't want to be just a private cop; oh, no. I wanted to be both Spenser and Hawk, both tough and smart. So, I got a Sociology degree from City College, where I met Yolanda who was getting a business degree, then I spent four years as a New York City cop walking a beat. Now I was back home, in my own neighborhood, a private cop in the service of people who very often didn't think much of the public ones but who had sufficient complexity and challenge in their lives that Yo and I hadn't had a really slow week since we opened.

One of the lucrative jobs that we just finished was an ongoing security check for the various departments at New York University. The head of security there liked and trusted us and the more satisfactory work we did for them, the more work they gave us. One of the bare bones jobs that we just finished was for two Nigerian men, brothers, newly arrived in the U.S., working to earn enough money to support the wives and children who were waiting for visas to enter the country. The brothers had a small deli and grocery store on a raggedy, run-down street close to the East River, under the tracks of the J train. Gentrification hadn't found that block yet, and the paint had long since faded and cracked and peeled off every building in the vicinity. The old-timers had either died out or moved on. The newcomers, mostly Spanish-speaking with a few Eastern Europeans and Middle Easterners thrown in, were a volatile, surly group who didn't seem to have sense enough to appreciate having a grocer in the neighborhood. Especially one that stayed open around the clock: The brothers worked twelve-hour shifts. The only day they closed was Sunday. And they were getting robbed at least once a week and sometimes twice. They couldn't afford to close the store and walk away from their investment, and even if they could, they couldn't afford to rent better space in a better neighborhood. So, what they needed was for the robberies to stop.

It had taken the better part of a month and some very creative undercover and sting work by Eddie Ortiz and Mike Smith, two retired NYC cops who worked for us, but we had made it happen. After several arrests and a couple of major ass whippings laid on the thieves by Eddie and Mike to serve as a deterrent against future bad behavior, the robberies had stopped. The Nigerians were so pleased that they sang the praises of Phillip Rodriquez Investigations throughout the community of their countrymen. As a consequence, we had appointments scheduled not only with Nigerian small-business owners in each of the five boroughs, but at the Nigerian Embassy as well. I had asked Yolanda what she thought an embassy would want with us and she'd said she didn't care as long as I got a haircut and wore a suit to the interview. "If we start getting work at embassies and another of the universities, Phil, we'll be able to help more of the little guys. You know, like lawyers do? Pro bono."

"We do any more work for the rates we gave the Egwim brothers and Mrs. McInerney, we might as well call it pro bono." I'd sounded a little grumpy at the time, but I secretly agreed one hundred percent. To be able to help Ma Mac, as everybody in the neighborhood called her, and not have to worry about expenses, would make us both very happy. Ma Mac's brother, Aloysius McKinney, was eighty years old and still built like the longshoreman he was for more than fifty years, but his mind was gone. She'd been trying to take care of him since her husband and his wife died, but he was too much for her. He'd get out of the house and start to roam—always headed for places that still existed only in his fractured memory. We'd found him this time in a biker bar in Hell's Kitchen, and I was still sore from wrestling that tough old bastard into a taxi for the ride home. He'd punched and kicked and cursed me, calling me a stupid, stinking Spic and mumbling about how he told me he'd get even. Crazy old bastard. I stood up, stretched, and sauntered back to Yolanda's hide-out behind the screens.

"I hope you're coming to talk to me about food."

"I heard your stomach growling. Soup and a salad okay?"

She stopped what she was doing and turned all the way around to look at me over the tops of her glasses. Then she let go a big, deep belly laugh, like I haven't heard from her in a while. "Connie deLeon gets the gold medal, Brother Man! In a matter of just a few months, she's converted you from a double death burger with cheese, a large order of fries, and a triple shake to soup and a salad?" She jumped to her feet and did a little dance that involved lots of booty wiggling. "Yes, Phil, and thank you. I'd love soup and a salad. What kind of soup do you recommend? And what dressing for my salad?"

She was still laughing when I stalked away from her en route to get my hat and coat. I made a detour to the bathroom and therefore didn't hear our version of the tinkling bell over the entry door—a discreet though definite buzz that sounds in the back of the room, everywhere but in the bathroom. So, when I emerged, I heard voices—not Yolanda on the telephone but her talking to someone in the office. It was a voice I recognized and though I hadn't heard it in many, many years, the sharpness of the memories it evoked made it feel like yesterday.

"Ah, Phil Rodriquez," he said. "You're a dead ringer for your Grandpa. The Vega one, not the Rodriquez one."

I walked toward him, hand extended. "Hello, Mr. Epstein," I said. He ignored my hand and pulled me into a bear hug. I hugged him back and felt the bony body of an old person. Like my *abuelitos* and *abuelitas*. No matter how strong and powerful they once had been, old age reduced them all to these vessels that merely stored their fragile bones. All except for that damn Aloysius McKinney. "You sure got here quick."

"Ellie called me this morning at five, I was on a plane at seven." Suddenly, all the energy left him and he slumped. I still had an arm around his shoulder and he sagged into me. I caught him, supported him, and led him to one of the sofas.

"Did you have any breakfast, Mr. Epstein?" Yolanda asked him and, judging the answer from the look on his face, "Do you prefer coffee or tea, and a bagel or an English muffin? Cream cheese or strawberry preserves?"

He looked up at her and managed a rakish grin and a come-hither twinkle. "I heard about you, Miss Aguierre. I heard you were a real looker. But I gotta tell ya, your notices don't do you justice." He slowly dropped the lid of his left eye closed, then opened it again. "Coffee, black, and a bagel, toasted, with anything you got that'll taste good on it. I trust your judgment."

Yolanda returned his wicked wink, asked if I wanted bagel or muffin, and retreated to the kitchen, where I knew she wouldn't miss a word of whatever David Epstein and I were about to discuss. And he got right to it. "This business with Sammy." He started but couldn't seem to get any farther.

"Still no word?"

He shook his head and wisps of snow white hair danced about. I sat in one of the desk chairs and rolled it across the carpeted floor to the sofa, placing myself directly in front of Epstein, so close that our knees were touching. He'd always had gentle brown eyes and bushy dark eyebrows and lots of bushy dark hair. He wasn't a big man, or tall, but he'd had a forceful personality and he'd always radiated energy. Just now, for a moment, we'd been treated to the energy and the personality, but it had been for Yo's benefit. Once she disappeared, so did the Epstein of old. "Tell me what you know, Phil," said the old man looking at me with watery eyes topped with white eyebrows. A heavily veined, age-spotted hand grabbed mine and let me know that strength still resided with David Epstein. I told him what I knew, what I thought, what I suspected, and what I feared. When I finished talking, he sat staring straight ahead at nothing.

"We had four children, Esther and me. Two girls, two boys. Sammy is all we've got left." He hadn't been staring straight ahead, he'd been looking back, into memory. "It will kill Esther if we've lost him, too."

There was nothing I could say to that so I didn't try. Instead, I thought of my own grandparents and tried to imagine how they'd react if all their children had died before them. I looked again at Epstein. Esther wasn't the only one in danger of expiration.

"A hand, please, Phil," I heard from the kitchen. I got quickly to my feet and with a pat on the shoulder for David Epstein, hurried back to help Yolanda, who, I was certain, didn't need any help from me.

"He thinks Sam is dead?" She had two trays loaded with coffee, juice, bagels and English muffins and she really did need my help. But she also wanted to know before we faced Epstein again whether I shared the old man's fears.

"I think he's had so much practice preparing himself for the worst that he just does it automatically. And who knows? Maybe it's not a bad way to approach things."

Yo picked up a tray and I grabbed the other one and followed her out. "It's an awful way to approach things," she muttered.

Epstein looked asleep as we approached him. His head was thrown back and his legs were stretched out in front and his hands were folded on top of his round little pot belly, but his eyes popped open when we reached him with the trays. He sat up straight and sighed deeply. I used my foot to move one of the tables toward him and he reached for it and pulled it in close, then he watched Yolanda place his food on it—orange juice, coffee, two toasted bagels with cream cheese and strawberry preserves. "Thank you, Miss Aguierre," he said.

"You're welcome, Mr. Epstein," she said, and none of us said any more until the food was history and we all were on our second cups of coffee. Epstein looked revived and I felt that way. He wiped his mouth and hands on a napkin, then folded it neatly and placed it dead center on his plate, right beside the knife and fork. My friend Mike Smith, the ex-cop, did the exact same thing and I asked him about it once. He wasn't even aware that he did it. Then he shook his head and gave a little laugh and told me that if I was lucky, one day I'd know what it felt like to have been married a lot of years to a good woman. "You pick up good habits from good women," Mike had said.

"You said Sammy wanted you to do him a favor," Dave Epstein said quietly and gravely. "People in business don't do favors or they won't be in business very long. I want to hire you. I can pay whatever you charge. I want you to find Sammy and bring him home, and I want you to find out who burned that restaurant. If it was Sammy . . ." He shook his head. "I still can't believe he'd do something like that, but if he did, well, I need to know that. But more than anything, I need him back. We need him back, Esther and me. Because he's all we've got left. Him and Sasha." Then he was crying.

I gave him a moment and he struggled to pull himself together. Enough that I could be certain he understood what I was telling him. "You should file a missing person report with the police, Mr. Epstein."

"No way!"

"Why not? The police have experts in missing persons . . ."

"He's not missing! And I don't want the cops sticking their noses in this."

I gave him a moment again, hoping he'd realize how ridiculous what he just said was. He didn't. "If he's not missing, Mr. Epstein, where is he? Sam's a little old to have run away from home. And you don't want the cops sticking their noses into what?"

"You know what, Rodriquez! I tell them Sammy's missing, I gotta tell 'em about the fire and how you think Sammy did it!"

I felt like I was standing in a shit pond in my bare feet. "You don't have to tell them anything but when, where, and with whom Sammy was last seen. Then, if they get far enough along in an investigation and arrows start pointing in a specific direction, and that direction is a burned out restaurant, then yeah, you've got to tell them, if they ask, that Sam had a connection to the restaurant."

"I'm not filing a missing person report because my son is not missing."

"But you're paying me to find him."

The old man exploded. "If he's scared, if he's embarrassed, if he's hiding somewhere, you can find him and tell him to come home, tell him nobody's mad at him."

Which would be a lie because if he torched the Taste of India I was mad as hell at him, but I couldn't take it out on an old man. "Mr. Epstein, you have to know that the chances of a positive outcome lessen the longer a person is missing." He began to cry again, silently, with tears running down his face. I loaded the trays and took them to the kitchen and did the dishes while Yolanda got Mr. Epstein back in control of himself. I heard her assuring him that he had nothing to apologize for, tell him that we understood his feelings, tell him that we shared his fears, promise him that we'd do everything possible to find his son. Then I heard him go into the bathroom and Yolanda came to find me. I was almost done with the dishes.

"Keep that up, Connie might marry you," she said.

There was time in my very recent past when those words and the thought they produced would have caused a gag reflex. "You think?" I said, and she wrapped me in big bear hug from behind and I would have bet money that I heard her stifle a sniffle. "Do you want to draw up a contract while I take the old man back to the cleaners?"

"He needs to go home and go to bed, Phil. He's about to collapse."

"Yeah, I know. But he won't leave Ellie alone in the store."

"And he will leave Sasha alone in that apartment? He needs to get some rest and he needs to be there when she gets home from school."

"He needs to call the cops and file a missing person report."

"Maybe when he gets some rest, he'll be thinking more clearly. But right now, he's got to make Sasha his top priority."

She had a point. The store wasn't a fourteen-year-old girl who'd lost her mother and now may have lost the uncle who was her rescuer. They could pay somebody to help run the store—promote one of their long-time employees who already knew the business. It wasn't so easy to find a suitable stand-in parent for a grieving girl. I heard Epstein come out of the bathroom.

"Yolanda's going to draw up a contract for you, Mr. Epstein, and bring it to you. And I'll take you home so you can get some rest . . ."

He waved me off. "I gotta get back to the store, give Ellie a hand. I told her I'd come back and help her close up."

"Mr. Epstein, I'm going to need all the help you can give me on this, and you're going to need all your strength to get us both through it. That lady who was helping Ellie this morning—"

"That was Viv. Vivian Henderson. She's been with us for over twenty years."

I nodded. "I could tell. She worked the cash register and the customers like a pro. Make her an assistant manager, give her a raise, let her take some of the weight off Ellie. And off you. You need to rest, sir." And I need you to let me inside that apartment, into Sammy's private space, into Sammy's computer, into Sammy's head.

He looked at me with eyes that no longer were old man's eyes but the sharply focused, flinty, unblinking gaze of one who knew the score of more than one of life's games. Then he blew air through his lips at me. "You might look your grandpa Vega but you got stones like the Rodriquez one. He was one tough customer, I gotta tell ya."

"I've heard that about him," I said.

"I've seen it in action," he said.

"Tell me about it."

"I'll tell you one story. This happened way back before you were born, when your Pop used to bring the uniforms for cleaning. Only this one Saturday your Grandpa brought 'em in. It was during a heat wave, I remember that. Even at six in the morning we had the doors and windows open and still couldn't get any relief from the steam coming from the back. We had just opened and your Grandpa's one of the first in the line. Behind him is Mrs. McKinney. She's dead now, and better off for it if you ask me, married all those years to that sorry excuse for a man, Aloysius McKinney. She's waiting to pick up her husband's work clothes—this is back when we did as much laundry as dry cleaning. Now I know and she knows he's gonna be late 'cause he's due on the docks at seven. He shoulda picked up his clothes the night before but he always went to some watering hole after work instead of going home like a good husband and father. She worked at one of the hotels way up on the East Side cleaning rooms and she didn't get home until after we closed. Anyway, here she is, gettin' his clothes and he roars in, still drunk from the night before, cussin' and screamin' and callin' her all kinds of names. She tries to calm him and quiet him and what does he do but give her a slap, right across the face. Your

Grandpa grabbed him and heaved him outta the door like he didn't weigh close to two hundred pounds." Epstein stopped his story to catch his breath, then he finished his story, speaking slowly and not in the jumble of words like before. "So, like I said, the door's wide open and everybody in the store can hear McKinney out on the sidewalk, still cussin' like a madman. Then he yells, 'You stupid, stinkin' Spic! I better not ever see you again!' And what does your Grandpa do? Strolls out the door, kicks McKinney in the ass, then offers to walk Mrs. McKinney home." And Epstein held his right arm out, crooked at an angle, like he was waiting for a woman to join arms with him, and began a mincing stroll-like imitation.

I was laughing so hard my stomach hurt. "There's a second part to this story," I managed to say. "I'll tell it to you on the way to your place."

Epstein loved my Aloysius McKinney story so much he made me tell it three more times in the taxi on the way to his—to Sammy's—apartment, and he howled with each telling, clapping his hands and rubbing them together. "You gotta tell your Grandpa that story," he said, and I promised that I would. "He'll love it," the old man said. We were outside the door to the apartment he'd lived in for over forty years and he hesitated before putting his key into the lock. "Sasha might be home," he muttered, then rang the bell and inserted the key at the same time.

Sasha was home. So was Frankie Patel. She looked up, expecting Sammy and for a moment she couldn't react. Then her face reacted in about a dozen ways, from surprise to happy excitement to dread: If Grandpa was home, that meant that Uncle Sammy was . . .

Epstein and his only grandchild rushed each other and their embrace made both me and Frankie avert our eyes. "Your Grandma misses you so much."

"I miss her, too. And you, too, Grandpa! And where's Uncle Sammy? What's happened to him? Why hasn't he come home?"

Old Dave Epstein wasn't about to have that conversation in front of a stranger. He eyed Frankie. "Who's this young man?"

"This is my friend, Frankie Patel—"

"Oh!" Epstein was speechless for a moment but he recovered like a champ. "I'm very sorry about what happened. Is your family all right?"

Frankie swiped at his eyes with the back of his hands, both eyes simultaneously, and nodded his head. "They don't have any place to live, Grandpa, and no clothes or food or anything, and they're all piled into one hotel room," Sasha wailed. "And Frankie's laptop and books and school stuff got burned up." Frankie's tears started again and he just stood there, letting them fall, not making a sound, not trying to wipe them away, just looking down at the floor and silently weeping. I was feeling helpless and useless. Dave Epstein wasn't. The man, was after all, the father of four children. He put his arms around these two and drew them into him and held them and let them cry out their pain and fear and sorrow and whatever else they were feeling, all the while saying things to them in a low, soothing voice that I couldn't hear but that must have made a difference to Sasha and Frankie because they stopped heaving. Dave looked over at me, his eyes filled with compassion and love and his own sorrow, both for his loss and for Frankie Patel's loss.

"We could use some wet towels here, Rodriquez," he said, and I hurried to the kitchen, wet a handful of paper towels, and hurried back. Eye drying and nose blowing took a moment. Then Epstein said, "There's a large apartment over the cleaners and nobody's living there right now. You and your family are welcome to stay as long as necessary, Frankie."

"We don't have any money to pay you, and maybe we won't ever have any. The insurance people think my father started the fire so they won't pay the claim."

"I'm not looking for money, son. Make sure you tell your parents that, and I'll tell 'em myself later tonight or tomorrow. In the meantime, you all get settled in. There's some furniture there, and sheets and towels and kitchen stuff. And it's clean—or it should be. It better be!" Epstein was in his element now. He took a key off the ring in his pocket and gave it to Frankie. He wrote down the alarm code. Then he took a wad of bills from his wallet which Frankie first refused to accept. "You said your folks didn't have any money and you need food and . . . and . . . things. There are things you gotta have to live. Now take the money, son, and go to your folks and help 'em get their bearings. Go on," he said pushing the money into Frankie's hand and pushing him toward the door. The boy stopped and hugged the old man, then he looked at Sasha and gave her a smile that almost made me fall in love with him.

"I'll come with you, Frankie," she said.

Epstein held her back. "They need to be alone as a family right now, sweetheart. You can see them tomorrow."

Sasha wanted to argue but her heart wasn't in it. She watched Frankie leave, then turned away from me and her grandfather and headed down the hallway to what I guessed was her room. "What do you make of that business about the insurance?" Dave asked as soon as his granddaughter was out of earshot.

"They know it was arson and they have to be certain Patel didn't torch his own place. They'll make his life miserable for a couple of weeks, checking his financials, digging into his lifestyle, poking through his sock and underwear drawer." I'd done enough of this kind of work for insurance companies to know that they'd be looking for signs that the Patels spent more money than they earned at the Taste of India, that he had a gambling habit or that she was a shopaholic or that everybody had a coke habit. And after the adjusters satisfied themselves that the Patels weren't the arsonists, they'd pay up. But it wasn't the insurance company I was worried about; it was the Homeland Security knuckleheads. Once they got fixated on an idea or a theory, no matter how absurd or unlikely, they didn't let go. They were Rottweilers in that respect. So I first had to find out why the Feds were interested in this particular fire, then, if I could, divert their attention away from the Patels. And, of course, there was the Sammy factor. I didn't think the Patels burned their own restaurant, but had Sam Epstein done it? And how would I manage any of this and keep myself off the Homeland Security radar, because Yolanda was dead-on right in her assessment of how things worked these days. I damn sure wouldn't be of any use to anybody in a cell five stories underground.

"That was some deep thought," Epstein said.

"That was a very good thing you did for the Patel family," I said.

"It was the least I could do."

Yeah, right, I thought, especially if it was your son who destroyed their home. "I need to see Sam's room, and I need to talk to Sasha about the last time she saw him."

He hesitated for just a moment; he knew what I was asking and he didn't like it, the idea of a stranger pawing through his son's private belongings, but he also knew he didn't have a choice. He'd hired me to do a job, and he needed to let me do it. He nodded and walked out of the room, following Sasha's earlier path. I took advantage of the chance to scrutinize the Epstein home. I'd never been inside a Stuyvesant Town apartment before, despite its massive, looming presence as practically the gateway to the neighborhood. For almost sixty years the complex has stood, virtually unchanged, except that it now rents to people of color; but for many years, like many other places in New York and America, non-whites were personas non grata. And I, like many other black and brown people, still carry around a lot of the hurt and anger born of that time and place. But in this time and place, a man whose family had lived in Stuyvesant Town almost since its inception was paying me a lot of money to do a job for him, and I needed to keep my focus on the fact that the Epstein apartment was on the southwestern side of the Stuyvesant complex, right at 14th Street and First Avenue, about ten blocks due north of where the Taste of India now was a smoldering, stinking, ugly hole. I walked to the window and looked down. The Epsteins lived on the tenth floor and looking out, all I could see was more Stuyvesant Town: The place was its own city, its own town, in reality as well as in name. Almost nine thousand apartments in three dozen buildings, eating up eighteen square blocks of Lower East Side Manhattan. As insular as this place was, I knew that nobody would ever tell me if, when, or whether they'd seen Sam Epstein yesterday, the day before, or at any time in the more than thirty years he'd lived here.

Dave Epstein returned and my cell phone rang at the same time. I raised a finger to Dave, and took what I was certain would be Yolanda's call; it was. She had Epstein's contract ready and wanted to know where to bring it. I put the question to Epstein, and he hesitated before answering. "Sasha's not doing too well right now. She doesn't want to talk to you. I'm sorry." I quickly processed that information and just as quickly made a couple of decisions. I told Yolanda to bring the contract here, closed the phone, and gave Dave Epstein a taste of what he was paying for.

"I can only imagine how shitty that kid must be feeling right now, but I really need to talk to her while things are still fresh in her memory. I'll check Sam's room first, to give her a few more minutes to compose herself. By that time, Yolanda will be here with your contract, then we can get out of here and give you two some time alone. Like you said earlier, there are times when family needs to be with family." I could tell the old man wasn't enthusiastic about my decision-making but he knew he didn't have any wiggle room. He also knew that throwing up roadblocks in an investigation before the contract was even signed was not the best way to begin a new relationship.

"If you think this is the best way, Phil?" He made it a question.

"Yes, sir, I do." I gave him an answer.

Chapter Four

Though Yolanda and I hadn't met until college, our maternal grandmothers had been best friends as young women in Spanish Harlem and still harbored the hope that one day she and I would become partners of a different kind, even though Yo had stopped being secretive about her sexual orientation many years ago: She was happily and proudly gay and everybody who knew her, knew that. "Deal with it or vacate my space," was a favorite saying of hers. And even though we now both lived way downtown from East Harlem, Yo was relatively new to the area. Her family had remained Uptown while mine had migrated Downtown before I was born, so I have no personal history connected to living in Spanish Harlem. Alphabet City and Chinatown and the parks and playgrounds of the East River were my natural habitat, so Yo found the Stuyvesant Town history lesson of particular interest. "I've got to go exploring over there."

"It's an interesting place. Some people think it's too cookie-cutter, too utilitarian, while others think it Utopian."

She tilted her head to the side and gave me an appraising look. "I forget sometimes that you were a Sociology major, Phil." Her glasses slid down her nose. She took them off and hooked the arm on to the front of her sweater. "How many people did you say lived there?"

"I don't know exactly how many. Twenty thousand, maybe? Maybe more. I know there are almost nine thousand apartment units in there, and that they all look the same, and that there's grass and trees and fountains and that kids couldn't play in the grass." I knew this because after a certain age, kids, especially boys, chafe at the rules and restrictions of their lives, and lots of white—mostly Jewish boys—who lived in Stuy Town often sought out my group of friends to play ball and shoot marbles and go fishing with. And when we'd wonder why they wanted to play in the street when they had grass and fountains, they told us they couldn't play in those parts of the complex. So, they played in the streets with us and we opened the fire hydrants or jumped into the East River to cool off in the scorching hot summer months. I smiled at the memory, the happiness of it almost eradicating the painful aspects of memory that I'd experienced the night before.

"Life's an interesting journey, isn't it?" Yo said.

"That didn't sound very much like the musings of a business major," I said.

"Life can't be all numbers."

"Let me write this down: Date, time, place. Yolanda Maria Aguierre actually said that life can't be all numbers. Remember this next time you're hassling me about expense accounts and receipts."

"Speaking of which," she said, returning her glasses to the bridge of her nose and peering at me over the top of them, "it's Thursday and I haven't received a single receipt from you this week, and I know you've been in taxis and out to lunch." She stuck her hand out toward me and wiggled her fingers.

Muttering curses under my breath, I began my weekly receipt hunt: Digging in jacket and pants pockets, the folds of my wallet, the drawers of my desk. Where was that envelope I kept for receipts . . .

"Front door, Phil," Yolanda said quietly and I looked up, certain that I was watching Frankie Patel's father enter. Tall, thin, turbaned and bearded, he walked toward me with confidence, though as he got closer I could see the fatigue in his eyes and a slight slump in his shoulders.

"Mr. Rodriquez?"

"Mr. Patel?" He smiled and I could see the source of Frankie's thousand-watt grin. We shook hands and I took his coat and offered him coffee or tea. He said he'd appreciate a cup of tea, if it was no trouble, and I went to the back to hang up his coat, make his tea, and confer with Yolanda. She raised her eyebrows in a question and I raised my shoulders in the only answer I had. Maybe the guy just wanted a cup of tea. But Yo's curiosity was piqued. She told me to go talk to Patel, and she'd bring the tea when it was ready. I followed orders.

Patel was standing where I'd left him and I led him to one of the sofas and waved him down. He sank gracefully and, I noted, gratefully. The man clearly was exhausted. "My partner will bring your tea, Mr. Patel."

"Thank you for seeing me, Mr. Rodriquez," he said in a movie-star resonant voice, without the slightest hint of an accent. "I didn't destroy my livelihood and my home and kill my cousin," he said, making the reason for his visit crystal clear.

"I don't think you did those things, either, Mr. Patel, but I'm not the one who needs convincing."

"But why must I convince anyone of anything? I'm the one now reduced to living on another man's charity. For which I'm extremely grateful." He looked as if he couldn't believe he'd said such a thing; as if he couldn't believe the need for having to say it.

"I'm sure I don't have to tell you that the world—that this city—has more than a few dishonest people, Mr. Patel. And, hard as it may be for the honest ones like yourself to accept, the system is geared to deal with the dishonest ones. So, when a business burns to the ground in a matter of minutes and a large insurance payout is hanging in the balance, the insurance company looks very carefully at the situation." I took a deliberate beat. "And I'm assuming that the insurance payout is large." It wasn't a question, and Patel didn't answer what I hadn't asked, which was all the answer I needed. "I promised Mr. Epstein that I would do what I could to speed the process along and I'll do that, Mr. Patel, but understand that your idea of 'speed' may differ from the insurance company's."

Patel looked sad and grim and angry. It was the angry that interested me; and as if he knew that, he said, "Then you should know that the Homeland Security people think that I'm a terrorist."

I was speechless. So was Yolanda, who was bringing the tray with Patel's tea, and she halted mid-step. He looked up, saw her, and jumped to his feet to help her with the tray. They introduced themselves and Patel fixed himself a cup of tea while I rolled over in my mind the idea that the Federal government's unleashed Rottweilers had Patel's scent up their nostrils. Not only did this not bode well for him, his presence here had just dropped me into the shit pile, and I could tell by the look on Yo's face that she'd reached the same conclusion. "Why do they think that, Mr. Patel?" Yolanda asked.

"Because somebody called and told them. That same somebody or group of somebodies has reported at least half a dozen Hindus and Sikhs that I personally know to Homeland Security as potential threats to the country, and there have been others that I've only heard of."

"Other what?" I asked.

"Other reports that innocent people are terrorist threats."

"Like who?" This was starting to stink worse than the Fulton Street fish market.

"Like some of the Muslims in Brooklyn and Queens, and the Buddhist monks in the Village, of all people!" This seemed to upset him. "Of all the unlikely people to accuse of being terrorists, these idiots point to the Bikshu Buddhists."

"What kind of Buddhists?"

"Beggars!" He almost shouted the word. "They go out every morning with their bowls and beg. For food, money, whatever people wish to give, and whatever they get is all they have. They are among the most peaceful people in the world and some . . . some . . . evil-minded . . ." He couldn't think of the words to describe people who would make such a dangerous accusation in the current climate, but I could, though they probably would be words that Patel had never spoken in his life. Maybe even were words he'd never heard.

"Why would they target you, or the others?"

He touched his head. "Because of this, because I am Hindu and my wife wears a sari, and because the Muslim women cover their heads and bodies, and because the Buddhists wear saffron robes and shave their heads and wear sandals even in winter."

I knew that what he was saying was possible but the pieces weren't fitting together logically. At least all the pieces I had on the table. I could believe that hatred would ignite a fire and destroy a home and business. I could believe that hatred would wrongly accuse people because they behaved differently from the accuser. What didn't fit was the setting fire to the unjustly accused. If Homeland Security thought that . . . what was Patel's first name? Frankie? If Homeland Security thought he was a terrorist threat, would they think he'd torch his own place? Wouldn't siccing Homeland Security on somebody be punishment enough? I'd be suspicious if a supposed terrorist all of sudden became a victim of terrorism. But suspicious of whom?

"You're not convinced, Mr. Rodriquez?"

"I'm confused, Mr. Patel."

He looked at me for a moment, and then he laughed. "My son said he liked you. I trust his judgment. He has excellent instincts for one so young." The lightness left him. "I would like to hire you to discover who destroyed my property. I have some savings, most of it in municipal bonds and Treasury notes. For Frankie's college. I don't know how long I'll be unable to earn more money, but I can pay you to begin, and if I run out of money, you'll have to stop. It is due solely to Mr. Epstein's kindness and generosity that I'm able to pay you at all, because otherwise I'd be paying a hotel, but I must feel that I'm doing something more than sitting and waiting for some external force to return my life to me."

I understood that as completely as if the thought had come through my own brain and out of my own mouth.

"Mr. Patel, what is your first name, if you don't mind my asking?" Yo asked then.

Patel was surprised but he clearly didn't mind answering Yolanda's question. In fact, I've yet to encounter the man who minded anything she said or did. "My name is Ravi," he answered, and looked expectantly at her.

She smiled and demonstrated that she could crank out the wattage, too. "I'm interested to know how Ravi Patel has a son named Frankie."

If they'd been in a high wattage contest Ravi Patel might just have won, so appreciative was he of Yolanda's shifting of the tension, and placing his interest in what clearly was a more pleasant place. "He was named for his grandfather, my father." And Ravi Patel told us how his grandfather and great uncle, brothers and the sons of Indian immigrants to England were named after Winston Churchill and Franklin Roosevelt; their sisters were named Eleanor and Elizabeth. Then the brothers left England for Canada, and Franklin eventually found his way to New York. "They were remarkable men," Patel said. "They considered it a great privilege to have had the opportunity to exchange British citizenship for Canadian and American citizenship, and to have had the ancient heritage of the Hindus of

India as a cultural launching pad. I am as American as the two of you are, and as Indian as you are Puerto Rican."

I didn't say what I wanted to say because it would have sounded too much like a cliché. In fact, even thinking it felt trite and cliché-ish. But so what? I'd think it anyway: That's what being an American meant—that blend of the unique and the ordinary, men and women who'd come here from all the places on the globe, ordinary people bringing with them the unique aspects of their homelands, and blending in. I thought of my own family, and of the people I knew and cared about and respected: Basil Griffin and Arlene Edwards, Blacks from Trinidad and Jamaica, and Jeffrey Dahl, a white man born in Barbados; Jill Mason's parents and Sandra Gillespie's grandparents, Black American southerners whose ancestry may have been lost and destroyed but whose ancient history permeates every aspect of American culture; David Epstein, whose grandparents perished in Nazi concentration camps and whose daughter is buried in Israel; Carmine Aiello, a first generation American whose elderly mother, despite more than sixty years here, still is more comfortable speaking Italian; the Nigerian grocery store owners who work around the clock to earn a living for their families; and half the people I do business with in Chinatown—unique and ordinary, every one of them.

"I'll draw up Mr. Patel's contract, Phil," Yolanda said, rescuing me from the murky labyrinth of my thoughts.

"And I'll bring it to you later today. I need to see Epstein and if it's convenient, I can drop it off . . ."

He interrupted me with one of his smiles. "When you come to dinner. Both of you, and anybody you'd like to bring. Please! The lodgings provided by Mr. Epstein are almost exactly what we had above our restaurant and my wife feels so much at home that all she wants to do is cook. But without the restaurant, there's nobody to eat so much food. So you must come to dinner. Everybody must come to dinner!"

It was quite a feast the Patels laid on. Despite having been in residence less than twenty-four hours, Indira Patel had transformed a previously unoccupied space into an elegant home for her family. A few strategically placed rugs, pieces of fabric, statues, and wall hangings, along with the soft strains of sitar music in the background and the delicate scent of aromatic incense wafting all around, combined to create an elegant and peaceful yet comfortably homey setting. Yolanda and her long-time lover Sandra Gillespie had brought arm-loads of flowers, and Sandra, once a principal dancer with the Alvin Ailey Company, had brought a framed poster of women of all cultures dancing. Indira Patel, delighted, immediately got busy hanging the art and sent Frankie and Ravi to find vessels to hold all the flowers. Connie and I had stopped at a Puerto Rican bakery and bought one of everything and Mrs. Patel had to suspend her picture-hanging mission long enough to steer Frankie away from the dessert. A fifteen-year-old boy was a fifteen-year-old boy all over the world, and dessert before dinner had never spoiled the ability of one to eat like a racehorse when the dinner bell rang.

Just as the flowers were arranged and the picture hung, knocks on the door signaled the arrival of the Epstein family. "Now we can eat!" Frankie yelled, and Ravi opened the door. Sasha, Ellie, and Dave entered and their eyes widened and their mouths opened and didn't close for several seconds.

"Wow!" Ellie said.

"Amazing!" Dave said.

"Holy shit!" Sasha said. And the party was on. It took all the women in the room—and there were more of them than there were of us—to get all the food to the table, and at that, there were still several pots on the stove with big ladles in them, ready for dipping. The Epstein family had brought a dozen bottles of wine, juice, seltzer, and cider. We filled our plates and glasses and found places to sit—most of us on cushions on the floor. Then we all filled our plates and glasses again. And again. And I'd thought I didn't much care for Indian food. Where had I gotten that notion? When I whispered that thought to Connie she whispered back that I must not have been in the proper company on my visits to Indian restaurants. "Good food requires good company," she told me with such a serious expression that I seriously began to consider the notion, until she poked me in the ribs with her elbow. She might have been joking but I think she was onto something.

Ravi Patel stood up and made a toast that had everyone sniffling and wiping their eyes. Then the men cleared away and washed the dirty dishes while the women made coffee and tea and got the dessert trays ready. Again Mrs. Patel spent most of her time shooing Frankie away from the sweets. I managed to grab a few private words with Ravi, Dave, and Sasha. It was almost midnight when we left. I hadn't enjoyed a meal and the company of that many people since Thanksgiving. In fact, it had felt very much like a holiday gathering, greatly improved this time by the fact that Connie agreed that it would make sense for her to spend the night at my place since it was so late, rather than go all the way Uptown to the Bronx.

She woke me the next morning before the alarm sounded with a punch to the arm. "Ow," I mumbled. "What?"

She was sitting upright in the bed looking like something was seriously wrong. "I can't wear the same clothes to work today that I wore yesterday."

I didn't see the problem but was wise enough not to say so. In fact, I didn't say anything. I still had an hour of sleep left and I really wanted to claim it. Connie reached across me, grabbed the phone off the stand and started punching numbers. That got my attention and got me half awake. "Who in the world are you calling this time of morning?" It was barely six o'clock.

"Yo, Sis," she said. "Sorry for the early call but . . ." Yolanda must have spoken because Connie stopped suddenly, then started to giggle like I'd never heard her do. I've said it once, I'll say it to anybody who'll listen: It is the height of arrogance and stupidity for men to think they're superior to women. They know things in ways that we'll never know or understand. Until I started seriously dating Connie a couple of months ago, she and Yolanda had never met. Now they were calling each other Sis and giggling on the phone at six in the morning? She punched off the phone, kissed me good, then scrambled out of bed.

"No fair!" I yelled. And it definitely wasn't.

"Gotta go, babe. Yo's lending me clothes to wear to work so I've got to get to her place, get dressed, and get to work. Besides, you've got breakfast with Carmine this morning." She blew me a kiss this time and in seconds, I heard the shower running. Yep, women definitely were the superior species.

Carmine Aiello agreed wholeheartedly with my assessment and added his own bit of wisdom: He said he knew better than to ever let a woman know that's what he thought. "And if you're as smart as I think you are, Rodriquez, you'll keep that thought to yourself, too. Bad enough broads got all the power, but the only way we keep control is if they think that we think we got the power, too." He sat back with great self-satisfaction and sipped his espresso.

I'd met Carmine a few months back when he hired me to find out who was hurting Dr. Jill Mason, but I'd known about him for most of my adult life. Carmine had always boasted of mob connections but nobody believed him because he ran his mouth too much and everybody figured that anybody who was really connected wouldn't have to brag about it. He also claimed familial connections to the *Sopranos* actor, but nobody believed that, either. But then Carmine got me a sit-down with Carlo Portello, the ninety-year-old head of the Little Italy mob and made a believer out of me. But the real reason nobody liked Carmine was that he was the kind of asshole who went around calling people Spics and niggers. So when he said he wanted to hire me, I refused. After all, I was a Spic and Jill Mason was a nigger and why would he want to put money in my pocket to help her? Then I found out why: Carmine's young daughter was one of the victims of the serial rapist and Jill Mason was the shrink treating many of these young girls and helping them heal. Carmine Aiello, whom I'd previously only thought of as a fat, mean racist, took his beloved daughter for her sessions with the shrink at night and sat and waited for her and took it personally when somebody wanted to hurt the woman who was helping his daughter. I then saw Carmine Aiello as a husband and a father and part of the group of parents who figured out that the cops weren't doing much to find out who was raping and murdering little girls. As luck would have it, I did find out who the bastard was and I did make sure he paid. But it didn't happen overnight, and during that time, Carmine and I learned how to talk to and listen to each other. And we became friends. We have breakfast every Friday morning at little restaurant in his part of the old Little Italy neighborhood that has the some of the best coffee, and truly the best Napoleons, in New York City.

We settled on Friday mornings because, no matter how hectic and unpredictable my week gets, I always manage to get to the gym on the weekends; and after the number of Napoleons I eat on Friday mornings, the gym on Saturdays and Sundays is a must. Carmine, on the other hand, had stopped worrying about his weight about seventy pounds ago and as he snagged another cannoli—his third—from the plate of pastries in the center of the table, he asked about Yolanda. He's one of the many men who, at the sight of her, lose all contact with their store of common sense. He paid us double our usual retainer when he hired us because he was showing off for Yo. Being the pragmatist that she is, Yo had smiled and taken the man's money.

"She's fine and that reminds me," I said, opening my carryall and removing a gift-wrapped package which I extended to him across the table.

"What the hell's this?" he groused, reaching for it.

"A birthday present for Terry. And Yolanda says give a hug from her."

The fat man's face went all mushy. "How's Miss Aguierre know about Terry's birthday? I'd forget myself if it wasn't for Theresa."

"Women know everything, Carmine. That's what I'm trying to get you to accept. They know everything, they do everything right, and we're at their mercy."

Carmine studied the pretty package, then looked up at me. His eyes narrowed. "You better hurry up and marry that broad, Rodriquez, so you get the proper perspective on this thing before it's too late." He chewed some cannoli, still staring slit-eyed at me. "Though given that goofy, shit-eating grin your face is wearing, I'd say it's probably already too late for you."

On more than one occasion with Carmine, I'd been attacked by a case of the teenage boy giggles. I felt an attack coming on. The look on his face and the movie-mobster tone of voice he adopted rendered me all but helpless. "What perspective would that be, Carmine?" I asked, knowing I'd regret it.

He lowered his voice further and leaned across the table toward me to make sure that the waitress, who I discovered was a cousin of his, couldn't overhear. "It's only when you're in love with 'em that you're blind to the truth. Once you go to bed with 'em and wake up with 'em year after year, the truth comes clear, and the truth is, Rodriquez, that they're dangerous. All of 'em. Grown women, little girls, all of 'em. You know what I hadda get that kid for her birthday? What she and her mother insisted and demanded that I get her?" He now had a wild-eyed, deer-in-the-headlights look.

The giggles had control of me. I covered my face with the napkin, grateful that it was cloth and larger than a tissue, but my heaving shoulders must have given me away because the waitress sidled over to our table, hands on ample hips. "What shit is Carmine spouting now?" But she laughed with us, asked about Yolanda, Carmine showed her the present, and she went to get us more coffee.

I took advantage of the moment to tell Carmine I needed his help, and when I gave him a brief outline of what I wanted, he grew immediately serious. "Yeah, I know Joey Mottola. I know his old man better than him, but I know him. And I gotta tell ya, Rodriquez, he ain't gonna sit face-to-face with you." Carmine shook and sighed deeply, as if he couldn't understand such behavior, when less than six months ago, he wouldn't have been caught dead having coffee and pastries with me at his favorite coffee bar.

"Then will you ask him for me if he knows where Sam Epstein is?"

"When was the last time somebody saw this Epstein?"

"Tuesday night, when he closed the cleaners."

"I know that place, that Epstein Cleaners. They got the only plant in the Village now and they're making a fucking killing. Every dry cleaners around sends their stuff out to Epstein. They got people working almost around the clock."

I didn't want to know how Carmine knew what he knew, so I just said, "Add to that the fact that it's been his family's business for fifty years, and I know that's why he didn't just walk away from it," I said, and sat back to give Carmine time to think about things. I knew he didn't respond well to being rushed or pushed, and that he liked, whenever possible, to be the instigator of thoughts and ideas and plans. A bit of a control freak was Carmine.

"Casey and McQueen ain't gonna go face-to-face with you, either. They don't like Spi . . ." Carmine caught himself, cleared his throat, and continued. "They don't like nobody but their own. Tell you the truth, I'm surprised they're even hooked up with Joey." He thought about it some more. "And I'm surprised Joey's hooked up with them." He played with his spoon, his brain figuring all the angles, and I could tell he was as confused by the picture he was getting as I was. "Lemme do some askin' around over the weekend, Rodriquez, and I'll get back to you. And the only reason I'm not real worried about Epstein is that Casey and McQueen are involved. If it was just Joey . . ." Instead of completing the sentence, Carmine slapped his hands together in an up and down motion, meaning that Sam Epstein would have been finished on Tuesday night. Done with. Over. And on that cheery thought, I paid the bill and left.

On the walk to my office, I gave in to the worry that Carmine's confusion caused. This was a man who was weaned on crooked deals and scams and I wasn't in the least consoled by the fact that his dislike of the picture I painted confirmed my own suspicions. Then, mid-thought and mid-stride, I changed directions and headed back to the café, creating disruption on the narrow, snaky sidewalk on the narrow, snaky Bowery side street. However, I was just thankful that I'd remembered to go back for the breakfast receipt before I'd gotten too many blocks away so I wouldn't have to endure both Yolanda's scorn and a trip all the way back over here later to get it. I wouldn't have time later, anyway. I had a full day ahead of me.

This time, because of the time wasted on the return trip, I took a taxi when I left the café, and I remembered to get the receipt. I wanted to be in the office at nine straight up so that I could put in a call to a claims adjuster I knew at Big Apple Business Insurers. His name was Bill Calloway and I'd worked with him before. I didn't know if he had the Patel fire but I guessed that he did, and I hoped that he'd agree to see me. I was betting, based on discussions with Ravi Patel and Sasha Heller the previous night, that I knew things—important things—that he didn't know. And if that proved to be the case, then I was counting on the fact that he'd feel some sense of obligation to me for telling him, and to demonstrate his gratitude, he'd stop screwing around with Ravi Patel's insurance claim check. Of course there was always the possibility that Calloway knew everything I knew and was either ignoring the information or discounting it, or not giving a damn, in which case I'd have to figure out a way to show him the error of his ways. But based on what I knew about Bill Calloway, I didn't think I had to worry.

I expected Yolanda to give me a good ribbing about the early morning phone call she received but she surprised me. Instead, I got a big smile and a warm greeting and big dose of the warm fuzzies about the evening with the Patels. She and Sandra, she said, hadn't enjoyed themselves so much since Thanksgiving. "But it was a really weird feeling, too, Phil, considering that everybody there was a client. With the exception of Jill Mason, we've never socialized with clients, have we?"

"I don't think so. And you're right; it does feel kinda strange to enjoy spending time with people who're paying us. And by the way!" I apologized for the abrupt change of subject, then asked her if she'd known that before last night, I'd thought that I didn't like Indian food. "I know it sounds silly. It feels silly. But I was just wondering . . . I guess what I'm asking . . . well, dammit, people change, right? I mean, we grow into and out of likes and dislikes, and I was just wondering if it's possible that I woke up yesterday morning and didn't like Indian food, but then I ate it, just to be polite really, and it was wonderful! Is that how change happens, you think? Why it happens? Out of necessity?"

Yolanda came over to my desk, kissed the top of my head, and asked whether I'd brought her a Napoleon and remembered to give Carmine the birthday present for Terry. I gave her the pastry box with two Napoleons inside and she grinned like a little kid, then left me sitting at my desk while she went to get a cup of coffee to accompany her pastry.

I got my contact list out of the desk drawer, looked up Bill Calloway's number, and called him. He answered on the first ring. He was surprised and pleased to hear from me, and readily agreed to meet me for lunch without asking why. But I knew why he agreed so readily when he said he'd be in my "neck of the woods anyway around lunch time." I guessed that was because he'd be meeting his investigator to discuss the Patel fire and to plan the investigation into the family's background. Part of me was annoyed that I hadn't gotten the job, but I quickly admitted to myself that I'd much rather be working for the Patels than against them. Of course if Calloway had called me before Ravi showed up in my office, I'd never have gotten the chance to formulate a preference. What's that Yolanda said: Life's an interesting journey.

I spent the rest of the morning writing out my notes. I had three days' worth. I didn't like to get that far behind but there had been little private, quiet time in the last three days when I could just sit at my desk and commit to writing everything that I could recall about what I'd said and done, whom I'd seen, and where I'd gone. I realized that I found it difficult to write about the encounter with the Homeland Security agent and I wasn't certain why. I was fairly certain, though, that I hadn't seen the last of him. Perhaps that was the source of my difficulty: Since I knew I'd be seeing him again, and since to see him again almost certainly meant an adversarial situation, I'd either have to suck up to him and kiss his ass, or get busted. No wonder I couldn't write about it. So, I decided to do something pleasant instead. I called Connie. We'd sort of drifted into the habit of spending Friday nights together at my place, and since we'd spent Thursday night together, I wanted to make sure that tonight was still a go. And I had something to say as well.

"I was just thinking about you," she said. "And before you ask, don't ask what I was thinking because I can't tell you." The warm humor in her voice gave me the warm humors all over and I realized—like being struck by the proverbial bolt of lightening—why Yolanda didn't rib me about this morning: She knew before I did what I was feeling.

"So, how about I tell you what I'm thinking?" I asked.

"Fine, as long as it doesn't make me blush."

I knew that meant that her office door was open and that there were people wandering in and out, which was a regular Friday occurrence as she organized the week's files and reports and did what she called general housekeeping. Her office was private but part of a system of counselors and social workers at Beth Israel Hospital that dealt with victims of rape and sexual assault. Her door was closed only when she was with a client. The rest of the time it was open. Like now. "Okay. Two thoughts. Questions, really. If you'd consider leaving some things at my place so that what happened this morning won't happen again. And if you'd consider staying there on the nights you work late so you won't have to go all the way uptown so late at night." I finished talking and thought I knew what that writer meant about waiting to exhale. I waited for a good, long few seconds that felt like a couple of hours.

Finally she said, "I like it when you have brilliant ideas, Phil, even if you think they're questions. And I don't think I'm blushing but I am grinning like a Halloween pumpkin, and I'll have to call you back later. Bye."

I probably looked a lot like a pumpkin, too, as I hung up the phone and continued with my notes, the conversation with Connie having had the desired effect of lightening the heavy feeling I was having about Homeland Security agents. The process also helped me decide on an approach to take with Bill Calloway and clarified some of the confusion I had about the players in this odd game. I certainly was still confused but I think I was beginning to understand clearly why. I didn't understand at all, though, Mike Kallen's odd behavior, and as I shifted gears and began to work on the Avenue B apartment building security analysis and recommendation, I realized that I didn't like Kallen. More than that, I actively disliked him, and I didn't think it had anything to do with his vacillating about signing the contract and everything to do with the man as a person. Then I told myself it didn't matter whether I liked him or not; I wasn't getting paid to have personal feelings for the guy. So I put the feelings on the back burner and busied myself doing what I was getting paid to do. No way, though, I would turn my back on that stove until I knew what was simmering in the pot on that back burner.

Chapter Five

Bill Calloway and I hooked up at twelve-thirty sharp at a trendy vegetarian restaurant on First Avenue. He was dressed in jeans, Timberland boots, and wore a hooded sweatshirt under a parka, which confirmed my suspicion that he was on an investigation. I'd met Calloway a couple of years ago while doing some undercover work for a gay nightclub on the West Side. The place was huge—a warehouse with six bars, three game rooms, two video rooms, and three dance floors on three levels, and the owners were raking in so much money that it had taken them months to realize that at least two of their employees were engaged in a sophisticated skimming scam that was costing them three or four thousand dollars a week. I thought that it must be nice to be making so much money that you didn't miss four grand, and was happy to legally separate the owners from a few of those thousands in exchange for shutting down the illegal payday. I was alternating undercover kitchen work with Mike Smith and Eddie Ortiz. It was my night and I'd gone outside on the loading dock to catch some fresh air. I heard a scuffle in the alley behind the club, heard somebody curse, heard somebody yell, and went to check it out. Three dudes were kicking the shit out of a guy on the ground who'd curled himself into a ball. The three doing kicking were calling the guy on the ground some ugly names, most of them beginning or ending with faggot. The guy on the ground didn't utter a sound. I picked up a wooden board and started swinging it around and yelling about calling the cops. The three macho types scattered and disappeared into the darkness like the cockroaches they were. The guy on the ground was Bill Calloway.

"I'm not even going to ask why you called out of the blue and offered to buy me lunch," he said, shaking my hand. He was long and lean—he looked like the marathoner he was—and he wore his hair close-cropped and he wore tiny gold-rimmed eyeglasses and, depending on his dress, he looked like a college professor or a college student. Today was student day. "I'm just glad to see you, Phil."

"Same back at you, Bill," I said, sliding into the booth across from him. "It's been way too long. And out of the blue isn't so bad if you're getting a free meal out of the deal. Especially at your favorite veggie pit stop."

"So true, so true. So, how've you been, Phil? How's business and how's the lovely Yolanda Maria? And if you see that Sandra Gillespie wench anytime soon, tell her it's rude to not return phone calls from old and dear friends."

Bill was a motor-mouth. I never had to worry about holding up my end of a conversation when I was with Bill because he could, would, and did hold up both ends quite ably. "If we'd had lunch yesterday I could have delivered your message to Sandra, because I saw her last night. Yo is wonderful, and business is good but it could always be better." I had to stop and catch a breath. "In fact, it would have been improved if I'd gotten the Patel fire investigation."

Bill was a dark-skinned Black man but I watched him first blanch, then redden. "How'd you know I had that?" He'd whispered the question as if he feared being overheard.

"I didn't know, I guessed. And relax, dude. Resume inhaling and exhaling. I was just razzing you a bit. I'm not being serious."

But Bill was major-league serious. He actually looked around the restaurant, then leaned across the table and, still whispering, said, "I wanted to use you. I would have used you but they told me not to. They said I couldn't."

"What 'they' told you not to? What are you talking about, Bill?"

"Homeland Security, man. They're all over this thing. Giving me major pain in the ass, too. I wanted to call and ask you what you did to piss them off so bad but they tap people's phones and shit and I don't need the aggravation, you know?"

Oh, yeah, I knew. "Tall skinny blond guy with crooked teeth?" I described the Fed I'd gone toe-to-toe with the morning after the Taste of India fire, and Bill, looking, if possible, even more disturbed and worried than before, nodded. "I didn't do anything but refuse to kiss his ass," I said.

"They don't do failure to kiss ass so well, Phil. In fact, they don't like that at all." Bill looked around again, as if expecting Fed faces with crewcuts to pop out of the wall sconces.

"How did he know to jerk my chain? I only had a few words with the guy but I never told him my name," I asked, and Bill explained how, the morning following the fire, the Fed—his name, I learned, was Petersen—showed up at the insurance office, asked to see the claims adjuster for the fire, and requested Bill's cooperation, which Bill took to mean cooperate or else.

"I thought it was a little unusual but I didn't get worried until he opened your folder, took one look at your ID photo, and started blowing smoke out of both ears and both nostrils. I thought he was going to explode."

"Did he tell you why he wanted to be involved?"

Bill shook his head. "They never tell you anything—they don't have to—and they never share information. They just demand in the strictest secrecy." Bill's worry had changed to disgust. A couple of days of Federal agents in your face will do that to the mildest of men, and Bill Calloway was a mild-mannered man.

"Then let me tell you a few things, Bill, starting with the fact that some idiot has taken to calling Homeland Security and claiming that certain people are terrorists. People like Hindus and Muslims and Sikhs and Buddhist monks. People whose dress readily sets them apart, but whose dress is a reflection of their religious beliefs, not their political ones."

"And Ravi Patel . . ."

"Was served up to Homeland Security on a dirty platter. But that's not the good part, Bill. Try to wrap your mind around a victim of the World Trade Center disaster being a terrorist."

Bill had picked up his water glass and was ready to drink. On hearing my words, his action halted, glass in mid-air, mouth open to meet the glass. He looked like a tank fish anticipating feeding time, and if there were any room for humor in this situation I'd have laughed at him. But there wasn't. "How is Patel a Trade Center victim, Phil?"

"Taste of India Too. It was a little café on the ground level of Tower One. It was owned by Ravi's cousin, the son of his father's brother. Ravi and his cousin were as close as brothers and their only children as close as brother and sister. That entire family perished, including the daughter who normally would have been at school but on this day, of all days, she'd gone to the restaurant to help out that morning because one of the regular staff had a baby the previous night."

Bill looked sick. Like most New Yorkers, even these five years later, his hearing some aspect of that event not previously known impacted him like those first moments and hours and days and weeks. "You think Homeland Security knows about this?"

"Damn right, they know!" But as soon as I said the words, I knew I might be wrong. What the Federal investigative agencies didn't know at any given moment could topple another few skyscrapers. Not only were they notoriously secretive, they were that way even with each other; secretive and proprietary. If one agency knew something, the last thing it would do would be to share that knowledge or information with another of the agencies for fear the other agency would get the credit. Not get the bad guys, but get the credit. Add to this stupidity the fact that the Department of Homeland Security didn't exist at the time of the September 11th attacks, and yes, it was entirely impossible that Petersen of Homeland Security didn't know that half of Ravi Patel's family was obliterated in that disaster. It was also possible that he knew and didn't care; he had a bone between his teeth and he wasn't about to let it go. "It doesn't really matter what they know, Bill. The only thing that matters is that you conduct the kind of solid investigation that I know you will. And if you do that, I believe you'll find that while arson almost certainly was the reason for the Taste of India fire, you'll also find that the Patels had nothing to do with it. These people are victims, Bill. Again."

The sick look slowly drained out of Bill, taking all his energy along for the ride; his shoulders sagged and he slumped down in his seat. "So are we all, Phil. I let some jerk I'd never seen before convince me not to hire you, a man who saved my life!"

"Don't beat yourself up, Bill. You know as well as I do that if you'd refused him he'd have gone over your head and spread a lot of crap about national security, then you'd have your boss's bad breath on the back of your neck as well as Petersen's. At least this way you get to run your own investigation in your own way."

"How and why are you so sure the Patels are clean?"

It was step carefully time. "I've got two clients with interests related to this case, Bill, and what I know, like I told you, is that certain people whose race and religion mark them as different have been reported to the government as terrorist threats. There may have been other fires . . ." I hadn't had that thought until this very moment and I didn't know where it came from but I'd bet the mortgage that it was true and I'd most definitely be looking into the possibility because all of a sudden pieces were connecting and forming a picture. ". . . other fires with these same people as the targets." I stopped talking. I either was digging a very deep hole into which I'd have to jump if I was wrong, or I'd stumbled upon a truth that didn't bode well at all for one of my clients. "I would tell you more if I could, Bill." But, I finished the thought in my head, I don't know any more. I don't even really know what I just told you, but it makes more sense than anything I've thought so far. Then I did a Yolanda and changed the subject. "So, are we gonna eat or do I get to escape this lunch with having bought two glasses of water and a free basket of blue corn chips and salsa? Yolanda will be so pleased."

Bill quickly picked up his menu.

It was a quick walk from the restaurant to Epstein's Cleaners, burdened though I was by the hefty receipt for lunch at the vegetarian restaurant. Trendy vegetables are expensive and marathoners have very healthy appetites and they apparently need to eat lots of trendy vegetables to fully nourish themselves. Bill and I parted on good terms; better than good, actually. He didn't say it in so many words but I knew he'd expedite the Patel investigation and that he wouldn't allow anything but the facts to influence his decision. At the end of the day, that's all I could ask of him, or of anybody, for that matter.

There was a line at the counter when I entered the cleaners and Vivian was at the register. She saw me and motioned with her head that I should go through to the back. I took off my coat and she shifted to the side so that I could get behind her and into the back room. It was every bit as steamy, hot, and smelly as before. I hurried myself to the back of the room and up the narrow staircase to the box. The door opened before I could knock, and Dave waved me in. Ellie was on the stool in the corner and they both looked a few degrees past miserable.

"Tell me you've got something to tell me," Dave said.

I didn't react to his attempt at humor, and that told him a lot about what I had to tell him. "There may have been more fires. I'm still checking. And there's reason to believe that the people who are burned out are first reported to Homeland Security as terrorist suspects." Both Dave and Ellie were momentarily speechless, then Dave's mind went to work. Before he could get too far, I said, "Did Sasha ever tell you how she and Frankie Patel met?"

"At school, wasn't it?" Ellie said.

"Not the way you mean," I said.

"How many ways are there?" Dave demanded, not pleasantly. This whole thing was taking a toll on the old man, and he was showing the wear and tear.

I decided I could afford to overlook the unpleasantness. "The school they both attend has a high percentage of students directly affected by the Twin Towers collapse. Affected in that they lost family . . ."

Dave cut me off. "Last time I looked, Frankie Patel's mother was alive and well and cooking dinner for her family. Sasha's mother is not."

"Neither is Frankie Patel's aunt, uncle, and cousin, who was like a sister to him." And in the heavy moment that followed, there was absolute silence in the soundproof room. Dave's shoulders sagged, just as Bill's had done in the restaurant such a short time ago, and all the anger drained out of him, leaving just the hurt and the sadness and the sorrow and the fear. "I came to tell you that I think it's highly unlikely that you've given shelter to an arsonist, and that I think I'll have some word about Sam on Monday."

"Monday! This is Friday! How can you know something about Patel so soon and not know anything about my Sammy?"

"Because the insurance adjuster would talk to me, off the record, but the people who may know something about Sammy, won't."

"Why the hell not?"

"Because they don't talk to Spics and niggers, Dave, that's why." And as soon as I said the words I regretted it, wished I could take them back, because it was too much for the old man. He began breathing heavily and tears leaked from his eyes.

"When did things get so bad? How did this happen?" Ellie had her arms around him and she looked at me, as if waiting for an answer.

"You mean when did the Irish and Italians start hating Blacks and Puerto Ricans?" I knew I should shut up but I was too scrambled inside for common sense and common decency to have any chance of keeping my mouth from speaking what I was thinking and feeling. I knew Dave Epstein was scrambled inside, too, which is why he would say something so asinine. The man was a Jew who'd lost half his family to another bunch of cowards, and maybe having that happen twice in one lifetime is too much. I didn't know how much was too much for another person, but I did know that I was tired of people blaming the current resurgence of racism on the cowards that destroyed the World Trade Center and their masters. I also knew that logic and grief didn't cohabit; I couldn't talk sense to a man who was on the verge of losing a good part of what was left of his family. "I'll be in touch if I hear anything about Sam before Monday," I said, and left two generations of the Epstein family in the soundproof box to try and bring some comfort and consolation to each other.

I left the cleaners, turned left, and rang the bell on the next door over. It was answered almost immediately by Ravi Patel who buzzed me in when he heard my name. As I climbed the stairs and entered the temporary home of the Patel family, I marveled again at the lack of heat and chemical odor. I'd have expected the spoils of the business below to penetrate and permeate the upstairs living space, but I suppose that the Epstein family had, long ago, figured out a way to keep the smell of work from following them home. I declined Patel's invitation to come in, remove my coat, sit down, and have something eat or drink. I told him what I could of my conversation with Bill Calloway and tried to curb his excitement. I wanted him to understand that I was making no promises, and he said he understood. He just wanted me to know how good it felt to know that there was hope and that he could, with honesty in his eyes, face his wife and son and express that hope. Then I asked him if he was aware of any other fires having destroyed Hindu-owned businesses. If he found the question odd or upsetting it didn't show. What did show was the considerable thought he gave the question.

"Noooo . . ." he said slowly, shaking his head. "Of course the Hindu community in New York is very large and we don't all know each other, but no, I don't think—wait! Yes! It was some months ago but yes, there was a store that sold fabrics and rugs and jewelry. An import and export business, it was. On Seventh Avenue, in Chelsea." He was pleased to have remembered and so was I.

"Do you know the people, or know anyone who knows them? I'd like to talk to them. As soon as possible."

"I suppose I can find out something."

I gave him my card. "As soon as possible, Mr. Patel, please. Call me as soon as you know something," I said, and almost ran from him, leaving him staring, surprised, after me. I had to run because as soon as he mentioned the fire almost a year ago, I knew what it was that put me on to the fire thing in the restaurant with Bill Calloway: About a year ago the Middle-Eastern café two doors from my gym was torched. Everybody knew it was arson and while nobody was ever arrested and charged, suspicion hung over the owners, two Lebanese who, because of their proximity to the gym, became body builders, which is how I came to know them.

I did something I disliked intensely, something I criticized others for doing whenever I saw it: I called Yolanda on the cell phone while I was walking down the street. I thought walking down the street and talking on the telephone was almost as stupid as driving and talking on the telephone—almost because you couldn't kill anybody while walking and talking. As I punched the numbers I hoped nobody was looking at me and thinking I was an absolute asshole. "Yo!" I said when she answered. "Do a search, going back at least a year, for fires in the businesses of . . . of . . ." Who? People who wore something other than jeans and sneakers to work. "Hindus, Muslims, Sikhs, and whoever else dresses like them. I'm on my way in." I snapped the phone shut and began a slow jog toward the office, just as pellets of ice and flakes of snow began a slow drift down from the heavy, dark clouds that had hovered all day. I found myself wishing that it would just go on and snow, just dump the ten or twelve wet, mushy inches that are typical of March snows and get it over with. Then spring could happen.

As soon as I saw the package on my desk when I rushed into the office I knew that momentarily I'd be crashing back to earth from the high I'd experienced, thinking I'd tumbled on to something important and relevant about the fires. As soon as I saw Yo's face I knew I was right. "You get any hits on the fires?"

"Not yet, but the package on your desk is from KLM. They want you begin the security evaluations Monday."

"Whoopee."

"Let's see a little more appreciation, if you don't mind, for the job that's going to pay our bills for the next year."

I produced a sickly grin and did some half-assed jumping jacks. "How's that? Now, any hits on the fires?"

"Yes, as a matter of fact." She gave me several printed-out pages from her internet searches then demanded to know what was going on in my head. I filled her in and watched her process it all. No wonder she liked computers so much; her brain worked just like one, moving all the bits and bytes around until they found a logical place to fit. "In its own warped way, it makes sense, Phil."

I took the papers to my desk, turned on the lamp, and started to read. I knew that I'd need to go to the big wall map of the city that hung in the back of the room and stick pins in the locations of the fires, but one thing was instantly clear: My hypothesis had all the fires occurring in the southern part of Manhattan, below Chelsea. The fires literally were all over the map. Of course, it would require a lot more checking to determine for certain that the targets of all the fires fit the category I had in mind, but this was a start. I scanned the list and found what I thought was the import-export business that Ravi Patel had mentioned and marked it with a yellow highlighter. Then I put the sheaf of papers in my desk drawer and put the Patels, the Epsteins, and the fires out of my mind and turned my attention to the package from KLM Properties and Mike Kallen. Most of my attention anyway, for it was Friday afternoon and my weekend could officially begin in another couple of hours. If nothing strange or bizarre happened, that would mean two whole days spent with Connie deLeon. Given that prospect I didn't mind that Mike Kallen wanted to meet me at seven o'clock Monday morning at an apartment building on East 29th Street and First Avenue.

My cell phone rang and I jumped. I turned around to look at

Yolanda, to see if she was testing my reflexes or some other silly thing; she was the only person who ever called me on the thing . . . except Connie. I snatched it off the charging stand, answered it, and heard, "You know who this is?" My senses needed a moment to synchronize. I knew the voice—I heard it most mornings but I'd never heard it on the telephone. Why the hell was Willie One Eye calling me on the telephone?

"I know who it is," I said, sounding as cautious and suspicious as Willie. "Is something wrong? Are you all right?"

"Everything is good, *hermano.* Thank you for asking. My nephew has words for you. He's working nights now through Monday."

If cell phones had dial tones I'd be listening to one. Willie was gone, and even if he hadn't been, I couldn't have asked him what his nephew wanted to talk to me about. The fact that he did was its own message. The nephew, whose name I didn't know, was, I knew, an ex-addict with the tattoos that branded him an ex-felon as well. He was a thin, quiet, still man. Motionless, even. It was Willie's nephew who had provided the tip that led me to Jill Mason's assailant and, by default, to a multimillion-dollar drug and theft ring that operated out of a barber shop. If Willie's nephew had words for me, I'd definitely find time over the weekend to listen to them, but since I couldn't possibly imagine what they would be, I didn't spend any more time thinking about it.

"Front door, Phil," Yolanda said quietly as the door opened. I immediately opened the top right drawer of my desk and stood up.

"Can I help you?"

"No," snarled my visitor, "but I can help you." He hadn't closed the door behind him and it didn't take long for the cold to reach me.

"Close the door and tell me about it," I said. I wasn't a

judgmental man, my intention to see Willie One Eye's nephew as soon as possible just one example of that, but what had just walked in my door guaranteed that I wasn't about to step away from the desk and the open right-hand drawer where my Glock sat within easy reach. He looked like a refugee from a Hell's Angels training camp, a refugee because he looked too stupid to even have made the cut in that fraternity of dubious reputation. This guy was tall—over six feet—and he'd obviously never met a carbohydrate he didn't like or an exercise program that he did. He was probably still in his twenties but his gut hung over his belt like that of an old man. He glared at me through watery pale blue eyes.

"How much you pay for information?"

"Depends on the information," I said. "Close the door and tell me what you've got." I made sure he got that I wasn't asking for a favor and he slammed the door. "So, what are you selling?"

"I want five bills," he said in his snarly voice.

"You and every other low life in the East Village."

He took a couple of steps toward me, confirming my suspicion that he was drugged to the gills. He could barely place one foot down and lift the other and keep his balance. "I'm trying to do you a favor, asshole."

"I think I can live without it," I said. "Close the door on your way out."

Faster than should have possible given what I believed to be his drug and alcohol blood level, he grabbed a chair and flung it against the wall. I grabbed the Glock from the drawer and aimed it at him. That got his attention with about the same intensity as the chair meeting the wall got Yolanda's. She had rushed out into the front room in time to see me point a gun at our visitor.

"Phil! What's going on?"

"Oh, wow! You're the dyke, right? I heard about you. Yeah,

you're a fine piece of ass, all right. Bet I could change your mind, though." He leered at Yolanda and grabbed his crotch and made a wiggling motion that if hadn't been so stupid-looking would have been too obscene to watch.

"Go ahead and shoot him," she said.

"It'll mess up the carpet," I said.

"I bet his mother'll help us replace it," she said.

I chambered a round in the Glock, a sound our visitor obviously was familiar with but just as obviously found not to his liking. He backed up toward the door. "You'll be sorry, asshole." His hand behind his back, his eyes locked on the weapon in my hand, biker dude opened the door and backed out, leaving the door open.

"I'll get over it," I said to the gust of wind that blew in. I hurried to close the door but hesitated a moment, listening for the roar of a chopper starting. Car horns was all I heard, confirming my assessment of our visitor. I carefully locked the door and pulled down the shade; it was Friday afternoon and we could safely call it a week. Yolanda was looking at me in total disbelief. "Don't ask because I don't know," I said.

"You'll be sorry for what?"

"I don't know, Yo," I said, not bothering to curb my exasperation. "He said he had information to sell and he wanted five hundred dollars. I laughed at him and he threw a chair."

She walked over and looked at the brick wall, then at the chair that had bounced off the brick wall. She returned the chair to its proper place, rubbed her hand against the rough wall, then looked at me. "We're connecting the intercom. Immediately. No more people walking in the door unannounced and unexpected."

"What about legitimate clients, paying clients, like . . . like Ravi Patel, who walked in unannounced the other day. And Dave Epstein."

"Legitimate clients like Ravi Patel and Dave Epstein won't mind giving their names and stating their business. Pieces of garbage like the one who just left don't ever need to be inside this office, Phil." And the way she closed her mouth after she finished talking made it clear that there was nothing more to be said, so I didn't say anything. "Isn't that part of your security evaluation? Isn't that what you tell all our clients, that they should be sure they know who they're letting in the front door?"

"You're right. I'll call the Henrys on Monday . . ."

"I'll call the Henrys right now," she said, and retreated to her lair to make the call.

Henry Smith, my cop friend's brother, and Enrique Cruz, owned the security company that we referred our clients to. They also did our personal security work. Naturally we called them the Henrys, and I didn't doubt that by Monday morning the intercom box on the front of the building that rang Yolanda's loft on the top floor and the yoga studio on the middle floor would ring Phillip Rodriquez Investigations on the ground floor, and we could ask who was buzzing before we buzzed them in.

I returned to my desk, returned the Glock to the drawer, and returned my now quite divided attention to the KLM property file. I'd already completed the analysis of the Avenue B building and sent it by messenger to Kallen, and I'd read enough about the building I was to assess on Monday morning to know that I didn't need to read any more, but I all of a sudden really did need to know what Willie's nephew wanted to tell me. I also really wanted to know what the hell Mountain Man wanted, because I didn't believe he'd showed up by accident or mistake. He wanted to tell me something. Question was what could he possibly know that I'd care about? Not that a Hell's Angel couldn't have information worth paying for; it just wasn't likely one of them would want to sell it to me.

"What's on your mind?" I hadn't heard Yolanda approach. She was standing right beside me and I hadn't heard her. I told her what was on my mind. "Exactly what I've been thinking," she said. "The Hell's Angels part, not the *sobrino* part. I didn't know about that part. But now that I do know, I'm still thinking exactly what you're thinking."

I looked at my watch. Could I get to the doughnut shop and back to my place before Connie was due to arrive? Not likely in Friday evening after work traffic. Yolanda heard that thought, too, and I could tell that she wanted to say something. I could also see the effort her restraint was commanding. "What?" I said.

She shook her head. *"Nada,"* she said, and walked away.

I picked up the desk phone to call Connie and the other line rang. I knew that Yolanda would answer it so I punched in Connie's number and got her voice mail, but before she could finish asking me to leave a message, Yo was standing beside me again. "Ravi Patel needs to see you right away." In my other ear I heard the voice mail message beep on Connie's phone signaling me to start talking. I hung up the phone.

"He needs to see me right away why?"

"He found the people in Chelsea whose business was torched and he thinks you need to hear what they have to say. And the thing I was going to say? If she had a key it wouldn't matter what time you got home."

Had I not thought to myself a mere fifteen minutes ago that if nothing strange or bizarre happened I could look forward to a wonderful, peaceful weekend with Connie? And everything that had transpired since I had the thought had been either strange or bizarre or both. I returned all the KLM papers to the folder and dumped the thing into the bottom desk drawer, the deep one, and slammed it shut. I got my Glock and my cell phone and turned off the desk lamp. I went to talk to Yolanda. "You ready to call it a week?"

She took off her glasses and squeezed her eyes shut. Before I could tell her we had to find a way to keep her from spending so many hours starting at a computer screen, she told me not to mention the hours she spent staring at a computer screen. I used to worry about her being inside my head like that, but she did the same thing to Sandra, and even Connie has mentioned how Yo can sometimes read her thoughts. Not that it was any less weird when she did it, but it least I wasn't the victim. She turned off her computers and the lights, stood and stretched. "Call me later, after you've seen *sobrino* and Patel and before you see Connie." I tried to give her a dirty look but couldn't pull it off. Instead I helped her close all the shades and dim the lights. The kitchen was already clean since I hadn't eaten lunch in today and Yo could eat a multi-course meal and not make a mess.

"You're going out the front?" I asked as we donned coats, hats, and scarves. Nobody but us and Sandra knew that there was a hidden stairway leading directly up to Yolanda's loft, and she wouldn't need outerwear to go home that way.

"I've got to shop and if I don't do it now, Sandra'll be really grouchy because there's no half-and-half for her coffee in the morning, even though I'm the one who'll have to get up and go to the store." I found myself wondering how it would feel to share that kind of intimacy and domesticity on a regular basis, then thought maybe I'd be finding out in the not too distant future.

Yolanda set the alarm and turned off the front lights and I locked the door behind us. "Did you talk to the Henrys?"

"One of them will be here tomorrow evening," she said, giving me a hug. "Hi to Connie," she said, and we parted, heading in different directions. I took the presence of an empty, cruising taxi headed in my direction to be a good omen, a change from the bizarre strangeness of my recent life. Then I thought, what could be more bizarre or more strange, than an empty cruising taxi on Friday night?

Connie wore her surprise at seeing me better than I had expected. I knew that her colleagues ribbed her about our new relationship, and that there were numerous jokes about her "personal private dick." I spoke to everybody by name, which impressed them and Connie the first time I did it. We went into her small office and closed the door. She kissed me quickly, then pushed me away and sought the safety of the chair behind her desk. I sat in the visitor chair, where I'd sat the first time I met her. Just like it was Willie's nephew who'd given me the tip that led to Jill Mason's assailant, it was Connie who'd supplied the tip that eventually led to the serial rapist and murderer of little girls. "I'm sorry to barge in on you like this."

"I'm not sorry at all," she said. "I am sorry that I'm going to have to toss you out in about three minutes, though." I took an envelope from my pocket and placed it on the desk in front of her. "What's that?"

"Door keys and the alarm code. I've got to see a couple of people tonight, late developments that I can't put off . . ." I all of a sudden felt tongue-tied and confused about what to tell her. This definitely was a first. I didn't discuss my work with anybody but Yolanda, and I discussed every aspect of it with her. "I'm sorry, Connie . . ."

"No apologies necessary, Phil. You don't work a nine-to-five job. I know that and I understand what that means. All I want is for you to take care of yourself, to be safe. And anyway, I was going to be later than I told you. I've got to stop by the store . . ."

I cut her off this time. "I went shopping!" I was proud of myself. I'd not had so much food in the refrigerator or in the cabinets since I bought the place. "I've got all kinds of stuff, including those ravioli things you like, and a case of seltzer water."

She got up and came around the desk and hugged me. "I can't wait to explore the cabinets, but I've got other stuff to get. Like a toothbrush and deodorant and a razor . . ."

"I've got plenty of razors."

She pulled me to my feet and pushed me toward the door. "Make you a deal: You don't use my razor and I won't use your razor." Then she opened the door and pushed me out. "See you when I see you," she said, and I promised myself that would be sooner rather than later.

I exited the hospital through the visitors' door, knowing I'd have a good chance of finding a taxi, then cursed myself as I got in, remembering that I'd forgotten to get the receipt from the previous ride. Then I thought that a cab ride to see my girlfriend wasn't a legitimate business expense and felt better. I also shifted—forced my mind to shift—from thoughts of Connie to the *sobrino* . . . and I'd have to ask the guy his name. I couldn't keep calling him the nephew. Or maybe I could, because there was a very good chance that he wouldn't tell me his name. Willie had never volunteered it, and certainly the *sobrino* himself had never told me.

The cramped little coffee shop was doing good business for so early on a Friday night. Like most places of its kind, it catered to a mix of the gently poor and the nearly destitute, most of them far enough along on life's journey that they'd probably forgotten more than they were likely to have to remember ever again. The younger clientele tended to be, like the *sobrino* himself, recovering from some addiction, or recovering from relapsing back into the addiction. I took one of two available places at the counter and watched my man work. He was, I realized, a damn good short-order cook. He had several piles of hash browns and a couple of burgers going, along with some pancakes and eggs. He was flipping and turning and cutting and squaring the food with calm, even movements. Then I realized something else: This man had been a professional cook somewhere, and I was guessing the military. I'd made him an ex-con junkie, a junkie ex-con, and had given no thought to who he really was, but as I watched him now, I noticed how straight he was, how precise and ordered. I'd always noticed how calm and still he was, even now, as he was putting coffee and a couple of doughnuts on the counter in front of a guy who looked a lot like Stephen King. He looked my way, saw me, and turned back to his grill. He'd get to me when he could. My ex-cop friends, Mike Smith and Eddie Ortiz, wouldn't give the *sobrino* the time of day. They both believed that you could never trust an ex-hype, who, of course, believed that you could never trust a cop, ex or otherwise. I wondered if they'd have a different opinion of an ex-military man, since in addition to being ex-cops, they both were ex-Marines.

A cup of coffee and two chocolate-covered doughnuts appeared in front of me, followed by the metal cream container and bowl of sugar packets. I nodded thanks and busied myself doctoring my coffee. As I recalled, it wasn't bad here. And though I'd rather be sitting down to dinner with Connie, I was hungry enough that a couple of doughnuts would go down nicely. I was finishing them when I chanced looking around. *Sobrino* was cleaning his empty grill and everybody in the place was eating something. I drained my coffee cup, wiped my mouth, put some money on the counter, and stood up. *Sobrino* moved his eyes toward the hallway that led to the restrooms and the pay phones and I headed in that direction.

He followed seconds later, pushing a mop and bucket. He got close to me. "See a guy named Jackie at the back of the Furniture Depot main store on 10th Avenue, on the loading dock. He's there Monday through Friday, eats his lunch twelve-thirty to one. Skinny white dude, looks like a young Clint Eastwood. He can tell you something about the fires. Something nobody knows but the ones spilling the gasoline."

Those were the words he had for me. All of them. *"Gracias, sobrino,"* I said, and put my hand out. He took it briefly, long enough to take what was in it. Then he looked directly at me and a slow smile slid across his mouth, lifting his lips at the corners.

"Raul," he said, and pushed his mop and bucket down the hallway. Until this moment, I knew that his tolerance of me was owed solely to my relationship with his uncle Willie. I now was the proud owner of my own relationship with Raul. And while I didn't doubt for a second that Jackie, the Clint Eastwood look-alike, possessed some useful if not pertinent information, whether he'd willingly share it with me was another issue, and *sobrino* Raul wasn't a guy who answered questions. Ever. So, for all I knew, I could walk up to the Furniture Depot loading dock at lunchtime and Jackie would blow my brains out. He'd still know whatever it is that he knows, but I'd be none the wiser and all the more dead. And, I'd have asked Raul if given the chance, did Jackie's knowledge of the fires extend to the whereabouts of Sam Epstein? Because the longer I went without word of Sam, the worse it had to be for him. No matter what the television programmers said, people did not just disappear. Not regular, ordinary people with businesses and lives and people who depended on them. In my experience, and I'd done more than a little skip tracing and missing persons work, the people who "disappeared" didn't just vanish; they organized, planned, and orchestrated relocations . . . unless they were dead. Sam Epstein was either dead or he was guilty of vicious, racist crimes and he planned his own relocation. I didn't believe that, so I had to believe he was dead, and I didn't want to believe that. I had to find him.

I was meeting Ravi Patel at a restaurant in Chelsea, near the store that had burned last year, so I hopped the subway. I hadn't been underground all week and I missed it. I loved riding New York City subways. The London Underground was always made to seem romantic and sophisticated while our city's subterranean transit almost always was portrayed as dirty and grimy at best, and flat out dangerous at worst. Wrong on both counts. NYC Transit was the great equalizer. No matter where you lived, how much rent you paid, how much money you earned, when you got on the subway you were the equal of everybody else on that train. And if your money bought you taxi or limousine rides, quite often people down below got where they were going a lot faster because there were no traffic jams in the subway tunnels. True, taxis for me often were faster than walking, which was my usual mode of locomotion, when I was moving about the Lower East Side. But if I was headed north, as I was now, the subway was my transportation of choice. Tonight, the F Train to 23rd Street. It was packed, standing room only, and not much of that, people heading home after work. The Wall Street crowd, identifiable by the starched shirt collars peeking out from beneath cashmere coats and scarves and the shiny wingtips, would disembark en masse at 34th Street or Rockefeller Center, then transfer to the Long Island Rail Road or to the shuttle that would take them to the Upper East Side trains. The assistants and secretaries and messengers to the cashmere coats would get off at 42nd Street and transfer to the trains heading Uptown to Harlem and the Bronx, or stay on the train and cross the East River into Queens. However, the F Train ride would be a completely different experience in two or three hours; Chelsea was a popular destination with movie theaters and legitimate theater and fitness clubs and health food stores and new restaurants that seemed to open every day and it was Friday night.

I was to meet Patel at one of new restaurants. I got off the train at 23rd and walked west. Like in my own neighborhood, both sidewalk and street were jammed, the pedestrians reaching the end of the block before the vehicles. The restaurant, Tandoori Oven, was in the middle of the block. When I reached it the door opened and Ravi Patel waved me in. It was a pretty place but it was not elegant. There were about fifteen tables—an equal number, it seemed, of fours and twos—and they all had pale pink tablecloths, contrasting napkins, and little vases with a single white flower. There were no diners yet, just the staff bustling about, making sure all was ready. Patel indicated that I should follow him and we walked through the restaurant, through the kitchen, down a cramped and musty-smelling storage room, and into an equally cramped and musty-smelling office. A round man wearing a turban and what I knew was an expensive suit sat behind a desk. When we entered, he removed his eyeglasses and stood up.

"I am Jawal Nehru. Thank you for coming. Please sit down." He sounded like Winston Churchill. Come to think of it, he looked like Winston Churchill, only browner. I sat in one of the chairs in front of the desk; Patel took the other, and we both had to turn our knees sideways to keep from cracking our kneecaps on the desk front. Since it was clear that Mr. Nehru wasn't one for small talk, I dispensed with it, too.

"Please tell me about the fire at your business, Mr. Nehru."

His eyes flashed and the muscles in his jaw worked. "It was early the morning of September thirtieth. I remember the day so well because I had spent virtually the entire night before with my business manager and my wife finalizing our quarterly tax documents. We left the building at just before three a.m. The business manager lives in Queens and my wife and I persuaded him to come home with us." Nehru's voice had become fainter and weaker as he talked until it finally petered out altogether. I waited for him to continue. Then I looked to Patel for guidance.

"I believe this is the first time that Mr. Nehru has spoken of the event since it occurred," Patel said and Nehru nodded. I waited.

"We took a hired car home . . ."

"Which is where, Mr. Nehru?" I interrupted to ask. "And do you remember the name of the livery service?"

"Seventy-seventh and West End Avenue and the Star of India," Nehru said, and waited for a moment to see if I had more questions. I signaled that he should continue, and he did, relating that he, his wife, and the business manager got home at approximately three-twenty. His wife prepared the guest room for the business manager and they all collapsed into sleep, unworried about the coming business day because the day manager would open the store as usual at eleven o'clock. "We had barely gotten to sleep when the telephone rang. It was the security company. There was a fire . . ."

It took the better part of half an hour but I finally got the rest of the story from Nehru. He still had not recovered from the loss, financially or emotionally, because the insurance company hadn't settled his claim, and that was because two months before the fire, the Department of Homeland Security was advised that the Nehrus were terrorists. The investigation into that charge hadn't been completed at the time of the fire, and had yet to be completed. "The only positive in this scenario is that the tax documents we'd worked so feverishly to complete that night we had taken with us to the accountant later that morning. Otherwise we would no doubt have had the IRS on our backs as well." The anger in that statement was thick as molasses, but the sorrow was so deep that I doubted the man himself could see to the bottom of it.

"Do you have any idea at all, Mr. Nehru, who would want to cause you this kind of grief? Any hints, any rumors, any speculation?"

Nehru had started shaking his head when I started asking the question and he kept shaking it, more and more forcefully. "I have harmed no one, ever. I am an honest businessman, and a fair one. I am a good father and a most lenient grandfather, and I was a good husband. Until all this happened . . ."

Nehru lost control again, and turned again toward Patel, who leaned toward me and whispered that Mrs. Nehru had fled to India and refused ever to return to the U.S. "More than forty years she'd been a citizen of the United States," Nehru said. "We came here together, young and full of hope, immediately upon graduation from university."

"I'd like copies of any business papers you have left, Mr. Nehru, especially anything from the insurance company . . ."

For the first time since I arrived, Nehru's round face lost its shroud of sadness. He reached into his pocket and brought out a fountain pen on a chain and dangled it before me. "My daughter is a computer genius. She designs software programs. My son builds computers. Between the two of them, I have every new high-tech toy before even the manufacturers. This . . ." and he dangled the pen on the chain, "is every document that ever existed pertaining to every aspect of my life—home and business. This is called a flash drive. It holds more memory, my daughter tells me, than I'll ever need."

He tossed the thing across the desk to me and I caught it, looked at it, and put it in my pocket. Yolanda, no doubt, would have loads of fun with it but I'd already forgotten what it was called. "I'll get this back to you, Mr. Nehru."

He dismissed my promise with a wave of his hand and I heard Yolanda inside my brain chanting her always back-up everything mantra and knew that if he gave me documents in a fountain pen, he had back-up files. "Do you think you can help me, Mr. Rodriquez?"

I took my time answering. "There seems to be a pattern here, Mr. Nehru, and 'seems' is the operative word. I have no proof. And even if I find proof, I have no assurance and I can give you no assurance that I can change anything for you."

"But you are looking for proof."

"Yes, sir, I am."

"And from what Patel and others tell me about you, you wouldn't be looking if you didn't think you could find it, this proof. If you didn't think it existed, you wouldn't waste your time looking for it. And, from what I hear, you wouldn't put forth the effort to find the proof if you couldn't change anything."

Here we go again, I thought. "What 'others,' Mr. Nehru?"

He tilted his head to the side and gave me an up-and-down look. "The Nigerian Embassy, for one." I waited for numbers two and three, but obviously one was all I was being offered. I didn't even bother to ask how an Indian Hindu import-export merchant would have any idea what the Nigerian Embassy was up to, and not so much because I didn't expect he would tell me as because I really didn't want to know. Things had gotten much too complicated. And dangerous. Arson was one thing—one ugly and dangerous thing. Terrorism was another hideous and dangerous thing and it was in a class all by itself. I didn't mind whatever effort I had to expend to find out who burned these men's businesses but I minded like hell being on Homeland Security's radar screen.

A cell phone chirped and all three of us touched our pockets. It was Nehru's. He flipped it open, listened, and stood up. "Kusala Bikshu is here." Then he extended his hand to shake mine, which he hadn't done when I arrived. He stepped away from the desk and started to open the door. I stopped him.

"Is this your restaurant, Mr. Nehru?"

"My wife's brothers own it. They have been kind enough to employ me as manager while they tend to their other enterprises." Then he opened the door and left the office. Patel and I followed, back through the funky store room, back through the kitchen which now was hot and bustling, and into the dining room, where almost every table was taken. At one table for two on the wall nearest the glass-walled partition that shielded the customers from the fire-breathing tandoori oven, sat a bald man in orange robes. He stood up as we approached, put his hands together, and bowed to us. He was introduced as Reverend Kusala Bikshu from the Village Buddhist Center.

"Mr. Rodriquez. I'm pleased to meet you. I've heard many good things." And I guess my face assumed the here-we-go-again look because he told me that Patty Starrett was a member of his temple. Patty Starrett whose beautiful young daughter Pamela was a victim of the serial rapist. I had not known that Patty was a Buddhist. Now I did. Nehru led us all to a table and started ordering food from a waitress who suddenly appeared. I had to insist that I couldn't eat and then had to explain that I had dinner plans.

"Ah, yes, Miss deLeon," said Patel and I nodded. "You're a very lucky man, Mr. Rodriquez. Miss Aguierre at work, Miss deLeon at home." Nehru's head whipped around and the Buddhist monk's eyes widened and Ravi Patel, through a hearty chuckle, hastened to explain the circumstances of my good fortune and the men agreed that I was indeed fortunate to have two women in whom I could place trust and confidence. Then Mr. Nehru's shoulders heaved.

"Don't ever forget to express your gratitude to and for them, Mr. Rodriquez."

The restaurant was crowded now, and the noise level

excluded the possibility of meaningful conversation. I gave the monk my card and took his phone number and address and made an appointment to see him on Tuesday morning, and then I left. I all of a sudden had to get out of the Tandoori and into the cold night air. I felt overwhelmed, like there was too much to do and I had absolutely no idea how to do it, like I had taken money from people under false pretenses. Though I knew nothing about them as people, as individuals, I didn't believe for half a second that any of the men I'd just walked away from were terrorists or that Patel or Nehru would destroy businesses in which they had invested considerable sweat equity, that Jawal Nehru would take any action that would cost him the presence of his wife. I knew quite a few people who lived their entire lives in danger of toppling off one edge or another, some of them practicing criminals, and I considered myself a good judge of character: I knew a slimeball when I saw one. But did I know a terrorist when I saw one? Was Sam Epstein a terrorist or merely a man so blinded by grief that he'd lost his sense of direction . . . or was he both?

I stopped walking so fast. Maybe if I slowed my pace, the thoughts in my head would follow suit. When I reached the corner an empty taxi was stopped at the light. My mind being in the state of upheaval that it was, I almost sprinted for it. Then I noticed the glowing green globe of the subway. That's what I wanted, what I needed—a major reality check. Time in the great equalizer. I recalled the fear and anger that gripped the city following the destruction of the Towers, and again following the train bombings in Spain, and again following the bus and train bombings in London, and the questions we New Yorkers asked ourselves about the safety of our trains and busses. Some of us had walked or taken taxis for a while, and a few of us bought bicycles, but most of us resumed our routines and habits and secretly wished we could catch some fuckin' terrorist in the act of setting a bomb in one of our trains. Yolanda's Sandra summed up the New Yorker's sentiment when she was asked late one night whether she really planned to ride the subway home to Brooklyn. Formerly a principal dancer with the Alvin Ailey company, she'd retained her diva personality. She tossed her head and replied, "Since I'm not Jesus, I can't walk across the East River so, yes, I'm riding the train home to Brooklyn."

I heard my train screeching into the platform. I had my transit pass in hand when I reached the turnstile and I grabbed it out on the fly, and squeezed into the train car as the door was sliding shut. It was Friday night in NYC and the subway train was as packed now as it had been three hours earlier, but now the energy wasn't about exhausted people hustling home at the end of the work week; this energy was about many of those same people seeking relief from the source of that exhaustion, and I was willing to bet that not a single one of them had given a single thought to terrorists when boarding this train, so I pushed the thought to the back of my brain. I couldn't afford to push it completely out—and wouldn't have succeeded if I had tried. Like it or not, at least for the short term, that was a new part of my reality.

Chapter Six

I was intentionally early for my meeting with Mike Kallen on Monday morning. I wanted to see the building and the neighborhood at a busy time, and six-thirty on Monday morning fit the bill. I'd taken the J train to Canal Street and transferred to the No. 6 train for the ride north, getting off at 28th Street. I had a long crosstown walk to First Avenue but it was time well spent as I got a ground-level sense of the neighborhood. Security for a residential building is as much about what goes on outside the building as inside. For example, in a block with considerable foot traffic and any level of crime but low, you don't want a tenant to spend more than a couple of seconds getting into the front door, so a keypad or a quick turn key and a quick-close pneumatic door are basics. There was a lot of foot traffic on 28th Street, all the way east to First Avenue, where the vehicular traffic was dense and relatively swift. I turned left and slowed down to watch the people and the cars. Lots of women alone, which was a good sign, and the men were dressed for going to work, not for hanging out and doing nothing. The cars parked on the street were well-kept, there were virtually no out of state license plates, and most surprisingly, not a single windshield sported a parking ticket. A group of upstanding, law-abiding citizens.

When I reached the building in question, I walked past it, to the corner, crossed the street, and studied it from a distance. It was a plain Jane—not unusually ugly but certainly no architectural gem. It was a ten-story elevator building sandwiched between similar structures. There were two groceries, a dry cleaner, a video store, a martial arts studio, and three restaurants in the two-block area. Unless Kallen's building was a dump inside, the morning's exercise would be a piece of cake; in and out, painless and hassle-free. I checked my watch, looked up again at the building, and Kallen was coming out of the front door. And I thought I was getting a jump on him. I waved at him, jogged across the street against the on-coming traffic, and met Kallen on the sidewalk in front of the building. Despite the temperature he wore a tight black T-shirt and even tighter black jeans and his chest and arm and back muscles bulged and rippled every time he moved. His hair was wet and he smelled like soap and deodorant and he looked bright and alert, which I hoped meant he wanted to get through this as fast as I did. He did, but for different reasons.

"Good morning, Phil." Then, "Is it all right if I call you Phil?"

"Of course. And good morning to you." We shook hands, both of us aware that we didn't really like each other but equally aware that we had business to conduct and that a pleasant façade was better than no façade. "I walked around a bit, checked out the block. This seems a secure area."

He nodded. "I saw you, and yes, it is."

"So," I said, "shall we get started?" And I followed him up the steps, watched him unlock the door, watched the door close and lock itself, and took my tape recorder out of my pocket, ready to make observations, suggestions, and recommendations.

"I don't expect this to take very long," Kallen said, "and if you've got time, I'd appreciate it if you would spend a few minutes with me at the Avenue B building. We've acted on some of your suggestions and I'd like your frank reaction to what we've done."

"We just sent the report on Friday."

He gave me a smug look. "These are suggestions you made on your first visit. I remembered everything you said and got immediately started. To tell you the truth, I'm very proud of what we've done in such a short time, which is why I want you to see. I suppose I'm seeking your approval."

I tried to picture Kallen in an approval-seeking mode and couldn't, so as I followed him into the building I wondered instead why he'd obviously just had a shower. Did he live here? I called to memory the employee list from KLM and couldn't recall seeing any information on Kallen. Maybe he didn't consider himself an employee; after all, he was the guy in charge and I didn't suppose it mattered what he called himself or where he lived. He was right about one thing, though: The security evaluation of this building didn't take long. It was a well-maintained facility. Like the outside, it was nothing special inside, but it was clean and quiet, everything was in proper working order, the elevators had been recently inspected and the boiler serviced, the laundry and trash rooms looked and smelled clean. If I had a complaint—and I did but I didn't voice it nor would I put it in writing in my report—it was the building manager. He was, according to Kallen, in his eighties and had been the building manager since its initial occupation more than forty years earlier. I had no bias against senior citizens; my problem with this octogenarian was that he could barely walk and he smelled like a brewery. If there were any kind of emergency—a fire or a tenant in some kind of distress—he would be useless, but it wasn't a violation of the New York City housing code or any state law to have a useless building manager. Anyway, if Kallen did, in fact, live here, it wouldn't matter who was listed as the manager.

"You're right, Mr. Kallen—Mike—this is an A-1 building."

He smiled, pleased. "Good thing, since I live here. And if you'll give me two or three minutes, I'll get a jacket and call for the car." And without waiting for a response, he turned left and jogged across the lobby and down the hallway.

I called Yolanda, told her what Kallen wanted me to do, that I'd be later getting to the office than I thought. She told me I'd be even later than that because Carmine wanted to see me at the restaurant, and she made me promise not to bring back "any of that ass-widening pastry." I closed the phone, wondering whether Sandra had made any unwise comment about Yolanda's posterior and hoping she hadn't because I liked Sandra and didn't want her to be murdered. True to his word, Kallen reappeared zipping a black leather bomber jacket. He had changed from the black leather slip-ons he'd worn earlier to a pair of Doc Martens. The only color in his ensemble was a blood red scarf that I'd bet was cashmere. This definitely wasn't the suited-and-tied big-time property manager I'd met earlier. I followed him out of the building and down the steps as a black Lincoln Town Car eased around the corner and slid to a stop.

"That's our ride," Kallen said. He approached the car, opened the back door, held it for me, then slid in beside me. The car was rolling again before the door was closed. "I'm visiting all my buildings today. I do that every Monday," he said.

"Well, if the others are as A-1 as this one, you won't be late for lunch," I said, and he gave an appreciative chuckle. Then he reached inside his jacket and took a BlackBerry from his pocket and I took that as a sign that we wouldn't be sharing small talk and chit-chat on the ride downtown, which was fine with me. While Kallen scrolled through his messages, I scrolled through the thoughts in my brain. That Carmine wanted to see me so early either was very good news or very bad news; either Sam Epstein was alive and well or he was in pieces in the East River. I wished I'd asked Yolanda how he sounded when he called but knowing Carmine, he probably sounded like he was trying to be charming and anyway, Yolanda was focused on ass-widening pastries, not Carmine Aiello's tone of voice. I knew, though, if he'd sounded tight or tense, she'd have picked up on that and mentioned it. Could be Carmine was just doing what he said he'd do, which was get back to me on Monday. I had been avoiding thinking about what to say to Dave Epstein; no point in making myself crazy. I didn't have anything to say to him until I heard what Carmine had to say, but if Carmine had no info, good or bad, on Sam's whereabouts, then I knew I'd have to insist that Dave file a missing person report. And I'd have to be prepared to file it on his behalf if he refused, which could drop me naked in a vat of boiling oil. I wasn't on the best of terms with my unfriendly neighborhood guys in blue. In fact, some of them actively disliked me. I could just imagine their response to my filing a four-day-old missing person report.

"What the fuck . . . ?" Kallen's shout jolted me out of my daytime nightmare and I tuned in to see that we we'd reached the Avenue B building and that there were three squad cars blocking the street. Just as the car cruised to a stop and I noticed that two cops were holding on to a skinny, old bald guy and two more were holding on to a Goth-looking young guy who was screaming at the bald guy, the driver of our car threw it into park and jumped out, running for all he was worth away from the police action. "You son of a bitch! You come back, you son of a bitch," Kallen yelled at the long-gone driver, then he let loose a stream of what I was sure was profanity in what sounded like Russian, but could have been Czech or Polish or Lithuanian or anything else Eastern European. He opened the car door and hurled himself out, slamming the door so hard the car shook, and he barreled toward the fracas in front of his building as fast as the driver had run from it.

I jumped out of the car, closing my door a bit more gently, and hopped into the front seat and closed that door, too. I whipped out my phone and punched the button that got me

Yolanda in a hurry. I told her what had just happened and flipped the visor and read her the info on the livery driver's license. Then I quickly got out of the car, ran to the rear, read her the license plate number, and threw myself back into the driver's seat. Yolanda asked me what I thought was going on and I told her the truth: I didn't know but I was about to go find out. I closed the phone then pulled the big Lincoln out of the middle of the street and over to double-park beside a row of beat-up and battered-looking cars. I switched off the ignition, grabbed my carryall from the back seat, and hustled over to the growing crowd on the sidewalk. The Goth-looking kid was still screaming, only now it was Kallen screaming back at him instead of the bald guy, and the two cops who weren't holding anybody were trying to get Kallen and the Goth to shut up. Then the larger of the two, a Ving Rhames look-alike, whipped his handcuffs off his belt and dangled them in the air in front of his face, and silence reigned.

"Who wants to go to jail?" he purred, sounding like a Bengal tiger. "Nobody? Good, 'cause I don't feel like all that paperwork first thing on Monday morning. Now." He looked at Kallen. "Who are you, sir, and what do you know about this young man?"

Kallen shot the Goth a nasty, withering look, then turned his attention to Officer Bengal Tiger, whose name tag read T. JETTER. "My name is Mike Kallen and I work for the company that manages this building and I don't know who this is but I do know that he doesn't live in my building."

"Yes I do!" the Goth screamed. "Apartment four-twelve!" He was too tall to be so skinny and he had way too much dirty black hair for my taste and I didn't much care for his wardrobe choices, but this was no East Village street urchin, addicted to drugs and/or alcohol since he could walk. His teeth were beautiful, his skin and eyes were clear, and his nails were manicured.

Kallen held out a hand toward the skinny bald guy who, upon closer inspection, wasn't old at all, just prematurely bald, and the guy passed over a sheet of paper from the rolled up sheaf of papers in his hand. Kallen read it, then looked at Officer Jetter. "The tenant in four-twelve is named Rosemary Days and she lives alone . . ."

"I live there with her! She's my girlfriend!" Goth screamed. Every time he opened his mouth it was at top volume. I was waiting for the Bengal tiger to smack him but Officer Jetter obviously was too well trained for that.

"Rosemary Days is the only name on the lease," Kallen said, deliberately and very calculatingly keeping his tone moderated, "and only the people named in the lease can legally live in the building." And he shot Goth-boy a gotcha look.

"Fuck that shit, man! I live in apartment four-twelve with Rosemary Days. She's my girlfriend! I come home this morning and there's some fuckin' lock on the fuckin' door and I can't get in! I'm knocking for somebody to open the door when this bald asshole shows up talking about he's the building manager and I don't live here and he's gonna put me out! This fuckin' building don't have a fuckin' manager and I do fuckin' live here!"

I looked at the building and sure as shit, there's a brand spanking new door. Then I looked at the skinny bald guy and sure as shit, he's got a ring of keys attached to his belt and a copy of the tenant list he'd given to Kallen. No wonder Kallen looked so smug earlier. He'd transformed the building from a dangerous dump to a safe haven for tenants like Rosemary Days.

Officer Jetter also did a visual inspection of the new door and asked the question that I was thinking: "When did the new door go up?"

"We started the work on Friday and completed it on

Saturday," Kallen said. "But all the tenants got their keys Friday night."

"Are you sure about that?" Jetter asked.

Kallen nodded and pointed to the bald guy. "Boris personally delivered the keys to each tenant and got a signed receipt for the keys from each tenant."

Boris nodded and rifled through the sheaf of papers he had rolled up in his hand and pulled one out and extended it to Jetter who took it, read it, and returned it. "When were you last here?" the cop asked the Goth.

"Thursday night," the boy answered, not screaming for the first time, but still too loudly and very nearly smart enough to see where this was headed. He might behave like a street kid but he definitely didn't have street kid smarts.

"It's Monday morning," Jetter said. "You haven't been here since Thursday? And you wonder why you can't get in? It's a wonder Miss Days didn't change the lock on her apartment door."

"She did," Boris said, speaking for the first time. "Or rather I did." He rifled through his sheaf of papers again, pulled out what I could read as MAINTENANCE REQUEST FORM. "She said somebody had tried to break into her apartment." Here he shot a poisonous look at Goth. "The lock looked tampered with, and it was old, so I changed it. She paid for it. Or she will." He passed the paper to Kallen. "It will be added to her rent."

I looked at Goth boy, hoping he'd have sense enough to keep his mouth shut. He didn't. He started whining about needing to get his stuff and how he'd already paid for half of this month's rent and the bitch better give him his money back, getting louder with each whiney word, until finally Jetter did smack him on the back of the head.

"You got ID on you?" Now the boy got some sense but it was

too little, too late. He slowly and reluctantly reached into his back pocket and retrieved a battered wallet attached to a silver link chain, like a dog collar. He opened the wallet, took out what looked like a student ID card, and gave it to Jetter who looked briefly at it, then passed it to his partner. "I hear about you being over here again, Allen Copeland, I'm gonna lock your ass up. Understand me?" Allen Copeland nodded miserably. "Where does Rosemary work?"

"At NYU. She's a graduate assistant in the math department."

Now everybody looked at Allen. A graduate student at NYU was hooked up with him? Jetter shook his head in the disbelief we all felt. "I better not still be a cop when my daughters start dating because if they ever bring home anything that looks like you, I'll shoot 'em. No, I won't. I'll shoot what looks like you if it's standing in my living room looking for one of my daughters. And I'll lock your ass up you go near that girl's job, you understand me, Copeland?"

Copeland gave everybody dirty looks but he kept his mouth shut, nodded his head that he'd heard Jetter's warning, took back his ID, and loped off down the street. He had a funny-looking walk, rising up on his toes and bouncing along. Then Jetter looked around at everybody and said to nobody in particular, "That little creep is a grad student at NYU, too." And he walked away as did the other cops.

"You sure know how to throw a surprise," I said to Kallen.

"I hadn't planned on it being quite so dramatic," he said.

"I'm no less impressed," I said, and meant it, and then turned my attention and extended my hand to Boris. "Phil Rodriquez," I said.

"I am Boris," he said, shaking my hand, no last name offered which is what I wanted since I already knew the Boris part. Boris with an Eastern European accent. I'd bet money he could cuss up a blue streak like Mike did in the car when the driver tucked tail and ran. Bet the driver could cuss in the same language because I'd also bet not only didn't he speak much English—his fear of cops was the real thing—his arrival to these shores was recent and probably not legal.

And thinking about the long-departed driver made me remember to dig in my pocket and retrieve a key ring, which I extended to Kallen. He hesitated. "The keys to the car. I moved it and locked it after the driver, ah, departed."

The big man's face contorted and clouded over and I expected more foreign language profanity, but he willed himself in control, took the keys, smiled—a real smile—and thanked me. "I'd forgotten about the car, with so much other stuff going on. Thank you, Phil."

He was being really and honestly pleasant now and all I really wanted was to get away. I didn't like the feeling I was having about Kallen and his building, and that feeling wasn't helping the feeling I was having about hearing what Carmine had to say. "I know you've got a few things on your mind this morning, Mike, so why don't I come back, say, Wednesday or Thursday? I'm really anxious to see what you've done. Maybe Boris won't mind showing me around?"

"I'll do it myself! Thursday morning? About ten?"

We made a date and I trotted to the corner to find a taxi.

Carmine was reading the racing form and picking his teeth when I got to the coffee shop. He didn't look stressed or worried, but then again, he wouldn't; Sam Epstein was my problem, not his. The plate of pastries was in the middle of the table and the waitress was topping off his cup. She looked up, saw me, smiled, and said something to Carmine. He looked up, motioned me over to the table. I hung my coat on the rack in the front of the place and stood there for a moment, inhaling.

This little restaurant, coffee shop, pastry shop—whatever it called itself—was the best-smelling place in New York City. Cinnamon and yeast and butter and vanilla and . . . and . . . did warm have a scent? Because this place also smelled warm. Carmine's mother's sister owned the place and it was his de facto office, although as far as I knew, I was the only non-Italian allowed to meet him here.

"Rodriquez. How's it hangin'?"

His standard greeting. We shook hands and I sat down as the waitress put the soup-bowl sized cup of cappuccino before me. "*Buon giorno,* Senora Geruso."

"*Buon giorno,* Senor Rodriquez," she said, and walked away.

"You look like you just shot yourself in the foot," Carmine said.

"You've got a way with words, Carmine," I said, "but you make the point, and I'd rather that's what's wrong with my foot than maybe what I just stepped in."

"Which is what?"

"Russians, maybe."

He gave a low whistle of serious dismay. "What the fuck did you do that for?"

"It wasn't on purpose! I thought it was just a job. Now it's looking maybe like it's Russians, or some kind of Eastern Europeans." I drank some of my coffee and stared at the plate of pastries, imagining my ass widening and wondering whether Connie would comment if it did. "I'm hoping I can tread lightly, finish the job, and back out of the door before what's so far only a bad feeling turns into something really bad."

He gave me a strange look. "Epstein's connected to fuckin' Russians?"

That deserved an out-loud laugh, and I gave it one. "No way, Carmine. Separate issue all the way around."

"Good thing 'cause I wouldn't give him back to you if he

was. I hate fuckin' Russians."

I choked on the big gulp of cappuccino I'd just taken. "You've got him?"

He shook his head. "But I know where he is and you get him back all in one piece. But I need something outta this."

"Okay," I said, sounding much calmer than I felt. I tended to forget that Carmine was Mafia. Low-level but Mafia just the same. "Tell me what you need, Carmine."

"I need to keep my nephew and myself outta this."

"Joey Mottola? I didn't know he was related to you."

"He's related to my wife by marriage, which makes the little piece of shit related to me, otherwise you could drop him in it and I wouldn't give a flyin' fuck."

I thought for a moment. I didn't give a flying fuck about Joey Mottola, either. I was hired to find Sam Epstein and if Mottola could lead me to him, I'd let him lead me. I had only one problem but it was a big one. "You know a man died in that fire." I made it a statement, not a question and I didn't add what I was thinking, which was if there's a worse way to die I don't know what it is.

Carmine was nodding his head; he knew where I was going. "McQueen started the fire. Casey was the front lookout and Joey was in the back, watching the alley."

"Where was Epstein?"

"Tied to a chair to keep him from runnin' to the cops."

"And what's to keep one of them from coming after Epstein next week or next month?" I looked at Carmine, waiting for an answer. He looked back at me with the answer in his eyes. Now I was doing the nodding. I believed Carmine only because I was sure he'd slapped the Mottola kid around a bit to get the true story and that kid wouldn't risk lying to him. Not if he wanted to keep walking without a limp. And McQueen and Casey wouldn't risk crossing Joey Mottola if they wanted to keep walking, period. "All right, Carmine. I don't have a problem with that, with keeping Mottola out if it."

"You're keeping me out of it, too, Rodriquez. I don't know nothin' about no fires, I don't know nothin' about that Epstein asshole, and if comes down to it, I don't know nothin' about you, either." And he meant every word of that.

"You know I don't talk about you out in the world, Carmine!" I hoped I sounded more offended than terrified. I wouldn't tell anybody but Yolanda that I had asked Carmine Aiello for help, and I wouldn't have told her if I could have gotten around it. "This is private, Carmine. Whatever happens between us stays between us. Always." He gave a satisfactory nod and I exhaled relief. A moment too soon, as it turned out.

"And stay the fuck away from fuckin' Russians. Whatever it is you got goin' with those assholes, Rodriquez, drop it. Let it go."

He was serious, which made me more nervous about Kallen than I already was. "Why, Carmine? Exactly."

" 'Cause they're assholes, exactly, is why. Every one of 'em. They lie, they cheat, they steal, and you can't trust one of 'em as far as you can spit. Is that exact enough for you?"

I couldn't believe what I was hearing; didn't want to believe it. Then, I remembered—again—who Carmine really was. I kept forgetting, because I liked the guy, considered him a friend. But he was—had been most if not all of his life—a small-minded, petty tyrant where issues of culture and race were concerned. His dislike of Russians was race-based: They weren't Italian, ergo they were assholes. My thoughts must have been reflected in my face because Carmine was getting mad, and that really did make me nervous. He slapped the table with the palm of his hand, making the silverware dance.

"I know what you're thinkin' and you're wrong, Rodriquez."

"What am I thinking, Carmine? And why is it wrong?"

"You're thinkin' I gotta lotta nerve, what with the Russians bein' just like us, but you're wrong. They're nothin' like us. They got no rules, they got no organization, and they got no morals."

"You're right: I was wrong. I was thinking you were on a racist rant, just hating the Russians because they're Russian, when all along you were comparing the relative merits of the Italian versus the Russian . . ."

"Don't you say that word, Rodriquez," Carmine growled at me.

I raised my hands, palms out, in surrender. I certainly wasn't going to voice a preference of one group of mafia mobsters over another, whether I said the word or not. "So, where's Epstein?"

"I do hate Russians because they're Russian. And all the rest of that Eastern European flotsam and jetsam. You oughta see what they've done to Italy, swarming all over the country like . . . like a, like I don't know what."

He was giving me the same kind of headache Sam Epstein did. "I gotta go, Carmine. I need to collect Sam Epstein and get to work."

Carmine leaned across the table and whispered, "We never bought and sold women for sex, Rodriquez. That's what the fuckin' Russians do."

It took me a second to catch on, but when I did, I got pissed. I leaned across the table and whispered back, "You guys made billions off prostitution, Carmine!"

"Prostitution ain't slavery, Rodriquez."

I didn't have a response for that, so I changed the subject. "Epstein?"

He reached under his plate and slid a piece of paper across the table toward me. I let it sit there. "Nobody there but him, only he don't know that. He's tied up, gagged and blindfolded. The door's unlocked. Get him and go, and the sooner the better."

I stood up and put some money on the table for breakfast, including a gigantic tip for the waitress. Carmine nodded his thanks. I picked up the piece of paper, nodded mine, and headed for the front door and my coat. I had it on and was halfway out the door when I turned back toward the table. The waitress had the money in her hand and a big smile on her face. She waved me good-bye. I had realized that I didn't have a receipt but I sure as hell wasn't going back to ask for one. Yolanda would have to create one. Or two, since nobody spent or tipped that much for a cup of milk and coffee.

I crossed the street and ducked into the deli on the corner, went all the way to the back of the place, and called Yo on my cell phone. I filled her in and told her I needed Mike and Eddie to meet me right away to grab Sam. I gave her the address and she said that was a shitty block. I said considering that it was Casey, McQueen, and Mottola, Epstein was lucky the place had running water and a toilet. Then I thought, this being New York City, maybe it didn't. Then I remembered that he was supposed to be tied to a chair, and thought, it didn't matter one way or the other. I closed the phone and kept walking, through the storeroom, looking for the back door and hoping it wasn't chained or bolted shut. This time of the morning—ten o'clock—Carmine's people would be on the street and I didn't want them to see me. More importantly, however, Carmine didn't want them to see me. He kept our relationship more secret than I did. And given the conversation we'd just had, I supposed I should be honored that he talked to me at all, and be grateful that I wasn't Russian. The whole thing pissed me off again: Here I was, ducking out the back door of a shitty store, into a stinking alley, dodging filth and mean dogs until I could safely travel the sidewalks again, all to avoid being connected to Carmine Aiello.

I switched my mind away from my stupidity and was trying

to picture the block Yolanda thought was so shitty and not coming up with much. I knew the area around Times Square had cleaned up a lot, to the dismay of those who preferred it, I believe "gritty" was the term they used. I didn't like that particular part of town at all—never had—gritty or otherwise. I'd take my grit down here in the narrow part of town. I emerged from the alley on Allen Street and couldn't figure out where I was for a moment. I walked the wrong way for a block, got my bearings, turned and ran to Second Avenue and the F train. I took it to West Fourth, transferred to the A train, sat down, and spent a few long seconds just breathing. In and out, in and out. I learned that from Sandra. I closed my eyes and inhaled deeply, then exhaled slowly and completely. Then I opened my eyes and checked my watch. It had been almost fifteen minutes since Yolanda had called Mike and Eddie. They no doubt already were headed uptown and probably would get to the location before I did, and if so, I hoped they'd go in and get Sammy Epstein and get him outside in the cold air. Let him breathe in and out for a few moments and collect himself. Before I kicked his ass.

When I turned the corner onto 44th Street, my first thought was that Yolanda was right, this was a shitty block. My second thought was that I didn't see Eddie or Mike and that worried me because I knew they should have gotten here before I did. Then I saw them, coming down the dirty stone steps of the dirty brick building, Sam Epstein between them, obviously needing the support they provided. I ran toward them just as a livery car pulled up to the curb, the car between me and them, and I had a moment of pure panic. It died when I saw Mike beckon to me over the top of the car. Sammy already was inside, in the back seat, and Mike squeezed in next to him. I got in on the other side and Eddie rode shotgun. Yolanda had sent a car.

If there were three things to choose to do—good, better, best—Yolanda always managed to choose best, usually without having to give thought to the matter.

"Thanks, guys," I said to Mike and Eddie when I got into the car. I spoke to the driver, whom I knew from seeing him around but whose name I didn't remember. I knew he was somehow related to the owner of the car company, which was a client of ours. Then I turned my attention to Sam Epstein. He was a little bruised and battered and he was a lot dirty. In fact, he stank. He was wearing the same clothes he'd been wearing the last time I saw him. He looked as if he hadn't slept or eaten since the last time I saw him, either. He also looked completely and totally defeated.

Both Mike and I were hugging our doors, trying not to get too close to Sam, and we both lowered our windows despite the cold. Sam seemed oblivious. He kept his hands tightly clasped in his lap and he rocked back and forth a little. The driver started the car and his eyes met mine in the rearview mirror, his eyebrows raised in a question. "I don't know yet where we're going. That all depends on Mr. Epstein. Just drive."

Sam jumped when I said his name, then he turned his head to look at me and seemed to really see me, to recognize me. "You made them let me go," he said. "They said they were going to kill me. They beat me up and said they were going to kill me."

"You're going to tell me everything, Sam. The whole story, from the beginning, leaving out nothing. I want dates, times, places, everything. You tell it all and you get to go home to Sasha and your dad instead of to a jail cell . . ."

"My dad! What's he got to do with this?"

"How about he hired me to find you?"

"He knows?" The man clearly was in shock. I told the driver to go to my office, then I called Yo and told her we were en route, told her that Sam needed to shower and some clean clothes to wear, told her that we all needed to eat, and thanked her for being her usual incredibly wonderful self. She liked that but I didn't have time to congratulate myself for turning my good thoughts about a person into good words to that person because Sam Epstein was coming back to life. "You said my father hired you, that he knows that I was . . . where does he think I was and how does he know?" He sounded like a teenager busted for taking his father's car without permission.

"He's here, Sam. Ellie called him . . ."

Anger was now taking the place of shock and Sammy was becoming his usual excitable self. "What the hell did she do something so goddamn stupid like that for?"

"Because Sasha refused to go home with her and she couldn't leave a fourteen-year-old child alone in the Stuy Town apartment. Because she couldn't run the business by herself. Because she didn't know where you were and she was afraid. That's why Ellie called your father, Sam. Now, let's talk about why you did something so goddamn stupid like siccing Homeland Security on decent, law-abiding citizens, or, even more goddamn stupid, why you destroyed people's businesses and livelihoods. Suppose somebody torched the Epstein Dry Cleaners and Laundry. What about all those people who work for you, Sam, who've worked for your family for twenty, thirty years? Alfred Miller and Vivian Henderson. What about Ellie? You want to talk about goddamn stupid, you piece of shit! You've got a lot of nerve!"

"I'm sorry. Oh, God, I'm so sorry! It all just got out of hand."

"Yeah, that happens with something like hatred. It's hard to make it stay curled up, nice and neat, in its box. It likes to get out and roam around, misbehave, break the rules." I was red-hot mad and it wasn't all at Sam Epstein—I still had the conversation with Carmine Aiello reverberating in my brain—Sammy just happened to be a handy target. He was by no means, though, the only deserving target so I decided to shut up until I could spread the mad around a bit more evenly, making the ride downtown to the office a quiet, if freezing cold journey, because now both the driver and Eddie in the front had their windows open, too, against Sam's stench. You couldn't be mad at a guy, though, for things that weren't his fault, and it wasn't his fault that nobody had let him bathe or change his clothes. Add to that three or four days of terror-induced sweat and even a *GQ* model would stink. None of us wanted to curse Sam so we cursed that traffic that had come to a stand-still on Seventh Avenue. Nothing moving and no way for the driver to change lanes. It took almost fifteen minutes to crawl four blocks and clear the congestion caused by delivery trucks double-parked on both sides of the one-way avenue, but it was smooth—and quick—sailing after that.

The car pulled up in front of the office and into a space just vacated by a green panel van that looked vaguely familiar but I couldn't focus on that; we all bailed out of the car as quickly as possible, and the driver left the windows down to air it out. As soon as we walked inside, though, we forgot the immediate past and its discomforts. Our olfactory senses were bombarded with good food smells. Yo hadn't merely ordered food—sandwiches or burgers. She'd gone all out. Six bags from El Caribe were piled on the front tables. That was the green panel van! Bradley Edwards, son of El Caribe owner Arlene Edwards, no doubt delivering the rush order Yolanda had phoned in.

She exchanged warm greetings with Mike and Eddie, whom she hadn't seen in a few weeks. Her relationship with them—and theirs with her—was changing, warming. She initially hadn't liked them, she said, because she found what she called their super macho, ex-cop, testosterone-overload energy taxing and tiring, not to mention very often offensive. They hadn't liked her, they said, because she was too prudish, too prissy, but

I suspected their testosterone-loaded macho energy didn't relate well to the fact that Yo's a lesbian, and I suspected that she knew that. But because they worked for us more and more, they were thrown together more and more, and mutual respect grew. "Sam, you come with me," she said to Epstein, leading him back to the bathroom.

The rest of us hauled the bags of food back to the kitchen and got busy unloading them and fixing plates. Mike and Eddie knew there were sodas and juice in the fridge and they so informed the driver, whose name, it turned out, also was Eddie. I heard Yo come out of the bathroom and close the door. I told Eddie the driver to have a seat out front; I needed a word with Yolanda, Mike, and Eddie. "I'm feeling that I've got to go find this Jackie guy today," I said, and told Mike and Eddie, before they could ask, that Yo would fill them in. "You all will have to deal with Sam. He tells it all or he goes to jail. Period."

"Tells what, *hermano?*" Eddie asked.

"Yolanda will fill you in, bro. I've gotta eat and run. I can only catch this Jackie guy on his lunch break, from twelve to one, and I've gotta go back uptown. Dammit!" Then I remembered the car and driver and Yolanda saw me remember. I took a plate of food out front and told the driver we were back out the door as soon as we finished eating. He jumped to his feet and I waved him back down. "Eat," I said. "We're not in that big a rush. Besides, this food is too good to waste."

"It's the best Island food I've ever eaten," Eddie the driver said.

"It's the best Island food in Manhattan," I said. "Right, Mr. Smith?" I said to Mike who was chewing as he joined us. And because he's such a well-bred gentleman, he didn't try to talk with his mouth full. He waited until he'd finished chewing and washed it down with a big swallow of ginger beer, and then he agreed with me, and kept on talking.

"We think it's a good idea if I go with you to meet this Jackie." I heard what he said, the way he said it, and also what he didn't say. It was three against one. No way I was going to meet some dude named Jackie that none of us knew without Mike Smith's back-up company and assistance. Truth be told, I was glad to have him and instantly was more relaxed than I'd been so far that day. Now I could give some time and attention to all the stuff moving about inside my head. Sam Epstein appeared contrite enough that he'd tell everything he knew about the fire at Taste of India and he'd own up to any other fires he and his buddies had set—at Jawal Nehru's import and export business maybe—and about anonymous calls to DHS. I could now think seriously about who Jackie was and how he tied into this thing. If he tied into it. He knows something about the fires, Raul had said. Something only those spilling the gasoline would know. I didn't doubt Raul's information or his motives. He'd have no reason to drop a false tip on me. So either Raul had received bad information, or whatever it was that Jackie knew, it had nothing to do with Sam Epstein and whatever it was that he knew. Which meant that I might have solved one problem only to stumble headfirst into another one.

Chapter Seven

The Furniture Depot occupied an entire block. A huge parking lot ran along the front of the building and it was almost full. Glass-fronted showrooms displayed living room, dining room, and bedroom furniture in half a dozen styles and wood finishes. There also were plasma-screen televisions and the furniture for speakers, CDs, and assorted other high-tech gadgetry. We drove through the parking lot, from one end of the building to the other, then out and around the corner. The side of the building was a solid brick wall, no doors or windows. The back of the building wasn't accessible from that side, so we drove around the block. There were windows at the top of the building and some kind of duct or venting system. When we turned the corner to come back to the front, we stopped hard and the car lurched as Eddie the driver slammed on the brakes. Four semis blocked the narrow street.

"Loading dock," Mike said, opening his door. "Meet me in the front parking lot," he said as he got out of the car. "I'm dressed for it, you aren't," he said to me before I could object, and closed the car door and jogged away. He followed the line of trucks up to the loading dock entrance and disappeared behind the cab of a semi bearing the name of a North Carolina furniture factory. Mike had at least ten years on me but he moved like a man ten years younger than me, which shouldn't be possible considering that he'd walked a beat as a New York City cop in Harlem for more than twenty years. He was a muscular guy, though, not a tank like, say, Mike Kallen, and he was quiet and intense and he had a great sense of humor, though it was quiet and intense, too. And he was usually right about things, like being better suited than me to recon a loading dock at lunchtime. He was wearing gray cargo pants, a black turtleneck, black high-top hiking boots, and a three-quarter length wool overcoat that was flapping in the breeze. He also had on this goofy-looking knit cap that he wore in the winter that he would pull down over his ears when it was really cold but which would stand up in a floppy point when it wasn't, like it was doing now.

Eddie drove slowly so that I could get a good look at the loading dock. Nothing to see because, like Raul said, it was lunchtime. I had wondered about eating lunch on an exposed loading dock in March but I had in mind an exposed concrete platform; this was more of a huge room with the door left open a little. I could see a couple dozen guys sitting on palettes and crates eating lunch. In the cabs of the semis drivers were eating, reading, napping. Mike was right: The way I was dressed, I'd have been as out of place as an olive in rice pudding. Eddie took the car back around to the front of the building and found a place in the parking lot where we could watch the corner of the building and the showroom entrance. Smart move on his part. I'd keep him in mind if I needed a car and a driver in the future. He lowered the windows a bit and turned off the car. We waited. And I turned this puzzle cube around and around in my mind, realized that wasn't helping at all, decided to call Yo. She wasn't ready to talk to me.

"I'll call you back, Phil. We're at a crucial point with Sam. He doesn't want to talk—he's terrified that he'll be killed if he does. We're trying to get him to see that he'd already be dead if you hadn't made a deal to keep him alive. He almost believes us. But Phil, I don't think whatever Sam was into has anything to do with anybody named Jackie. What he was doing started and ended with Mottola, Casey, and McQueen."

I closed the phone wishing I could feel better about the positive outcome with Sam Epstein. After all, I'd done what I was hired to do and we'd clear a healthy profit. I also didn't create any debt with Carmine Aiello, something that had worried me from the beginning and had flat out scared Yolanda. She didn't want us asking him for favors, but the reality was we couldn't go into Irish and Italian communities asking questions and expecting answers. This wasn't television. Mottola, Casey, and McQueen wouldn't have given me the time of day, and would probably have kicked my ass for being bold enough to go on their turf asking questions, especially about their activities. I needed Carmine. Simple as that. Being able to keep Joey Mottola out of the picture came as an unexpected gift. Now I didn't owe Carmine and he didn't owe me, and that thought cheered me.

So did the sight of Mike Smith rounding the corner of the Furniture Depot. He was walking normally, not hurried, not as if he expected somebody to be on his tail. I didn't have to tell the driver to start the car; he did it on his own, shifted into gear, and let the car drift slowly toward Mike, who opened the door and hopped in while the car was in motion. "Go out the other end," Mike said, and the car turned slowly and smoothly in the other direction and joined the queue exiting the parking lot into the Ninth Avenue southbound traffic. "You're a damn good driver," Mike said.

"Thanks," Eddie the driver said. Then, realizing that he was expected to explain it, he did. "I took this defensive driving course. I was working for this singer and he was worried because a couple of his buddies got popped, so he bought this armor-plated limo, thing weighed a ton, then paid for me to take this defensive driving course. It was interesting, tell you the truth.

Some ex-CIA guy taught it. I don't know what I was thinking, though, because the first time somebody shot at my guy everything I learned went right out of my head. I just wanted to get away. My guy was happy—he thought it was the defensive driving techniques that got us away—but I knew it was fear, the kind of fear I smelled on your guy this morning. I quit the second time we got shot at and went to work for the car service. They like it that I've got this training, but I refuse to drive rappers, gangsta or otherwise."

Mike and I were both laughing by the time Eddie finished his story. It was a good one, and I knew it was true. We didn't accept work from celebrity clients of any stripe for the very reason that they often were targets—of adoring fans as well as the competition. Then Mike turned serious. "If I had to guess I'd say your boy Jackie has met a bad end." And he related his experience on the loading dock. Jackie's name was French, spelled JACQUES, last name Marchand, he was twenty-six or thereabouts, his supervisor thought. And the supervisor, whose name was Jerry Talbot, also thought Jackie was, here lately, in some kind of trouble. "He couldn't be specific," Mike related, "except to say that he was so preoccupied he dropped one end of a ten-grand plasma TV."

"Preoccupied or clumsy?" I asked.

"The supervisor, Talbot, swears that Jackie's a straight arrow, pays attention to his work, is always on time, doesn't bullshit with the other guys, smoking reefer, drinking beer, and listening to rap music when he should be working. Which is why the guys on the dock called him Jackie instead of Jack."

I wasn't sold and said so, though I didn't tell Mike why; he already didn't like that I used Raul as a source. Mike had been a cop too long to ever be able to trust an ex-con, especially one who was an ex-addict. And while I did trust Raul's information, I wasn't certain that somebody like him would know or associate with a guy described as a straight arrow. Especially a twenty-something with a name like Jacques Marchand. "Is he French, then? Jackie?" I asked.

"French Canadian by birth, according to the supervisor, but here long enough to have dual citizenship and work his way halfway through NYU."

I heard an alarm bell but couldn't pinpoint the source. "How long's he worked at Furniture Depot, and how does dropping a TV translate to meeting a bad end?"

"A year and a half and never missed a day, according to Talbot." And the way Mike said that I knew something about this story was chafing him, too, so I stayed quiet and let him work through it. "Okay, here's the part that doesn't add up for me. Talbot says Jackie didn't enroll in school for the current semester because he wanted to work full-time and save enough money so he could go to school full-time in September."

"Makes sense to me," I said. "Loading and unloading furniture for eight hours straight is back-breaking work. He wouldn't have energy left for school."

Mike was frowning, shaking his head. "This job was part-time. He'd got himself a second part-time job and Talbot said that's when Jackie started behaving strangely."

"Strangely how?"

"Coming in late, calling in sick. And now Talbot says he didn't show up at all today and didn't call, which was so unusual that Talbot called him. Busy signal on his home phone since early this morning."

"That doesn't necessarily translate into bad news, even if the guy's a saint. He's still a guy, a twenty-something in sin city. Maybe he met a girl over the weekend and hasn't gotten out of bed," I said, liking the thought of that much better than thoughts of bad ends. "And did Talbot call the second job? Did Jackie show up there?"

"He doesn't know where it is, just that it's with some insurance company, doing salvage and reclamation work."

Another alarm bell sounded, this one louder than the first, both of them insistent now, and I got the messages: Foreign-born person and insurance company. "Where's he live? And did Talbot know anything at all about this insurance company?" I knew I was grasping at straws and that was because I now shared Mike's feeling that Jackie, if he hadn't already come to a bad end, was moving in that direction.

"*Nada* on the insurance company. I pressed Talbot pretty hard on that, especially on the salvage angle, but came up dry. He did know, though, that the kid lives off First Avenue somewhere . . ."

"East Second," I said.

Mike looked at me. "Yeah. How'd you know?"

"That's where Raul works. That's how he knows Jackie."

The remainder of the day just . . . happened. I was present but I didn't feel like a participant in events as much as an observer of them. Yolanda and Eddie had taped their conversation with Sam Epstein and were certain that he'd told them all he knew, so I took him home, but I'd had to read him the riot act first. He was still pissing and moaning about his father being involved, still criticizing his cousin Ellie for calling him. I don't know what came over me but I couldn't listen to another sentence. "You ungrateful, useless piece of shit," I said to him, getting his full attention. I stood in front of him, making him look up at me. "Your old man sat right there, in that same chair, and cried like a baby because he was afraid you were dead. You're all he has left, Sammy, you and Sasha, and he thought you were dead. Do you understand what that means? The man had four children. By now he thought he'd have a dozen grandkids. Instead, three of his children are dead and your sorry ass was missing. Your mother's in such a state that she couldn't even make the trip. She couldn't bring herself to come here only to find out that you were dead, too, like three other of her children. And all you can do is whine and complain. That old man will be so grateful to see you that he won't care if you did burn down that restaurant and kill that delivery man. He just wants you, his only remaining child, to be alive. Now go get in the fuckin' car and stop your fuckin' pissing and moaning."

Everybody was looking at me like I was some new species of being, even Eddie the driver, and I was feeling like a new species, maybe like a mutation of Carmine and my regular self. Except my regular self seemed to have taken a leave of absence and all I had left was the mutation. Yolanda insisted that Mike and Eddie go with me to return Sam to his family, and insisted that we come right back. She had things to tell me, she said. So we did what we were instructed to do. Dave Epstein and Ellie and Sasha were so glad to see Sam that they didn't even notice that we'd left. When we got back to the office Yolanda told Eddie the driver that we were finished with him and gave him such a large tip that he stuttered for several seconds before he could express his thanks. "Anytime you folks need a driver, please ask for me," he said. "And tell dispatch to call me if it's my day off. I mean it. I'd drive for you folks anytime."

Finally it was just the four of us. Yolanda locked the door and pulled the shades even though it was barely four o'clock. We were closed to the outside world, and inside we had a world of trouble staring us in the face. I was content to let Yolanda do all the talking and explaining. She began by playing Sam's tape for Mike. She and Eddie had done such a good job of questioning him that Mike didn't have any questions, but he had lots of commentary, though it was nothing I hadn't said to myself, the most salient of his comments being, "You have really stepped into a big pile of elephant shit this time, bro."

I considered defending myself but was glad I didn't when Yolanda dumped a thick file folder in the middle of my desk. "Arson fires in businesses owned by non-white immigrants in the last year. There are seven. Three of them Sammy admitted to setting with his friends, but he says he called DHS and reported all of these business owners as suspected terrorists."

Silence reigned, but I was certain it was only external because I knew that the other three brains were spinning and sputtering as loudly as mine and coming up with the same balls dropping into the same slots: There were two sets of arsonists, a fact Sammy had neglected to mention, which suggested, at least to me, a mastermind, which Sammy also neglected to mention. Maybe he didn't know? I replayed the Sammy/Yolanda/Eddie tape in my mind. They had let Sammy talk, then they had pushed for the information they suspected he was withholding; Yolanda pushed gently but insistently, Eddie pushed hard and mean when necessary. They believed, and I agreed, that Sam Epstein had told them all he knew about the fires, including the fact that they were set because Homeland Security didn't seem to be doing anything about the terrorists among us. Yolanda had asked him why he thought those specific people were terrorists. "All you have to do is look at them," he'd replied. "Look at the clothes they wear, listen to them talk."

There was a brief silence after that, then Eddie's nastiest laugh. "So did you report the Hassidic Jewish community in Brooklyn as terrorist suspects? They dress funny, talk funny. Or would you like for me to make that call to Homeland Security for you?" It had taken several more minutes but they finally got Sam to admit that all those reported to DHS as suspected terrorists were people of color, and that focusing on them had been McQueen's idea.

"And what did you think would happen to those people?"

Yolanda had asked, and Sammy had replied, "They would be sent back home." Then Eddie must have made a sudden move because Sam cried out, "Please don't hit me!" and Eddie had shouted, really screamed at the top of his lungs, something I'd never heard him do, "I ought to kill you, you cowardly piece of shit! Those people are home! This is their home, just like it's your home!"

But there hadn't been a specific question to Sam about the other fires, whether or not he knew about them, though Yolanda had asked whether other people were involved with the four of them—himself, Mottola, McQueen, and Casey—and he'd said no.

"So what are we gonna do, bro?" Mike Smith asked.

"I'm for serving up Epstein's sorry ass to the Homeland Security assholes. They deserve each other," Eddie said.

I agreed but Sam Epstein no longer was a concern of mine, Ravi Patel was our paying customer and it was the New York City Fire Department and Big Apple Business Insurers who needed to be convinced that Patel hadn't torched his own building, which meant finding a way to drop Tim McQueen into the elephant shit pile since he was the one who started the fire. For sure Sam Epstein wouldn't point the finger; he shook and trembled every time anybody said the words, McQueen, Casey, and Mottola. Mottola was out of the picture, due to my deal with Carmine. I had to find another way, which led me right back to Jackie Marchand.

"Find Jackie Marchand. Get the loading dock supervisor to violate his rules and give you the guy's address, bribe him if you have to. Then go find him. I need to know what he knows." Mike nodded and Eddie looked expectantly at me so I told them about Raul and before they could react the way I knew they would, I told them not to. "The dude is righteous whether you two think so or not. I'm telling you he is, and if Mike's bad feeling about Jackie Marchand is right, and knowing Mike it probably is, then I need Raul's help. Talk to him *mano a mano,* Eddie, not like cop to perp . . ."

"Phil?" Yolanda gave me a look I couldn't interpret, so she had to spell it out. "If you need something more from Raul, you should be the one to ask him for it. He just got to the point of trusting you, he's not going to trust Eddie, and you'll lose him forever."

She was right and I knew it. I nodded and Mike stood up, stretched, slipped into his coat which was hanging on the back of his chair, and headed for the door. "I better try and catch Talbot before he leaves," and he was out the door.

"There's something Eddie can help me with," Yo said, shocking him and me, but he nodded warily. "The tenant and employee files Kallen submitted for the Avenue B building; there's something not right about it but I can't figure out what it is. Eddie, you're good at reading between the lines. Would you take a look?"

"Sure," he said, "bring it on."

"What's this pile on my desk, then?" I asked; I'd thought it was the KLM/Kallen stuff that Yolanda had just asked Eddie to look at.

"The Patel and Nehru records. Very detailed, as you'll see; wish all our clients were so organized. You'll also see that Mr. Nehru is a very rich man. His idea of import-export isn't trinkets you buy at street fairs and flea markets."

Yolanda and Eddie disappeared behind the screens and I followed them, but I stopped at the map of the city on the wall next to the kitchen. Every street and alley, every train track and subway tunnel, clearly marked. I took the list of fire locations and marked each one with a red push pin. Then I added a yellow pin to the fires set by Sammy and Company. I already knew that all the businesses were owned by non-white immigrants, so the only other pattern I could discern was location: All the fires occurred in a slice of the southern part of the city, between 34th and Canal Streets. But was that really a pattern? I stood there looking at the map for a long time, visualizing the streets and the neighborhoods, both East Side and West Side, searching for meaning. I didn't find it. If it was there, it was going to make me work to uncover it.

I went back to my desk, switched on the lamp and opened the Patel file, which seemed to contain every piece of paper ever generated pertaining to the purchase of his building and the opening of his restaurant. I couldn't imagine that anybody could look at this file and see a terrorist, or a man who would destroy everything these pieces of paper represented. I'd read some of the terrorist profile information that flowed like water downhill from the Federal, state, and city police agencies after the declaration of war on terrorists, and Ravi Patel didn't have a toenail that would fit one of the profiles. I knew a little bit, too, about arsonist profiles, especially those who torched their own homes or businesses, usually to collect on the insurance. Again, no Ravi fit or match. The government spent millions of dollars developing and generating these profiles; did anybody in the government ever read them? Did the damn government agencies themselves even believe them?

I closed the Patel file and opened Jawal Nehru's. It was the size of the Manhattan yellow pages. Clipped to the first page was the fountain pen–looking thing that really was for backing up files, and beneath it an arrow pointing to it and, in Yolanda's handwriting, "It's called a flash drive, Phil, not a thingy." I chuckled to myself and started reading the first document, which was the quarterly tax return prepared the night before the fire that destroyed Nehru's life. "Holy shit!"

Yolanda and Eddie came running from behind the screens. "What?"

"Nehru lost inventory worth more than three million dollars in that fire!"

"I told you he was no street peddler."

"Yeah, but . . ." I didn't know what to say. No wonder Mrs. Nehru felt compelled to leave if anyone seriously believed she and her husband would intentionally destroy that kind of net worth, to say nothing of the lifestyle it bought.

"And they've got the receipts for every item on that inventory, Phil. They'd already bought and paid for that stuff, and now the insurance company won't ante up."

"What's their premium?" I asked, already turning pages.

"Read it and weep," Yo said.

"Holy shit!" I said again. And I thought my insurance premiums . . . "Wait a minute . . . did you see this, Yo? Big Apple has Nehru and Patel." She started toward my desk but the phone rang and she went back to her own. I heard her out of only one ear; the bulk of my attention was on Nehru's Big Apple insurance file, pages and pages and more pages of documents. Then there was the insurance coverage on their West End Avenue apartment . . .

"Let's roll, *hermano.*" Eddie was standing beside my desk zipping up his jacket. "That was Mike on the phone."

He didn't need to say anything more. I strapped on my gun, went to the back and got my jacket, grabbed the cell phone out of the charger, and joined Eddie waiting for me at the front door. I turned back toward Yolanda but found she'd followed us to the door. "Is this a police matter yet?" She shook her head, no, and gave me a piece of paper with an address written on it. I hoped it would stay that way, at least until we had searched for anything helpful to our case.

"Mike's inside," Yolanda said, both sounding a warning and issuing a plea, and I heard both, loudly and clearly.

Eddie and I both knew that at this time of day our feet would get us over to First Avenue and Second Street faster than any form of motorized transportation. We both started running, dodging cars and people as we moved from street to sidewalk. We took the one-way streets whenever possible, traveling the opposite direction. In about twelve minutes we were standing outside of Jackie Marchand's apartment building. No sign or sound of cops present or en route. I was about to press the buzzer to Jackie's apartment when Eddie nudged me in the ribs with his elbow and signaled with his head that I should look inside the door. I did, and saw Mike Smith coming down a dimly lit hallway at a trot. Eddie and I both backed up down the steps and were headed up the block when Mike caught up with us but we didn't speak for another block. If Mike was in a hurry to get out of that building, there was a good reason for it. We turned a corner, spied a bodega, and headed for it. There were too many people inside for us to talk about anything, so we each bought something—chips for Mike and me, gum for Eddie—paid and left. We walked another block, slower this time, Mike and me eating our chips, until we reached a small park. It had benches so we sat.

"Jackie Marchand's been dead long enough to stink," Mike began. "Beat to death, looks like." He dug in his pockets, came up with a grubby manila envelope folded in half. He opened it, spread it out across our three laps, and shifted the pieces of paper inside so that we all could see and read them: Transcripts from New York University that showed Jacques Marchand to be a dean's list student; documents from the Department of State of the United States showing Jacques Anatole Marchand to be a naturalized citizen of the United States; essay and term papers marked A or excellent; and pay stubs. From Furniture Depot dating back more than a year, just like the loading dock supervisor said, and from Big Apple Business Insurers, dating back to December. "The place was tossed," Mike said. "Somebody was looking for something. I don't know if they found it. This was all I found, and I had a pretty good look around before I called it in."

The screech and scream of sirens split the air. Jackie Marchand's death now was a matter for officialdom. "How'd you get in, Mike?" I asked, "and where'd you find this stuff? Must've been hidden pretty good."

First question answered first. "Picked the lock. Whoever did him, he let 'em in, but when they left, they just shut the door behind them so the top two locks weren't engaged. I couldn't have gotten in otherwise. As for this stuff," and he tapped the folder still spread across our laps, as if none of us wanted to be the one to close the file on Jackie Marchand's life, "it was inside a boot, one of those heavy, fur-lined things, the kind they probably wear in Canada, or up in Buffalo or Syracuse, 'cause even our worst winter here wouldn't require anything like those shoes. And it was obvious he hadn't worn them in a while. The top of the box they were in was all dusty."

"If he let in whoever beat him to death," I said, "he either wasn't afraid of them or he didn't believe he was a threat to them."

"Or he didn't know he was a threat to them," Eddie said. We all thought about that for a moment, then Eddie tapped the papers in our laps. "I mean look at this! This boy was no threat to anybody! All he did was study and work."

I swallowed hard and closed the file on Jackie Marchand's life. This was getting to me, in the same way, only more intensely than the death of the Taste of India delivery man had gotten to me. I thought I understood that one—I'd first thought that a fifteen-year-old boy had been murdered for so stupid a reason that it didn't warrant trying to understand. I didn't understand this one at all. Aside from the fact that he was a human being who didn't deserve to be murdered because no human being deserved that—okay, most human beings didn't deserve that—why should I be affected like this? I didn't have an answer. I only knew that I felt these murders were coming too close to home.

Mike got to his feet and Eddie and I followed suit. "I promised Talbot at the loading dock I'd let him know something," Mike said.

"Are we sure he won't blame you?" I asked.

Mike nodded. "He already was having a bad feeling. He really liked the kid. I just don't want him to suffer any longer than necessary."

"I'm going back to the office, then. Finish helping Yolanda," Eddie said.

Mike gave him the same kind of look that I had but didn't say anything. "I guess I'll head over to the diner and fill Raul in," I said. I gave Jackie Marchand's folder to Eddie. "Give this to Yo. She'll figure out if it can help us." And how to keep the cops from finding out we'd broken into a murder victim's apartment and stolen evidence I thought, but didn't say. And we split up, heading off in three different directions. If there was an up side to the situation it was that my destination was only two blocks away. I walked slowly, wondering how to break bad news to a guy I barely knew. I didn't know how well Raul knew Jackie, didn't really know how it happened that Raul knew Jackie. Didn't know how Raul knew that I was looking into the fires in the first place. I called up to memory the phone call from Willie One Eye, Raul's uncle. All he'd said was that his nephew had words for me, and when I went to see Raul, all he'd said was somebody named Jackie knew something about the fires. And now Jackie was dead. Because he knew something about the fires?

I opened the door to the diner and before I could go in, three people came out, two of them thanking me for holding the door. Who said New Yorkers weren't polite? I realized, once I was inside, that I didn't know if Raul was working now or not. He wasn't at the grill and I didn't want to make myself obvious by looking for him, so I took a seat at the far end of the counter, kept my eyes down, and took a business card from the jacket pocket. I wrote my cell phone number on the front, where the office number already was imprinted, and on the back I wrote: We need to talk, Sorbino. It's important. Call me any time. I was capping the pen when I thought to add, *Gracias.*

I looked up to see the counter man watching me. It wasn't Raul. I made a circle with the thumb and forefinger of my right hand, then raised the index and middle fingers. He quickly brought me two doughnuts and a cup of coffee and he didn't walk away immediately so I looked up at him. He was an old white guy, lined face, hard, pale eyes, unlit cigarette in the left corner of his mouth. He had tattoos up and down both arms just like Raul did; just like most cons did, and I was certain that if I studied his I'd find the Aryan Brotherhood or some other white supremacist prison protection group. He met my eyes, then looked down at the card I'd written on for Raul. "Want me to give it to him?" the counter man asked in a near whisper.

"Is he all right?"

"Layin' low," came the answer, not one I was happy to hear. I took a twenty from my wallet and put it on top of the card, nodded my thanks, and picked up my coffee cup. I missed Raul doubly, because this counter man made a lousy cup of coffee. As always, though, the doughnuts were fresh, gooey and good. I bought a bag of them to go.

I walked back to the office wondering why Raul found it necessary to be laying low. Something to do with Jackie's murder? I hoped he was just laying low and not laid out somewhere. That would be problematic in more ways than one, the one being that his uncle might blame me. On that cheery thought I zig-zagged across the street against traffic that was at a standstill and jogged the rest of the way to the office. I pushed the buzzer, told Yolanda it was me, and walked in to the scent of freshly brewing coffee. Eddie must've suggested that no way I'd go to a doughnut diner and not bring back a bag and he stuck his head around a screen as I came in and peered at me over the tops of black-rimmed reading glasses. He looked like a hairy academic. I tossed the white bag at him and he was grinning in anticipation before the bag reached him. "Told you!" he said with a little kid's glee.

When we all had a mug of coffee and Eddie a plate of doughnuts, we slouched on the sofa, our feet on the table, and I laid all my doubts, worries, skepticism, and fears on the two of them. They listened and contemplated. Eddie chewed. Yolanda said she wasn't that worried about people knowing that we were looking into the fires. "You know, this is nothing but a small town, Phil. Everybody in the East Village knows everybody and knows everybody's business, and they especially know the people who help and people who hurt."

Eddie was nodding vigorously but his mouth was too full of doughnut to talk so he had to keep nodding while we waited. Finally he said, "Yo's right about that, Phil. And I'll tell you something else about down here." He said "down here" like he was talking about a foreign land, and in a way, he was: When his folks finally left East Harlem they moved further north, like Connie's family did, up to the Bronx. "People down here live close to the ground. You got no fifteen-, twenty-story apartment buildings down here, block after block of 'em. You got these little short, squat, narrow buildings, people can't have a decent marital spat or case of diarrhea without the neighbors knowing about it."

Yolanda gagged in mock disgust and punched him on the arm and they both giggled like they were back in junior high. I covered my surprise at the ease of their banter. Until four months ago, these two had barely tolerated each other. I was glad of the change. Yolanda was my right hand; no, more than that—the exhalation to my inhalation. Without her there would be no Phillip Rodriquez Investigations and I didn't fool myself about that. But Mike Smith and Eddie Ortiz were important to the business and as it grew, they were becoming crucial. I needed them and relied on them more and more and it had been tough, the two of them and Yolanda at odds. It was so much better being able to have these brain-airing sessions with them together instead of with Yo, then with Mike and Eddie, then blending and balancing their differing views and opinions to come up with some kind of whole, rational approach.

"So you all are saying that despite our professional obligation to maintain secrecy, confidentiality, for our clients, we can't do that because everybody knows what we're doing anyway, sometimes even before we do it?"

"Not saying that, *'mano.*"

"What we're saying, Phil . . . for instance . . . about the rapes? Everybody knows you did the cops' job for them, finding that rapist, but it's not public knowledge who the rape victims were, except for the ones who were murdered." Yolanda didn't finish. She still got really emotional around this case because it cut too close to home for her.

"And nobody knows who beat the shit outta that lowlife scum bag who raped those other little girls and put him in the hospital on life support. People just know that you're the one who found him for the parents," Eddie said.

"And nobody knows the cops knew who he was and could have arrested him before he raped and killed another child," Yolanda added angrily.

"But people think I'm the one who beat him."

Both Yo and Eddie were shaking their heads. "No, they

don't," she said. "They think one of the fathers did it but they don't know which one—the even money is on Carmine because of who he is—and they don't really care. All they care about is that somebody—you, Phil—found out who was hurting little girls and put a stop to it."

"But they do think I castrated Itchy Johnson."

Now they were back to giggling and punching each other like high schoolers. "Yeah, well, whatcha gonna do, *hermano?* It's hard bein' a hero," Eddie said.

"And that's another example, Phil, where everybody knows you're the one who saved Jill Mason but nobody knows who hired you to do that . . ."

"And nobody cares about that part, Phil, the confidential part," Eddie said. "It's the results that matter to people. You find out who's burning these businesses and put a stop to it, that's what people will care about, not the confidential client part. That's what people will remember long term."

"But we can't do business confidentially if everybody knows we're doing it!" Their attempts to soothe and reassure me were having the exact opposite effect. "Suppose that's why Jackie Marchand is dead, because somebody knew I was looking to talk to him. That makes me, in a way, responsible for his death."

"You're reaching, dude," Eddie said, and though both his tone of voice and his words were gentle I felt a bit of a sting. "If, and I say IF, that boy's death is related to these fires, then it's because he was ready to rat somebody out, not because you're doing the investigating. Get clear about who the bad guys are, Rodriquez, and you ain't one of 'em. The bad guys are whoever is setting the fires. The bad guys are whoever beat that boy's head in. The bad guys are reporting innocent people to fuckin' Homeland Security. That wuss we just took home to his daddy, for my money, he's a bad guy, and it's a good thing I'm working for you and not the New York City police department

’cause his sorry ass would be in a cell right now. Then he’d have something to whine about.”

“Eddie’s right, Phil. People in the neighborhood know that you’re the one to come to when there’s a problem and they automatically assume that if something’s getting fixed, you’re the one doing the fixing.”

I looked from one to the other of them, saw the resolve and right in their eyes. “I’m not doing the fixing alone,” I said.

“You finally said something that makes sense, *’mano,*” Eddie said, and ate the last of the doughnuts. “So, what’s up for tomorrow?”

I looked at Yolanda for the answer. “You go see the Buddhist monk in the morning, then swing by Avenue B to see Kallen . . .”

“Aw, shit! I just left Kallen! What’s he want now?”

“He’s seeking your approval—his words, not mine—about the steps he’s taken in the building, and to tell you the truth, I want you to take a look, because Eddie doesn’t like what he’s seeing in his files any more than I do.”

“And what are you seeing?” I asked, praying that the answer wouldn’t be a glimpse of the Russian Mafia. They scared me more than Carmine ever did or could.

“Seven new tenants, all women, all under twenty-five, all white, all employed by the same temp agency. Two new employees—a handyman and a porter—both with out-of-state references, both early thirties, both white.” Eddie looked at me, waiting for me to get it. I did.

“White janitors in buildings in this part of town. A bit unusual,” I said.

“No shit,” Eddie said.

“What about those girls, the tenants?” Yolanda asked.

“Seven new tenants, all at the same time, sounds a little suspish to me. And all of ’em single, white, twenty-something females?” He wobbled his hand from side to side.

I shrugged; didn't seem that unusual to me, given what I'd seen of Kallen and what I thought about him based on what I'd seen. "I can see Kallen renting to a bunch of single women. He probably thinks he's a player. And besides, Eastern Europeans have a reputation as being more than a little racist. Maybe they don't hire or rent to non-whites."

Yolanda thought about that. "Maybe that's why he tried to fire us? He found out we didn't meet his pigmentation requirements?" She thought for another moment, then said, "Okay, I'll buy their illegal and racist rental practices—everybody in town is guilty of that—but the only apartment building in this town with seven vacancies at one time is the one still under construction."

She definitely had a point. "What about Boris?" I asked.

"Who's Boris?" Eddie asked.

"The resident manager. I told you about him, Yo."

She was shaking her head. "No Boris in the files."

Eddie was giving me a negative, too. "No resident manager in the files, either."

"Well, maybe Kallen will give me some paperwork on him tomorrow. And these other people—they all have socials?" Yolanda said she was still checking them. "Was Mike planning to come back here?"

"He's going home," Eddie said, "which is where I need to be going if I'm going to have dinner ready when Linda gets home."

"You can cook?"

"Damn right I can cook! Red beans or black, you haven't had beans and rice until you've had my beans and rice. I'll bring you some tomorrow."

"I'll bring my appetite," Yo said, and disappeared behind the screens.

"You ever seen her eat? You better make an extra pot of beans," I whispered, and it was the two of us, Eddie and me, giggling like high schoolers. I walked him to the door, thanked him for his good work, and got a pat on the back and wink and the reminder that I paid him very well for his good work, which was thanks enough for him. I turned off the front lights and lowered the shades, feeling better about things. Not quite relieved, but better. I loaded the Patel and Nehru files into my carryall and turned off my desk lamp. "You going to Sandra's?" I called out to Yolanda.

She appeared already wearing coat, hat, and scarf, my question answered. I opened the door, she set the alarm, and we left. I walked her to the subway, then turned east and headed home. It was, I realized, still daylight. The cold weather was hanging on but it would have to give up soon. Spring definitely was coming.

Chapter Eight

I looked in surprise at the tiny building that housed the Village Buddhist Center. I must have walked past it dozens of times if not hundreds. Off Broadway, it was situated between the Villages, East and West, in an old clapboard house that was a throwback to the century before the last one. Pots of colorful spring flowers lined the porch; Buddhists, like most New Yorkers, hastened the arrival of spring. Pairs of shoes also lined the porch, at least a dozen of them, too many, I thought, to belong to residents of the little house. I looked at my watch. I was six or seven minutes early. I walked up on to the porch. The door was closed and no sound emanated from within. In fact, there was no sense of movement of any kind. I looked for a doorbell or knocker, didn't see either. I raised my hand to knock, thought better of it, and was glad I did because at that moment I heard bells inside, a tiny tinkle, three times, then more silence and stillness, and then movement. If I had knocked I'd have disturbed a religious ceremony.

The front door opened and people spilled out—young, old, male, female, all colors, one in a wheelchair. Some carried shoes in their hands but most were in their sock feet and I moved out of the way so they could put their shoes on. "Mr. Rodriquez!" I heard, and found Patty Starrett smiling at me. "Phil! What a surprise!"

"Hi, Patty," I said, and was pleased that she embraced me instead of offering me a hand to shake. "How's Pam?"

I got an even bigger smile and her eyes sparkled with tears. "She is an amazing little girl and she's doing really well, with Dr. Mason's help."

"And yours, too, Patty. The kid's got an amazing mother, don't forget." And I meant that. If it could be said that any good could come from something as horrific as the serial rape and murder of little girls it would be that the people who loved and cared for those little girls found within themselves reserves of strength they probably didn't know they had—people like Patty Starrett and Carmine Aiello—and that strength rubbed off on people like me and I'm better for it. I know this is true. "Give Pam a hug for me."

"I will, Phil, and she'll be sorry she missed seeing you. You're her hero, you know. You are!" she insisted when she saw me start to protest. "She knows you're the one who got the bad man who hurt her, and the bad man who hurt Dr. Mason. You're all the X-Men rolled into one for her."

I was still being warmed by the memory of Pamela Starrett, a smaller version of her mother, when I heard my name called again, this time by the monk I was here to see.

"Good morning, Mr. Rodriquez. Come in, please."

"Should I leave my shoes out here?"

"You can remove them inside. There's a bench just inside the door."

I followed him inside and the first thing I saw, at the end of the room directly opposite the front door, was a large altar in the center of which was a large golden Buddha statue in front of which was a huge golden bowl of fruit. And there were flowers and candles and incense. There was a raised platform just beneath the altar and a dozen or so pillows faced each other across either side of the altar. I wasn't certain what I'd expected, never having been inside a Buddhist place of worship before, but I didn't expect it to be so . . . church-like. With the exception of the pillows instead of pews, it looked and felt like church. I sat on the bench just inside the door and took off my shoes while the monk waited for me, then I followed him through an arched doorway into a surprisingly large, bright kitchen.

He was a big man, this monk, tall and obviously muscular beneath his robes. He was bald and he wore wire-rimmed glasses and I didn't think there was anything fake or phony about the smile constantly on his face. He waved me into a chair at the table in the middle of the kitchen floor. "Coffee or tea?" he asked.

"Whatever you're having is fine as long as it's hot," I said.

He put two big mugs and a couple of plates on the table, then a platter of some good-looking muffins, spoons, and some napkins. He didn't seem to feel the need to say anything, and he didn't seem bothered by the silence. I didn't mind it either, so we both just waited for the water to boil. When it did, he put some loose tea into a pot, poured the water in, put the top on the pot, and brought it to the table. It was like something out of a British mystery novel or a PBS special. "Eat as many of those muffins as you like," he said. "Patty made them."

I looked at the muffins. "What's wrong with them?"

He laughed, and it was a good laugh. "They're delicious is what's wrong with them and if you don't eat them, I'll end up eating them, and that's the other thing wrong with them: They are totally irresistible. You can't eat just one."

I put a muffin on my plate, broke it in half and took a bite. Before I was done chewing I put another muffin on my plate. "Better than delicious," I said with my mouth full. "Sinful." I chewed a moment. "Do Buddhists have sin?"

"No, and I'm really glad we don't because I'm happy thinking that the only thing really wrong with me eating three or four of these at one time is that I don't need to gain another pound."

I gave my own mid-section a pat, thought about Yolanda and

her ass-widening comment about the Napoleons, and took another bite of muffin. "What should I call you?" I asked the monk.

"My name is Kusala."

"Thank you for seeing me, Kusala," I said, then waited for him to pour the tea. It had a rich, spicy smell, like it would go really well with the muffins. I put some honey in the tea, stirred it, sipped it, and wondered if I could get Patty to make muffins for me and where I could buy this tea. "I need your help but I'm not sure what to ask you."

"Suppose I just talk, then if you have questions you can ask them?" And when I nodded, he told me that during the first week of January, two Homeland Security agents interrupted the morning meditation and demanded to see his proof of citizenship. "I think they were angry because they'd knocked, then pounded on the door—all they had to do was open it—but nobody stopped meditation to get up to open the door. I finally did and when I opened the door they showed me their identification, asked for me by name, though they mispronounced it, and demanded the proof of citizenship. It just so happened that we had two lawyers and a newspaper reporter present that morning. I'm sure I don't need to tell you what transpired in the next several moments."

I grinned widely, imagining three barefoot defenders of freedom going up against two DHS agents that early in the morning, but I quickly sobered. "They're not known for their well-developed sense of humor, those guys."

"They definitely were not amused, especially after I showed them my passport. They had trouble believing I'm an American—born and raised in upstate New York—and they had real difficulty with my frequent travel to Thailand, Tibet, and India. They asked all kinds of questions, and they were asked all kinds of questions from the people whose morning meditation they had interrupted. And DHS agents aren't accustomed to answering questions, but they finally got around to telling me that I had been reported as a possible terrorist suspect. DHS agents also don't like being laughed at."

Buddhist monks apparently don't like being called terrorists, either, because for the first time I saw the man's serenity crack. He didn't quite look angry but he definitely hadn't gotten over the experience. "So, after they got laughed at, you must have said something that convinced them they'd received erroneous information?"

"They absolutely refused to discuss the accusation, who made it or exactly what was said. They left and I've heard nothing further."

"Nobody from DHS ever told you that you're no longer a terrorist suspect?"

He shook his head with a heavy sadness. "But I can't travel. My name is on some kind of list. My passport is blocked for foreign travel and the airlines have my name on some kind of domestic watch list."

"What were their names? The Federal agents?"

"I have no idea. They never gave their names, they only flashed their ID cases, and to tell you the truth, I was so startled I didn't think to look for names."

"Do you remember what they looked like? Can you describe them?"

"One of them I can, the angry, belligerent one, because he stood so close to me I thought we'd merge," and he described to a tee my friend from the Taste of India fire. Angry, belligerent, and in your face. That's him.

There was a contractor's van and a plumbing truck parked in front of Mike Kallen's Avenue B building when I got there, and Kallen himself was standing at the top of the steps, arms crossed at mid-chest, legs widespread and feet planted, as if he planned to block entry by a whole army of plumbers and contractors. Only his eyes moved, restless, scanning, searching. For what, I wondered? Me, maybe, because when he saw me he relaxed his stance and beckoned for me to join him. "Thanks for coming, Phil," he said, as if I'd accepted an invitation to breakfast.

I pointed to the trucks. "Spending the company's money early, I see."

"What is that saying, you must spend money to make it, yes?"

"And it's a true saying from what I can tell."

"Then let me show you how the money is spending," he said, and turned toward the front door—the new front door that had been an early morning surprise to one shallow young man—and pressed a button. After a moment there was a beep.

"Who is there?" said a voice from the buzzer box.

"It's me, Boris. Please open the door." And there was a louder buzz, a click, and Kallen pulled open the heavy door. He gave a satisfactory nod of his head, smiled at me, then closed the door. It swished closed and clicked loudly as it locked. "No more people coming into this building who don't belong," he said. Then he took out a key ring, selected a key, and unlocked the inner door. He stood aside so I could enter first, and it wasn't out of politeness. He wanted to see my face as I saw the transformed lobby.

"Wow," I said, and meant it. The walls and ceiling had been painted a warm and friendly pale yellow, the stairway banisters stripped, sanded, and polished, the tile floor repaired and polished. The bare bulb in the ceiling was replaced with a multi-light ceiling fixture that threw out a lot of light, and smaller versions of the fixture now lit the stairway. The mailbox room, off to the right of the lobby, had been painted, too, and the brass boxes cleaned and polished. I walked around, looked up and down, touched the glowing wood of the banisters, the brass of the mailboxes, looked through sparkling clean windows out to the street. "This is truly impressive, Mike," I said.

"I, too, think it is very beautiful. Come," he said, heading toward the stairs. I followed, noting that the improvements carried all the way down the first floor hallway and included installation of a new, heavy-duty metal door leading down to the basement, which is where we were headed.

New paint, here, too, and bright fluorescent ceiling lights. The steps still were too steep and narrow for my liking, but the hand railing had been replaced. The basement floor was concrete and sections of it had been painted. We followed the painted floor to the laundry room, which now required a key for entry, and which now had bright fluorescent ceiling lights, a new folding and sorting table, and a bench. The machines had been cleaned, as had the sink, and the mildew smell that had permeated the air on my first visit was gone. "You've got a good plumber," I told Kallen.

"For what he charges he should be able to make the East River drinking water."

Kallen led the way out of the laundry room toward the trash room, which also now was brightly lit but where lots of work still needed to be done. "I'm trying to figure out how to fix this," he said, waving his hand at the stacks of newspapers and bins of plastic, glass, and aluminum. "I hear from the tenants that they don't want to have to use a key to unlock the gate to the recycling bin. They just want to toss the stuff in and go." He shrugged, a weighty, elaborate gesture that lifted his massive shoulders all the way to his ears, then slowly dropped them.

"If what I've seen this morning is a guide, whatever you decide will be the right decision, Mike. What you've done in such a short time is really to be admired." I knew I might be spreading it on a bit thick, but I also meant what I said, and

Kallen truly deserved the compliment. He also liked it. He did everything but blow on his nails and buff them on his chest, but he didn't have a chance to comment because his cell phone rang. He flipped it open, listened, and his mood shifted way too fast for my comfort level.

"I pay you to handle these things, not to bother me with them. I won't always be here to hold your hand. Then what will you do?" Then he said something in a foreign language and slapped the phone shut. "I apologize, Phil, but I must go take care of a matter. You know the way out, and I'll call you when you can view the finished product." And he turned and ran up the narrow steps two at a time. I couldn't figure out how he did it. He was bigger than me, so his feet must be bigger than mine, and it was only with care that I got back upstairs to the first floor. One step at a time.

The lobby was empty so I took my time examining the work. It was very well done, real professional work, and good paint, not the cheap, shoddy stuff that's so prevalent now in commercial construction and contracting.

"Hey, you, housing department guy!" I heard behind me and turned to see a short, wide woman coming down the stairs, holding the railing tightly with one hand and waving at me with the other. "Wait just a minute." She was probably mid-sixties, I guessed, but part of the new breed of what used to be called seniors. The energy flowed out of her like water from a faucet. Her hair was dyed a little too black but everything else about her was age-appropriate, including her expectation that I'd do as told, which I did: I stood where I was and waited for her. "I see you looking all around, up and down, inspecting, but don't be fooled by the cute little cosmetic touches." She whipped a fat envelope out of her purse and thrust it at me. "You can save me a trip to the post office and give this to your boss and make somebody come here and deal with Mr. KGB. Tell him he's not back in Russia. This is the United States of America and people still have rights. Don't we?" Her question demanded an answer and she was waiting for it.

"I think so, yes."

"And people have the right not to be moved out of their apartments where they've lived for many, many years, I don't care how much fresh paint and pretty lights the KGB bring in. You tell your boss to tell that to Mr. KGB." She looked at her watch and headed for the door.

"Wait! Miss . . ." I followed her to the door and out. "Miss!"

"I don't have time, young man, if I miss my bus I'll be late for work. Anyway it's all there in the letter, all spelled out for you. All you have to do is read it." And she hurried off down the block. I looked at the envelope she'd thrust at me. It was addressed to The New York City Department of Housing, Bureau of Inspections. All it needed was a stamp. I turned it over. It wasn't sealed. So, I'd put a stamp on it, seal it, and mail it. I stuffed it inside my carryall and headed toward the office, wondering if the lady had ever called Kallen Mr. KGB to his face, decided she probably had. She didn't appear to be the type to be intimidated by secret police. Then I had another thought: Suppose Mr. KGB wasn't Kallen at all, but Boris, who had been strangely invisible this morning. Kallen wasn't in residence here, Boris was. And come to think of, he did bear a striking resemblance to Vladimir Putin, who had been, in a previous incarnation, the head of the KGB. An interesting thought to be sure, but one I had no intention of indulging. My job wasn't to help foster warm, fuzzy feelings between Mike Kallen and Boris and their tenants; it was to help KLM Property Management make sure their buildings were safe and secure, and as a result, protect them from negligence lawsuits. It just so happened some of those safety and security measures corresponded with housing department regulations. Maybe the tenants had complained to the housing department before and saw the recent improvements as a response to their complaints, and when the tenant saw me this morning inspecting the work, she reached what for her was a logical conclusion. Logical but erroneous, which she'd find out soon enough. As impressed as I was with what Kallen had accomplished in so short a time, however, I still didn't like him and I still wanted to be finished with him and KLM as soon as possible. And I wanted to turn my full attention to Jackie Marchand and to Raul. If I didn't hear from him today I'd suck it up and pay a visit to Willie, ask him where his nephew was.

Dave Epstein was walking out of my office door when I turned the corner and, fortunately, he headed in the other direction. I didn't want him and his problems in my head, either. I was finished with him and his son . . . unless his son had something to do with Jackie Marchand's murder. I didn't think so but then I'd never have thought Sam Epstein would burn down a man's business because of the color of the man's skin or his religious beliefs. A Jew hating a man because of his religion. A Mafioso hating a mobster because of his nationality. What was the world coming to?

Mike and Eddie were inside and Yolanda looked happy. The only thing that could have made the scene any better would have been for Connie to be there, too, but a man can't have everything, or so my Papi always told us. But as I'd learned, my Papi hadn't been a happy man so his take on things left a lot to be desired. "*Buenos dias,* and what's happening, y'all," I said.

"Y'all?" Mike Smith laughed at me. "You borrowing pages from my Georgia kinfolks' dictionary, bro?"

I laughed with him as I dumped everything I'd been carrying on to my desk and shrugged out of my coat. That was a sure sign to me that I'd had enough of winter—when winter wear became burdensome. "I like that word. Y'all. It has a nice sound to it, a warmth to it, you know? I wouldn't greet just anybody that way. It's a word for the people you like the most."

Mike was laughing even harder now. "If you're thinking that Southerners only call family and friends y'all, you've got another think coming, bro. Southerners call everybody y'all—people they like and people they don't. A Southern cop walking into a room full of rapists and murders and general lowlifes would say, 'What the fuck are y'all doin'?' "

We all were laughing now. I guess we all needed to, to slough off some of the ugliness we'd been splattered with the past couple of days—a cleansing of sorts before we had to go wading in the cesspool again. "What did Epstein want? I saw him leaving."

Yolanda looked even happier, rushed back to her desk and rushed back out, waving a check. "He came to 'settle his account,' to use his words."

"We billed him already?"

She shook her head. "Nope. I hadn't even finished tallying up the charges, but he had the check made out. Told me to take it and if it wasn't enough to call him. I told him it was probably too much, but he said no price was too much to pay for his son's return."

I looked at the check, whistled. I wouldn't have paid this much for Sam Epstein, but then he wasn't my kid. "We gonna keep it?"

"Damn right, we're going to keep it!" Yolanda snapped. She wasn't a mercenary person. In fact, she was just the opposite—kind, considerate, generous—but for her, business was business. We'd done what we were hired to do and if the client wanted to pay more than we billed, damn right, we'd take it, not to enrich ourselves but to make it possible to help people who didn't have Dave Epstein's kind of money. "Now, what are we doing to earn

Mr. Patel's money?"

Mike and Eddie gave her a look, then exchanged one between themselves, then gave me one. "If you didn't have her you'd still be walking a beat on the Upper East Side, *hermano,*" Eddie said.

Since we all knew that was true I didn't see any need to respond. Instead I behaved like the private eye businessman I billed myself to be. "McQueen and Casey aren't going to present themselves at the Precinct and confess to torching the Taste of India which means that we're going to have to find somebody else to drop them in it. I was hoping that would be Jackie Marchand. Now I'm hoping that Raul knows more than nothing."

"I still think we ought to drop that little asshole, Sammy Epstein, into the shit."

"Let the check clear first, bro." He looked at Yolanda. "I'll walk with you to the bank, you want." Everybody laughed but me.

"Might not be a bad idea. If we don't turn up anything else, Sam's all we've got. I don't owe him anything." I was still mad that he thought I'd beat up a kid, and doubly mad since I'd met the kid. Who could hurt Frankie Patel? If I had a niece or a daughter, Frankie's the boy I'd want courting her.

Yolanda gave me a speculative look but she didn't budge; I knew she wasn't worried about Dave Epstein's check, and not because she trusted Epstein. She had some kind of computer program that allowed her to put a hold on funds in a bank account until the actual check was deposited and cleared. Dave Epstein couldn't block payment of his check now even if he wanted to. Yo's look wondered whether I'd really turn Sammy in to help Ravi Patel, and I knew she knew that I would. "The police don't have any forensics yet on Marchand or his apartment, but they're treating it like a burglary gone bad."

Mike nodded. "I can see how they'd think that, given the scene, but that theory falls apart when you look at the building. Nobody looking for anything worth stealing would think to look in that building, and nobody would pick that apartment in that building—Jackie Marchand's apartment—unless they knew he worked two jobs. And if Jackie Marchand was the target, then it was more than just a burglary gone wrong."

"And that may or may not enter into the investigation, depending on who's doing the investigating, so we can't count on it," Eddie said. "Next thought."

"Then I go talk to Willie, see if he's heard from Raul."

"And if he hasn't?" Yolanda asked, already knowing the answer.

"Then I'll sic Bill Calloway on Sammy Epstein," I said, then added as an afterthought, "I thought I'd have heard from him by now."

"He called this morning, Phil . . . and your cell phone's dead again, right?"

Shit! I fished it out of my pocket and flipped it open. Low Battery read the message on the screen. I plugged it into the charger. Day late and a dollar short. "What did he say?"

"He wants you to call him but not at the office. He actually sounded a little upset, which is unusual for Bill. You know what Sandra calls him, right? Still Bill."

Appropriate, I thought. "Where am I supposed to call him, then? The office is the only number I have for him. Unless . . ." I leaned across the desk and put my face next to the cell phone on its charger and flipped it open. The little green charger icon was moving from side to side, doing its job. I pressed the message button and put my ear next to the phone. Two messages: Bill and Yolanda telling me that Bill had called. "Write this down," I said, and rattled off the cell phone number Bill had left for me.

"Slick move. You must be some kind of detective or something," Eddie said.

"He wants me to meet him behind Taste of India at eleven o'clock," I said, looking at my watch. "If I leave right now I won't be more than a few minutes late." I grabbed my coat. "I'll stop by Willie's when I leave Bill." I headed for the door.

"Phil!" I turned around and just barely caught the cell phone Yolanda tossed to me. "You really can't be unreachable out there, Phil." Her no-nonsense tone chafed but I knew she was right. Good thing she had as many cell phones as computers.

"You want some company, *hermano,* in case the *federales* are still hanging around?" Eddie asked, but he wasn't waiting for an answer. He and Mike both had their coats on and Mike whipped his cell phone off his belt and flipped it open.

"Charged and ready, Miss Aguierre, in case you need to reach me," and he ran out the door ahead of any impending retaliation for his wisecrack.

"Find us a taxi, *'mano,* 'cause I'm not walking all the way over there," Eddie said.

"It's not that far," I said.

"I know you're into this walking thing, think it's faster or hipper or . . . or . . ."

"More egalitarian," Mike offered, ignoring the hostile glare I shot him.

"Right," Eddie said, "but it's not. It's just dumb to do all that walking when you could ride. And you don't even have to pay for it! You bill the clients. The three of us take a taxi and that nice Mr. Patel pays for it." His eyes hadn't stopped scanning the street and he released a shrill whistle from between his teeth. A taxi screeched over to the curb and we all climbed in. "This way, *'mano,* you won't be late for your appointment and my feet won't be hurting."

And we weren't late. We exited the taxi across the street and a block from the restaurant, receipt in hand, at eleven o'clock straight up. "Why does he want you to meet him behind the place?" Mike wanted to know.

"I suppose because that's where the fire started. Maybe he's found some new evidence or information."

"I'll stick with you. Eddie, you take the front. Is the crime scene tape still up, you think?" Mike was a tactician at heart and there was no such thing as a simple task.

"Like you would care," Eddie said at the same time I said, "Like that would stop you." But it wouldn't be an issue, we saw. We now were directly across the street from the burned out restaurant. The downstairs door and windows were boarded up, the windows of the upstairs apartments just empty, vacant. Eddie and I kept walking, crossed the street in the middle of the block, cut through an alleyway between a grocery-deli and a four-story walk-up with a beauty-shop-cum-nail-salon at ground level, and angled around to the rear of the Taste of India. The scent of charred, burned material still hung in the air, smelling old and unpleasant now. We could see trash and debris piled in the space behind the restaurant and I wondered what Bill could have discovered here that he wanted me to see. Then I noticed that the board securing the back door of the restaurant was off and in the same instant that I began to process the possible meaning of that, I heard gunshots. Two of them. Mike had his gun out and was running toward the restaurant, was inside, when there were two more pops. I had my gun out and was about to follow when I heard, "I'm down, Mike! I'm down! Take cover! Take cover!"

I crouched low and crab-walked toward the restaurant using the pile of debris as cover. I stopped and my breath caught in my chest. Bill Calloway was lying on his back in what had been the back door, the kitchen door, of the restaurant. The hole in his chest and the blood pouring from it told me he was dead. I knelt beside him and touched his neck anyway, hoping, praying there still was blood flowing through his jugular vein. He was warm but he was dead. I closed my eyes, sick and dizzy. There was something in Bill's shirt pocket, something that looked familiar. I grabbed it and then ran inside the restaurant and tripped over a huge kettle in the middle of the floor. I caught myself on the side of a stainless steel counter, got my balance, and moved more slowly through the muddy, ashy sludge on the floor. Mike was sitting on the floor in what used to be the dining room of the restaurant, holding Eddie in his lap. My heart thudded so hard it hurt.

Eddie's eyes were open and he looked more mad than hurt, but he definitely was hurt. Mike's hands were pressing against the upper right corner of Eddie's chest and he was breathing hard. "Did you call it in?" I asked, and he nodded. I slipped off my jacket, sweater, shirt, and finally my undershirt. I folded it, and as Mike lifted his hands I put the thick pad of the folded cotton shirt on Eddie's chest and pressed down hard and saw the blood spurt in the instant before the T-shirt and my hands stanched it.

"In the back, that's Calloway?" Mike asked.

I nodded and Eddie said, "What's wrong with Calloway?"

"He wasn't as lucky as you," Mike said. "And if you know what's good for you you'll stay lucky, because I'll kick your ass if you die on me." Eddie tried to make a witty comeback but it got lost in a rattly cough and Mike shushed him and rubbed his head as if he were a child and Eddie's eyes fluttered, then shut. "Open your eyes!" Mike yelled, and Eddie complied, briefly.

"Where's the fuckin' ambulance . . ." The sirens' scream overrode me. "Take the pressure, Mike," I said, and he slid his hands beneath mine on top of the blood-soaked sweater. I stood up and headed for the front door.

"Shoulder your piece, Phil," Mike shouted at me. "They'll

shoot your ass you run out there with a gun in your hand."

I went out the front door with my hands in the air. Mike had already kicked the board away; it was lying on the sidewalk. The paramedics came first, saw the blood on me, and stopped short, but I waved them forward. Then came the cops. I started talking as soon as they got close enough to hear me and kept talking until one of them finally agreed to do what I was asking over and over and over for them to do: Call their captain, Bill Delaney. He knew me. He didn't like me but he knew me. He was my desk sergeant when I walked a beat on the Upper East Side and now was the captain of this precinct. We'd butted heads and traded insults a few months ago but Delaney knew enough about me to listen to what I had to say. And I knew enough about cops that telling them there was a DB at the back door would shift the focus from me for a while.

The EMTs rolled Eddie out the front door on a stretcher at full speed. It was three hours before Mike and I could follow, and when we got there, to the ER waiting room, four women gasped at the sight of us: Eddie's wife, Linda; Mike's wife, Helen; Yolanda and Connie. We'd forgotten that we were both covered in Eddie's blood; anyway, there'd been no time or place to clean up. We looked at each other, looked at the women looking in horror at us. "We should find a bathroom," I said.

"We're going to find a bathroom," Mike said to the women, and we hurried down the hall, attracting horrified stares with every step. "He must be okay. The women aren't crying."

"You know that was meant for me."

Mike stopped walking. "You think Calloway set you up?"

"I think somebody set us both up."

Mike contemplated that for a moment, then said, "That's Miss deLeon with Yolanda, right? What are you thinking about her, bro?"

"I'm thinking maybe she's the one, Mike."

We used all the liquid soap and most of the paper towels and a good bit of the hospital's water supply so we didn't look like slasher movie extras when we rejoined the women. Linda Ortiz wouldn't let me apologize, didn't want to hear an apology. She hugged me, told me that Eddie loved me, and said she loved me, too, because I gave him something to do. Otherwise, she said, he'd just be a retired cop getting on her nerves, making her life miserable because he was miserable. Helen Smith hugged me, too, and told me not to do anything silly like blame myself for what happened. Then Yolanda hugged me, just hugged me tight, didn't say anything. Then Connie hugged me and didn't let me go. "What's the word?" I asked.

"He's in surgery," Linda said. "They think the biggest problem is blood loss. The paramedic said you two—you and Mike, Phil—definitely saved his life with the compression on the wound." Then she started to cry and all the women, Connie included, wrapped their arms around her. I felt cold without her arms around me.

I walked a little away from the circle of women and Mike followed. "Sounded like Eddie got off a couple of rounds out there," I said. Mike and I had not had a chance to talk—cops wouldn't give us a chance, kept us separate to see if our stories matched.

He nodded. "There was a car, Toyota or Honda, silver or gray, four door. Guy leans out the back window, fires two at Eddie, one hits him. He goes down, rolls, pulls his weapon, fires twice. Doesn't know if he hit anything. If he did, he says, it was the trunk, the back windshield at best."

"One shooter?" I asked, trusting Mike's gut opinion as much as anything before we had any forensics, and given Bill Delaney's chilly reception and treatment of me, I had no reason to hope that the cops would tell me whether the gun that killed Bill Calloway also put a hole in Eddie Ortiz's chest.

"My guess would be yeah, especially if, as you speculate, you were the intended target. And the more I think about that, the more I think you're right. But that doesn't really get us anywhere, bro. No place good, anyway."

"I don't know how good the place is, Mike, but we know two things: The shooter isn't from this neighborhood because he doesn't know what I look like; and wherever he's from, he thinks all Ricans look alike."

"You fuckers do all look alike. You look just like that hairy-faced bastard . . ." He couldn't finish. I grabbed him, wrapped my arms around him, and held him tight. And he let me. Mike was bigger than me. Older, tougher, smarter, stronger than me. I looked up to him and Eddie though, technically, they were my employees. Right now, in this moment, we became real friends. Not the more-than-twenty-years kind of friendship that he and Eddie shared, but important and real enough.

The women came then and added their emotional weight to Mike's hug. I didn't know if he felt any better but I certainly did. Then Linda saw the doctor and we all rushed her. She didn't flinch at the horde of humanity charging her, and she started talking as soon as we were within reach: Eddie would be fine. Eventually. He'd lost much too much blood but the arteries severed by the bullet were patched up enough to stop the blood loss and he was being transfused. When he stabilized enough, the arteries would have to be repaired, one, perhaps, replaced, and then he would be fine. But he wouldn't wake up any time soon, she said, so we should all go home and get some rest.

Linda Ortiz said she'd stay, and Mike and Helen Smith said they'd stay with her. Yolanda, Connie, and I eventually left. I walked between them, an arm around each of their shoulders, each of them with an arm around my waist. We were holding each other up. Or maybe they were just holding me up because

I thought if they stepped away from me, I'd just collapse.

We climbed into a taxi that fortunately was right outside the ER door. We dropped Yo first, then crawled in the evening rush hour traffic to my place. Then I crawled up the stairs to my apartment and collapsed on the couch. Connie left me there for a few minutes, and I was vaguely aware of familiar sounds—in the kitchen and in the bathroom—but I couldn't focus on them, couldn't connect them to reality. Then Connie was back. She took off my shoes, then sat me up and took off my jacket, sweater, and shirt and I started to shiver. She led me through the bedroom and into the bathroom and when she opened the door, a wonderful scent rushed at me on a cloud of steam. She unfastened my pants and let them drop to the floor; my boxers followed. "I can't pick you up and put you into the tub," she whispered. I heard the smile in her voice and tried to give her one back; don't know if I succeeded, but I did step out of my pants and into the warmth of the water and bubbles and oil. An extra long and deep tub I'd had installed and this was first time I'd ever sat down in it and covered myself in liquid luxury. I leaned back and my head was resting on a pillow. I had a bath pillow?

I started talking. The words spilled from my mouth like the blood had gushed from Eddie's chest. And Bill Calloway's chest. I said everything I was thinking and feeling and worrying about. Connie sat on the floor beside the tub, held my hand, and listened. She didn't say a word. I kept expecting her to comment or question but she didn't say a word. She just listened. Then I realized—understood—that she was doing what she knew I needed her to do. I needed to talk and I needed somebody I trusted to listen. She was, by profession, a counselor, a therapist, and she knew when to talk and when to listen.

The water cooled and Connie ran more hot into the tub.

Then she washed my hair and scrubbed my nails. Then she scrubbed my back with one brush and my feet with another one. Not only a pillow, but different kinds of brushes, too. I smiled at her and she smiled back at me and stood up. "Rinse and dry and put on your nighties and get into bed. I'll be right back."

She left and I did what she told me to do and then she was back with a tray. I wasn't hungry; in fact, I was anything but hungry. I was trying to think of a way to say that without hurting her feelings when I saw what was on the tray: A big bowl of tomato soup, a grilled cheese sandwich, and a beer. I was ravenous. "Thank you, Connie," I said. "For everything."

"You're welcome, Phil. For everything." She picked up the remote and flicked on the television, surprising me; she wasn't much of a TV watcher. "It's snowing. I want to see if it's just a tease or if we're getting a real March blizzard."

I was chewing and nodding. "Blizzard," I said, when I could talk without offending. "I felt it earlier today, outside the Taste of India, before . . ." I had, for a few brief and wonderful moments, managed to put the day's events on a back burner. Now it was all back. "Whoever killed Bill Calloway is not getting away with it. Jackie Marchand's murder hurt because he was a kid, just getting started in life, but Bill was a friend and this cuts way too close."

"How will you find out why he called you?"

I sat up so fast I made myself dizzy and almost knocked over the tray. "That pen. There was a pen in my pocket . . . I think it was in my pocket . . ."

Connie hurried out of the room and was back in seconds. "This flash drive?" she asked. Did everybody but me know what a flash drive was?

Chapter Nine

"First Mike breaks into a murder victim's apartment and steals crucial documents that might be evidence, then you steal what definitely is evidence from a murder victim's actual body . . ." The way she said "body" and glowered at me almost made me contrite. Almost.

"Don't forget, the first message in Bill's flash thing-y was addressed to me . . ."

"Which you didn't know at the time you stole it."

"I wish you'd stop saying that word!"

"What word, Phil? Steal? That one?"

I knew Yo was well and truly pissed, but at the moment I didn't care; I was too focused on what we'd learned from Bill Calloway's treasure trove of information, and what I thought was in store from Raul. I'd walked my usual route to work this morning, and made my usual stops along the way, including at Willie's newsstand. Far from being upset or angry with me, he'd fixed me with his one-eyed stare and told me his nephew had "important words" for me, told me when and where. I told him I'd left my card with my numbers on it for Raul but Willie told me that Raul didn't use the telephone. Not ever. I didn't bother commenting on yet another of Willie's nephew's peculiar eccentricities; I was just glad he wanted to talk to me. I worried that he still was laying low, staying away from his job at the diner, and I was thinking maybe the reason would connect some of the dots that I saw leading from the fires to and from Big

Apple Business Insurers, because Bill Calloway's message to me had been that he'd been removed as the investigator of the Taste of India fire. No reason given. He also included e-mails from his immediate supervisor removing him from investigating three other fires in the last year. We weren't certain yet but Yolanda thought all were on her list. And we knew that Jackie Marchand's time sheets were signed by Thomas Kearney—the same Thomas Kearney who was Bill Calloway's boss.

"What do you want to bet that if I'd left that flash thing in Bill's pocket, it would right now be in a paper bag locked in an evidence room and we'd never know why Bill wanted to see me."

Yolanda gave me an exasperated look. "That doesn't make it all right, Phil."

I looked over at Mike, looking for some support, but since he already was on her list for the break-in at Jackie Marchand's, he had no intention of opening his mouth, causing her attention to be directed at him. He intensified his concentration on the *Times* editorial page.

"Okay, Yo," I said.

"Okay, what, Phil?"

"I promise no more breaking and entering the apartments of DBs and no more removing evidence from DBs—but that's only if no-damn-body else in this sorry show gets killed." I was all but shouting. Yolanda doesn't like shouting, a holdover from her childhood when her father spent most of his waking hours shouting, so I apologized for mine and almost immediately realized the reason for it, the source of it: I'd been afraid that *sobrino* Raul was not just laying low but was somewhere lying dead. My relief at hearing from Willie this morning literally felt like something enormous had been lifted off my shoulders and back, allowing me to stand upright.

"You're really letting this get to you," Yolanda said.

"I'm not letting it, Yo, it's just there, up close and in my face and very, very personal, and I don't like it. It's too close."

Mike rattled his newspaper, closed it, folded it, and stuffed it into his back pocket. "I say we go check on Ortiz, make sure he's not recovered enough to be grabbing on nurses, then go find your friend, Raul, see what he has to say for himself."

Mike's good at that, almost as good as Yolanda, at saying what it is I'm thinking. I finished my coffee and my orange juice, then took my cup and Mike's to the kitchen and washed them. Mike and Yo had their heads together when I came back out front and I left them alone; whatever they were saying about me I didn't want to hear. Besides, I still was so happy that the three of them had decided to like each other, I didn't mind if they occasionally put their heads together to discuss me. As long as they didn't make it a habit. I got my phone off the charger and spent a panicked moment wondering why my gun wasn't in the desk drawer until I remembered that the cops had it. They had to make certain that it wasn't my weapon that had killed Bill Calloway and wounded Eddie Ortiz.

"Let's go, Mike!" I was back to the raised voice that almost was shouting.

Yolanda walked toward me. "I'll need the rest of today and probably a good part of tomorrow to analyze everything of Bill's and Jackie Marchand's, see where their paths cross those of Patel and Nehru. And I need their files, Phil."

I got them from my desk drawer. "These men didn't destroy their own businesses and I'd be a terrorist before either of them would."

"Don't say things like that, Phil! Not even as a joke. You never know who's listening."

"Speaking of listening, Yolanda, can you give me one of those remote devices?"

I jumped in before Yo could respond. "For what, Mike?" I demanded.

Mike Smith doesn't intimidate. "You're not going to let me sit in on your meeting with your pal, Raul," he said calmly and matter-of-factly. It wasn't a question so it didn't require an answer. "So, if I can't be right there next to him, I will be close enough to hear every word." He looked at Yolanda and she went behind the screens to the supply closet.

"Why can't you cut the guy a break, Mike? He's put his past behind him, why can't you do the same thing?"

Mike sighed deeply and I saw more than two decades of walking a beat uptown in Harlem flicker through his memory, his eyes being the projection screens, the lines in his dark brown face as readable as captions. "Once a hype, Phil, always a hype. They try, they really do, some of them, to change; to be and do different. I believe your guy, Raul, is probably clean right now, maybe even been clean for a couple of years. He's got a job he goes to and someplace clean to live. But I'll bet you he wouldn't recognize his own kids on the street, his wife stopped talking to him years ago, and his parents, if they're still alive, probably love him but they won't let him in the house. They gave him too many chances too many times and lived to regret all of them."

"I'm not his wife or his kids or his parents, Mike."

"No, Phil, you're not; you're just a guy who does a lot of good for a lot of people who will suffer if, because of Raul, you go down. I don't have to trust Raul and I don't and I won't, but I will watch your back. That way, you can trust all the Rauls of the world all day long."

Yolanda was back with the remote transmitter. I stuck my hand down inside my sweater and shirt and put the transmitter inside the pocket of my T-shirt, and Mike turned on the receiver. Without a word, we walked away from each other, me talking to nobody and being glad I was inside so nobody could see me losing my mind.

"At some point, Phil, would you pay Mr. Patel and Mr. Nehru a visit and tell them that I need to talk to them? And sooner rather than later. Please," she added.

"Is that your way of saying you'd appreciate it if I didn't come back here today?"

She gave me a high-wattage Yolanda smile and Mike and I headed for the door. "I don't suppose you'd complain, though, if a lunch delivery from El Caribe interrupted your work?" I tossed over my shoulder as we left, and I heard a few loud smacks follow us out the door, which indicated that Yo was blowing us kisses.

"I'll kiss you, too," Mike said, "if you're buying me lunch at El Caribe."

Eddie wasn't awake when we got to the hospital, though his nurse said he had been earlier—awake, conscious, and lucid long enough for Linda to be convinced that he wasn't going to die, so she'd finally gone home to get some sleep. Neither Mike nor I was allowed inside the ICU, not being family—the only reason we got any information at all was because the charge nurse knew Mike's wife—so we sat out in the waiting area, reading our newspapers and not talking about the things we were thinking about. The not talking part was fine with me because I realized that I couldn't talk about it without getting angry and that getting angry didn't help connect any dots. The meeting with Raul wasn't until eleven, in Washington Square Park.

"Why do we have to meet this guy in the park? What's wrong with a restaurant or a coffee shop? The library, even? Your office, for crying out loud! But a park, sitting right out there, exposed to the world . . ."

"Mike? Calm down, bro. It's not a setup . . ."

"How do you know that, Phil? You don't know, not for sure." He jumped up and began pacing, looking over at Eddie through the glass every time he passed the ICU suite. I waited for him to collect himself and sit back down.

"Mike? Eddie's going to be fine and nothing's going to happen to me. Or to you either, for that matter. And I know because I know, all right?"

Mike wasn't anywhere close to being convinced. "You were set up yesterday, Phil. You and Calloway. I think you were right in your assessment: Eddie got what was meant for you, and we can only be thankful that in addition to being stupid, most low-lifes also can't shoot worth shit."

"But it wasn't Raul who set me up, Mike."

"Dammit, Phil, you don't know who it was!"

Nothing I could say to that. If anybody was keeping score and giving prizes for being right, Mike would win it for this round. I didn't know who wanted me dead, to say nothing of poor Bill Calloway. Or Jackie Marchand. I looked at my watch. Despite what it felt like, an hour hadn't passed since last I'd checked. I stood up. "Let's go eat some doughnuts. There's a Supreme King Doughnuts over near Washington Square Park."

"Now you're talking, bro," Mike said. He walked over and looked at Eddie through the glass. "If it was one of us lying in there, Eddie would go eat doughnuts until he thought of what to do to make things right."

If there was such a thing as a perfect doughnut, the Supreme King people made it. The coffee, though, wasn't much better than that at Raul's diner—when Raul made it. But the coffee didn't matter when the doughnuts were this good. Mike nodded his agreement. "Though they're about to go out of business," he said, chewing.

"Who's about to go out of business?"

"Supreme King Doughnuts. Stock tanked." Mike knew things like which stock was up and which was down—he and Yolanda could always discuss the market, even when, a couple of years ago, they couldn't find anything polite or civil to say to each other.

"I thought everybody loved these doughnuts."

Mike gave his head a disgusted shake. "So did the Supreme King Doughnuts people." He bit into another doughnut, this one lemon filled. "I don't understand that kind of greed. They're already making money hand over fist, opening up new outlets across the country, but they gotta have more. Wasn't enough to be making lots of money, they wanted to be making more than lots. That's how businesses get into trouble: fueled by greed."

"But they exist to make money, Mike, right? Isn't that what it's all about?"

"Yeah, but at some point, somebody's got to decide what's enough money and draw the line. They also gotta pay attention. When the hamburger and chicken joints started selling salads, the doughnut people should've seen the handwriting on the wall."

"You make a good point, Mike."

He started laughing. "Greed is a killer, man." He laughed harder. "You hear about the fool who opened a pizza franchise somewhere in Africa?" He was holding his sides he was laughing so hard, and I joined in, the two of us putting our own takes and spins on ordering and delivering pizza in a place where food itself was a luxury, to say nothing of telephones on which to call in the order, and vehicles with which to deliver the order, and houses with doorbells for the pizza delivery person to ring. "I don't wish bad fortune on other people, but that guy needed to go broke."

We both felt better after the laugh and were probably intoxicated from the sugar in all the doughnuts we'd eaten. I decided I wouldn't get a receipt; didn't want to have to explain to Yolanda how Mike and I, just the two of us, no Eddie, had consumed a dozen doughnuts in one sitting. Yolanda is one of the people who would send the doughnut and the pizza people spiraling into bankruptcy. I looked at my watch and was thinking I'd head toward the park when I felt Mike snap to attention. I looked out the front window of the restaurant, following his gaze.

"That's Raul, isn't it?"

Indeed it was Raul, head down, hands stuffed into his pockets, walking swiftly toward Washington Square Park. Question was how did Mike know? I asked him.

"He was leaving Jackie Marchand's building when I was going in that day." He didn't need to explain what day: The day he'd found the kid's beat-up body on the floor of his apartment, smeared with pints of his own blood.

I dropped some money on the table and stood up. "Where will you be?"

He put his hand into his inside jacket pocket and I knew he'd activated the receiver to the transmitter I wore. "I'll sit here for another couple of minutes, let you get a good head start, then I'll follow, find a place that looks good. Just one thing, bro: Since this meet is out in the open, stay out in the open, okay? Don't let him get you to sit behind a statue or a wall."

I nodded and left, chin dropped and talking into my chest to be certain that I was transmitting. If there was a problem, I knew Mike would have caught up to me before I was half a block away; caught up to me and either insisted on joining me, or canceling the meet, and not giving a damn whether Raul ever trusted me again or not.

He was sitting on a bench in the middle of the park when I got there, head still lowered, hands still stuffed into his pockets. He wore jeans and high-top sneakers and a knit cap pulled low over his ears, and the scarf and gloves I'd given him a few months earlier when we'd had a similar outdoor rendezvous. That day had been bitterly cold and I hadn't realized until I questioned his lack of hat, scarf, and gloves, that he didn't possess any. I'd left mine for him on the bench between us.

Looking at him as I drew nearer, thin and hunched, he could have been a kid Jackie Marchand's age instead of a grown man my age. He looked up as I approached, then looked past me to see if anybody was with me. Up close he was thinner and much more hunched than he'd appeared at a distance. "You don't look so good, *sobrino,*" I said.

He tried to smile, couldn't make it happen. "I'm not feeling so good, Inspector."

The shock I felt must have registered on my face because now he did muster a thin, sickly smile. "That's what me and Uncle Willie call you. The Inspector." Then a look of panic widened his eyes. "It's meant to be respectful," he said.

"That's how I'm taking it," I said, and sat next to him on the bench. My butt immediately froze and I wished we were in his diner, or back at the Supreme King Doughnuts. "But I have been worried about you, when the guy on your job said you were laying low. That worried me, Raul, especially after what happened to Jackie."

He wouldn't meet my eyes, and he spoke so low that I barely heard him, wondered if Mike did. "I was scared he'd come for me."

I was confused. "Who would come for you, Raul?"

"The freak who killed Jackie. I saw him. I was there." The guy was shaking so hard he was stuttering, and he was stuttering so hard I could barely understand him. Part of it was fear, certainly, but he was cold and probably hungry.

"When was the last time you ate?"

He looked at me through squinted eyes, like he really was

trying to remember, then he gave up, shrugged. "I don't know. Since before Jackie . . ."

I stood up. "You like Island food, right? Ever eaten at El Caribe?"

"I can't afford food like that."

"I can," I said, standing up and turning around in a circle. I wasn't sure where Mike was but I needed to give him a heads up and a head start. "Let's grab a taxi on Fourth," I said to my chest, and saw Mike loping over to Fourth just ahead of us. I started to move toward Fourth Street and the warmth of a taxi but Raul didn't move a muscle. "Raul? Come on, man."

"Suppose he's out here, waiting for me?"

This guy was not just frightened, he was terrified. "Stick close to me, Raul. I won't let anybody hurt you. I promise." I looked him squarely in the eyes. He met and held my gaze, though his eyes were red-rimmed with fatigue, fear, hunger, and I hoped that was all; I didn't want Mike to be right about this particular hype, though I could well imagine that watching someone you cared about get beat to death would be enough to send even the strongest among us running for a fix, to say nothing of the weakest among us. "Nobody's going to hurt you, Raul."

He nodded, stood up and started walking with me toward Fourth Street and a taxi.

We got to El Caribe just as the lunch rush was starting. Arlene Edwards, the owner, was greeting customers at the door. "Phil! What a wonderful surprise!" She pulled me into a tight hug and I gave her one back. I introduced her to Raul. Then I whispered in her ear that we needed to eat in her office, if that was all right, that Mike would arrive in a moment and position himself in the hallway outside her office, and that I wanted lunch delivered to Yolanda. Bradley, Arlene's son, followed us into her office, moved a pile of papers off a card table in one corner, and in about three seconds, had a tablecloth, napkins, and silverware laid out. Then he was out the door, with a promise to return "in just a few moments" with water and menus.

Raul looked around uneasily but the cooking smells of the best Caribbean food restaurant in Manhattan had followed us from the front of the place to the back, and he was, it seemed, hungrier than he was scared. I took that to be a good sign. "Have a seat, Raul. I'm going to the bathroom. I'll be right back."

I wanted to make sure Mike was in the hallway; he was, and, surprisingly, worried about Raul. In a manner of speaking. "Hurry up and get the description of Jackie's killer before this guy strokes out on us. I don't think I've ever seen anybody that scared of anything. I thought you said he was a con? How'd he ever last in the joint?"

"Maybe that's why he'll keep himself from doing anything to get sent back."

Mike grunted a grudging acknowledgement. Arlene came down the hall with a tray and I opened her office door and followed her in. Raul jumped up from the table when the door opened but sat back down when he saw it was just me and Arlene. He watched her, watched her put down bowls of food.

"Raul's never eaten here, Arlene," I said.

"I hope you won't be disappointed, Raul," Arlene said.

He tore his eyes from the food to look at her, as if he expected she was joking. When he saw that she was serious, he let a real smile crack his face. "I don't think you have to worry about me being disappointed, madam," he said. "This already looks and smells better than anything I've ever experienced."

I looked at Raul like he was a new life form. In the first place, I'd never heard that many words come out of his mouth at one time. And madam? Experienced? Not that the guy couldn't be literate and well-spoken. I'd just had no reason to think he was. I looked from him to Arlene and thought maybe he didn't think I was worth the effort. Arlene Edwards, despite the fact that she was a grandmother, definitely was the kind of woman a guy would make an effort to impress. If he wasn't going to haul out his erudition but a couple of times a year, when Arlene Edwards was serving him lunch would be one of those times. But not only did she bring out the good manners in him, she also was having a calming effect. He didn't look or act quite so squirrelly and jumpy and he watched Arlene like he'd just discovered oil beneath the Union Square subway station, and he owned the station. And as hungry as I knew he was, he looked sad when she left. "I'll come back in a little while to check on you," she said, and left, not quite closing the door all the way. I hoped that Raul wouldn't notice.

He didn't; he was too starry-eyed about her. "That's one classy lady," he said, piling food onto his plate. "Pretty, too." I nodded. Arlene was indeed classy, but she was an awful lot more than pretty. I didn't feel the need, though, to share my thoughts and ideas about women with him. I'd made the mistake of doing that with Carmine. Once was more than enough. Besides, the guy had enough on his mind and we'd deal with all of it, one item at a time. Getting some food into him was the first priority, and he was making real progress on that front. I held myself back out of guilt; Mike was standing in the hallway waiting for us to talk. He couldn't eat until we finished. The least I could do was wait.

"Think you can talk some now, Raul?"

"Yeah." He wiped his mouth on his napkin and gulped some water. "I don't eat when I'm scared or worried or upset, and then I forget I haven't eaten. Goes on for days sometimes. It's not so bad since I've been working at the diner, being around food all the time. But since I haven't been there for a couple a days . . ."

"What's he look like, Raul?"

"Fat, stupid-looking white boy. Big, though."

The one who'd come to my office with information about the fires to sell, who then got mad when I wasn't buying and threw a chair against the wall. Good thing Yolanda insisted on keeping the door locked. "Start from the beginning, Raul. How you know—knew—Jackie Marchand, all the way to why you were at his place the morning he was killed."

He did as I asked. He was a very cautious and observant man, habits picked up, he said, in the joint, so he had a memory bank full of names and places and dates and practically verbatim conversations with Jackie to share. "That was one smart kid. He wanted to go to work for the UN. He spoke languages, you know? He was born speaking French, up in Canada. He learned English in school up there. Then he learned Spanish when he got here—just learned it. And he was studying Chinese. Used to go to Chinatown all the time and talk to people. There's different kinds of Chinese. Did you know that? Depending on where a person's from?"

"Dialects," I said.

He nodded. "Right. Dialects. He could speak two or three of 'em. Wanted to learn Japanese, too." He talked on about how brilliant Jackie was and I let him; I knew it was to keep from talking any more about the rough stuff, the painful stuff. He wound down.

"Did you ever meet Thomas Kearney? Ever see him?"

He shook his head. "I just know Jackie didn't like him, didn't trust him, said he was a drunk, and mean."

"Do you have any of this, any of what you've told me, in writing, Raul? Did Jackie have any papers or documents from the insurance company that you saw?"

"His laptop. He had a laptop. The freak who killed him took it with him."

I felt all the air seep out of me. Whatever had been in Jackie Marchand's laptop computer was history now. I tried not to wish too hard that I had that computer; Raul had told me enough that I could do some serious dot-connecting and I was grateful. That's what I wanted him to walk away thinking and remembering. That and knowing that I knew that he didn't have to talk to me at all.

He'd said something and I missed it. "I'm sorry, what did you say?"

"That it's not what you think. Me and Jackie."

"I don't know what you're talking about."

"Prison changes some men, you know? Emotionally, psychologically, sexually. I changed the first two ways but not the last one. That's not what it was with me and Jackie." I must have looked as dumbfounded as I felt because Raul gave me a totally disbelieving look. "Aw, come on, Rodriquez. Don't tell me you hadn't thought that."

I was shaking my head. I hadn't, not for one second. But immediately I knew that Mike and Eddie had. "I didn't, *sobrino.* Not once. Not even a passing thought."

He looked at me for some more long seconds, looking for the truth in my words. I guess he found it because he continued telling his story. "I wanted to help him because he was smart. I was smart like that when I was a kid and I had nobody to help me. My family—my parents and grandparents and brothers and sisters—they all laughed when I told them I was going to college. I was accepted, too. Even had a partial scholarship. But it wasn't enough for everything, and my papi said if I wanted to keep living under his roof I had to get a job, pay some rent. I couldn't pay rent and buy books." He shook himself, trying to slough off what must have been a more than twenty-year-old memory that was holding onto him like last night's bad dream. "So I moved out. I was going to college and nobody was going to stop me. That first semester I was living in the basement of the student activity center and everything was okay until the first night it got really, really cold. I snuck into the boiler room to keep warm and fell asleep. The janitor found me the next morning and that was it."

My papi wasn't convinced that I was really smart enough to go to college, and the idea of me in a college classroom really tickled him, so he got a second job to help me out. If he hadn't, I wouldn't have made it. I tried feeling what Raul must have felt, the despair, the anger, maybe even a little hatred. Then I tried turning all that inward—and understood instinctively that that's how some junkies get made. Not all of them, but probably way too many. "How were you going to help Jackie? You can't be making that much at the diner."

"I'm not, but I'm living at my parents' place now. Big two bedroom over by East River Park. I couldn't even go visit my mami until the old man died, then she let me move into the second bedroom. Then she died. Finally gets rid of that mean ass fucker and she ups and dies. Anyway, the place is mine. Rent controlled, right? So I told Jackie he could have the second bedroom, rent free. That's why he wasn't in school this semester: He was working two jobs so that in the fall he could go to school full-time."

Raul looked so proud when he said this it made my heart hurt. "That's one of the most decent things I've ever known one person to do for another."

He shrugged it off. "No damn good now, is it, being decent? The dude's dead. Never got a chance to live it."

"But he got a chance to feel it, Raul, to feel hope and joy. And that's something."

He looked at me again. This dude could really look at you,

like he was trying to read something written on your face, or trying to read something on the screen inside your head. "I hope you're right, Rodriquez. I really hope you're right." He stood up. "I gotta go to work. If I don't show up today, I'm out of a job."

I stood up, too. "I meant what I said earlier: Nobody's going to hurt you."

"You can't be with me all the time."

"I can put a man on you twenty-four seven," I said.

"You'd do that for me?"

"Yes, I would," I said, and was greatly relieved when he refused the offer; with Eddie damn near dead and Mike attached to me like a shadow to keep me from getting as nearly dead as Eddie, I didn't have anybody to put on him for half an hour to say nothing of around the clock.

"I appreciate that, Rodriquez, but it won't be necessary. I can't hide for the rest of my life. Jackie wouldn't like me being a coward. I don't even like me being a coward."

I had an inspiration: "How about this: I'll put you in a cab from here to the diner, and have a car pick you up when you're off and take you home. At least until I can find this fat, dumb white boy and whoever hired him and put them both out of their misery."

He was shaking his head but smiling. "Thanks, man, but no thanks. I'm really okay. Maybe I just needed to eat something, you know?" He gathered up all the dishes from the table and stacked them along his arm. "Get the door for me, will you?" I did and followed him out, down the hallway and into the kitchen. Mike was nowhere to be seen.

"My goodness!" Arlene exclaimed when she saw Raul. "You're a waiter?"

He bowed from the waist, still holding the plates up his arm, and he was so smooth the silverware didn't even rattle. "Yes, ma'am. And if you ever need any help, let me know. I'll work for food. You don't have to pay me money. Just let me inhale these aromas and eat once a week and I'm your slave. And if you teach me to cook food that smells and tastes like that, I'll slay a dragon for you."

Arlene was laughing. I was speechless. Raul put the dishes on a long counter that was stacked with dirty dishes and I followed him through the jam-packed restaurant and out the front door, catching Mike's eye along the way. I was keeping an eye out for a taxi but I had one more question for Raul. "Why did Jackie let him in, Raul?"

"He said he had a message from Kearney. About some extra work. I heard that much through the closed door, so I eased back into the bedroom. Out of the way, you know? That was business, after all." He closed, then opened his eyes. "How many people would be alive, would be healthy, would be sane, if only they'd had enough money?"

I whistled a taxi over to the curb, put Raul into it, dropped some money on the seat beside him. "Thank you, Raul," I said.

"Thank you, Phil," he said.

Mike and I were at the table in Arlene's office eating like we hadn't consumed a dozen doughnuts a couple of hours earlier. I guess that's what's meant by empty calories. Mike had been strangely quiet. Never shy about expressing an opinion, he hadn't voiced a single one about my conversation with Raul. I'd even asked him whether the receiver and transmitter had functioned properly; he told me they did, that he'd heard every word. And now not a word from him? "I know who the guy is who killed Jackie Marchand," I said. That got his attention.

"Know him how?" he demanded. I told him. "I agree with Yo. No way you can have people like just walking in off the street like that. And she's gonna have to get over her dislike of firearms, too. Son of a bitch like that just needs shooting."

"Not gonna happen, bro. Anyway, the door's locked now."

"Jackie Marchand's door was locked. He unlocked it and let his killer in."

"How do you think they knew Jackie was going to talk to me before they killed him and took his laptop?"

"And why tear up the place if the laptop was right there on the table, in plain view?" I watched Mike retrieve the mental picture of Jackie's ransacked apartment. "Mr. Dumb Fat Boy definitely was looking for something else, the way that place was tossed."

"A printout!" I said. "That's how they knew! He must've printed out a copy of what was in his computer and taken it to work with him at some point, in his backpack along with his school papers, and somebody saw it."

"Then you might have it, Phil. It might be with that stuff I took from his place. We thought it was just class papers—essays and term papers, things like that. But suppose . . ."

I was supposing. I was also imagining. Imagining police captain Bill Delaney making good on his threat—his promise—to lift my PI license because, in his words, I walk too close to the line and my toes keep crossing over. He wasn't happy that I was the one who had discovered Bill Calloway's murdered body in the back door of the site of an arson investigation. I wasn't too happy about it myself; but Delaney still was chafed and rubbed raw about my involvement in identifying the guy who was raping and murdering little girls a few months back. The parents had hired me after months of no response from the police, and another raped, murdered little girl. That one was personal because it was Arlene Edwards's granddaughter. But I also found out that the cops knew who the perp was and if they'd stopped him then, Arlene's granddaughter would be alive. Then the perp took an ass-whip that put him in the hospital for more than a month. Delaney wanted to believe that I'd done it but I hadn't and I could prove it. But I knew who did do it and so, to divert Delaney's attention, I gave him a multi-million dollar theft, fencing, and dope dealing ring on a silver platter. It had been operating out in the open, from a barber shop, for years, and Delaney and his cops had never known it. I hadn't either, but then I didn't get paid to notice criminal activity in a public place. I got paid to do things that some citizens felt the cops didn't care too much about, like who was calling them terrorists and burning down their businesses.

"You can't worry about what that asshole Delaney thinks," Mike said.

"You gotta stop doing that, bro."

"Doing what?"

"Walking around inside my brain like that. Speaking what I'm thinking."

"It's not like you're that hard to figure out," Mike said.

"Ouch," I said, really feeling stung.

"Stop bleeding, bro. Didn't mean it that way. What I meant was that you don't ever weave a tangled web around yourself or anybody else, and you always do the right thing for your clients, even if it's the wrong thing for somebody else. Like Bill Delaney and the police department."

"I won't be much help to my clients if Delaney pulls my ticket, Mike."

"I told you, Phil, don't worry about Delaney. I've got the antidote for him."

I envisioned a huge hypodermic sticking out of Delaney's butt and laughed. So did Mike, no doubt because he knew what I was thinking. Arlene came in then with dessert—bread pudding. We looked at it and I said, "What doughnuts?" And we both laughed some more and ate the bread pudding. Arlene pulled up a chair and we spent some time talking with her, telling her as much as we could about why I needed to feed Raul in her office and why Mike was hiding in the hallway listening to the conversation.

"Will he be all right?" she asked of Raul, and we told her we thought he would, that we'd do everything we could to make sure that he was. "Good," she said, "because I really do need a waiter. Do you think he'd work out all right here?"

I was about to answer when Mike jumped in. "I think, next to your own son, Raul would be about as good a guy to have here as you could find."

She nodded her head once. It was a done deal. "Would you give him my number and ask him to call me?"

I left El Caribe wishing that Jackie Marchand could have lived to attend college full-time, could have lived so he could have a home in the spare bedroom in Raul's apartment, could have lived to see Raul waiting tables and cooking in El Caribe; and hoping that it wasn't too late for Raul to reclaim some sense of his long-lost self. "Let's go see Eddie."

"Yeah," Mike said. "I want to talk over this shitty case with him."

"He can't talk back, Mike."

"That's why I want to talk it over with him: He'll have to listen for a change."

Eddie was awake when we got back to the hospital. Linda was sitting beside him, holding his hand, and a cop was standing outside the ICU suite. Not just any cop, though. This was Assistant Chief Eric "The Ace" Spade. I'd never met him but I sure as hell knew who he was. Every cop in the city knew who he was. He was in full dress uniform, standing at parade rest, feet apart, hands behind his back, hat in his hands, looking at Eddie in his bed. He turned when he heard Mike and me approach and his long, thin face broke into a smile.

"Well just look at what the cat dragged in!"

"How're ya doing, boss," Mike said, shaking hands with Ace Spade.

Spade clapped him hard on the back. "I thought you two did everything together. How'd he get nailed and you didn't?"

Mike clapped me hard on the back. " 'Cause I was covering his sorry butt," he said, and introduced me. We shook hands.

"Heard a lot about you, son. Pleased to meet you."

"I've heard a lot about you, too, sir, and the pleasure's all mine."

"Do you know yet who shot Ortiz?"

I hesitated, but only briefly. "I think I might, sir."

"But what? Can't prove it?"

"Can't tie him to the paymaster. Not yet."

Spade's blue-gray eyes narrowed and his lips compressed into a tight, straight line. "You saying somebody paid to have Ortiz shot?" Before I could answer him, though, he said, "The dead insurance guy in the back door. He was the target and Ortiz was just collateral damage? Is that how you're looking at it?"

"Not exactly," I said, probably sounding as uneasy under his probing as I felt.

"You were the target," he said, the words sounding pinched off through his compressed lips. "And since all Spics look alike, Ortiz took the bullet meant for you." Spade's eyes turned a darker shade of gray and narrowed into mere slits and he turned them on Mike. "You see it that way, too?"

"That's how it's smelling," Mike said.

Slitty eyes back on me. "That stinks, all right, but it doesn't explain why you're at the top of Delaney's shit list, why he's pissed off enough to take your weapon."

I didn't know if he expected an answer, but I sure as shit wasn't about to give him one. Anyway, I was working too hard to avoid making eye contact with Mike. So all three of us stood there looking through the glass at Eddie. The energy field must have been intense because Linda turned around, saw us, whispered something to Eddie, then came out to join us in the hall. We all hugged her, she thanked us for standing by her and Eddie, told us what we wanted to hear: That Eddie was making good progress and that he was going to be just fine.

"I've got to get back to pushing the pile of papers on my desk," Spade said. He gave Linda another hug, Mike another clap on the back, and me another one of those slit-eyed looks. "You call me if you need anything," he said. "You can call or Mike can call." And he was gone.

"I can't believe he's still standing up for you two," Linda said.

Mike looked wounded. "What, we're not worth standing up for?"

She punched him on the shoulder. "You know what I mean. Not only are you guys retired, but he wasn't even your boss for the last half of your tour."

I looked at Mike. "Spade was your boss?"

He nodded. "Our first sarge, then our lou. When he made captain they moved him out of Harlem to some place more, ah . . . appropriate. Then he started moving up and just never stopped."

"And never stopped keeping in touch, either?" I asked.

"They were a really close group of guys," Linda said. "So close that a lot of the wives got close, too, and stayed close even after the guys retired."

"Walking a beat in Harlem, back in the eighties . . ."

He didn't need to say any more. I didn't join the department until the mid-nineties but I'd heard the stories about Harlem and Washington Heights and the Bronx in the eighties. The cops were afraid to patrol in cars, to say nothing of on foot, and Ace Spade would, legend had it, walk the beat with his cops. At least I'd thought it was legend. I also thought I'd known a bit about Mike Smith and Eddie Ortiz, but apparently what I knew didn't begin to scratch the surface of who they were and what they'd experienced. "When do you think we can see him, talk to him?" I asked Linda, to have something to say that wouldn't sound stupid.

"Tomorrow, I think. If he has a good night, they'll move him to a private room."

"We'll be back to check on him later," I said.

"Tell Yolanda and Connie thanks," Linda said. "I'll tell them myself when I see them, but just let them know how appreciative I am."

I nodded but kept my mouth shut because if I opened it, whatever came out would be stupid since I had no idea what she was talking about. And sure as shit, when we got outside, Mike asked me what Linda was thanking Yolanda and Connie for, knowing that I didn't have a clue. "Shut up, Mike."

"So, where to now?" he asked politely to hide his smirk. "Since Miss Aguierre won't let us back into the office."

"Let's go see Nehru first, then Patel. And while we're there, I want to pop in and see Sam Epstein."

"I'd like to pop Sam Epstein . . . right upside his sorry head."

"That's no way to treat the clients, Mike."

"The things we do for money," he said, which reminded me of what Raul had said about Jackie and why he opened his door to his killer.

"And we could always go looking for a fat, dumb white boy."

"And the sooner we find him, the better. I need to smash something and you won't let me have my way with Epstein."

Jawal Nehru greeted us like royalty, and when I told him that we would have questions for him tomorrow, he got so excited that he could barely talk, and when he did speak, it was in a much more heavily accented English than I'd heard from him. "If you can make right this situation, Mr. Rodriquez, my wife will come back home," he said, clapping his hands together. "I called her and told her that somebody who believed us was helping us and she said that yes, she would come back if this could be made right."

We received a similar greeting from Ravi Patel and his wife. Patel hurried across the wide expanse of the living room and into a back bedroom, then hurried back with two yellow legal pads, both filled with lines and lines of script. "We have been talking, remembering, and writing down everything, just as you asked," Patel said, waving the pads at us, his excitement as great as Nehru's. Of course, his wife was by his side, and she was beaming, every bit as excited and determined as her husband; as Jawal Nehru. They all seemed so certain that I was just steps away from, as Jawal Nehru put it, making things right, and I was anything but certain. Then I had a jarring thought: Patel didn't know about Bill Calloway, didn't know that there was a chance he'd have to start his claims process all over again. A remote chance, given that I had all of Bill Calloway's files and would make them public if I had to, but one I didn't want to have to take. I also wasn't going to be the one to tell them about Calloway.

"Is the name Thomas Kearney familiar to you?" I asked.

They consulted their yellow pages. "All names we have written here," said Mrs. Patel. "Everybody we have talked to . . . and no, no Thomas Kearney. There is a Francis Kearney, but no Thomas."

"Who's Francis Kearney?"

"A leech!" Ravi Patel said, the corners of his mouth dropping down in distain. "A parasite! Called the other day offering to buy our restaurant! A burned out shell, he called it. He even had the nerve to say it would never be anything but a burned out shell and we'd be smart to accept his offer."

"Do you have a phone number for him?" Mike asked, then added, "Though I'd understand if you ripped it up and flushed it down the toilet where it belongs."

Mrs. Patel looked at Mike as if she wanted to hug him—probably would have had her husband not been in the room. "I was going to do just that but Ravi stopped me," she said, giving one of the legal pads a good shake. A blue-green colored piece of paper fell out and fluttered to the floor. Mike picked it up and held it out to Mrs. Patel but she waved it away. "It's from him. Francis Kearney."

Mike moved closer to me so we both could read the paper. It was an eight-by-ten flyer advertising FRANCIS X. KEARNEY PROPERTY DEVELOPMENT and the fine print said the company specialized in the purchase of condemned or fire-damaged property at "fair and reasonable prices."

"May we keep this?" Both Patels nodded. "And you called him at this number?" This time both Patels shook their head in the negative.

"He called us. This . . . this thing was in with our mail. Then, the same day we received it, he called us that night."

"How did he know your phone number?"

"That is a very good question," Ravi Patel said in his logical-sounding voice.

I had quite a few more questions but the Patels didn't have the answers and I didn't want to spook them, or give them any false hopes, so we thanked them, told them we'd probably be talking to them again the next day, and left.

"You should've told them about Calloway," Mike said when we got downstairs. We were standing on the sidewalk in the space between the door leading upstairs to the apartment where the Patels were staying and the door leading into the Epstein Dry Cleaners and Laundry.

"Maybe," I said. I wasn't certain whether I should have or not; I just knew that I didn't want to have to tell them that a second person had been killed in the back door of their restaurant, and if I could prevent them ever finding that out, I would. I opened the door of the cleaners, the bell over the door tinkled, and Sam Epstein, who was behind the counter, looked up. He didn't quite scowl when he saw us, but there was no happy smile of welcome and greeting, either.

"Sam," I said. "How are you?"

"Getting better every day, Rodriquez," he said to me, with a nod in Mike's direction. "What brings you to my humble establishment? I mean, I don't see an armload of dirty clothes," he added, trying to cover for his rudeness. Like I needed a reason to visit his humble establishment. How about the fact that we kept Tim McQueen and Pat Casey from killing his sorry ass? We needed more reason than that?

"Where can we find Thomas Kearney?" Mike made it a demand to know and not a request for information, and Sam turned such a sickly shade of green I thought he was going to throw up. I'd been prepared to merely ask Sam if he knew Kearney. Clearly Mike's approach was the best one. We waited for an answer, and when it seemed that there wouldn't be one, at least not immediately, Mike pulled the blue-green flyer from his pocket. Sam knew immediately and exactly what it was. His coloring was a contrasting match to the paper. Mike waved it in his face.

"We'll tell Kearney we got this from you," I said.

"You can't do that!" Sam yelled.

"I can and I will," I said. "I'm sick of your crap, Epstein. People are dead because of you, one of them a friend of mine, and another friend is in the hospital. Because of you. Because you're a wuss and a coward. If it weren't for the respect I have for your father, I'd have turned your sorry ass over to the cops and let them charge you with burning down that restaurant and killing that delivery man. That can still happen. The statute of limitations on the arson clock just started ticking, and if you watch the TV crime dramas, you know the one on murder ticks along forever."

Epstein was watching my mouth like he could see the words coming out, like maybe the words would have a different meaning if he could see them. I felt Mike's fist tighten and I knew he was about to destroy Epstein's orthodontics. I also knew that I wouldn't stop him. Then the curtain parted and Dave Epstein appeared. Sammy snapped to. "Oh, hey, Pop," he said.

Dave said something back to him in what I assumed was Yiddish and Sam's head jerked backward as if Mike had punched him. Dave looked as us. "What do you need from Sammy? He knows something that can help you?"

"Yes, he does," I said, and nodded to Mike, who gave Dave Epstein the Kearney Development flyer. "This guy's in the business of buying buildings at fire-sale prices," I said, and waited for Epstein to find the meaning. It didn't take long. He looked at his only son with such disappointment in his eyes that it hurt my feelings.

"Tell them what they want to know, Sammy. Tell them everything."

Sammy was sweating. "You don't know these people, Pop . . ."

"And I don't want to. It's bad enough that you know them."

I could almost feel sorry for the guy. He was sweating fear bullets, caught in the crossfire between the Old Testament anger of his father and the even older kind of anger fueled by irrational and baseless hatred. Almost but not quite. Mostly what I felt for Sam was anger and it was raw enough that no component of forgiveness had snuck in yet. "So, Sam?" I said. "What's it going to be?"

"You can't turn me in! They can't do that, Pop! You already

paid them!"

"I didn't pay them to break the law, which is what they did when they brought you home instead of taking you to the cops. That was a favor to me, I hope because of how I tried to treat people all my life." The old man was getting emotional. I put out a hand to calm him but he pushed it away. "This business that pays you such a good living was built treating people like human beings. Everybody who walked in this door was Mr. or Mrs. Somebody, no matter what color they were or how much or how little money they had . . ." He stopped talking and I thought he was about to cry, but what he did, too fast for someone his age, was slap his son across the face. Sammy stumbled backwards. There was nothing to catch him but the curtains leading through to the plant, so he fell on his ass. The old man looked at us then followed his son through the curtain.

"You know what it takes for an old man to smack his grown son?" Mike said.

I shook my head. I couldn't imagine. I wasn't best pals with my old man but he hadn't hit me since I was ten or eleven and that was for stealing peaches from a fruit stand, then lying about it, which, as far as he was concerned, was worse than the stealing. I didn't know what Mike's relationship was with his father—didn't know if his father was still alive—but I could tell neither of us could imagine, at our age, being slapped by the man we called pop or papi or dad. "I don't think they're coming back," I said.

"Where to?" Mike asked.

"The office," I said. "See if Yo'll let us in."

She did, and she was glad to see us, though looking as harried as I'd ever seen her. Her glasses were riding low on her nose and her hair was, well, disarranged, and there were three pencils sticking out of it at weird angles. She had on sweat clothes and the thick wool socks that were her chained-to-the-computer wardrobe, especially in winter. "This is some truly ugly stuff we've got here, my brothers, but I can tell you already know that," she said. "So. How ugly is it out there at street level?"

"The one who killed Jackie Marchand is the same one who came in here that night looking to sell information about the fires."

She barely took a beat. "Do we have a name?"

The look on my face was her answer. With Sam Epstein in a catatonic state of fear, there was nobody to leverage. It was all but certain that the Kearneys, whoever they were, weren't going to roll over on each other—at least not at my request—and anyway, we couldn't get to the Kearneys without help from Patrick Casey, Tim McQueen, Tommy Mottola, or Sam Epstein. Four strikes puts you out of the game . . . out of the whole damn ball park. "Maybe some of the ugly shit you dug up will combine with some of the ugly shit we dug up, and give us a way to put a name to his face . . . speaking of ugly." And since he already tried to sell out his masters once, I was betting it wouldn't take much to get him to do it again.

While Mike and I hung up our coats and got sodas from the fridge, Yolanda was organizing stacks of different colored papers on my desk. She'd started with the colored paper to help me follow threads and connections, which came as easily to her as tying her shoes. Her brain functioned like a computer, mine more like a slot machine: Different images and pieces rotate through mine, each having its own significance, until . . . ding, ding, ding, three of a kind! "You want a juice?" I called out to her.

"I've got some ginger tea left . . . oh, and thanks for lunch! It was wonderful, as usual. How'd Raul like it?" And that got us off on a discussion of Raul. I let Mike do most of the talking, his way of apologizing for his up-to-now intractable views of hypes in recovery. "You think he was serious about working there?" Yolanda asked.

"I think so," I said. "I think the diner job was what he could find when he got out of the joint, and I think he didn't bother to look further because he didn't feel that he had a reason to look further."

"Until Jackie Marchand," Yo said.

"Those papers from his place, where are they?" Mike asked.

Yolanda got up to get them, returned quickly. "Raul thinks something's here?"

"We think it's possible," I said, quickly paging through papers that were exactly what they appeared to be: Essays and term papers and book reports, most of them from high school, all of them marked "A" or "Excellent" or some other suggestion of genius.

"What did you hope to find?" We told her. "Good thinking," she said. "Makes sense. There had to be a reason to kill him, and thinking he was about to tell you what he knew would be a pretty good one."

"But what did he know?" I asked. "And how did they know what he knew?"

"And how did they know he planned to tell you?" Mike added.

We spent the next couple of hours trying to answer those questions, and others; and each time we found an answer, we found also that it led to more questions, the main one being who was the wizard behind the curtain? The Kearneys—Yolanda's research had discovered they were first cousins—were front men. Thieves, crooks, and liars for sure, but the trail didn't end with them as much as it just petered out. We figured that Mottola, Casey, and McQueen were just errand boys for the Kearneys; and we already knew that Epstein was barely a player. But somebody was a murderer and somebody ordered those murders, the same somebody who decided which businesses to torch and then withhold the insurance settlement, forcing the business owner to sell on the cheap so the Kearneys could buy low and sell high. I wanted that somebody.

"Eddie's awake," Yolanda said, standing and stretching, "and I'm hungry. Let's go see if he saw the shooter and the car, and then let's eat."

Chapter Ten

I couldn't sleep, so instead of tossing and turning and keeping Connie awake, I got up and sat in the living room and watched the traffic moving back and forth across the Brooklyn and Manhattan Bridges. It was the middle of the night, in a city with one of the greatest subway systems in the world, and I could swear that at times there were as many motorized vehicles here as there were in Los Angeles. And where were these people going at three o'clock in the morning? Three forty-two to be exact. To work? Home from work? Home from a night out? As usual, the view soothed me and began smoothing out the jagged edges of worry that were preventing sleep. One of Yolanda's many brilliant ideas had been that I buy two units in what was, at that time, a shabby building in an even shabbier neighborhood, which now was being called the New SoHo, and my building, which stuck out into the East River and provided the magnificent view, was some kind of yuppie haven. So trendy, in fact, that the rent I get for the smaller of the two units I own pays for itself and my top floor digs. That thought soothed, too.

Barely a month ago, if I'd been sitting here this time of night, enjoying the view and my wise investment, part of the reason for my nocturnal musings would have been loneliness. I'd had plenty of female company over the years, but no companionship and that got old and then I worried that I would, too, before I found someone to share life with. Yolanda always told me that stressing over a situation only made it worse, that the woman of my dreams would walk into my life while I was focused on other matters. And she'd been right. Again. So, tonight's sleeplessness had no angst attached to it; just the fear that I would not be able to save Ravi Patel's and Jawal Nehru's property for them. I could tell them who destroyed it and why, but I was completely powerless over the insurance company.

I stood up and paced, both propelled and pursued by my thoughts. Everything hinged on the mysterious "someone" pulling the strings in this operation, and my worst fear was that it was the mob. I had no proof of that and nothing to point in that direction other than Tommy Mottola's involvement. Was he there to deliver messages from his boss, and to keep an eye on things? Or was he just another hate-mongering little creep who got off on other people's misery? I hoped it was the latter because if it was the former, there would be nothing I could do to help Patel and Nehru and the others. Ever. I couldn't help them, the cops couldn't help, God couldn't help them. Not if it was the mob who was controlling Big Apple Business Insurers.

I stopped pacing so I could call to mind Yolanda's research on the company. Can't walk and think at the same time. It was a well-seasoned outfit, started out half a century ago small, insuring mom-and-pop stores, and grew into one of biggest and best insurers of small- and medium-sized businesses in the five Boroughs of New York City. No hint of Mafia stink attached. So why would a reputable, fifty-year business risk its reputation? Even if it was just Kearney who was crooked, wasn't it somebody's job in the company to watch him? To make sure he was doing the right thing? And not having the answers to these questions, and not being able to get the answers, was what was frustrating the very hell out of me.

No, that's not true. What was frustrating the hell out of me—and scaring me and making me mad—was that I was in either way too deep or in way over my head. Whichever analogy applied. I started my business to help the people of my neighborhood, New York's Lower East Side, the East Village, Alphabet City—the places that touch and nudge the more well-known neighborhoods of Chinatown and TriBeCa and SoHo and The Village and Little Italy. Those are places where people who need the kind of help I provide live, but who are unable to pay the kind of money that TV and movie PIs get. The people in my neighborhood have the same problems as people in those other places, they just have less money to throw at the problem—either to resolve it or to make it go away. True, Ravi Patel and Jawal Nehru had their businesses in my 'hood, but the source of their problems was well beyond my reach. I couldn't help them any more than I could help that very nice Buddhist monk get his name off the terrorist watch list. How do you fight back against that kind of nastiness? How do you win against people who play dirty in the dark?

And I knew the answer! With apologies to the monk, whose name I didn't remember, I knew the answer! And I mentally apologized because I knew that kind and gentle man would never do what I was concocting; he couldn't even bring himself to be angry. But I could.

"So, have you got it all worked out?" Connie's arms slipped around me and she rested her head against my back.

I turned to face her. "I think I do," I said.

She nodded her head against my chest. "I thought you would," she said. "You were getting close to it at dinner and I knew you wouldn't sleep until you worked your way through it."

I was about to ask her how she knew that, but instead I said, "Will you marry me?"

Then the phone rang. We broke apart as if caught in an illicit act, and we both looked at the phone like it was crazy. I picked up and looked at the caller ID strip and my insides froze. "Yo?

What's wrong?"

Connie was by my side, her nails digging into my arm. I was holding the phone to my ear listening to Yolanda tell me that there was a fire but my brain wasn't working. Connie took the phone from me. "Yolanda. What is it?" Then she said "Oh, God," and punched off the phone. "Come on, Phil."

I didn't move. I couldn't move. My building was on fire.

Flames were visible on the second floor, but it was mostly smoke. Thick, dark, billowing smoke whooshing out from the windows like a big wind was behind it doing the pushing. I still don't know how Connie managed to get us both dressed and out, but she managed it all by herself because I was of no use or value. I was swinging back and forth between feelings of despair, terror, and rage: Despair for the end of a dream if the building was gone; terror that Yolanda would be hurt; and rage at whoever had set the fire, because I knew it had been no accident. But it wasn't until I was standing across the street, behind yellow tape, watching my building burn, that the significance of the fire's location slapped me in the face: The second floor housed the Dharma Yoga Studio, run by a couple of Sikhs.

It took less than half an hour for the Fire Department to call the thing under control. They were rolling up their hoses as Yolanda and I stood holding on to each other, telling ourselves and each other the lie that the building didn't matter; that what mattered was that we both were safe. That was true, but the building mattered. It mattered a lot. We'd looked for a suitable location for months, me at first just wanting to rent an office somewhere, Yolanda insisting that if we were going into business for ourselves, we needed to own our own building. Then we'd seen this little place—narrow and run-down and dirty and ugly—and we'd known it was meant to be ours. We transformed it into a place where she lived on the top floor and where we both spent the majority of our waking hours on the ground floor and which signified for both of us that dreams can and do come true. The building mattered.

"Phillip," I heard behind me, and turned to find Jill Mason at my shoulder. It was six-thirty in the morning and she was standing there wide awake and fully dressed. I was about to ask her what the hell she was doing there when I saw she wasn't alone. Carmine was behind her, and Patty Starrett was there; so were Mrs. Campos and Willie One Eye and Raul. Yolanda started to cry and sought refuge in Sandra's arms. Connie held me and I reached out a hand to Jill.

Mrs. Campos was handing out fresh juice to everyone, and Raul and Willie were handing out hot coffee. Carmine and Patty were passing around bags of pastries. Nobody was talking; everybody looked as stunned as I felt, all of us shivering in the cold morning air. Grateful, yes, for the food and drink, but all eyes were on the building that had brought all these disparate people together. But, it really wasn't the building, was it?

Mike Smith pushed his way through the crowd and grabbed me, pulling me away from Connie and Jill and holding me at arm's length, his big hands squeezing my shoulders until the bones hurt, looking me up and down. Then he let me go and grabbed Yolanda away from Sandra and did the same thing to her. Then he looked across the street at the building. Didn't say anything, didn't do anything, just looked. It was Jill's, "Good morning, Mr. Smith," that jolted him back to something resembling a normal awareness.

"Dr. Mason," he said, and offered her his hand. She took it in both of hers and he left it there. Shrinks must be able to soothe with their hands as well as their words because Mike's shoulders dropped from up around his ears, and his clenched jaw relaxed, and Jill let go of his hand. "It's good to see you," he said to her.

She smiled at him, then turned to me and Yolanda. "I'll be at my office if you need me, then I'll be home tonight," she told us, and she walked through a crowd that parted for her, a beautiful, elegant woman who had endured hatred because of her race, and had slogged through a minefield of grief following the deaths of her husband and children, to emerge capable of always being willing and able to offer solace and assistance to someone else.

I watched her go, then turned back to watch my building some more. It was still smoking and that made me think of the Taste of India fire, and remember the smell of the smoke. I didn't smell anything right now, and I knew that I should. My building was burning but I didn't smell a thing. Connie took my arm and walked me a little away from the crowd.

"If I stay here I'll just be in your way, won't I?"

I pulled her in close and rested my chin on top of her head. We both liked it when I did that. "Thank you for getting me here. I think if you hadn't been there, I'd still be standing in the living room holding the telephone." She tightened her arms around my waist. "Yeah," I said finally, not wanting to let go of her. "I think it's better if you go on to work. I'll keep in touch."

She squeezed me again, then released me, took a step back, and looked into my eyes. "You think it's the same arsonist, don't you?"

"Yeah, I do."

She kissed the tips of her fingers and placed them on my lips. "Be careful, please," she said, and turned away.

"You didn't give me an answer," I called after her.

She turned back, smiling at me. "Yes, I will," she said. I watched her walk away, my heart thudding in my chest so hard it hurt. What a way to start a day.

I turned to look for Yolanda and Mike, found them huddled together, their heads almost touching, encircled by Sandra, Carmine, Raul, Willie, Mrs. Campos, Patty, and Arlene Edwards. A wall of protection. It really wasn't about a building.

Carmine broke away from the group and hurried toward me, his face screwed up into an expression that wasn't quite angry, but could be on command. "Tommy have anything to do with this?" he said when he was close enough for me to hear him. " 'Cause if he did, I'll kill him. I promise you that."

I looked at my building again; I couldn't keep my eyes off of it. The second floor was a dark, smoking hole; the front door was standing wide open, firefighters in heavy, wet boots tromped in and out, dragging hoses and axes, and I all of a sudden was acutely aware of how noisy the scene was: The motors of the fire trucks and constant crackling of the two-way communication system. "It's hard not to think that this isn't connected to the other fires," I said, "but I can't point any fingers at anybody right now, Carmine."

"The same thing I like about you, Rodriquez, is what pisses me off the most about you. That bein' fair shit. There's some people you can't treat with fairness."

"You're right, Carmine, but right now, I don't know if Tommy's one of 'em."

The fat man's face smoothed out and he chuckled, then he looked across the street at my building, then he looked at me. "Gimme another phone number." He took an expensive pen and a leather notebook from his pocket and I gave him my cell phone and home telephone numbers. "I'll call ya," he said, and walked away. I had felt no sympathy for Sam Epstein in the face of his father's wrath, but I found myself conjuring up an ounce of pity for Tommy Mottola. Carmine really would kill him.

I was beginning to feel my synapses and senses beginning to function again and I went to find Yolanda; we needed to talk to the fire marshal. We needed to get inside our building. We needed to call the people who ran the yoga studio and tell them they were out of business for a while. She and Sandra seemed to be having the same kind of parting that Connie and I had: Sandra knew she wasn't needed here, knew that Yolanda would be fine without her. I approached them, gave Sandra a hug, and put an arm around Yo's shoulder. "Let's go get on somebody's nerves," I said.

We went looking for the fire marshal, found the arson investigator instead, and introduced ourselves. His greeting was harried but polite. Why couldn't cops behave more like firefighters? "How bad is it?" I asked. I recognized him from the Taste of India fire. I looked for his name stenciled on to his coat: McNamara.

"Thanks to the first-rate renovation you guys did, not bad at all," the investigator said. "Fire contained on the second floor so it's pretty much a mess. Some smoke damage to the top and bottom. You get somebody over here to suck out the smoke, no reason you can't use those floors."

"How did it start?" Yolanda asked.

McNamara pointed to the gaping hole that had been the second floor bay window. "Two big rocks tossed with some force through that second-story front window. Once they got the glass broken, they followed the rocks with accelerant. Your alarm system made a silent call when the first rock hit. The cops were here when the actual fire started, and they called us." He was about to say something else but stopped himself. He saw me watching him. "I was about to tell you all how lucky you are, but it wasn't luck that saved your building for you, it was smarts: Pouring concrete between the floors, installing that alarm system that'll detect a rat pissing on a cotton ball, and the bulletproof glass on the first floor front windows. If they'd gotten that accelerant inside the first floor, things might've been a little dicier."

"I thought you said the second floor was the target," I said.

The inspector shook his head. "I said the second floor is where it started, but the first floor is what they wanted." He started walking, waved for us to follow him. "Look here," he said, pointing to the sidewalk in front of the building. There were two very large rocks there, as large as cantaloupes, each with a numbered yellow tag beside it. "And look here," McNamara said, pointing to scratches on the glass. "This is where those rocks bounced off the glass."

I peered at the scratches, then down at the big rocks. Where did somebody get rocks like that in New York City? You'd have to go way out into the countryside to find rocks that solid and that big. "You said there were rocks like these upstairs?"

"Yep," he said, nodding, "two more. River rocks, these are, and it would take somebody big and strong to heave a stone this size not only up that high, but with enough force to break through safety glass." Then he pointed to door. "Tried to get in this way, too. See the scratches on the panel? Whoever started this fire knew a little bit about what he was doing."

"Can we get into the building?" Yolanda's voice sounded so small and distant that I could barely hear her, and she was standing right beside me. I looked over at her; I'd never heard her sound small before.

"Sure," McNamara said. "We're almost done here."

Yo grabbed my arm and pulled me away, in a hurry to get away from our building and I knew why. "That was about us, Phil, not the Sikh owners of a yoga studio."

Now I smelled the smoke, the harsh, throat-burning, acrid smoke of fire, and it was about the building again. Even as I looked at the people who had come here this morning before dawn out of care and concern for Yolanda and me, this attack was on the building because the building represents us and what we do . . . oh, shit. "The computers, Yo, will the smoke hurt the computers?"

She held up the canvas carryall that hung diagonally across her body and which contained her master computer, the one she'd asked me to sign a blank check to purchase, then unzipped a side pocket and pulled out four of what I now recognized to be those flash things. "The entire building could have burned to the ground and we wouldn't have lost a single client, business, or personal file," she said. "Not that I want some perverted son of a bitch burning down my building!"

I blew a kiss at the computer, whose cost she had assured me I didn't want to know, ergo the blank check, though I had a pretty good idea: Any expenditure of more than five thousand dollars required both our signatures on a check. The computer had just paid for itself. "We need to call . . . I can't ever remember their names . . . the yoga people."

"They're gone for the month. I told you that . . . yes, Phil, I did! They're in India for some kind of Sikh festival. This could all be cleaned up by the time they get back."

"Yeah, unless fuckin' Kearney thinks we tried to burn the thing ourselves." My cell phone rang and I whipped it out of my pocket, expecting Connie. It was Raul. I looked around and he told me to be cool. Then he told me that Jackie's killer was standing a block and a half away, watching the crowd. I nodded and told him to hang up, then kept talking like I was still on the phone. "Call Mike," I said, looking at Yolanda. "Tell him Raul just called and told me that Jackie Marchand's killer is standing a block and half away, watching. Turn and face the other way, Yo, and make the call, then give me your phone." I closed my phone and palmed Yolanda's and walked a little away, Mike and me trying to figure a way to get to the guy without being made. I couldn't look his way; he'd see me. Mike could look in that direction but he couldn't see around the corner. "Fuck this,

Mike! I'm going to him. I think he's too fat and too drugged to outrun me. He can't see you, so you get the head start. When I see you reach the corner, I'll start running. Okay? Go!"

I turned and watched Mike head for the corner, watching our prey out of the corner of my eye. He was just standing there, hands in his pockets, watching. Mike had turned the corner and I had started running toward him before he registered what was happening. Then he took off. So much for being too fat or too stoned to boogie. Mike gave up the chase before I did, and I gave it up a block later, and huffed my way back to where he was bent over, hands on his knees, breathing hard. "I'm way too old that for kind of shit, running down perps," he said through deep breathing.

"That makes two of us," I said, adding, "dude's fast for a fat boy."

"But he's a twenty-something fat boy," Mike said. "Youth. Makes all the difference."

I shook my head; I was still winded and more than a little pissed off that I'd been out-run by a guy sixty pounds overweight, no matter how young he was. Mike's breathing was almost back to normal and he was standing up straight. "You ever seen a tank on maneuvers?" he asked, and kept talking because he knew that I hadn't—except in the movies. "A tank is a big, ugly animal that looks like it should barely be able to roll, but it can damn near outrun a camel and can turn and change directions like a Jaguar—the car—and stop on a dime."

This was not the time or place for Mike's expressions of admiration for the military tank. "Why are you talking about tanks?"

"Because that boy who just smoked us is just like a tank: Big and fast. And did you see him turn that corner? Like he had wheels on his feet." The admiration for the military tank now was transferred to a guy who'd just tried to burn down my building? "I got one quick glimpse of his face and a real long look at his back, but I'll know him if I see him again," Mike said, reading my thoughts again.

"If he's not spooked," I said, sounding as disgusted with myself as I felt. Suppose my brilliantly failed plan of attack scared him off for good?

"He's not smart enough to stay spooked for long." We started walking the four blocks back. "What are you going to do?"

Until Mike asked, I wasn't sure, but whoever said the answer was in the question knew what he was talking about. "I'm going to work, Mike."

The rubber-neckers and nosey-roseys had scattered when we got back, and the people left were those who cared about us. Arlene and Raul had their heads together; Patty Starrett, Mrs. Campos, and Willie One Eye were having what looked like a serious discussion, and it appeared that the women had one opinion and Willie another; and Yo was talking to McNamara and the fire marshal. Everybody stopped talking and looked at Mike and me, everybody but Yolanda and Raul wearing expectant looks, and that was because only they knew why we'd run off and that we hadn't been successful. I walked around talking to people, thanking them for the show of support, and being vague in the extreme about what I thought had happened. And one by one, they all left, except Raul. I knew he wanted to talk and that he didn't want to talk in front of Mike and Yolanda, but I thought it was time for him to get over that. I walked over to him.

"We couldn't catch him," I said.

"You will next time," he said. "Guys like him always come back."

"That's what Mike said."

"He's a cop," Raul said, pointing with his head in Mike's direction.

"Used to be," I said. "So did I." I gave him a moment to feel whatever it was he was feeling about that piece of information, then I said, "And so what, Raul? You used to be a hype and a con but you're not now. You're a solid citizen with a job and a home and family and friends. It's time to stop acting like a perp, *'mano.*" I walked back to where Mike and Yo were standing. Raul followed and I made the introductions. He shook hands, said polite things.

"I remembered something. About Jackie. I can't stop thinking about him, you know? And I remembered that he had this little book that he wrote in, his journal, he called it."

I felt Mike straining not to react. He hadn't recovered a journal. "What's it look like, Raul? Did you ever see it?"

"It was thin, about like this," and he made a shape with his hands suggesting four inches by six inches, "and it had a brown leather cover, but no dates or months, just blank pages. He wrote in it every day."

"Where did he keep it?" Yolanda asked.

"Usually in his back pocket," Raul said, patting his own back pocket. "And up on the shelf in the closet when he was home . . ." He blushed, embarrassed. "I picket it up once and flipped it open and he grabbed it from me. Said it was personal, private. Then he laughed and gave it back to me, told me to go ahead and read it but I wouldn't, not then. He said I couldn't anyway because it was all in French, but after that, he always put it up on the closet shelf."

If Kearney had seen Jackie regularly writing in a journal, that would have been enough to consider the kid a threat, whether Kearney could read what he'd written or not, and the existence of something in writing would have motivated the search of Jackie's apartment. Question was, had Tank found the journal, and if not, was it still on the closet shelf in Jackie Marchand's apartment? "Thanks, Raul," I said.

He nodded, told Yolanda and Mike it was nice meeting them, and turned to walk away. "You going to work for Arlene?" I called after him.

He turned back and it was a different man looking at me; the happiness on his face had transformed him. "I start tomorrow. And she's going to teach me how to cook."

We watched him walk away and nobody but me knew that the head up, shoulders back, quick stepping dude leaving us was a new man, a man with purpose. I was a man with a purpose, too, though my walk to the front door of my building was more foot dragging than quick stepping; part of me didn't want to see what was inside. Even though the fire inspector said the damage was limited to the second floor, I'd seen enough fire aftermaths to know the kind of damage firefighters do in their efforts to contain a fire. Yolanda and I must have both been holding our breaths because we both exhaled loudly when we got inside. Except for a thick layer of smoke hanging in the room like fog over San Francisco, everything looked normal. We walked around, not touching, just looking, Mike following us, his gun in his hand, and I was grateful for his willingness to display his unease. If Delaney didn't return my weapon soon, I'd have to get another one.

"So, would I be right in thinking that if the second floor window was broken and that's how the fire started, that's also how the firefighters got into the building?"

"Or through my place," Yo said. "The ladders stretched all the way up." The small voice was back.

I wrapped her in a bear hug and asked the question I should've asked two hours ago. "The alarm woke you and Sandra?" I felt her head nod up and down against my chest, then I felt the warmth of her tears. I held her tighter.

"The alarm scared us half to death, then we smelled the smoke. I was in some kind of catatonic state, couldn't move, couldn't think. Sandra was up and moving, got us dressed, grabbed the essentials. I didn't want to leave, Phil! She had to drag me down the stairs. I couldn't believe—no, I couldn't understand—what was happening! When we got outside and saw the fire trucks, it still wasn't real. It was all so dreamlike." She shivered.

"Let's go upstairs, Yo, take a look. If it's like this, like the inspector said, it'll be all right. Smoky, but all right."

She shook her head. "I can't, Phil."

"It's okay. I understand. I'll go check it out."

"You'll tell me the truth, won't you? Even if it's bad, I want you to tell me, Phil. I don't want to see it, but I do want to know."

I headed for the back stairs, the ones nobody but the two us knew existed. I saw the surprise on Mike's face. "I'll be okay, Mike. Stay with Yo, will you?" I knew what she was thinking: That it was bad enough that firefighters in their dirty boots had invaded her space, but enough was enough.

The smoke was deep and thick in the stairway, especially on the second floor, but as soon as I got to Yolanda's door, I could feel it begin to dissipate. I could also feel cold air. I opened the door to her space and marveled, as always, at the beauty and elegance she'd created here. It was, in a way, like Jill Mason's loft, only Jill's had cost a couple of million dollars more. Yolanda's open space felt open—the only walls and door were to create the bathroom. The kitchen was open and shared a fireplace with the living area. The sleeping loft was invisible unless you knew where to look. The hardwood floors, usually gleaming, showed imprints of heavy rubber boots and the drag marks of hoses. So did a couple of the Chinese rugs. But nothing was broken except the front window—broken from the outside so all the glass showered in. If we got the window boarded up and the utilities back on, she could stay here tonight if she wanted to. And I knew she would, and that's what I told her when I got back downstairs.

"Thanks, Phil," she said in her normal voice. Then she pushed an envelope at me. "I forgot all about this until just now. What's this all about?"

"What is it?" I asked, but before she could answer the door swung open and a Tom Selleck look-alike from his *Magnum PI* days waltzed in. All this guy needed was a flowered shirt and some short shorts. Mike's gun was in his hand again.

"Damn, Smith. You gonna shoot me before you say hello?" Guy even sounded like Selleck, even had the same smart aleck grin beneath the same thick lip rug.

Mike stared, put his gun away, and shook his head. "I thought I left all my bad habits behind when I retired." He shook hands with our visitor, then introduced him. "This degenerate is Detective Second Grade Abraham Horowitz, and what the hell are you doing here, man?!"

"Actually, these days it's just plain ol' Abby Horowitz, and Ace sent me." He looked around, then raised his nose and sniffed the air like an expensive and well-bred hound. "Gas and kerosene mixture would be my guess," he said.

"Ace sent you for what?" Mike queried. "And you put in your papers? When?"

"I've been a private citizen since the first day of January. And Ace thought you and your friends might need some help." He stuck his hand out, first to Yolanda, then to me. "He didn't say what kind of help but he knows how bored I am already, and how sick my wife is of me already." He shook his head sadly. "All those years of marriage about to go down the drain, just because I pulled the plug on the NYPD."

Mike offered up a commiserating and wry grin. "Took my wife about the same length of time." Then he looked at me. I looked at Horowitz, then at Yo. She looked at Horowitz and I could see her brain doing its computer thing. She was about to say something when the door swung open again.

"Dammit, I'm calling the Henrys!" is what she said. "Who are you?"

The guy standing in the door was too young to have the pot belly that stuck out over and hid his belt. He barely had facial hair. "I'm Rudy. Mr. Aiello sent me. I'm supposed to blow the smoke outta this place, then board up the windows."

I thought I understood exactly how little Alice felt on her tumble down the rabbit hole. First a deputy police chief sends me exactly what I need to work this case the way it should be worked, then a Mafia middleman sends me exactly what I need to get my office back up and running. I didn't much like the idea of being beholden to either one of them, but I also knew much better than to look a gift horse in the mouth. Whatever that meant in its literal sense.

"How many exhaust fans you got, Rudy?" Abby Horowitz was demonstrating his potential value.

"Two," Rudy said. "That's what Mr. Aiello said I'd need." He sounded slightly on the defensive, like we could blame Carmine if we needed more than two.

Horowitz, obviously a very smart man, looked at Yolanda. "You want to blow the smoke out from the top two floors first, and then get those windows closed up? Snow's in the forecast."

Yolanda gave him the look that conveyed absolutely nothing, then said, "Sure. Rudy, I'll open the front door for you and your fans," and she headed toward the front door, Abby Horowitz on her heels without a glance back, like he knew who he had to convince and impress.

I looked at Mike and he answered my question before I could ask it. "I had not a clue. Horowitz showing up here was as much a surprise to me as it was to you. But I'll tell you this: He's an okay dude. With him, what you see is what you get.

And because Ace sent him, you get Ace, too."

I knew why I thought Ace Spade thought I needed a guy like Horowitz, and even though he was right, I found myself resenting the assumption and the intrusion. "What did he work, Mike?"

"Bunko and white-collar crime."

White knight in shining armor. All that was missing was the horse. I could resent him until hell froze over; fact was I needed him. I couldn't go and I couldn't send Mike and Eddie to places Horowitz could go as a matter of right, like into the Irish and Italian neighborhoods of Long Island and Queens looking for connections to the Kearneys and the people who did their dirt for them. That's the way things were, the way they'd always been, and probably the way they always would be. My choices were few and they were boldly and brightly numbered: I could limit myself to work that kept me in my neighborhood, or I could be open-minded and receptive and let Abby Horowitz show me his moves. Or, put another way, I could have Deputy Police Chief Ace Spade in my corner, or I could have precinct Captain Bill Delaney breathing down my neck, making my life and work uncomfortable if not miserable. I also could stop thinking about things I couldn't change and do something useful like calling the gas, electric, and water companies to get service restored. I picked up the desk phone: Dial tone loud and clear. I punched in Carmine's number, listened to it ring, listened to Theresa, his wife, give their we're not at home message, and left my own, thanking Carmine for his generosity and his consideration in my time of need. Carmine likes shit like that; he's very old school that way. I think he also likes that his wife gets to hear people calling her husband a nice guy, which can't be something that happens with great regularity. Or maybe it was; maybe Carmine did unexpected and nice things for people all the time. Besides, it was the only telephone number I had for him. I could have called the pastry shop and left a message but that would have me feel a little lower down the food chain than I cared to be.

"It's cold in here," Mike said. "Call the utilities and get the heat back on."

"Why? You afraid it's going to snow?"

Mike threw back his head and laughed. "Don't blame the messenger."

Yolanda and the messenger came back in then and as soon as the door was opened, I could hear the roar of the exhaust fans. "I was just about to call the utility companies," I said. I looked at Horowitz. "They've been saying it was going to snow for a week."

"They've got to get it right eventually. What would you bet you'll get the blizzard the very time your windows are busted out?" The man made a lot of sense. I picked up the phone but Horowitz waved his hand at me and shook his head. I put the phone down. "The fire department shuts off power from a master switch outside." He reached into his pocket and pulled out a fat ring of keys, picked one and held it up. "One of my all-time favorite things to do would be to turn off all the power just before raiding one of those so-called smart crooks. We'd stage the raid for three, four in the morning. Cut the power and hit the door. No electricity, no alarm, no bedside clock, can't find the eyeglasses or the lawyer's phone number, can't open the electronic safe or the panic room. And you'd be amazed at the number of them who'd spend a small fortune—tens of thousands of dollars—on those fool-proof security systems and then neglect to spend four or five hundred bucks for a back-up generator." He laughed. "Watching those creeps crawl around in the dark, crying and cursing, alternating between mad and scared—see, we're inside their burglar-proof home and we look like space aliens in our night vision goggles—it was better than sex." Still chuckling to himself, Horowitz went back outside.

Yolanda watched his exit and then stared at the closed door for a long moment before she said, "Those fans really work. They're powered by a generator on the truck. You can actually see the smoke being sucked out," she finally said. "If Rudy gets the boards up and Abby gets the heat and lights on, it could start feeling like home aga . . . dammit!" She whipped her cell phone out of her pocket and started scrolling for a number. "I keep forgetting to call the Henrys. Too much happening all at once."

It was another half hour before all the necessary phone calls were made—including mine to Connie and a group one to Eddie, who was in his own room and mostly awake and lucid—and the heat and lights were back on and we all had a cup of coffee and were seated in the living room area of the office. I don't know if Horowitz felt as calm and relaxed as he looked but I did know that Yolanda and I were wound more tightly than was good for either of us, and that Mike was tense from watching us. Yo and I had had a quick conversation in the kitchen, agreeing that we needed Horowitz and that we could trust Mike's assessment of him. Didn't mean we liked it, though.

Yolanda let me do most of the talking as we laid out our case and I found that talking through it was calming, in a way—it gave my anger something constructive to do for those minutes; harnessed it, focused it, gave it purpose. When I finished talking, nobody said anything—either because I'd done such a bang-up job of stating the facts, or everybody was waiting for the other guy to speak first. The only sound was the gentle roar of Rudy's exhaust fans. Finally Horowitz said, "What do you need from me?"

"Help finding the Tank, help ID-ing the shooters, and help nailing the owner of this scheme." Horowitz had been nodding his head in agreement until I got to that last part. He frowned at me.

"You don't think the Kearneys own it?"

I shook my head and he watched me, waiting for me to explain myself, but his impatience got the best of him. "Why not?" And the way he said those two words demanded that I'd better be right.

"Those two guys were nothing but a couple of putzes a couple of years ago: One of 'em selling tract houses to Eastern European immigrants in the ugly part of New Jersey for way more than they were worth, and the other one pushing papers in an insurance office, a barely functioning alcoholic. Then, all of a sudden, Francis has his own real estate office, and almost immediately becomes a developer? At the same time that Thomas becomes a supervisory claims adjuster?" I stood up and paced a few steps. "These aren't fast track twenty-somethings, Horowitz, these are forty-something nobodies who have become overnight players in a game that's way too sophisticated for them. No, I don't think they own it. I don't think they own their own toothbrushes and toilet paper."

Now Horowitz got up and paced off a few steps. "You don't think this is about greed, either, do you?"

"To some extent, yeah—people like that, greed's always a factor. But that's not all of it," I said. "Or even most of it. This is about hatred. Every one of those burned out buildings the Kearneys are trying to steal belongs to a non-white immigrant."

"I might be in over my head, then," Horowitz said. "I know how to run down and hog-tie dumb fuckers motivated by greed." He ran both his hands through his head full of salt-and-pepper hair, leaving it standing on end, then he smoothed it back down. "Hatred's new territory for me."

I liked him better in that moment. I wasn't in love yet, not even feeling any warm fuzzies, but I definitely was liking him.

"Dumb fuckers motivated by anything petty and stupid—and greed and hatred fall into the petty and stupid categories—make the same mistakes," I said, and I believed that. "And under the right circumstances, they'll talk to you, let you get close enough to bring 'em down. Me they wouldn't talk to if I was the last human on the planet. Why? 'Cause I'm the wrong color. Then they end up in jail surrounded by who? People the wrong color."

We all of us needed that brief moment of levity and laughter, but it was truly brief because the next words out of Horowitz's mouth brought all my tamped-down anger right back to the surface. "You gotta call the insurance company right now. Get the claim started, get Kearney moving."

Yolanda and I looked at each other. We'd avoided making the call, not wanting to see if Kearney would be arrogant and stupid enough to come himself, or whether he'd send an underling. We guessed the latter since he'd certainly know by now that our building wasn't destroyed, and therefore withholding our claim wouldn't benefit his scheme. She opened her cell phone and hit a button. "I've almost made this call half a dozen times in the last couple of hours," she said, walking back to her desk.

I looked at Horowitz. "Don't factor the greed out just yet, and keep the stupid factored in. Every one of those buildings the Kearneys set fire to was worth over a million dollars. Green is the one color that trumps all the others."

"Is that your way of saying this building is worth more than a million dollars?" Mike asked, and when I nodded in the affirmative, he said, "Hell, I might kill you myself, then." And we let that light moment carry us until Yolanda returned.

"Somebody'll be here 'as soon as possible.' I suggested that 'somebody' visit the arson investigator first, to save us all time and trouble. My suggestion wasn't appreciated. I can't imagine why." She headed for the front door. "I'm going to check on

Rudy and the fans." She opened the front door, then turned back to us. "It's snowing."

CHAPTER ELEVEN

Mike went to visit Eddie, Yolanda was upstairs keeping an eye on Rudy and his helper while they cleaned up the broken glass and boarded up the window in her loft, and I was sacked out on the sofa, waiting for the Henrys to come repair the alarm system and for the insurance adjuster to come do whatever he was going to do. I didn't know where Horowitz was, and didn't really care. I wished that I felt differently. He seemed like an okay guy; Mike liked him and that was no small thing. I knew exactly what the problem was, and it was mine, not Horowitz's: I didn't want to need him, but need him I did. It would have been easier to accept my resentment if Abby Horowitz weren't such a likeable guy and so obviously a very smart one. But he was those things, and I was a petty, irrational horse's ass.

"We really do owe Carmine a big fat smooch." Yolanda came in from the back.

"If anybody's smooching Carmine, it's going to be you." I sat up and held out my hand to her. "I need to tell you something, been wanting to tell you all day, but we haven't had two minutes alone."

She walked toward me, her face tired, scared, and worried. "Phil, what is it?"

I pulled her down on the couch next to me and held her. "Nothing bad. Just the best. I asked Connie to marry me and she said yes." Yolanda started to cry. Really and seriously weep, a major release of the day's pent-up emotion.

"I am so happy, Phil! You are such a wonderful man and you so deserve to be loved." She hugged me and kissed me, tears forgotten. The she jumped up and ran across the room. "I gotta call Sandra. And Connie! I gotta call my sister! And Jill! Jill will want to know!" She was jumping up and down like a little kid, which is what I felt like doing. Why couldn't guys jump up and down if they were happy? Maybe Mike and Eddie would know. I planned to ask them.

Horowitz came in then and Yolanda went back behind the screens. He shook the snow off his coat and hat and boots, hung everything up, and sat down across from me. He'd gotten a haircut and a shave. With short hair and a trimmed, preppy mustache, he could easily pass for a Wall Street heavy hitter. "You clean up nicely."

He gave me a Magnum PI grin, caterpillar eyebrows dancing up and down, and I knew I wasn't the only person who'd ever noticed the similarity. "I really appreciate the opportunity to work with you on this, Phil. I don't miss being a cop, but I do miss the work I did. I was good at it—I'm still good at it—and I think I can help you guys."

"I know you can help us, Abby, and I'm glad you're willing to."

"But you wish you didn't need my help."

"That's right. I do wish we didn't need your help. At least not for the reasons we need it."

"I didn't make the world the way it is," Horowitz said.

"No," I said, "you didn't."

"What were you planning to do before I showed up?"

"I've got access to a couple of reporters."

"Effective," he said with an appreciative nod and stroking his newly-trimmed mustache, as if trying to get used to its thinness. "Not a total solution, but certainly an effective one."

"Some days I'm really happy just to be effective," I said.

He didn't have anything to say to that and I didn't have anything to add, so we sat there in the quiet, neither of us uncomfortable, and I thought that was probably a good sign. I yawned, Mike came in looking like the abominable snowman, and Yolanda came back into the office from behind the screens. She kissed the top of my head three times. "That's from Sandra, Jill, and Arlene. Connie'll deliver her own message. *Mas tarde.*"

Mike and Abby looked questions at me. I wanted to tell Mike, couldn't do it without telling Abby, so told them both. They both pumped my hand, slapped me on the back, hugged me, congratulated me, and it made me feel good that these men who were older than me, who'd been married for lots of years, were happy for me. "When did this happen?" Mike asked.

"Last night, this morning . . ." Was it only this morning?

"This morning must feel like a month ago to you," Horowitz said.

"At least that," I said, then I stood up, yawned and stretched. "But this day isn't half over and I can't spend it sitting here."

"Where are you going, Phil?" Yo asked.

"I don't know, but I can't just sit around here doing nothing!" I suddenly was edgy and jumpy and exhausted and the anger had come back. "I need to be working."

"You need to be here, Phil. We both need to be here right now. Today."

"And I really need to be able to ask you some questions, to pick your brain," Abby Horowitz said.

"We already told you everything," I said.

"You told me all the facts. You didn't tell me everything."

I shot Mike a dirty look. He returned a blank stare that transmitted a volume of unspoken communication, like how dare I think he would violate my trust by revealing protected client information to Horowitz or anybody else; like how dare I take out my frustrations on him; like why didn't I stop acting like a jackass and get down to business.

"What is it you think I didn't tell you that you think you need to know?"

"How well did you know Bill Calloway and how much did you trust him?"

"Very well and without question."

"How did you get his files?"

"Protected."

"Can I have a copy?"

I looked at Yolanda. She hesitated, just briefly, then nodded. "What else, Abby?"

"How did you get Jackie Marchand's documents?"

"Protected," I said.

"Bullshit," Horowitz said. "Marchand wasn't your client but he was a murder victim and if you took anything out of his place, if you compromised a crime scene . . ."

I cut him off. "I didn't compromise a crime scene and I don't need a lecture on procedure from you. I completed the same police academy training that you did." I watched the surprise fill his face. "You didn't know?"

He shook his head. "I knew that you and Mike were friends but I didn't know how. And you know what? It doesn't matter. I don't care. I'm looking for a strategy here, for a way in to dealing with these Kearney characters."

"I was wondering whether Casey and McQueen were connected to the Kearneys, and I'd started doing a computer check, but I got distracted," Yolanda said.

"God, Yo, how could you let something distract you from connecting all those lovely Irish names to the same stinking scam? What was it?"

"The damn Russians!" she exclaimed, and ran back behind the screens.

"What damn Russians?" Horowitz was on his feet, on Yolanda's heels.

"Hey!" I yelled at him.

He stopped in his tracks, turned, came back and sat down. "What damn Russians?"

I told him.

Horowitz was rubbing his hands back and forth against each other as he listened, hunched forward, absorbing every word. His eyes glittered and he looked less and less like cute, cuddly Magnum, and more and more like a shark following the scent of blood in the water. Yolanda came back with a sheaf of papers. Horowitz stopped rubbing his hands together and held one of them out, then, aware of himself, snatched it back. Yolanda gave him her own version of a shark-like grin, and gave him the papers.

"Where's that envelope, Phil?"

"What envelope?" I asked, then immediately remembered. I stood up, patted my pockets, then hurried back to the closet. The envelope was in my jacket pocket. I got it out, looked at it, smacked myself upside the head. The letter to the housing department from the woman in Kallen's building who thought he and Boris were the KGB. "What's this got to do with Russians, Yo?" I asked. "Just because a disgruntled tenant calls the building manager the KGB doesn't mean he is. Maybe she's just set in her ways and doesn't like the new rules." Or, I thought, maybe, like Carmine, she doesn't like Russians.

"Read the letter," Yolanda told me.

I sat down, opened the envelope, took out four pages of single-spaced copy, and started to read. It didn't take long to get to the part that started making me nervous. Everything Carmine had said replayed itself in my mind: They lie, they cheat, they steal . . . they got no rules, they got no organization, they got no morals. Everything in this lady's letter to the Housing

Department could be construed to be confirmation of everything that Carmine had said and it was scaring the shit out of me. I wanted no part of any kind of mob—Carmine's or Mike Kallen's. Mike had come over and was reading over my shoulder. "Oh, shit," he said.

"No shit," I said, and passed the letter to Horowitz.

He read quickly, put all the papers neatly together, and returned the pile to Yo.

"Russian mob?" Mike asked.

"Almost definitely," Horowitz answered.

"Prostitution ring?" I asked.

"Something a little worse than that," Horowitz answered.

"Sex slavery," Yolanda said.

Mike and I looked at each other, then at Yolanda, the question written in large letters across our faces: Slavery? Damn you, Carmine. Right again.

Yo exhaled deeply. She was equal parts mad and sad. "All those young, single female tenants in that Avenue B building, yeah, they're prostitutes, but not by choice. They're probably in this country illegally and they don't see a dime of the money they earn."

Horowitz nodded, then looked from Yo to me and back again, then at Mike. "What interesting lives you people lead. I wanna play on your team. I really do. Just tell me what to do and I'll do it, no questions asked."

The three of us exchanged looks with each other, then looked hard at Horowitz. He looked like the last kid waiting to be picked for the team. "Look, Abby. Ace Spade sent you here to help us, and I appreciate that. I really do, resentment put on the back burner where it belongs. But I can't have somebody who reports to the chief of police in my house, pretending to work for me."

"I don't report to him . . ."

"Sure you do! He didn't send you over here just because he's a nice guy."

"That's exactly why he sent me over here, Rodriquez." Horowitz hesitated, then his shark grin joined his Magnum eyebrow lift. "That and the fact that he hates Bill Delaney and he knows I'm bored to tears and that my wife is ready to kill me. He thought I could help you and, along the way, I might find something that could help him get Delaney out of his command and behind a desk downtown."

I thought about that. "He's got somebody he'd rather have commanding this precinct?" Horowitz gazed at the ceiling and at the four corners of the room and we all knew the answer to the question. I wouldn't mind having somebody in charge at the local precinct who wasn't threatening to yank my license every fifteen minutes, and I could imagine that whoever Spade wanted to replace Delaney with might be easier to get along with. "You can't be reporting to Spade, Abby."

He raised his right hand in oath-taking fashion. "I swear to God I won't."

"And our first obligation is to the client, not the police department."

"I can make the adjustment."

"It's tougher than you might think, making that adjustment," Mike said.

"I decided years ago that I served the citizens of the city, not the department."

"We sometimes walk really close to the line, legally . . ."

Yolanda's snort stopped me short and Horowitz did a pirouette. "I dance really well," he said, "toes on the line being a specialty of mine."

I looked at Mike. He looked at Horowitz, then back at me, then at Yolanda, then back at me, and nodded his head. I looked at Yolanda and she nodded her head. "All right then," I said, and extended my hand to Horowitz. He jumped up and down, then did a little dance around the room, answering the question I'd posed to myself earlier about why guys didn't do little happy dances when they were happy. Then he hugged Yolanda, hugged me, hugged Mike.

Feigning a disgusted look, Mike pushed him away. "We've got two elephant burgers on the plate here, folks," Mike said. "How're we gonna go about eating them?"

"One bite at a time, bro," I said. "One little bite at a time."

"And who's going to take the first bite of elephant ass?" Mike asked.

"Who's got the sharkest . . . I mean sharpest . . . teeth?" I asked.

Yolanda gave another snort of disgust and walked away, leaving us giggling like the boys she thought we were. "I'm going upstairs," she said.

"The front way, Yo!"

She stopped, turned, and came back. "Right. Thanks."

We didn't want any more people knowing that there were back stairs; certainly not Rudy and his helper. "You got any surveillance equipment?" Abby asked.

"Some," I said. "Why?" But as soon as I asked the question I knew the answer: To watch the comings and goings at Kallen's Avenue B building.

"Is the front door the only way in and out?" Horowitz asked.

"There's the basement door, where the garbage gets picked up, but that area's too public. Laundry room and storage lockers. You wouldn't want johns wandering around down there . . ." I stopped mid-sentence, my thoughts following my memory.

"What?" Mike and Abby said at the same time.

"At the end of the first floor hallway there's a door that was bolted and welded shut, so I don't know what it leads to." I closed my eyes and visualized the building, front and back, and where that hallway would lead. "If that door functioned—and I told Kallen that the fire code required that it did—it would be a back door. It should be a fire exit. There's a small yard behind that building, and an alley running east-west."

"That would do it," Abby said. "Johns in the front, out the back. Or vice versa."

"Mike and I can handle this. What do you need to go after the Kearneys?"

"The paper. I always follow the paper, like crumbs on the forest floor, and it always takes me home."

"Get it from Yo."

"But keep the reporter close at hand," he said.

"What reporter?" Mike asked.

"From the Buddhist temple. You remember I told you . . ."

"Yeah, yeah, yeah," Mike said, nodding his head as the memory came back. "And speaking of which, where are your yoga people? I'd think they'd have shown up by now, given that their place of work is a wading pool."

"Yo says they've been gone for a month. I don't remember her telling me that, but she says she did. They're in India at some kind of conference."

"Who are we talking about?" Abby asked.

"The second floor tenants. They run the yoga studio."

"They go to this conference before or after Epstein and his asshole friends started siccing the Feds on innocent people?" Mike asked, and it was a really good question, one I hadn't thought to pose, and I should have, because the yoga studio is run by Sikhs. Like the Buddhist monk, they are American born; and like the monk, their wardrobe reflects their religious association.

"I should know the answer to that, Mike, but I don't. And what I'm wondering, now that you ask, is whether maybe they're in hiding, whether, like Mrs. Nehru, they just decided to go away. Rational, law-abiding citizens aren't comfortable being terrorized by their own government."

"So, you're thinking now that you weren't the target of the firebug after all?" Abby asked. "That the Sikhs were the target?"

I didn't know what I thought anymore. Nothing made sense. I walked to the front door, opened it and looked out. It was still snowing. Not quite a blizzard, but it definitely was more than a dusting. If it remained cold, the stuff would stick. Rudy's truck still was parked on the sidewalk, generator humming. The writing on the side panel read AIELLO BROTHERS GENERAL CONTRACTORS. Gee. The things I didn't know. I closed the door and walked back to where Mike and Abby were sitting. I heard the door open behind me and I moved quickly sideways as both men put their hands on their weapons.

A guy I didn't know came in carrying four large bags, followed by a guy I did know.

"Henry," I said to the security system guru, relief thick in my voice. Henry would take care of the door opening and closing like a stall in a public bathroom. Then I looked at the stranger with the bags, but my nose told me what was in them. "Arlene sent you."

He nodded and shivered; snow was melting and dripping off him. "Your food's probably cold, though—sorry. I had to walk the last four blocks 'cause a four-car smash-up's got traffic stopped in all directions. I bailed on the taxi driver."

Abby and Mike took the bags of food to the kitchen while I tried to pay for it, but he wouldn't take the money; said I didn't owe anything. So I gave him a hefty tip, for which he was heftily grateful. "I haven't seen you at Arlene's before."

"I'm a friend of Brad's, we go to school together, and I help out sometimes, but Mrs. Edwards, she's got some new guy starting tomorrow." He dropped his voice into a conspiratorial whisper. "Brad's grades were falling because he was working so many hours in the restaurant, and if you know Mrs. Edwards, you know she won't stand for that." I knew what he said was true. I walked him to the door and opened it, to find Henry standing outside with a flashlight trained on the buzzer panel. I waved the kid good-bye and asked Henry what he was doing.

"Somebody's tampered with this panel, Phil." But before I could react, he said, "But don't you worry. This whole wall would have to come down before somebody could bypass this system. Nobody has ever penetrated one of my systems, and nobody ever will. That's my guarantee to my customers. I put it in writing, as you know."

I did know; it was in the maintenance contract. Still. "When you say that somebody 'tampered' with the panel, Henry, what exactly do you mean?"

"I mean it looks like somebody took a screwdriver head or a chisel and tried to pry the panel up. But like I said, it's not possible. They'd have to take down the whole wall, and even then, they'd have to know what I know to disable or bypass the system. You're safe here, Phil. Yolanda, too."

"And the system at my building, at home?"

"Exactly the same," Henry said. "These systems are new, state of the art, and fire and police departments don't like 'em. The only way to stop 'em is to cut power to the entire building, like they did this morning, which is why I have to come and reset it, and which is why you paid so much money for it." He grinned wickedly. "Worth every cent, though, isn't it?"

I agreed that it was, watched him finish, signed the paperwork, and went upstairs to tell Yolanda that she was secure again. The visible smoke was gone, and the odor almost was gone, but it was icebox cold. Rudy had done a really good job and I told him so. "There's still some water on the second floor," he said, "but most of it's been sucked out. We'll get the boards up in here so it can start to warm up. The second floor, though, that's gonna take a while longer, and I gotta break my guy for lunch."

We watched them nail the plywood up to the front window and Yo had to turn on all the lights it got so dark. I told Yo she could set her alarm and the relief on her face told me what she had never and would never say in words: That she had been truly and completely terrified. My hands itched with the desire to wrap them around the carotid artery of the fool who set this fire and squeeze. We followed Rudy down the stairs and stopped on the second floor to check out the mess that had been the yoga studio. He was right: Most of the smoke and water were gone. We'd have our building back by the end of the day. We stepped over the hose that was sucking out the water and continued down the stairs and out the door. "By the way, the alarm system is back on," I told Rudy, "so you'll have to buzz us when you get back."

He nodded and they walked off. I used my key to open the office door for Yo and me. She smelled the food immediately. "You got lunch?"

Lunch. I felt like I'd been up since last week and it was only lunchtime. "Arlene sent food." And Mike and Abby had heated it up and had plates and napkins and utensils stacked on the cabinet and ready for us. Horowitz was going to be an okay fit, but he was no Eddie Ortiz, and I knew that Mike and Yolanda were missing him as much as I was. Yolanda put on some music and we ate, not talking much, each of us, I was sure, thinking through what had happened and what was yet to come.

The phone rang and we all jumped. I waved Yolanda back down and went to my desk to answer it. It was the insurance adjuster. He couldn't make it today; the weather was really a problem. He hoped we wouldn't be too inconvenienced. I told him as long as it was him and Thomas Kearney who were coming, I didn't care how long it took. I knew my remark surprised him because of the dead silence on the line. Then he wanted to know why I'd said what I said and I told him because Kearney had a reputation among city business owners, and then I hung up, hoping he'd report back to his boss.

"Was that wise?" Abby asked.

I shrugged. I didn't care if it was wise or not; it reflected how I was feeling. Besides, I didn't want some nameless claims adjuster, I wanted Kearney. "Remember, Jackie told Raul that Kearney was a mean drunk," I said.

Yolanda finished my thought for me. "And mean drunks usually are arrogant and stupid, too. He won't be able to let it rest," she said, which is exactly what I was thinking. And hoping. We finished eating and cleaned up the kitchen, then told Yolanda what we talked about and what we'd decided to do, and asked her what she thought.

"I think we should talk to Richard King first."

"Who's Richard King?" Mike and Abby asked in unison.

"The man who signs the check," Yo said, dry as the Kalahari.

"But if they're running a sex slavery ring out of that building . . ." Abby started.

"Then Richard King has himself a very big problem, which we have a legal obligation make him aware of, and which then gives him the opportunity to hire us to help him solve that problem." Abby got down on his hands and knees, crawled over to her, and kissed her feet. She pointed at Mike and me. "I wish you'd teach them how to do that."

"You're the boss," I said.

"Which is a good thing," Mike said, "otherwise we'd all be broke."

"However," Abby said, his brow wrinkled in concentration, "wouldn't Mr. King be a lot more inclined to hire us to solve his elephant burger of a problem if we had some proof of the evidentiary nature to show him?"

"In other words, not give him the opportunity to decide to

do anything but the right thing," I added, making it both question and comment.

Yo nodded and gave us a look that said there might be hope for us after all. "Make sure your surveillance video is date and time stamped, and that it's clear what the building is."

"We got it, boss," Mike said, and saluted her.

She stood up. "I'm going upstairs to start cleaning up the mess and reclaiming my home. Let me know when Rudy and Don Corleone come back."

"Who?" the three of us said, and Yo laughed.

"Guy's from Italy, speaks no English. I asked Rudy what his name was, Rudy didn't know. The guy's somebody's cousin and he needed a job. Rudy points at what he wants done, then he waves his arms and yells at the guy. You know how some people think that talking loudly will help somebody understand a foreign language better?" Then she demonstrated Rudy's tactics.

We were all laughing when Yo started up the back stairs to her place. We heard her coming back down quickly and we all snapped to attention. "I forgot to get the fires file for Abby." She gave him a foot-thick stack of material and he groaned. "You asked for it," she said, and left us.

Mike and I familiarized ourselves with the video cameras while Abby immersed himself in the fires file. He was so engrossed he didn't hear Rudy and Don Corleone return, didn't even notice the sound of silence when the generator and exhaust fans were shut down, didn't hear the suction hose being retracted down the stairs. The only thing that roused him was the front door buzzer. He and Mike went on alert. I opened the door. It was Yolanda in hands-on-hips mode.

"He wouldn't take any money!" Something she truly didn't understand. "I'm going to write Carmine Aiello a check and he's going to take it. You tell him that."

I nodded. I'd tell him, for all the good it would do. "Let's call it a day, guys, okay?" I was way past tired. I wanted to go see Eddie, and Mike and I were going to reconnoiter the Avenue B building at dusk, so we could determine the best angles for filming. Then I wanted to go home and fall on my face. I knew Yolanda wanted to clean up her place and do the same thing. I offered to help her clean. She said thanks but no thanks; she needed to do that for herself, and I understood.

"Are you taking all that paper home with you?" Mike asked Abby.

"Yeah. I'll take a cab."

"You won't get a cab tonight. Blizzard, remember?"

He looked truly disappointed. "Oh, yeah, right." He looked at the pile of paper and sighed deeply, then selected a couple of folders from the pile. "I'll finish tomorrow."

Yolanda walked us to the door, assured me that she would be fine before I could ask her, and I heard her lock the door and I knew she set the alarm before we walked away. It had been one of the longest and strangest days of my life, and it wasn't over yet.

It was practically dark when we got outside though it was just a little past five o'clock. Just last week it had seemed that the days really were getting longer, that spring really was coming. Now it was dark at five o'clock again. I was one of the few people who'd admit to liking winter, but when it was time for it to be over, it was time for it to be over.

"Let's do the Avenue B thing first," Mike said, "so we can hang with Eddie for a while. It's the first time he'll be awake and alert."

"Works for me," I said, and the three of us, hunched inside our coats and scarves, heads down as if that would keep the snow off us, walked east for a couple of blocks, then separated, Abby to head for the uptown train, Mike and me over to Avenue B.

"Hey, Phil. Thanks," Abby said in parting.

I waved at him. "See you tomorrow, Abby." I hunched down deeper into my coat and followed Mike as he zig-zagged and snaked his way through the traffic in the street and that on the sidewalk. Everybody just wanted to get home, to get warm, to get dry. I wanted all of that, and sleep. There would be no Connie tonight; she thought it wise to go tell her parents that she was engaged. I thought it wise to call mine in Puerto Rico and tell them that I, too, was engaged. I hadn't said those words out loud to myself yet. "Hey, Mike," I called out, and he stopped in his tracks, turned around and looked at me.

"What?"

"I'm engaged."

It took him a moment, then he grinned like a big kid. "I called Helen and told her and she's very happy for you. She likes Connie. Linda does, too."

"You told Eddie?"

"No, no, no! I told her not to tell him. You get to tell him yourself. Now come on, bro, it's cold out here!" And we walked as fast as we could. Fortunately for us, lots of people on that block of Avenue B were heading home so we were fairly inconspicuous as we strolled up one side of the street, then down the other, so Mike could get the lay of the land. Then we walked around the corner, made certain that nobody was watching us, and slipped into the alley. Kallen's building was the third one in, backed by a brand-new chain-link fence, with a brand-new eight foot wooden fence snuggled up next to it. Smart: People inside the yard would see an attractive wooden fence, people outside would see a double layer of protection. There was no way to see through the fencing to the yard. There was a gate in the chain-link fence which opened out toward the alley when the latch was lifted, and which provided access to a door in the wooden fence which was locked.

"Seen enough?"

Mike nodded but just as we were about to turn away, the entire area was flooded with light. We scurried up the alley and behind a Dumpster just as we heard the chain-link gate clatter open. Two men stepped out into the alley, buttoning their coats. They said something in what I assumed was Russian to someone behind the fence, then the gate clanged shut and the latch dropped into place, followed by the thud of the wooden gate closing and the click of its lock turning. The two men walked toward the mouth of the alley. Mike and I followed, grateful for the deep snow that muffled our footfalls. We waited a few seconds, then entered the street. There still were pedestrians about and cars moving on the street, slowly, looking for the impossible, improbable parking space. We'd lost the two men we'd followed, but it didn't matter; they didn't matter. Nor did the two who were entering the front door of the building when we sauntered past; we'd seen what we needed to see. Still, I risked a glance up the steps and there, opening the door to the two new arrivals, was Boris. I nudged Mike and he looked, got a good enough picture to remember the face, and we jogged up the street, away from Boris and his whorehouse. I wondered how he kept the law-abiding residents of the building from complaining, then remembered that at least one of them called him the KGB and had written a four-page letter to the Housing Department making accusations that she couldn't prove and that city officials, if they'd gotten her letter, probably would have ignored. Good thing, then, that she gave her letter to the wrong guy that day. But Mike and I would have to gather our proof sooner rather than later, get it to King, and hope that he would move to shut down this operation before somebody—our informant for starters—got seriously hurt. Nothing benevolent about the KGB's dictatorial practices.

"Come on!" Mike shouted. He was sprinting toward a taxi

half a block away, and was at the door by the time the couple exited and paid the driver, and inside by the time I got there. I slid in and shut the door and almost immediately began the thaw; the driver had the heat on inferno. Mike told him where we were going, then said to me, "What the hell makes that dude think he can get away with doing shit like that?"

"The fact that he is getting away with it, Mike, is what makes him think he can."

"And I'm lying here in the bed, helpless as a baby." Eddie looked pretty helpless, too. He was wan and pale and he'd lost weight—his cheeks looked hollowed out and his usually bright, shiny eyes were alert though they had a hooded look about them, as if keeping them open took effort. He still had IV tubes in one arm and a drainage tube in his chest. But he was awake and he was talking. Actually, he was carping and complaining: The food sucked, the television didn't have the soccer channel, and the nurses kept waking him up to ask him how he was feeling. "I keep telling 'em I'm fine. They keep telling me I'm losing too much weight. I keep telling them their food sucks. If I could get up outta this stupid bed I'd do-si-do with 'em." He was propped up in the bed, reading glasses pushed up on his head, glaring at us like we were the culprits. I was so grateful and relieved to see and hear him acting and talking like his old self I really didn't know whether to laugh or cry. I did a little of both.

"Get outta here if you're gonna do that shit, Phil," he said.

Mike clapped me on the back, I collected myself, and we told him about Abby Horowitz, and then laid out for him everything we knew about both cases. He listened like he was prepping for an exam, like we'd be asking him questions. Instead, he did the asking, and we had answers for most of them, including whether I trusted Horowitz.

"Not yet, but I think the guy's smart, and we need him, Eddie. Or somebody like him, if we want to expand our reach. Besides, it can't hurt to have a deputy chief on our side, especially if he can get Delaney off our backs."

"Did he give you your gun back?"

"No, and he's not going to until I ask for it. And he wants me to ask for it."

"You going to?"

"Nope," I said. And hell would freeze before I did.

Eddie gave me one of his looks. "Mike can't watch your ass for the rest of your life. You need your own piece, *'mano.*"

"Then I'll get another one," I said, mostly out of anger; then a moment of calm rationality took over. "And I'll bet if I ask nicely, Deputy Chief Spade will rush through a carry permit for it, bypassing Delaney and his minions."

"Now you're thinking, bro," Mike said, and we all enjoyed the moment in which we imagined Delaney's reaction to being outmaneuvered and being helpless to retaliate, which is the part that would really singe his shorts: Delaney lived for retaliation.

Linda came back into the room then and Eddie, taking advantage of his audience, got her to agree to let Mike take her home. I didn't know whether it was because she finally was convinced that her ornery husband wasn't going to die or that she finally was just too exhausted to remain upright in a chair for another night. I told her to have Yolanda arrange to have a car take Eddie home—he was being released tomorrow, though I didn't know how with a tube running out of his chest and I said as much.

"If they can't safely remove it tomorrow, he won't be going anywhere," Linda said.

"Which is why it's comin' out," Eddie snarled.

"I'll bring you some peas and rice and jerk chicken from El Caribe to celebrate your homecoming," I told him, not willing to argue the point and betting the doctor wasn't, either.

His eyes lit up. "That was almost worth getting shot for."

Linda's eyes bored into him with a look that would freeze spit and she walked out of the room without kissing him good-bye. He was still trying to explain how he hadn't meant what he'd said. She didn't want to hear it. Even I knew better than to joke about almost being killed and I wasn't even married yet—only engaged.

I turned around and ran back into his room. "I forgot to tell you: I'm engaged." Then I did a little dance while Eddie chanted, "Go Phillip, go Phillip, go Phillip."

Chapter Twelve

The snow was turning to slush. It had stopped snowing overnight, the storm that brought it having moved up the coast, leaving a respectable though far from record-setting twelve inches. This morning, though, it was warmer by at least ten degrees, and the snow was melting. I was making my usual morning walk to work under a bright sun in a brilliantly blue sky, convinced that New York City had seen the last of winter for at least the next eight months. My feet were warmly and dryly encased in winterized Doc Martens but up top, I had traded the overcoat and ear-warming knit hat for a leather bomber jacket and a Yankees cap. Of course I had on my long underwear beneath the jeans and turtleneck and sweater because I wasn't crazy, only hopeful, but I knew that all things were relative—that people who lived in Los Angeles or Miami wouldn't consider today warm—but we New Yorkers did. I wasn't the only one traveling lighter this morning. There wasn't a long overcoat to be seen among my fellow travelers as we picked our way carefully through the slush.

There was a crowd at Willie's newsstand this morning which meant that we didn't have the opportunity to talk, but he winked his one eye at me, and actually smiled, which was a first. Mrs. Campos's juice and fruit stand was busy this morning, too. Warm weather not only brought people out, it made them want to linger while they were out, instead of hurry to get inside, and a fresh-squeezed juice bar on an almost-spring morning was a great place to linger. I blew Mrs. Campos a kiss, grabbed the usual carrot juice for Yo, orange juice for me, and a couple of extras, just in case, and rejoined the throng of lingerers on the sidewalk. Walking, always difficult on the narrow East Village streets, was made treacherous as well by the mounds of snow left by the plows, and that shoveled to the curb by businesses and buildings. I gave up on the sidewalk and joined the slow-rolling traffic in the street, moving faster, most of the time, than it was.

For the first time since we'd bought it, Yolanda and I, I took no joy in the sight of my building when I turned the corner and it came into view. The boarded up windows up top and in the middle made the place look like the loser of a heavyweight title fight the day after the bout. There were smoke smudges on the upper façade, and some idiot, asshole, jerk had tagged the downstairs façade with some stupid, asshole graffiti! I was so pissed I almost dropped the bag of juice, looking for my keys.

Yolanda was inside when I got there. All the lights were on and some kind of gentle, sweet classical music was on the radio, and she was smiling and happy, and I really didn't want to sully the beauty and warmth of the room, but damn, I was mad! And she knew it. "Phil, what's wrong?"

"Some asshole wrote on the building."

"What!" She ran to the door and out, then back in and straight back to her desk. I heard her punching numbers, could visualize her, hands on hips, foot tapping, waiting for an answer on the other end. I heard her slam the phone down with a curse, then she stormed back out. "What time is it?" she demanded.

"A little after eight, Yo."

"Oh." She calmed then, and I guessed she'd called the insurance adjuster. "Do we have any paint? Or anything that can take that crap off the wall?"

"No, but I'll call Horace."

"Tell him he's got to handle this right away, Phil."

I went to my desk, picked up the phone, looked at the list of numbers in the speed dial, and punched the button next to Maintenance. Horace Gordon Janitorial Service took care of our building, inside and out. His wife, who ran the office, answered, and I told her what I needed. She said somebody would come immediately, and I knew that somebody would. Still, I wasn't expecting the door buzzer to sound two seconds after I hung up the phone. Yolanda asked—no, she demanded to know—who was there. It was Mike, and she buzzed him in.

"Some stupid asshole wrote graffiti shit on your building," he said by way of greeting. He, too, was dressed like a person who didn't want to wait another second for spring's arrival. He held aloft a brown bag. "Bagels, lox, and cream cheese, the bagels still warm."

I followed him to the kitchen, put the food and juice on one tray, plates, utensils, and napkins on another, and took them out to the table. Yolanda brought mugs and the pot of freshly brewed coffee. And the door buzzer sounded again. I answered this time. It was Horowitz and I buzzed him in. I didn't want to say anything, but this having to get up and go ask who it was every time somebody wanted in was getting annoying. Then I thought about the Tank being able to barge in unannounced again and got over my pique.

"Some asshole wrote on the building," Horowitz said as he breezed in. He stopped in his tracks when he saw the food. "That's from that deli on 51st."

Mike nodded. "Yep. Best lox in Manhattan."

"I know that," Horowitz said, "but how do you know that?"

Mike ignored him, spread cream cheese on one half of a bagel, put two pieces of the thinly cut fish on it, then spread cream cheese on the other half of the bagel and put it on top of the sandwich, and took a bite. He smiled as he chewed. Horowitz quick-stepped to the back to hang up his coat—he hadn't abandoned his overcoat in anticipation of spring's arrival—and when he came back out, I saw why. He had on a suit that I recognized because I'd thought long and hard about justifying the cost of it—even on sale at Barney's, its cost required justification. He'd gelled his hair so that it lay closely and neatly to his skull. He'd removed his galoshes to reveal beautiful, gleaming black wingtips. Yolanda gave him a wolf whistle, and Mike stopped chewing long enough to give him an admiring look.

"You sure you're in the right place?" I asked.

"If you saved me some breakfast I am."

Yolanda pointed to the tray. "There's your plate, cup, knife, and fork."

"You gonna eat food in that suit?" I was horrified.

"I learned how to eat without feeding my clothes when I was about five," he said, and proved it. He made the same sandwich Mike had and ate every bit of it, never dropping a single crumb. We all had a juice and cup of coffee and declared ourselves ready for work. I took the trays to the kitchen and Yolanda went to see if Horace had sent somebody to clean the front of the building. I was washing dishes and thinking about Connie when Yolanda called me to come out front. The tone of her voice said come right this minute. I dried my hands and went out front. We had a new arrival and instinct told me who he was before Yo did; the red, broken lines in his bulbous nose gave him away.

"This is Thomas Kearney," she said, "and he wants to know why we boarded up the windows before he had a chance to assess the damage."

"Were you in Miami yesterday, Mr. Kearney? Is that the reason you didn't get here to assess the damage caused by the arson fire on the second floor?"

"You think you're smart, don't you Rodriquez?"

I didn't say anything, then I realized he was waiting for an answer. I looked at Mike, who was sitting on the sofa reading the newspaper. His legs were crossed and he looked quite comfortable. I knew his gun was in his lap. Horowitz, now wearing a pair of tortoiseshell glasses I hadn't seen him put on, had his butt perched on the edge of my desk, long legs outstretched, arms crossed over his chest, the right hand inside his jacket, resting, I knew, on his gun. Yolanda's arms were crossed over her chest, too; tightly. She was controlling her weapon as well—her mouth. I knew what she wanted to say to Kearney and it was only strength of will that kept her lips tightly together. "I assume you have a copy of the fire inspector's report," I said to Kearney.

"You can assume whatever you want. I want to know why you thought you could go ahead and board up those windows before I had a chance to assess the damage."

"I want to know why you thought I'd leave my building wide open and exposed to a blizzard." I took a step closer to Kearney and he flinched. I enjoyed the moment.

"You just jeopardized your claim, Rodriquez. You shoulda left things alone."

"I don't think that's true," Horowitz said, pushing away from the desk and raising himself to his full height.

"Who the hell are you?"

Abby took a card from his pocket and flipped it toward Kearney as he said, "Abraham Horowitz, Esquire, at your service."

Kearney caught the card, read it, and turned even more red. "What do you want here? Who called you? You're not needed here!"

"I obviously am needed here, since you've threatened, in violation of several statutes and laws, to withhold payment of my clients' claim . . ."

"I did no fuckin' such thing!" Spit flew from Kearney's

mouth and I backpedaled. "We just have rules, guidelines that have to be followed," he shouted.

"Nowhere in your policies and practices manual, or in the client contract, does it say that property is required to be left open to the elements until after an adjuster's inspection. In fact, just the opposite is required." Horowitz sounded so believably calm that Kearney almost believed him.

"How do you know what's in my company's policies and practices manual?"

"I get paid to know things like that, Mr. Kearney."

"Then you know what it says about fires of suspicious origin?"

"If you read the arson investigator's report, you'll see that the origin wasn't all that suspicious. A kerosene and gasoline mixture, thrown through the second floor window, fire damage contained on that floor, smoke throughout the building."

"You don't know everything, do you, smart ass? Terrorist activity negates all other contractual provisions."

"And what terrorist activity would that be, Mr. Kearney? Unless you consider, as I do, that burning down somebody's business is an act of terrorism?" Abby said.

"I'm talking about the Patriot Act, smart ass. I'm talking about terrorists in our midst, out to destroy our country." Kearney was on a roll, puffed up and pleased with himself. Mike had lowered his paper and had his gun in his hand.

"And what has any of that to do with the fire here yesterday morning? Unless you consider Mr. Rodriquez or Miss Aguierre terrorists?"

"Not them, smart ass, the ones upstairs. They're terrorist threats, according to the Department of Homeland Security."

"And you know this how, Mr. Kearney?"

"Don't you worry about how I know."

"If you know anything about what's contained in DHS files, Kearney, you came by it illegally. Federal agents don't share their information with people who work for insurance companies." Horowitz no longer sounded calm. His voice sounded like the steel gate slamming shut on prisoners in, well, the slammer. "And by the close of business today, I'll have that little mystery solved. And by the close of business today, you'll have a check cut for Mr. Rodriquez and Miss Aguierre . . ."

"The fuck I will!"

Abby reached into his pocket and brought out what looked like a thin, silver cigarette lighter. He flicked it and it whirred. He flicked it again and Kearney heard himself talking about things he should know nothing about. He paled and tried to say something, sounding like a traumatized stutterer. "The fuck you will," Abby said, back to his calm, quiet voice. "Now get out of here."

Kearney turned and left. Silence reigned until Mike broke it.

"You're a lawyer? Since when?"

"For a while," Horowitz said. "I thought I'd need something to do when I left the Job. But that was before I met youse guys." He grinned as the New Yorkese slid from his lips.

"Good choice from where I stand," I said.

"How much of what you said to Kearney was bullshit?" Mike asked.

"Wonder how far he's going to get before he has to stop at a bar," Yo said.

"I'll bet he's got a half pint in his pocket," Mike said, and we all rushed to the door to see if we could catch Kearney drinking from the bottle down the block somewhere. What we saw was Horace cleaning graffiti off the front wall.

"Bless you, Horace!" Yolanda said, and ran back inside. "I'm going to call the contractor, what's his name, Phil? See if he can get windows in today. I felt imprisoned up there with that board across the front wall."

"Bulletproof all the way up," I said, following her back in.

"You ready to go surveil the KGB?" Mike asked.

"Chomping at the bit," I said. I looked at Abby. "I think you're a keeper, dude." Then I called out to Yolanda, "Can we afford to keep Abby?"

"If you and Mike can give KLM Property Management a good reason to expand and extend their contract with us, we can."

Abby made shooing motions toward Mike and me with his hands. "Go forth and collect compromising photographic images of corrupt Russians."

Mike and I got the cameras. We'd decided last night before we separated how we'd do this: We'd shoot both the front and back entrances today; I'd shoot the front door tonight; Mike would shoot the back gate tomorrow night; Yolanda would complete running the background checks on Kallen and on the limousine driver who'd bailed on Kallen and me the other morning; and we'd have a package ready to present to Richard King at KLM first thing Monday morning. I'd ask Shirley Golson, who referred us to KLM, to arrange the meeting. She'd do it, too, and make sure that Richard King didn't let on to Kallen that he was meeting us in secret.

Eddie, the car-service driver who helped us get Sammy Epstein home, was waiting for us outside. We'd asked for him, and told his dispatcher that we needed an inconspicuous ride—nothing too flashy, nothing too raggedy, just a regular New York City kind of car. Eddie was behind the wheel of a Ford Explorer that looked as if it had spent the previous night driving about in the blizzard, which it probably had. We climbed in, me in front, Mike in back. We told Eddie we were glad to see him, he thanked us for asking to work with him, and he asked us where our Eddie was. We told him our Eddie was home sick, and told him where we were going and what we needed to do. "Piece of cake," Eddie said.

And at first, it seemed that it would work just that way. We let Mike out in the alley beside the Dumpster that we'd hidden behind the night before. The absence of human footprints in the drifting and melting snow said it was an area not popular for foot traffic; all the footprints were outside the chain link fence and headed in the opposite direction. Eddie drove me back around to the front, the filthy truck double-parked across the street from building as if waiting for a parking space. I hunkered down in the back seat and shot video of men entering the front door of the building, admitted by Boris, and, thanks to the telephoto lens and the sparkling clean glass of the front door, watched as they walked through the lobby and toward the hallway where I knew the new female tenants lived. After an hour, we drove around the back to pick Mike up. If he'd shot the kind of video I had, we'd call it a day.

"How many girls did you say he had in there?" Mike asked, getting into the truck.

"Seven that we know about. Why?"

"There have to be more than seven. Either that or Boris is rotating johns through every half hour, which means those girls are being treated worse than slaves. Let's get outta here, I've seen enough. Or let me go in there and kick some sorry Russian ass." And this from a cop who'd walked a beat in Harlem during some of that neighborhood's worst days.

We drove back around front, slow enough to see, not so slow as to attract attention. "What's he doing?" Mike asked.

It looked like Boris was trying to stop a man from entering the building. "Maybe you have to have an appointment?" Mike lowered his window and stuck his head out.

"Don't do that, Mike!"

"Listen! The dude's saying he's trying to visit a friend, he's telling Boris . . . he's saying . . . 'you can't tell me who I can visit' . . . he's, it doesn't sound like he's one of johns," Mike said, just as Boris pushed the guy down the stairs.

I jumped out of the truck and hurried across the street, Mike on my heels. Mike bent down to help the guy to his feet while I hustled up the front stairs. "Hey, Boris!" I called out cheerfully. "Looks like you're having a little trouble. Anything I can do to help?"

He looked at me like I was a pile of alligator shit. I got in his face. I wanted him to do something stupid. Then he looked closely at me and his face relaxed. "You're security expert."

"That's who I am," I said. "Should I call Mike, tell him you're having some . . ."

"No!" Boris all but shouted. "No need to disturb Mik . . . Mr. Kallen. Everything now is okay. Is fine now." He was waving me away, would have pushed me down the steps, too, if he thought he could have gotten away with it.

"Who's that guy?" I asked, pointing to the man Boris had assaulted, because that's what throwing somebody down a flight of steps was: Assault.

"Is nobody. Doesn't live in building," Boris said, looking over my shoulder now, and peering up and down the block. Waiting for customers with appointments, I guessed.

"I came to see a friend," the man yelled up the steps at us. "She has the flu and I came to bring her medicine! She called and asked me to pick it up!" I turned around to see him waving a pharmacy bag. "This asshole won't even let me ring her door buzzer, to let her know I'm here! Keeps telling me I don't live in the building, like I don't know where the fuck I live!"

I looked at Boris. He looked at me. "What are you doing here, Phil? That's your name, right? Phil?"

"That's my name, Boris, and my friends and I were passing by and we slowed down so I could tell them about your wonderful building, and we saw what looked like a fight and I told my friends that I knew you and we stopped to help. Good

Samaritans, you know?" I stopped talking and left the weight squarely on Boris's narrow shoulders.

He looked past me toward the street, then at his watch. "No help is needed, thank you. You can go now."

"I'm going to give you some advice, Boris, for free. I'll call Mike myself and tell him I won't even charge you for it. It's this: In this country, you can't stop a person from visiting a friend. The man has the right to ring his friend's bell, and if his friend lets him in, you can't stop him from entering."

"You don't tell me who comes in my building," Boris said in the nastiest tone of voice I'd heard in a long time.

I whipped out my cell phone and flicked it open. "Now it's gonna cost Mike some money," I said, punching in some numbers. Boris made a lunge for my phone. I was expecting him to do something like that, and I sidestepped him. He almost fell face first down the steps. I grabbed him and pulled him back. "You've got a lot to learn about being an American, Boris," I said, and shoved him at Mike who caught him by one arm and twisted. Hard. I started punching numbers on my phone again.

"Nigger! You let me go!"

Mike snatched Boris' arm so hard and so far up his back the little Russian was standing on his toes, looking like he was dancing. "What did you say to me, you ugly piece of foreign dog shit?"

"Mike."

He looked at me. "How do people like him get into this country?"

I looked at Boris. "Maybe he snuck across the border. Is that what you did, Boris? Made a midnight run across the Canadian border when the Mounties were looking for terrorists?"

The Russian groaned and shook his head, then he looked down at the sidewalk, at the all-but-forgotten reason we all were engaged in our little dance. "Okay! Okay! He can go visit friend. You! Go! Go!" The bewildered visitor, still holding the pharmacy bag aloft as evidence, ran up the steps, past Boris doing his tippy-toe dance, and into the building, without a backward glance. "You go, too," Boris said to me. "And him," gesturing with his head over his shoulder to Mike.

"Should I let him go, Phil, or throw him down the steps?"

Boris give a shrill squeal. "No, no! Let me go!"

Mike looked at me. I shrugged; I didn't care whether he tossed the smarmy little bastard down the steps or not. Mike gave his arm another twist and let him go. Boris backed away, glowering.

"That's my friend, Mike," I said to Boris. Then I looked at the cell phone I still held. "And speaking of which, in all the excitement, I forgot to call the other Mike—your Mike."

"Is not necessary to call my Mike. I understand now," he said, rubbing his arm and smiling at me. I thought the smile was weird until I realized that someone was coming up the steps behind me. I stepped aside then turned to face the new arrival. I knew I'd be considered guilty of ageism in some quarters, but this was an old man. I heard Mike's snort of disgust so I turned around and headed back down the steps to Mike, and we headed for the truck.

"Whatever those girls earn, it's not enough for that."

"If they're slaves, Mike, they're not earning anything."

Yolanda was ready to call Shirley Golson to ask her to set up the meet with KLM's Richard King as soon as we told her what we'd seen and heard. "With what we've already got, why do we need nighttime video, too?"

"Just to emphasize the point, Yo. To show King that it's an around-the-clock enterprise."

"I don't think we're going to need to show King anything

other than proof that Mike Kallen, aka Mikhail Kalenski, is an international fugitive," she said.

"Do we want him to fire Kallen for lying on his resume, or do we want him to hire us to prove that Kallen is running a sexual slavery ring, and to keep the shit off him and his company when it starts flying? 'Cause if it's the latter, we need the night-time video, too, Yo," I said, feeding her back her own argument.

"You're right," she said, clenching and unclenching her fists at her sides. "I'm just so damn mad! But getting mad doesn't get us paid, does it?"

"Where's Abby?"

She rolled her eyes and shook her head as if I'd asked her about the latest antics of one of her many nieces or nephews. "He said he was going to pay a 'courtesy' visit to the Department of Homeland Security." I was waiting for her to look angry, but she didn't. I antagonize a DHS agent and she gets mad at me. Horowitz does the same thing and it's a schoolboy prank? She must've known what I was thinking because she said, "I think he wants to play his tape recording of Kearney's knowledge of a terrorist threat that nobody else seems to know anything about. Which brings up the matter, by the way, of our tenants: If they were targeted as terrorists, you could be right, they could have just walked away rather than endure the hassle."

The thought made me sad. I didn't know them well, didn't see them very often, but they were kind, gentle people, and they seemed to be building a good business for themselves. I really would like a hand-to-hand combat session with Kearney or Casey or McQueen or Epstein or whoever was responsible if their actions had frightened my tenants into leaving the country. My fist smashing into one of their faces probably wouldn't make Ravi Patel or Nehru or the Buddhist monk or my Sikh tenants feel one bit better, but it would do wonders for me. "Did you call about the window glass?"

"Installation first thing tomorrow morning."

"Good," I said. "That's good." I still wanted to hit something, somebody. The person selling women into slavery, the person turning American citizens into terrorist suspects, the person torching and stealing businesses from hardworking men and women: Any or all of the above would do.

"You got the paperwork for your carry permit?" Mike asked.

"You've already got a carry permit. Don't you?" Yo asked.

"Yeah," I said. "But Delaney has my weapon and I'll be damned if I'll get on my knees and ask for it back. So I'm going to a get a new weapon and ask my new friend, Deputy Police Chief Ace Spade, to rush through a carry permit for it."

"Brilliant, huh?" Mike said.

"If you say so," Yolanda said, and retreated to the back.

"What?" Mike said.

I shrugged. "I gotta get outta here, Mike, gotta go do something."

"Something like what?"

I'd been thinking of something, trying not to think of it, but not able to stop myself. "I'm wondering if Jackie's journal is still in his apartment." I was also wondering whether Carmine had had his little chat with Joey Mottola, but I wasn't going to tell Mike that. I wasn't going to tell anybody about my private Carmine conversations, including his feelings about Eastern Europeans.

"It probably wouldn't be tough to get into the building, but if the apartment is still sealed . . ." He shrugged and raised his palms. He didn't say we couldn't get into the place, though.

"Let's go see," I said. We told Yolanda we'd be back in a couple of hours, then left before she could ask where we were going. I didn't want to lie to her about what I was doing, and I didn't want her worrying, which she would be doing if she knew where we were going.

"I'm not walking," Mike said, and we hopped a taxi, then made the driver stop to let us out after a couple of blocks of him seeming to go out of his way to splatter slush on pedestrians. The light caught the cabbie at the corner and one of the guys he'd splashed just before we got out ran up to the taxi and threw a brick through the window, then ran off down the street.

"You can fuck with some of the people some of the time," I said.

"But you can't fuck with all the people all the time and get away with it," Mike said, and we walked the rest of the way to Jackie Marchand's building, keeping an eye out for drivers who got their kicks making pedestrians dodge cold, filthy water.

We stopped two blocks away from Jackie's building and eyeballed it from across the street, looking for signs that anybody was watching the building or guarding it. Nobody entered or exited for the few minutes we watched it; no cars stopped in front of the building; no cars left parking spaces near the building. "I'll take the first recon," Mike said, and moved off down the sidewalk toward the building. I watched to see if anybody was watching him. He passed the building and turned the corner. I gave him a couple of minutes, then I walked past the building going in the opposite direction. I didn't know exactly where Mike was but I knew he'd positioned himself to see if there was any reaction to my movement past the building. Nothing on both counts.

We reconnected at the corner. "I'm going in," Mike said, and walked off before I could argue with him, so I crossed the street and stood directly in front of the building so I could see inside. Not that seeing inside the front door would help much if Mike got into trouble inside Jackie Marchand's apartment, but I felt better for making the effort. I was thinking that this wouldn't take long because apartments are at a premium in this city; always have been, probably always will be. There was nothing special about this building—it wasn't luxurious or historic or architecturally interesting—but it was far from being a dump and it was in a decent neighborhood, the subway a block away. A one-bedroom unit would rent quickly and the manager would want to get it back on the market as quickly as possible.

I looked at my watch. Mike should have been back by now . . . if he hadn't been able to get in. My pulse quickened. He was inside Jackie's apartment. My pulse quickened again. Either that or he was laid out in the hallway, bleeding to death. "Stop that!" I made myself get rid of that thought, that image, and replaced it with a much more pleasant one—celebrating with Connie tonight. I looked at my watch again, wondered if I'd find Carmine at the pastry shop this time of day, saw Mike coming through the building lobby and willed my pulse to return to normal.

"You look like you didn't think I'd make it back out, bro."

"Get outta my head, Mike."

He grinned his shark grin, then waved his big hand in my face. I almost missed what was in it. "Am I good or what?" He dangled the brown leather book in my face.

"Better than an ice cream sundae in August, bro. Where was it?"

"In the same boot as the other stuff, but laying flat, all the way down in the toe part. That's why I missed it the first time. Second time's the charm, though."

Maybe not. "Is it really all in French?"

Mike sobered, too, then nodded. "Every word of it. Read it and weep."

I took the small book, opened it, and flipped through the pages of small, neat handwriting, line after line, page after of page, of words in a language I didn't speak or read. Half the people I knew spoke Spanish. For reasons I still didn't understand but which, Yolanda said, had something to do with not wanting to be predictable, Sandra spoke fluent German. Then there were Mike Kallen and Boris and the Russians. Why didn't I know anybody who spoke French? I had a thought, whipped out my phone, found my address book, and punched a number. I identified myself, offered a polite greeting, and asked her receptionist (whose name I never remembered) if Dr. Mason had a moment. She did, coming on the line almost immediately, happy to hear from me, thrilled about my engagement, wondering why I was calling. I told her. She laughed, said the way my brain worked was amazing, and yes, she spoke and read French and would be happy to help with a translation. She'd see me tonight after her last patient. I'd agreed and closed the phone before I remembered that I was to shoot video at the Avenue B building tonight.

"No sweat. I'll take care of that, then meet you back at the office, and we'll all go to Eddie's together."

Shit. I'd forgotten about going to Eddie's, too. I flipped open the phone again and called Connie. She said she'd be happy to help us welcome Eddie home tonight. I took a moment to wonder if there was anything else I'd forgotten to do. Then Mike and I split up, him going back to the office to review the video we'd shot and to help prepare the presentation for Richard King of KLM Property Management, me to the midtown gun dealer to pick out a new weapon, and then, perhaps, to the gym for a much needed and way overdue workout. It wouldn't do to get engaged and get flabby.

Unlike a lot of cops, I'd never been a gun nut. I didn't hate them the way Yolanda did, I just didn't love 'em. I didn't necessarily want them banned unless somebody could guarantee that no bad guy would ever be able to get his hands on one, and since I had no hope of that ever happening, the good guys needed to be able to keep the bad guys at bay. I wished I could be like Harry Potter and wave a wand and turn murdering, racist creeps into something—anything—but what they were. Since I couldn't, I'd do the next best thing, which was to buy myself a new gun.

Choices, choices. Who knew there were so many different kinds of guns, so many different gun manufacturers? When I left the cops, I'd bought a Glock 9mm because that's what I knew, what I knew how to use. I suppose I'd had choices back then; I just hadn't known I did. Now, wow. A guy I was certain was a former cop came over to help me. I admitted up front my ignorance, told him I'd just as soon buy another Glock since that's what I knew. He patted me on the back in a fatherly way, which didn't rankle because he was probably old enough to be my father—I put him late fifties to sixty—and asked if I minded a few suggestions. I told him I didn't mind at all. He asked, politely, if he could see my PI ID, and I politely showed it to him. Then he went back behind a display counter, looked at several shelves, made some selections, and came back to me with a box of handguns. A box of them. He saw my reaction, gave me another pat on the back, and told me to follow him down to the basement shooting range. Prepared to be bored and just wanting to get it over with, I followed.

I wouldn't admit it to another living soul, but I hadn't had so much fun in a really long time. I felt like a kid, loading one gun after the other and emptying it at the target. It also felt pretty good that I was a pretty good marksman, something I'd never given much thought to. It was a requirement at the training academy, and like the other requirements, I'd done my best to succeed, finishing near the top of my class. That's something I hadn't given much thought to, either, probably because it hadn't mattered in my family where I'd finished in my training academy class: Nobody related to me was proud that I was a cop. They'd learned to be proud that I was a college student, then a college graduate, but they couldn't figure out going to college to be a cop. In my neighborhood, cops weren't considered great intellectuals or worthy role models. No matter how hard I tried to explain the long term plan, they didn't get it. Or didn't want to, though all four of my grandparents offered major prayers of thanks that I didn't turn out to be a hoodlum. Better a cop than a hoodlum.

I surprised myself by purchasing two guns, neither of them a Glock. I bought a SIG Sauer 9mm and a smaller Sauer 25mm which I'd probably never use, though the salesman made a convincing argument for possessing a smaller, concealable weapon. I had no intention of ever wearing a gun strapped to my ankle. Okay, truth? I bought it with Yolanda in mind. Though she professed to hate them, she never let me go out on a job without mine, which meant that she knew and understood their usefulness. I thought that perhaps now, in the wake of the Tank's minor rampage in our office, and the fire, that perhaps she'd reconsider. And if not, should Bill Delaney ever have cause to relieve me of the SIG, I'd already have a backup.

I paid for my guns, filled out the necessary paperwork, said I understood about the mandatory thirty day waiting period, and left the gun shop fully intending to go to the gym, not realizing that I'd spent more than three hours shooting at moving targets. No time for the gym; barely time to grab a bite to eat before heading over to Jill Mason's office. I called Yolanda, told her where I was, what I'd been doing, and where I was going. She told me, gleefully, that Big Apple Insurers had had a messenger deliver a check. Then, something between worry and pique replacing glee, she said she hadn't heard from Abby and didn't know where he was, that all calls to his cell phone went directly to voice mail. Before I could decide whether or not to worry, though, she told me not to worry about it, told me she'd see me later at Linda and Eddie's, and disconnected the call.

The sidewalks and streets were even more of a watery, slushy mess than they had been earlier in the day. It had gotten warmer during the day than the forecasters thought it would and the snow melt run-off was moving faster than the gutters could handle all that water, and most drivers didn't seem to realize the connection between speed and a horde of attack-pedestrians: Reminiscent of the taxi driver earlier in the day, a guy driving a Subaru who had just sped down the block, drenching half a dozen pedestrians, got caught at the light at 4th Street and Avenue A. He was truly shocked when his car was pelted with ice and snowballs, but he wasn't angry enough to roll down his window to hear the curses thrown his way, too.

I wolfed down a sirloin burger and fries at a gourmet hamburger restaurant on Fifth Avenue, and bought a carton of chili and a French roll to take to Jill. If this had been a normal day, she would have worked right through lunch and wouldn't realize how hungry she was until confronted with food. Still healing from the loss of her husband and children, still adjusting to the move back downtown to her Lower East Side roots from the privileged existence of the Upper East Side, she tended to push herself beyond most reasonable bounds, tended to give more of herself than was wise. Like agreeing to meet me tonight to translate Jackie Marchand's journal: She'd have said yes to my request no matter how tired or hungry she was.

"Oh, bless, you, Phillip!" she said when she saw the bag with the food in it. "How did you know I was starving?"

"Anybody who's known you longer than fifteen minutes knows you forget to eat lunch most days," I said, following her through the now empty reception area, back to the warmly elegant office where she saw her patients.

"So, you've piqued my interest. What am I translating?"

"Nothing until you eat," I said.

She tried to shoot me a threatening look but it failed miserably, and as I often did, I ached for her and for the two little girls whose tragic deaths robbed her of years of mothering, which is probably why she gave so much to her patients. "Fine," she said primly. "If you insist."

"I do," I said.

She changed in an instant, rushing to wrap me in a bear hug, which would have been really funny if it hadn't been so endearing, given that she's barely a couple of inches over five feet and couple of pounds over a hundred. "Congratulations, Phillip! I am so very happy for you and Connie! You must tell me everything!"

"You already know everything," I said, sitting on the chair adjacent to her desk, while she sat at the desk and opened the chili. "It's the middle of night, I can't sleep, I'm in the living room pacing, Connie comes in, I asked her to marry me, then the phone rang. It was Yolanda telling me our building was on fire. Then Connie and I rushed to the office, the building didn't burn down, Connie said she was going to work, I said she hadn't given me an answer, she said yes, and Bob's your uncle."

Jill was laughing so hard she'd choked on a mouthful of chili and I had to get up and slap her on the back, then get her a bottle of water from the little refrigerator in the corner of her office, next to the bookcase. She drank water and I slapped her on the back some more, and she finally settled down. She was still laughing, but she wasn't choking. "That was just so romantic, until you got to the Bob part. Where on earth . . ." She started laughing again, this time patting herself on the back to keep from choking.

"I've always wanted to say that," I said, laughing too. "The British have the best sayings, don't they? 'Bob's your uncle.' I mean, what does that mean?" She was laughing again. "I'm going to the bathroom and I'm not coming back until you've finished eating." And I left the room, found the bathroom in the hallway between her office and the patient reception area, washed my hands and face, put some water in my hair and smoothed it down, and then went back to Jill's office. She was putting the empty chili carton and napkins in the trash.

"That was very good. Thank you."

"I should have gotten the big one."

She shook her head. "That was fine, though you'll have to tell me where you got it. I may want to get the big one to take home. Tonight's my television-watching night!" She sounded as excited as a little kid. She'd recently gotten a digital video recorder from the cable company and recorded the programs she wanted to watch. Then, once a week, she watched television, all her favorite programs in one night. "A big bowl of chili and some more of that good French bread . . . and speaking of which . . . ?"

I gave her Jackie's little notebook and she sat back down at her desk, positioned the lamp head for reading, put her glasses on, and began to read. She took a pad from her desk drawer, and pen. I may as well have not been in the room. She read several pages, then turned back and began to write. A couple of times she shook her head. Her brow furrowed. Once she looked surprised. She continued to read until she was finished, then she wrote, occasionally going back to check something, but writing swiftly and surely. When she finished she looked up at me, a sad, worried look. "Would you like to tell me what this is all about, Phillip?"

"Would I like to? No. But I will tell you." And I did tell her. All of it. When I finished she stood up, tore the pages of translation from the note book, folded them, stuck them inside the little leather notebook, and walked around the desk to stand in front of me.

"What you have here is vindication for Jacques Marchand. He writes that he saw one of the people in the insurance office try to read what was in this notebook. He writes that he realized how foolish it was to keep the diary when his colleagues suspected him, but he planned to collect enough evidence to bring them all down." She held out the book and the papers to me. "Vindicate this brave, foolish young man, Phillip."

"That's my plan," I said, "but I'd appreciate it if you'd lock this little notebook in your safe. I'll take the translated pages and hope we can use the information to leverage the proof we need to send some people to jail."

"Why can't you use the diary itself?" I hadn't told her quite everything, like how I came to be in possession of the diary. "Jacques didn't give you this, did he?"

"No, he didn't," I said, and she wisely asked no more. I stood up. "Thank you."

"You're welcome." She walked me to the front door. "The chili?"

I told her where to get the chili, gave her a hug, and went out into the night. It was dark and cold. Not frigid, not ass-freezing cold, but cold enough that if I saw a vacant taxi, I'd ride back to the office instead of walk back. I zipped my jacket all the way up and raised the collar and was turning the corner on to Second Avenue when a hard blow to my left shoulder staggered me. I whipped around, arms and hand instinctively up, and grabbed for what I saw ready to come down on me again. I took most of the force of the blow on my right forearm and managed to get a loose hold on whatever it was with my left hand. I pushed and pulled at the same time, throwing my assailant slightly off balance. Slightly because it was the Tank.

"You shoulda paid me the five hundred like I asked you, motherfucker." His breath stank of beer and hot dogs, and his person stank of the prolonged absence of soap and water. He was not much taller than me but outweighed me by maybe a hundred pounds. True, he was fat, but he was as strong as an ox, and pushing against him felt like pushing against one, too.

"What's the matter, Kearney doesn't pay you enough so you have to hustle me?"

He grabbed my jacket collar and yanked me toward him like I was a junior high school kid and not a grown man, older than himself. "What do you know about Kearney?"

"That he doesn't trust you with the big jobs, big boy."

"Yeah, he'd rather trust a Jew than his own blood." He loosened his grip and I took advantage of the opportunity and plunged my right fist into his belly and met nothing but layers and rolls of fat. He, on the other hand, hit me hard, with his fist, against the side of my head, and I saw stars. I stomped down hard on his instep and his high-top Chucks were no match for my Doc Martens. He yelled, cursed, and tried to dance out of the way, but I now was holding on to him instead of the other way around. I was pounding on his back, which was having no effect, and he wasn't about to let one of my feet near his again, so we danced around like that for a moment. Finally he gave me a good shove away from him and I lost my balance in the slush and went down hard. He kicked me but I was rolling over so the kick didn't land squarely, but the foot stomp to the ribs did. He was trying for another when I grabbed his foot. I knew he was coming down and there was nothing I could do to stop him from coming down on me. I couldn't breathe—not that I wanted to with him lying on top of me; his stink made me gag. The only positive aspect to this position was that he couldn't kick me again, but neither of us could move—me because of his bulk, him because of his bulk.

"I'm gonna kill you, motherfucker."

"Like you killed Jackie Marchand?"

"Yeah, motherfucker, just like I killed that little bitch."

"I don't think so," I said, and head butted him as hard as I could. I almost knocked myself out and stunned Tank enough that I could roll him off me, but that's all I could do. He must have cracked a rib or two when he stomped me because I couldn't get myself to an upright position. Tank was on his hands and knees, his butt to me, and when he turned around he had his weapon back—a length of pipe. The kind of pipe, maybe even the same pipe, that he'd used to kill Jackie. I kept trying to sit up, kept failing. Tank was grinning at me. He was on his feet, weaving a bit, but gripping the pipe. Then he made a mistake: He straddled me. I used the only weapon I had—a foot encased in a steel-toed boot. I fired it upward, into Tank's scrotum. He didn't make a sound when he dropped to his knees. I crashed my fist into his jaw and knew that it hurt me more than it hurt him. No way around it: I would have to take another dirty shot if I was going to leave here alive. Tank was on his knees, breathing hard, his eyes glazed but not tilted. He was shaking his head to clear it, and trying to stand up, something I knew I could not do. I flexed my hand and it hurt like hell; I couldn't hit him in the face or the head or the chest without breaking the rest of the bones in my hand. Only one thing to do: I shot my arm out from the shoulder and connected my fist with Tank's Johnson. He fell backwards and curled into a ball.

It was taking way too long for me to get to a sitting position, and I realized what I hadn't realized before, which was that I was soaking wet and freezing. My teeth were chattering. I reached into my pocket, looking for my phone, and knew that the pitiful mewling, moaning I was hearing wasn't all Tank. Every movement I made sent excruciating pain coursing through some part of my body. I knew I had broken bones in my hand, cracked or broken ribs, maybe even a broken skull. I also knew I couldn't go another round with Tank. I had to get up and get away before he collected himself.

I finally extracted the phone but couldn't flip it open. I was starting to shake. People were walking past, looking at me and

Tank on the ground, walking around us. I'm not drunk! I'm not crazy! But nobody heard the words because I couldn't make them come out of my mouth . . . Jill! That was Jill coming up the sidewalk . . . she'd see me . . . she wouldn't walk past someone lying on the sidewalk . . . not Jill Mason . . . talk, Phil! Dammit, open your mouth and talk! "Jill . . ."

She stopped walking and looked down at me, disbelieving, horrified, terrified, and she backed up, backed away. "No. No. No!"

"Jill . . . please."

She came back, leaned over me. "Phillip." The pain in her voice was more potent than the pain in my body. It was just what I needed.

"Please go call Yo. Tell her to get me . . ." Jill didn't move but Tank did. "Jill, go! Now! This is the guy who killed Jackie Marchand . . ." She turned and ran then, this good and beautiful woman who had suffered too much for one life but who had always managed to find enough caring and feeling to give to another person, and here I had just frightened her half to death. This is why I needed a gun. If I could have just shot this bastard, I wouldn't have had to frighten Jill Mason half to death.

Chapter Thirteen

"You frightened me half to death."

I was in bed and Connie was sitting on the bed beside me and I smiled. Then everything hurt and I stopped smiling and started remembering. I looked around at the room. This was not home. This was the hospital. "I'm so sorry, Connie. This is not a regular or routine thing, I promise you . . ."

She touched my lips with her finger. "I know. Yolanda told me. So did Mike and Eddie. You're not an adrenaline junkie and you don't go looking for trouble. This trouble came looking for you, which I'm sure he now regrets."

"Not half as much as I do."

"But he doesn't have me to help make him feel better."

I smiled again and this time it didn't seem to hurt quite so much. Or maybe it did because when I woke up again, Connie was gone and Yolanda was in the chair beside the bed. I couldn't read the look on her face. She stood up, leaned over and kissed me, then walked out. Eddie and Mike walked in.

"Ortiz, you hairy bastard! What are you doing here?"

He came and stood by the bed, took my hand, the one that didn't have a cast on it. "What were you thinking, *'mano?* You can't take down a big dude like that by yourself! That's why you got us!"

"How are you, Eddie? Really?"

"I'm really good. I get tired easily but I'm good. Linda let me off the leash just long enough to come see you. I'm going right back home." He raised his right hand as if taking the oath, which Linda no doubt had made him do.

"You up to telling us what happened?" Mike asked.

I didn't like reliving the experience but I knew it was necessary, so I told them everything I could remember. "Man, where did we ever get the idea that a fat boy was a wuss?" In one of my moments of semi-consciousness lying there in the freezing water, I'd had a really lucid thought, and it just came back to me: I was going to the gym every day, no matter what. I was not going to get caught without the strength to protect myself ever again. "For the first time in my life, I now know that if I'd had a gun, I would have shot another human being. That guy was going to kill me." I had to shake off that thought. "He told me he killed Jackie. Right before he told me he was going to kill me."

"We got the papers from your jacket, the stuff Dr. Mason translated."

"It wasn't all waterlogged and illegible?"

Mike shook his head. "You'd stuffed it deep in the inside pocket of your jacket. You were soaked through to the bone, but the papers were dry as a duck."

Eddie was giving me a funny look, kinda like the one Yo was wearing, and now that I thought about it, Mike was being much too cheerful. "What is it you guys aren't telling me?" I held up, or tried to hold up, my hands, and the pain that ran up and down my arms, both of them, told me they were still there. I raised my legs, one at a time, under the covers, and could see that they were still there, both feet still attached. I was looking at Mike and Eddie so I wasn't blind, and I still had Connie's scent in my nose so my other senses were working. So, what the hell was wrong?

"He got away," Mike said.

I'd thought my head couldn't hurt any worse but the pounding increased and intensified until I thought my skull would just crumble into tiny little pieces. I didn't say anything. I couldn't. There was nothing to say, but I was thinking that I'd just taken the beating of a lifetime for nothing.

"That's the bad news," Eddie said.

I looked at him, looked at Mike, still didn't say anything.

"The good news," Mike said, "is that Doc Mason took a picture of him with her cell phone, and you had his DNA all over you. We've got his large ass, bro. You didn't fight the good fight for nothing."

"Get outta my head, Mike," I said. "It hurts bad enough without you stomping around in there."

"You really head butted the guy?" Eddie asked.

I nodded, regretted the action, held up my right hand in its cast. "That's what happened when I hit him with my hand."

"Well, the head butt gave you a mild concussion."

"Is that why my head hurts like it does?"

Two doctors came in and Eddie made for the door. Can't say that I blame him, just having gotten out of the hospital himself. "Thanks, Eddie. I'll call you later." He left and Mike positioned himself at the door but he made no move to leave. I, however, was more than ready. "When can I leave?" I asked the doctors, looking from one to the other. The younger one busied himself reading my chart; the older one bent over and shone a light in my eyes and asked me to blink.

"I'd prefer you stayed another night, but if you have somebody to take care of you, you can leave today."

"I can take care of myself."

"Are you ambidextrous? Got another right hand in a drawer at home? No? I didn't think so. Then you can't take care of yourself." She walked out, followed by the young doctor.

"I'm gonna take Eddie home and then I'll be back," Mike said.

"No, you won't. Go home to your wife, Mike. Watch TV, get

some sleep, eat a decent meal. I'll be fine. I'll stay here another night, get rid of this headache, practice wiping my ass with my left hand, talk to Connie about babysitting me."

He started to protest, I waved him off—with my left hand—and he went away. Quite frankly, I was glad to be alone, to be alone with my thoughts. I didn't doubt that the mess they were making was contributing to the headache I had. I closed my eyes, then opened them again. I didn't want to go to sleep, I wanted to think. I just wanted my thoughts to be calm and quiet and orderly, not racing and screaming and doing wheelies off the walls of my brain. "Okay," I said out loud, "a half dozen fires, three murders, and who knows how many false calls to Homeland Security. Common denominator: The Kearneys. The fire starters worked for them; they either made the calls to DHS or had them made; and at least two of the murders are tied directly to them." That helped. I cranked the bed so that I was sitting upright, and that helped, too. I kept talking to myself. "The delivery boy at the Taste of India burned to death, presumably by accident; Jackie Marchand was beaten to death; Bill Calloway was shot, so was Eddie. Three different means of murder, three different murderers?" I swung my feet over the side of the bed and rode the wave of nausea, dizziness, and pain that swept over me like those Hawaiian surfers I like watching on television. Jesus Christ, I'm gonna pass out—or wipe out, I was thinking to myself. "Breathe, Phil, breathe," I said to myself.

"Good advice."

I opened my eyes. Connie was standing there with my overnight bag. I couldn't describe the look on her face for all the money in the world, but I won't forget it if I live to be a hundred. "Will you marry me tomorrow?"

"What's wrong with today?" She came over and hugged me and I held on.

"I know this frightened you, Con, and I'm so sorry."

"I know."

"I want to go home. Now, today. I told the doctor I'd stay tonight but I don't want to, Con. I want to go home. Will you stay with me? I promise I won't whine, complain, or cry when it hurts, and I'll wipe my own ass with my left hand. You will have to feed me, though."

At first she was crying, then she was laughing, and because I was sitting and she was standing, she was taller and she rested her chin on my head and I liked the role reversal. "I'll go find the doctor, then I'll help you get dressed." She put the overnight bag on the bed and unzipped it for me, and laid out my clothes. She'd thought of everything. Almost.

"Did you by any chance bring a phone?" She unzipped the side pocket of the bag and produced a phone. "Is Yo mad with me?"

Connie shook her head and now her face had something of the same sad expression that Yolanda's had had. "There are only three constants in her life, Phil: Sandra, you, and her home. You and her home swayed under her feet at the same time. Remember, the building that is your office is also her home, and you are more than her business partner. Her world suddenly felt not so stable, Phil. Not like such a sure thing." She kissed the top of my head and went to find the doctor. I looked at my clothes laid out next to me and opted to try and flip open the cell phone. I remembered trying to do that last night and wondered if that phone was still lying there in the slush. I got the phone open and was practicing using my left hand when Abby Horowitz came breezing in, still looking like an Upper East Side rich guy.

"I hope you're not in too much pain and misery to help slam the door shut on the cousins Kearney and their loving Aunt Mary Katherine." He pulled a sheaf of papers from his inside jacket pocket and waved them back and forth.

"You got 'em?"

"Yolanda laid the trail. I merely followed . . ."

"The paper."

He nodded. "Yup. You know why I never wanted to work the gang or drug task forces? Because those dudes are so much smarter than the smart fuckers. Your average drug wholesaler moves millions more than your average white collar criminal but nobody knows for sure how many millions more because there's no paper. Drug merchants don't write shit down. Your white collar fool, on the other hand, goes to great lengths to set up dummy and phony accounts and route money here, there, and yonder, to this overseas bank and that overseas bank. A computer genius like Miss Yolanda Aguierre in cahoots with a devious, pond-scum-hating bastard like myself on the trail of pseudo-smart crooks: They don't stand a chance."

"You really got 'em, Abby?"

"Signed, sealed, and ready to deliver to the DA's office."

My joy faded. "Are you crazy?"

He was genuinely confused. "No, I don't think so . . ."

"You don't work for the cops anymore, Abby, for the government!"

"We still catch the bad guys, don't we?"

"No! We don't! That's not what we get paid to do. We get paid—more money than the cops are ever paid, by the way—to get Big Apple Insurance Company to pay out Ravi Patel's and Jawal Nehru's insurance claims! And we want that to happen this week or next week, not in two or three or five years from now!" I was yelling and my head was pounding and I was dizzy and nauseous again.

Abby was watching me, probably waiting to see if I was going to faint or puke or something. When he saw that I wasn't, he came closer to the bed. "Does that mean we don't care if the fuckin' Kearneys don't get what's coming to them?"

"Oh, hell no, Abby!" I started to shake my head no. Big mistake. In fact, everything I did or said seemed to be a mistake. "No, Abby," I said in a whisper. "They'll get what's coming to them. After they pay our clients what's owed to them."

"But why would they do that?" Abby asked, frustration written in bold block letters all over his face. "What's in it for them?"

"We don't turn 'em in to the DA is what's in it for them."

"But you said they'd get what's coming to them."

"And they will. On the front page of the *Daily News.*"

Abby jumped up and hugged me before I could stop him. I yelped in pain, he backed away and started apologizing, still backing up, until he backed into Connie. Then he turned around and started a new round of apologies.

"Abby!"

"What?"

I put my finger to my lips and shushed him, then introduced him to Connie, and he was off and running again, congratulating her on our engagement, telling her how lovely she was, how pleased he was to meet her. She was trying hard not to laugh. "He's our new associate, is Mr. Horowitz, and clearly one of the most polite people on the planet." He and Connie shook hands, then Abby hugged her.

Amused and bemused, she came and sat next to me on the bed. "The doctor's coming to sign you out. She's not happy, but I promised her that I'd keep an eye on you and get you back in here immediately if you fainted."

"If I faint, don't bother bringing me back here, just dig a hole and roll me into it." I was feeling so good I thought I could stand up. I almost made it.

"You need to rest," Abby said.

"I need to eat," I said. "Lunch on me. Let's have something delivered to the office and have a feast. How about Indian food?"

"It's dinnertime, and you're not going to the office, you're going home."

I knew better than to argue. "So, Abby. Guess I'll see you *manana.*"

"Or the day after," Connie said.

"Tomorrow," I said.

"We'll see," Connie said.

Eddie the driver picked me up the next morning and took me to work. I hurt in places I didn't know it was possible to hurt but the ass-kicking headache had subsided somewhat and I didn't get dizzy and nauseous with every movement. I had to work to convince Connie that I really did feel up to going in, and I had to raise my right hand, cast and all, and promise that I'd come home if I felt faint. I almost cried when the car pulled up in front of my building and saw that the new windows were in, and I did get a little choked up when I opened the door to find Yo, Mike, Eddie, Abby and breakfast waiting for me. It hurt to talk, it hurt to laugh, it hurt to chew, it hurt to move, it hurt to breathe—and I had never felt better in my life. So glad was I to be in the company of these four people that I didn't mind that somebody had to open my bottle of juice, put cream and sugar in my coffee, and cream cheese on my bagel, put the tray holding my food on my lap, and tuck my napkin under my chin. I didn't mind having them do those things because they didn't mind doing them.

After I told the tale of my close encounter with Tank for what I hoped was the last time, I listened more than I talked; talking hurt and my associates now knew things that I didn't know, though I did have a couple of pieces of information to add to the discussion: I remembered the piece of pipe that Tank hit me with, that may also have been what killed Jackie Marchand, and that it might still be lying there on the sidewalk; and I remembered something that he'd said during the attack. "He'd rather trust a Jew than his own blood."

"Tank's related to Kearney, too," Yolanda said. "His name is William—they call him Willie—and they're all family—Casey, McQueen, Tank, the Kearneys, and Aunt Mary Katherine."

Yolanda had tied them all to a maintenance man who'd been killed in the World Trade Center that day, guy named Francis Kearney. Mary Katherine was the guy's sister, Francis and Thomas his sons, Casey and McQueen his grandsons, the sons of his daughters. Tank apparently was a grandson, too. It was Mary Katherine's survivor's money that had financed Francis Kearney's real estate development company, and Mary Katherine was the brains behind the scheme as well. We had all the pieces to this puzzle, everything we needed to leverage them into paying the Patel and Nehru insurance claims. What we didn't have was a solid ID on Bill Calloway's killer, and what we couldn't do was get back the properties of those merchants who had been forced to sell out because Big Apple wouldn't pay their claims. A smart lawyer, though, Abby said, could squeeze some serious money out of Big Apple because Kearney was acting for the company in denying legitimate claims. Abby thought he could convince those cheated merchants to hire us to make their case. That Horowitz was some fast learner.

When it seemed that we were finished with that case for the moment, Mike asked if we wanted to watch some home movies. "We're gonna have one hell of a show-and-tell session for the KLM people," he said, putting a disc into the DVD player.

We all watched in silent appreciation of what could be accomplished with the kind of digital video camera that anybody could use. It was almost like watching a movie.

"I sure wish we could get inside there," Abby said.

"This is great stuff," I said.

"Yeah, it is: Great stuff of guys going in the front door of a building and out the back door of the same building a half hour or an hour later. To Richard King, it'll look like enough to fire that Kallen character . . ." He stopped mid-sentence and turned a piercing, questioning gaze on Yolanda. "How, by the way, did you find out that he's not really Mike Kallen?"

"Fingerprints," she said. "I offered him a cup of coffee and he accepted. And when he left, I bagged the cup and sent it to our lab . . ."

"We've got a lab?" I asked, and expressed way too much surprise because the next emission from my mouth was, "Ow!" followed by—and there's no other adequate or accurate way to describe it—a whimper. The headache was back with a vengeance.

Yolanda jumped up and ran over to me. Eddie took the tray off my lap. Mike grabbed my coffee cup before I could add second degree burn to my vast array of injuries. It was agreed that what I probably needed to do was stretch myself out on the sofa. I let myself be out-voted and while the room was being arranged so that I could watch Mike's surveillance video from a prone position, I listened to Mike, Eddie, and Abby discuss the difficulty the cops were having policing the Russian criminal enterprise. I realized that I must have been dozing, drifting in and out of wakefulness. I realized that Connie was right, that I probably should have stayed home and slept today. Of course, it was too late for that now. I forced my eyes to open and remain that way, and tried to will the headache to subside enough to let my brain function, at least minimally.

"Say that again, about the Russians," I said, sounding so weak I didn't know if anyone heard me.

"What part?" Mike asked.

"The part about them not playing by the rules."

Abby pulled a chair over to the sofa where I lay. "They didn't think they had to. They thought they could just come here and set up their illegal enterprises—gambling, prostitution, drug dealing, counterfeiting, auto theft—you name, they did, and they did it on a grand scale and with a kind of ruthlessness that, at first, was startling. That's why they got away with it at first: Nobody could believe the balls on these guys. I mean, they'd get here—illegally, most of 'em—and set up shop. Go to work."

"You shoulda seen the Dominican dealers Uptown and the Jamaicans over in Brooklyn when the Russians started dealing!" Eddie laughed at the memory, then turned quickly serious. "The blood started flowing and didn't stop until finally the cops had had enough."

Heavy silence followed as the cops in the room relived that ugly period in the history of the New York City Police Department. I had never patrolled the streets where the blood had flowed and had not, until this moment, had a clear understanding of what had caused the turf wars because I hadn't wanted to know. What I knew and had always known was that the police department was a stepping stone for me—the best, most efficient way for me to become a licensed private investigator. "So, this was all the work of the Russian mob?" I asked, sounding like the student I was.

Mike was shaking his head. "Not the way you mean mob."

"How many ways are there, Mike?"

Mike looked at Abby, who answered the question. "For our purposes: Two. The Devil we know—our own organized crime *paisanos*—and the Devil we didn't know—the fuckin' Russians."

Carmine's words rushed back to me with such force it made me breathless: "They're nothin' like us. They got no rules, they got no organization, and they got no morals."

"You look green, Phil," Eddie said. "You look like I felt those first couple a days in the hospital."

"I'm okay," I said. "Really. And I want to see the rest of Mike's video," I said, and looked expectantly at the television that had been rolled over to the sofa to accommodate me.

Yolanda looked at me so long and hard I almost shifted my eyes, but she gave in before I did and restarted the DVD.

We all turned our attention to the screen again, me with a completely different attitude about what we were watching. Yes, I still wanted KLM's business; without us, Richard King would be hard-pressed to prove that the brothel Mike Kallen was running was his own enterprise and not a KLM-sanctioned enterprise: Men in the front door and out the back gate day and night; all of the social security numbers of all the new female tenants were bogus; Mike Kallen's identity was a sham; whoever Boris was, Boris wasn't his name; and the limo driver who cut and ran that morning, leaving Mike and me in the car, was a Russian criminal wanted by Interpol. Equally, though, I wanted some Russians to go to jail. Or, better still, back to Russia. And, unlike Carmine, not because they were Russians . . . at least I didn't think so.

"Are they really as ruthless as their reputations would have us believe?" Yolanda asked, her eyes never the leaving the screen but the coldness of her tone giving voice to her thoughts and feelings.

"Worse," Mike, Eddie, and Abby answered in unison.

"We were told that they'd rather die in a shootout here, or do a life sentence in one of our prisons, than go back where they came from," Mike said.

"They don't fear us—our law enforcement agencies—because, compared to what they're used to, we might as well be Santa Claus at Christmas," Abby said. "In fact, some years back, when we'd bust some of them on a misdemeanor and they were looking at being ROR, they'd assault a cop so they could go to jail. Three squares, a bed, and clean clothes—a better life than they'd ever had."

Yeah, I was thinking, back to the Motherland for Mike and Boris, when Abby jumped up so quickly that he knocked his chair over. Mike and Eddie jumped up, too, weapons in hand. Yolanda was on her feet and backing away. I couldn't jump up; I couldn't even sit up quickly, so I was the first to see that Abby's focus still was on the television screen, that his mouth was open in shocked amazement.

"You rat bastard! You low life piece of shit! Freeze that! Back it up a few frames!" He was roaring, hopping from foot to foot, and pointing at the screen.

I finally managed to get myself upright on the sofa and waved a hand at Abby; I wanted him to stop yelling and jumping; every sound, every movement, reverberated in my head. He understood, apologized, picked up his chair, then put his face next to the TV screen where the image was frozen, and pointed to the man being welcomed in the front door of the Avenue B building by a smiling Boris.

"That filthy, fuckin' rat bastard is Alex Sabzanov. He's a detective second grade. He used to work out of Harlem, but he's Downtown now, assigned, I heard, somewhere in the Village."

"He's also Russian," Yolanda said. "At least his name is."

"And he's probably getting freebies, the lousy rat bastard," Abby snarled, sounding more mean and nasty than I would have given him credit for managing.

We all stared at the frozen screen, at the frozen figures on the screen, and at Abby's face, which was still all but plastered there. Then he stood up, gave us a sinister version of the tooth-exposing, mustache-dancing grin and wriggled his bushy eyebrows up and down. "We are now inside Boris's little brothel," he said, and began dancing around the room.

"Why would he get you in?" Mike asked.

"What kinda hold you got over him?" Eddie asked.

"Is our equipment sophisticated enough for inside undercover work?" Yolanda asked.

"Are you totally crazy?" I said to Abby, and everybody looked at me. I struggled to my feet, waving off everybody's assistance, then had to accept it anyway as I swayed before I steadied. "Didn't you all just finish describing these guys as . . . as brutal beyond belief? And you want us to let you go inside there, and with a crooked cop?" I'd raised my voice, which was a huge mistake, and I had to sit down again.

"I won't be going in with Sabzanov, Phil, he'll just be gaining me entry: Me, another cop, and from Command—in a position to be really useful. Don't you think Boris will love it?" Abby was nodding his head as if answering his own questions, and rubbing his hands together.

I didn't feel much like explaining why I didn't like the idea of Abby Horowitz—or Eddie Ortiz or Mike Smith—going undercover alone into any situation, to say nothing of going into a den of dangerous Russians. Granted this was a new reticence on my part, no doubt born of my newfound knowledge of Russian behavior. And, I had to keep telling myself, it was not all Russians; probably not even most Russians. But the bad-ass ones, like Mike Kallen or whatever his name was, and Boris and the ones that made Carmine nervous, made me nervous, too, and I didn't want anybody who worked for me alone and unprotected in a place that.

Everybody was looking at me. I probably looked as irrational as I was feeling. I wanted my head to stop pounding so I could think, and then say what I was thinking in a logical and rational way. I couldn't tell them that if Carmine was scared of Russians, that was good enough for me, but I could—and did—claim my own fear. "I already got Eddie almost killed—"

"Dammit, I knew you were going there!" Eddie yelled at me.

"You can't make this about what happened to Eddie," Mike said, studiously not yelling.

"And what exactly do you plan on doing once you get inside,

Horowitz? If you don't go with one of the girls, Boris'll kill you, and if you do go with one of the girls, I'll kill you, and then I'll fire your ass, and I don't even know your wife."

"I've got a plan," Abby said, not yelling, either, but definitely not whispering.

"I don't want to hear it," I said. "You can't go in there, Horowitz, not without backup, and since nobody here can go with you, that means you can't go."

"Ah ha!" he said. "So that's it!"

"What's it?" I asked, but I knew; and he was right. I still had a lot of resentment about needing to hire Abby, even though I was glad to have him. I'd like to think I'd have hired him anyway, but because I wanted to, not because I needed to.

"You know what," Abby snapped at me; he was pissed and didn't mind showing it. "It's not my fault, man! What do you want me to do, apologize for being white? Or do you want to apologize for not being white? Or do you want major paydays from Big Apple Insurance and KLM Property Management? 'Cause we can have 'em both, but you gotta stop beating yourself up over shit you can't change. The world sucks, man, and there's nothing we can do about it but keep living how we live."

I looked at Yo and I'd never before seen the look on her face: Worry, fear, sadness, anger, and a little bit of confusion, as if she didn't know what to think or say or do. And that made me feel worse than I already was feeling. "Do we have the kind of equipment he needs to go in, Yo?"

She shrugged first, then she nodded. I looked at the guys; all three of them were looking at me. Damn, but I was tired. I felt that I'd sleep for a week if I closed my eyes.

"Mike and I will be outside the whole time he's inside, one of us at the front door, the other at the back gate. We'll be listening and if anything sounds funky, we'll go in and take

Boris's sorry ass down in the process," Eddie said.

"The shape you're in, you couldn't take down one of those girls in there," I snapped. Then added, "And neither could I. So that means," and I turned to look at Abby, "we've got no room for error, dude." He nodded, started to speak, but I wasn't finished. "You don't take this to Spade, Abby. You leave him out of it. And if you can't do that, then you stay out of it."

He was wrestling with that one; we all knew it and he knew we knew it. And the battle was costing him, though none of us had any way to know how much. One thing we could take straight to the bank, though: If Abby Horowitz decided he was in, he'd be all the way in. He dipped his head. We had our answer and everybody resumed breathing.

"When do we want to do this?" I asked, and when no answer was forthcoming, and when I realized why, I almost managed a laugh. "You don't think I'm going to let you three walk into the lions' den alone, do you?" I managed to make a passable scoffing sound. "I'm going to be in the vehicle, watching and listening. So. I repeat: When do we do this?"

Abby looked at his watch. "I need to find out when Sabzanov is on shift. I'll make a call and if he's on now, I'll go see him now. Give him a day to set it up—let's say day after tomorrow?"

I was okay with that. Maybe by then I'd have gotten some sleep and my head would have stopped pounding and I'd stop hurting every time I breathed or moved.

"What are you thinking?" Eddie asked. "Right a moment ago. What were you thinking? 'Cause, *'mano,* you shoulda seen your face!"

"I was thinking what bullshit it is in the movies and on TV when the PI takes an ass whip and he's up and about like nothing happened that same day and I can barely move."

"Maybe they're just tougher than you," Mike said.

"Could be," I said. "Or maybe they just never went a round

on an East Village sidewalk in the snow with Willie 'The Tank' Kearney."

That was it, everybody agreed, and got busy cleaning up and putting the furniture back where it belonged, then Abby got on the phone. I couldn't do much but sit and watch, so I went to my desk. Getting into and out of that chair was easier than with the sofa. I got my notebook out of the drawer and paged through it. I wouldn't be able to write anything for at least six weeks—until the cast came off my right hand. I couldn't write but I could think: Two really shitty situations apparently about to be resolved to our clients' benefit. Couldn't argue with that. Clients happy, us well paid, potential new work on the horizon. What's not to like?

"Phil? What's wrong? Are you in pain?"

"No, Yo, I'm fine, really . . ."

"No you're not!" Her eyes flashed and she headed right for me with Mike and Eddie on her heels.

"Okay, okay, I'm not fine. We don't know who murdered Bill Calloway and shot Eddie and I'm not fine with that. If one of the Kearneys did that, I want one of them to pay for it. I want whoever set the Taste of India fire and killed that delivery guy to pay for it. If one of those guys—McQueen or Casey or Mottola—did it, I want one of them to pay for it. Tank can't be the only guy to go down for murder. There were three of them, three murders, and maybe three murderers."

"Maybe Tank did all three," Yolanda said.

"I don't think so," I said, remembering how hurt he sounded beneath the anger: "He'd rather trust a Jew than his own blood." "He's a bit player. He didn't set the Taste of India fire and he didn't kill Bill."

"When we get the Kearneys here, we'll get it out of 'em," Mike said.

"How? What incentive do they have to rat out one of their own?"

"How about we can convince somebody to finger one of them for it?" Eddie asked.

"Convince who . . . Sam Epstein! That might just work, Eddie."

"I don't even think we have to convince him, Phil. I think we just have to tell the Kearneys that Epstein pointed the finger at them—we pick one of 'em, Thomas or Francis, I don't give a shit which one—and say our promise not to go to the DA with the info we have doesn't extend to murder." Mike was wearing his shark grin. "They'll give up the shooter."

"Even if it was a relative?" Yolanda asked.

I was up and walking, my brain adding an additional diabolical twist to Mike's plan. "I think they'll throw Sammy back at us, or Joey Mottola."

"Oh, shit," Eddie said. "Then it's on. If they drop Mottola in it, whether he did it or not, his people will go after the Kearneys."

"Yep," I said, "they sure will." And I had to fight not to check the look I knew Yolanda's face was wearing.

"What the fuck are you tellin' me, Rodriquez, that these Karney fucks are sayin' that Joey killed that insurance guy?" Carmine and I were drinking Sambuca along with our coffee instead of eating pastries, even though it wasn't yet noon, and I was really liking the warm, relaxed thing the liqueur was doing to my insides. Carmine said it would make me feel better and he was right.

"Kearney, and yeah, Carmine, they're trying to lay all the murders off on somebody else. We've got them cold on the fires and the insurance scam, but they figure they can ride that out. They've got plenty of cash. But they don't know how to do jail time. They could drop Sam Epstein or Joey in the shit. They chose Joey."

"Goddammit!" Carmine slapped his palm down on the table and the glasses and cups and saucers danced up and down.

"I'm letting you know, Carmine, before this hits the press . . ."

"What fuckin' press? What the fuck are you talkin' about, Rodriquez? How did this get to the press?" For the first time since I've known him, the fat man looked worried.

"I took it, Carmine. That's how I was going to get even with the Kearneys for the dirt they did and hurt they caused—expose them publicly. They're trying to leverage me the back way. They know I was working for Epstein, so they offered to keep him out of it and drop Joey in it. And since they're all the same family . . ." I didn't have to spell it out for him, him being such a loyal Family member himself.

"Shit!" Carmine hit the table again, though not as hard. "Fuckin' shit." He grabbed a couple of coffee beans, popped them into his mouth. Chewing, he asked, "How much time do I have?"

"Two, three days at the most."

"Okay, Rodriquez, thanks for the heads up." He already was finished being pissed off and working out in his brain how to fix his problem. "By the way, which one of those fucks did you? Couldn't have been Casey or McQueen, those skinny little bastards."

"Another cousin, we call him Tank."

"Fat, stupid-looking jerk? Looks like a Hell's Angel on a bad day?"

I tried not to look or sound excited. "That would be Tank," I said. "But how would you know him, Carmine? Why would you know him?"

"I don't know the little fuck. He hangs around Joey. The Kearneys treat him kinda bad on account of how he looks, and he's illegitimate."

I choked on my Sambuca. Who called anybody illegitimate anymore? Carmine was even more of an old-school guy than I thought. "He's what?"

Carmine grinned at me. He liked unnerving me, surprising me, saying things I didn't expect. "His mother's some old broad got knocked up by accident and this boy, Willie, or Tank, as you like to call him, was the result." Carmine's grin widened. "Tank's a much better name for him, though, than Willie."

"No shit," I said. "I can't tell anybody that a guy named Willie creamed my ass."

Carmine laughed, made me put my money away, and walked me to the door, which was a first. Then I saw why. A taxi materialized out of nowhere. "You ain't in no shape to walk," he said. "By the way, Rodriquez, why didn't you just shoot the bastard?"

"Delaney's got my gun. He took it after Calloway and Eddie got shot."

Carmine shook his head and headed back inside the little pastry shop. "That Delaney prick's even stupider than I thought he was."

Abby and I got back to the office at the same time. We entered to find Yolanda, Mike, and Eddie testing every piece of surveillance equipment we owned. Yolanda looked especially pleased, which pleased me no end. "Did we know that Tank was Mary Katherine's illegitimate offspring?"

"Illegitimate? Nobody says that anymore, bro," Mike said.

"I knew he was her son but I didn't find the . . . ah . . . illegitimate aspect," Yolanda said, and stopped herself before she asked me how I found out.

"You talk to Sabzanov?" I asked, as much to change the subject as to know the answer.

Abby did his shark imitation. "What was the thing you used to say, Mike, about a blind guy shitting and running?"

"He didn't know whether to run, shit, or go blind?"

Abby had started laughing when Mike started speaking and was holding his sides when he finished. "That's from Georgia, y'all. I love that, and it perfectly describes Detective Sabzanov's reaction to my little bombshell. I think he would have run if he could have, but since I had him cornered, he just shit his pants."

"But he's going to get you in?"

"Day after tomorrow. And no sex!" He gave me a look, then he grabbed my hand and shook it. "I appreciate the sentiment, Phil, truly I do. But my wife would've killed me a couple times over before you ever got the chance."

"How's that work, Abby?" Yo wanted to know. "How do you visit a brothel without engaging in sexual activity?"

"I'm going in as Sabzanov's boss who he had to cut in to guarantee the protection. We do this in the daylight. I go in, suit, tie, polished shoes—and not Russian—check the place out, count the girls, discuss the weekly take, and slam, bam, thank you ma'am, I'm out the door. We have it all on tape, Richard King writes us a check with lots of zeroes, and everybody's happy."

Almost happy. "If we could just find Willie the Tank."

Abby stood up. "Might be possible," he said, and headed toward the back.

"Where's he going?" Eddie asked. "Where you going, Horowitz?" he yelled.

"Be right back," Abby answered.

"He's weird," Eddie said.

"But effective," Yolanda said.

"Weird can be good," Mike said. "Right, Phil?"

"Why are you asking me?"

"Oh, I don't know . . . maybe because you do dirty deals

with Mafia lightweights?"

"This from a man who broke into a murder victim's apartment not once but twice and stole pertinent information, evidence." I made it a statement and let it hang. Mike and Eddie knew that I knew Carmine; they didn't know how or why or that I had breakfast with him once a week. My cell phone rang and I got up and crossed the room to take the call. Judging from the catcalls, they all knew it was Connie, who was taking seriously her caretaker role, for which I was grateful. I was tired and I ached and I wanted to go to bed. I told her I was on my way home.

"So, what? You gotta go home?" Eddie asked.

"As a matter of fact, I do," I said.

"Good God!" Mike said, and it wasn't commentary on my being summoned home. Abby had emerged from the back transformed. No longer the suited and tied and wing-tipped exec, he looked like an East Village biker boy: Grungy black jeans, black biker boots, black T-shirt, leather vest with metal studs, and hair no longer neatly combed and gelled but sticking up in spiked points.

Yolanda was speechless. She walked a circle around Abby, looking him up and down, seeing but definitely not believing. "If I passed you on the street, Abby, I wouldn't know you. I wouldn't want to know you."

Abby beamed. "Thanks! I guess that means I can scout biker hangouts and bars in search of Tank. Or Willie, as I'm sure he's called in his own environment."

I walked over to him, got really close, and sniffed. "They'll make you in a second and toss you out on your sweet-smelling ass, Horowitz. You don't stink, man! You gotta stink if you're gonna hang with the Tank!"

Chapter Fourteen

It was dark when I woke up. I just lay there, assessing my body, thinking maybe I felt better, hoping it wasn't just wishful thinking. Then I became aware of two things: Connie wasn't beside me and the low hum of the street noise was louder than it should be for this time of night. I turned my head to check the clock: 7:42 the red dial glowed. That didn't make sense; it had to be later than that if it was night—which it was because it was dark. It would be light if it were morning.

I raised myself to a sitting position and braced for the headache. It came but it was a much tamer version of its predecessor. I took a deep breath and that was a mistake. Shallow breaths were better. I worked my butt to the edge of the bed, planted my feet, stood. No nausea or dizziness. This was good. Walking to the bathroom was even better as it no longer hurt just to move. So, now that I was fully recovered, I needed to find Connie.

The door to the living room was closed, another one of those things I'd have to get used to. Not the door being closed but having somebody else in the place who also was considerate enough to close the door while I napped. And who also cooked! The delicious scent of food cooking met me when I opened the door, beating Connie by only a few seconds. She hugged me close and tight then quickly released me with an apology for hurting me. I grabbed her back and hugged her even tighter.

"You're better."

"Much."

"You hungry?"

"Starving, and whatever you're cooking, I'm ready to eat it."

"Well, it's not ready to be eaten yet, but we've got some snacks that'll take the edge off until it is," she said, leading me to the sofa. "Sit and put your feet up." I did and she arranged pillows behind and beside me until I was comfortable. "Phil?"

"Hmmm?" I was settling into the sofa, thinking about snacks. And maybe a beer.

"You know you slept for twenty-four hours . . . ?"

"What?" But as soon as the words registered, I knew they made sense. The last thing I remembered was . . . what? I struggled to call up the memory . . . Abby looking like shit but smelling like a rose. At four or five o'clock . . . yesterday. I came home after that and it now was 7:42 and it wasn't morning. "How'd I do that?"

Connie looked a little sheepish but not at all apologetic. "Pain pills. I gave you two when you got home last night and you were out cold in about half an hour. You have very little tolerance for drugs, you know?"

I nodded. I did know, which is why I had refused to take them. "So, how many of them have I taken?"

She laughed the laugh that I loved, kissed the top of my head, and headed for the kitchen. "Do you want a salad or green beans with your roast chicken and rice?"

"Both, and lots of it. And I hope you made a chicken for yourself."

I was soaking in a tub of hot, aromatic, herb-infused water the next morning when Connie brought me the telephone. "Who is it?" I growled, not yet wanting to be "into the day." In fact, I was thinking I could enjoy being an invalid for another day or so, sleeping, eating, bathing.

"I don't know, Phil," she was saying, when it rang again. I almost dropped it in the aromatic water. She punched it on for me and I answered. It was Carmine and he got right down to business, the central point being that Patrick Casey, Tim McQueen, and Willie Kearney were, and would be, at my disposal for as long as I needed them to be. I couldn't tell, from his tone of voice, whether they'd still be alive, and I couldn't ask him that in front of Connie, so I asked her to please write down the address and phone number Carmine gave me, then I gave her the phone because he'd hung up. "Is everything all right?"

"My building was torched by accident," I said, repeating the repeatable part of what Carmine had just told me. "Accident's the wrong word, I suppose. The yoga studio had been targeted but when the Kearneys found out that I owned the building, they cancelled it. But Tank, wanting to prove himself to his more accomplished family members—and wanting to get back at me—took the job on himself."

"Who was that on the phone?"

I hesitated for just a second before telling her about Carmine. Not everything, but the salient points. She didn't say so but I thought she recognized his name and his daughter's name from her work counseling the families of rape victims. She also didn't say anything about Carmine's familial affiliation. What she said was, "If you're going to have breakfast with him every week and eat three or four Napoleons, then you're definitely going to have to go to the gym every day. Now, let's get you out of this tub."

We'd devised a means of getting me out before I got in: She looped a towel over the towel bar and I used my good arm to pull myself up while she stood behind me and pushed. All of this after the water had drained from the tub. It worked, too, which I was very happy about because even though I did feel better with each passing day, I was stiff and sore mornings, and the hot soak in whatever those herbs were just took all the soreness away.

Eddie the driver picked us up. We dropped Connie at the hospital first, then he took me to work. I missed my morning walk, especially now that mornings were warmer and brighter. Connie said we'd go for a long walk Saturday morning and then to the gym and if I didn't die from the exertion, I could get back to my normal routine. I was looking forward to it. I'd called Yolanda after talking to Carmine, and she'd called the guys, and they all were waiting for me. Abby, thankfully, no longer looked like Tank's best buddy, but he did look like a Wall Street banker: He had a busy day ahead of him, what with his rendezvous at Boris's brothel and our meeting with brothers Kearney. The rest of us looked our regular selves. Except for me, I suppose, with the cast on my arm and the green-purple-and-blue-colored face. I was ambivalent about whether I wanted the Kearneys to see what Tank had done to me.

"That's the same place where we picked up Epstein," Mike said.

"What do you want us to do?" Eddie asked.

"Take a camera and go talk to 'em," I said.

"What if they don't want to talk?" Abby asked.

"Be persuasive," I said.

"You're not going?" Yolanda asked.

"No," I said. "I'd start out in persuade mode."

"Maybe they should, too, so we can have show-and-tell for the Kearneys when they get here," Abby said.

He was going to be all right, was Abby Horowitz.

Francis Kearney was a slightly more refined version of his brother Thomas, but only slightly. He was younger and his alcoholism hadn't had as many years to progress, so perhaps by the time he was Tom's age, he'd look like shit, too. Both, though, were belligerent and sullen and snarling. They both were also at the meeting, on time. We didn't bother with the niceties—no offering of refreshments, no introductions and handshaking. They were offered seats but both preferred to stand, which was fine by me. I hoped they wouldn't be there long enough to need to sit.

"You, Thomas Kearney, are going to pay the insurance claims to Ravi Patel and Jawal Nehru today. By the close of business today . . ."

"Fuck you."

"It's you, both of you, who are going to be fucked," Abby said, emerging from behind the screens with an armload of paper and a DVD, which he inserted into the player.

"That's the fuckin' lawyer I told you about!" Thomas said to Francis. "You ain't no fuckin' lawyer!" he yelled.

"I certainly am," Abby said. "Now listen carefully while I outline the legal case against you." And when he finished outlining it, holding up pieces of paper along the way that proved everything he was saying, Thomas had nothing more to say, and Francis had yet to utter the first word. "Now, as Mr. Rodriquez said, you're going to make good on the insurance claims of Mr. Patel and Mr. Nehru today or this information goes to the District Attorney tomorrow morning."

Nobody said anything for a very long moment. Thomas was shaking, he needed a drink so badly. Francis finally roused himself. "And suppose we don't?"

Yolanda waved the television remote at the Kearneys to get their attention then pointed it toward the screen and hit the button. The faces of the Kearneys' nephews filled the screen. Then Yo turned up the volume and Thomas reached into his pocket for the half pint of hooch he kept there. He downed half of it in one long gulp. Yo switched off the TV. "The paper goes to the DA and the videotape goes to the police," she said.

"And if we do what you want, pay those claims, do we get that file and the tape?" Francis was doing all the talking now.

I looked at Thomas. "Is he going to be able to take care of the checks?"

Francis looked at Thomas, too. He stood up, snatched the half pint bottle away with one hand and slapped the shit out of his cousin with the other. "He'll take care of it."

"Then you'll get the file and the tape."

"When, exactly?" Francis wanted to know.

"When Mr. Patel and Mr. Nehru tell us their checks have cleared," Yolanda said.

"Why do you want to protect them, help them?" Thomas was slurring his words and his eyes were pink and he whined the question, but the hatred was palpable.

"Why do you want to hurt them?" Yolanda asked, her fury barely under control.

The Kearneys looked at her, hatred, anger, confusion merging with the years of alcohol abuse to blur their features. "Because they're un-American," Francis finally managed.

"They're not the ones who are," Yo said quietly, and turned away, headed for her den.

Abby clapped his hands together and rubbed them back and forth. "So, if you have no more questions, gentlemen, we'll have to ask you to leave. We've other business to take care of."

If Francis Kearney had had the nerve, he'd have popped Abby right in the chops, but guys like the Kearneys only had behind-the-back kind of nerve. They looked down on Tank but he was the only one of them in that family with enough nerve to look somebody in the face and do them dirt. The Kearneys left and Mike got the air freshener from the bathroom and sprayed the room. Yolanda called our clients and told them it was possible that they'd get their insurance claim checks that afternoon, and asked them to call the moment they did. I knew without her telling me that she'd ask for some numbers off the checks, and she'd ask for some numbers off their bank accounts, and then she'd do that thing she did to credit the Patel and Nehru accounts with their insurance claim money before the checks ever left their hands.

We were satisfied with the work we'd done, but not yet pleased. Abby and Yolanda, thanks to the information on Bill Calloway's flash drive, had managed to penetrate Big Apple's data base and were looking for denied claims. We had gotten an idea from Casey and McQueen how many calls they'd made to Homeland Security and how many fires they had set. We'd be pleased with ourselves when we'd been hired by the people the Kearneys had cheated out of their property to pressure Big Apple Insurers into reimbursing them. Abby was sure we could make the case that the company was complicit in the illegal acts because we had Bill Calloway's memo to Kearney's boss suggesting that Kearney was up to no good. But this process would take time; maybe a lot of time, as in years. So, in the short term, we'd settle for being satisfied, and move on to the next item of business.

Richard King alternated between anger, disbelief, outrage, sagging defeat, and threats of murderous revenge. He swung from emotion to emotion like an out of control pendulum. Then he wept like a child at the thought that the business his father had founded and built would be lost on his watch. "Oh, God, what have I done!"

"Mr. King, Mr. King!" I had to shout at him to get his attention. "That's why we're showing you this video, why we collected the documentation to back up what we think is happening—so you can take the necessary steps to stop it, and to bring the perpetrators to justice."

He looked at me. He looked at Yolanda. He looked, in turn,

at Mike, Eddie, and Abby. "But I hired him. Kallen. I hired him. Doesn't that make me guilty, too?"

"Not if you didn't know what he was doing," I said.

King shot up out of his chair like he'd been fired from a cannon. "Of course I didn't know! That's what I'm trying to tell you! I had no idea—"

Yolanda took King by the arm and led him back to his seat. "We know you didn't know, Mr. King. That's why we asked you to come here for this meeting. If we thought you were involved, we'd have gone directly to the authorities, because otherwise, they'd have thought we were involved, too. Do you understand?"

King looked at her, nodded his head, then buried his face in his hands. "What should I do? Tell me what to do!"

Yolanda went to the back. I didn't know what she was doing, but I hoped she wasn't making more coffee. King had already had four cups and was bouncing around like a pinball. But no, not coffee, wise woman that she is. Two fingers of brandy in a little snifter. "Drink this, Mr. King, and calm yourself so we can talk." King took a big swallow of the brandy and shuddered. Then he sipped it slowly, like the gentleman he probably was under normal circumstances.

"What should I do?" he asked again. "What do you recommend?" We told him. He listened. "You're certain you can take this to the police and they can stop him, stop them, stop what's going on, arrest those people, without making my building and my company look bad?" He was looking at Yolanda when he asked the question, so she answered.

"Yes, Mr. King, we can do that. We will do that."

"All right, then. Bring the contract." Yo brought it and King signed it. Then he brought out his checkbook and wrote a check. He was calm now, and relaxed, no doubt owing in part to the brandy, but also because he was back in his comfort zone. He was doing business the way business should be done, aboveboard and with contracts and retainers. "I feel really bad that Kallen bamboozled me the way he did. Now I know why Shirley and Eileen insist on having you people run extensive background checks on all employees, not just the maids and janitors."

"It's not just maids and janitors who commit crimes, Mr. King."

"Oh, of course not! I know that. But I didn't think . . . well, I thought it was just the Mexicans that we hear so much about who are illegal aliens. I didn't think Russians and people like that were, too."

"Probably half the Eastern Europeans in New York City are here illegally, Mr. King," Abby said. "Maybe more than half. And a good number of those are engaged in illegal activity of one kind or another."

King gave a snort of disgust and got to his feet. "So what the hell are the Homeland Security people doing?"

"Keeping our borders safe from Buddhist monks, Hindu restaurant owners, and Sikh yoga teachers," I said.

Since he had no idea what I was talking about, King didn't bother to respond to that. At the door he said, "I really appreciate what you did for my business. I won't forget it." He shook all our hands and headed out into the world, head up, shoulders back, a spring in his step. Then he stopped and turned back toward us. "Those women. What will happen to them?" he asked, and in that moment, I liked Richard King. I respected him. He was a businessman, yes; but he also was a human being.

"Social Services will take care of them," Abby said.

King nodded in satisfaction and left us almost as pleased with ourselves as King was. Before we met with King, Abby had gotten assurances from Deputy Chief Spade that he personally would take charge of the investigation into Kallen's operation because he thought that there most likely was more than one such set up, and that no matter what turned up, the Avenue B building and KLM Management wouldn't get splattered when the shit hit the fan. But Spade couldn't promise that he'd shut down the operation right away, which meant that the legal and law-abiding tenants of that building would have to endure Boris and his KGB mentality for a while longer. I understood Spade's position: If he shut down the Avenue B operation immediately, Kallen probably would roll up the other components of his operation. Which is why I worked for clients and not the cops: I wanted the Avenue B residents not to have to endure another hour of Boris and his sleazy johns. And if the women in those apartments truly were sexual slaves, I wanted them not to have to spend another moment enduring physical, emotional, and psychological abuse and torture. But we'd made the deal we'd made and I'd have to live with it. Didn't have to like it, but I did have to live with it, as peacefully as I could manage.

The five of us probably looked as if we were being led to our executions as we got off the subway at its last stop. We trudged up the steps, not talking. There was nothing to say; we'd said it all before deciding to make this journey. None of us had been to Manhattan's tip since that horrible day in September of 2001. None of us had been able to look, up close and personally, at the hole in sky where the Twin Towers of the World Trade Center had dominated the landscape. Mike and Eddie and I had talked a lot about how we'd love to get our hands on some terrorist son of a bitch intent on doing harm in or to our city again—some crazy suicide bomber looking to become a martyr. But in truth, how would we know what one looked like? Sure, we knew that Indian restaurant owners and Buddhist monks and Sikh yoga teachers weren't terrorists looking to destroy our country and our way of life. But did we—could we—really know what a terrorist looked like unless we actually saw the bombs under his shirt or saw him park the car in a suspiciously illegal place?

We were above ground, looking north, back toward the city, instead of south, toward the water. As if on cue, we all turned toward the empty space and still no one spoke because there was nothing to say. I was thinking, though, what I'd do, if I got the chance, to get close enough. . . .

Chapter Fifteen

Yolanda, Sandra, Jill, and Arlene had joined forces to throw an engagement party for Connie and me at Jill Mason's place. Jill had the penthouse loft in a SoHo building that could have—should have—been featured in one of those magazines that depicts how the really rich really live. I'd been there once, in the dead of winter, and while I'd seen how truly magnificent the place was, I hadn't seen the rooftop garden. I also hadn't seen these people that I knew and cared so much about dressed elegantly, in an elegant setting, celebrating anything. That they were celebrating me, that all the stops had been pulled out for me—on the other hand, maybe it was for Connie, and I could stop trying to find words to express emotions I didn't know I had.

Arlene's restaurant catered the affair, but Arlene and her son Bradley and her daughters and their husbands were guests. Raul Delgado, in a white dinner jacket, was the banquet master, easily and adeptly overseeing a staff of a dozen. He looked like a movie star from one of those 1950s high glamour pictures, suave and cool.

Sandra Gillespie, who'd been a dancer for twenty years and who always was regal and beautiful, was more elegant and gorgeous than I'd ever seen her, and I'd seen photos of her in performance. She was as happy for me as Yolanda was; so happy that she'd brought her grandmother to the party, which was a statement in and of itself. Well into her seventies, and maybe even eighty, Mrs. Gillespie was regal and elegant herself, and she greeted me with genuine warmth and affection, and greeted Connie the same way. She had helped me out on a case a few months ago and had been kind and polite to me, but I hadn't known that she really liked me.

I met Jill Mason's parents for the first time. They, too, were quite elderly and I knew from conversations with Jill that both senior Masons were infirm, but they were bright and cheerful this night, and obviously having a good time.

For the first time I saw evidence in Carmine and Theresa Aiello of the benefits the money their familial connections must bring. Carmine's suit, shirt, and shoes were Italian and so well made that he looked a foot taller and fifty pounds thinner; and Theresa's dress, one of those filmy summer things that look as if they were made by magic instead of with material and thread, certainly hadn't come off anybody's rack in anybody's department store.

Mike and Helen Smith, and Eddie and Linda Ortiz, people I've known and seen for years, looked like strangers, like people in a glossy magazine spread advertising yachts or island retreats. Eddie looked strong and robust again though he still tired easily and occasionally looked a little sad; twenty years as a New York City cop and he'd never been shot and then, on a job with me. . . . And we met Abby's wife, Lisa, a tall, raven-haired beauty who laughed as easily as he did and who, like her husband, never met a stranger. My parents and Connie's parents, who had been stiff and formal with each other, even relaxed and loosened up when introduced to Abby and Lisa and then were overrun by Abby doing nothing but being himself. I could see how his arrest record was what it was: He simply out-talked the white-collar criminals he was after.

The people from Connie's life and job blended and meshed with those from my life and job as well as Connie and I blended and meshed together. Her best friend, Carmen de la Cruz, and her husband, Miguel, started off the toasting. Carmine ended it:

"You all know Rodriquez so I don't have to tell you anything about him. Except this: He was always worried that he wasn't going to find the right woman. No matter what else he was doing right and good, he was always worried about that one thing. No matter what I tried to tell him—that he should count his blessings while he could."

The roar of laughter drowned him out but he kept a mostly straight face and kept his champagne flute aloft. He looked down at Theresa and gave her a barely perceptible wink. "And since you all know Rodriquez, you know he couldn't let well enough alone, so here he is tonight, engaged to Miss Connie deLeon." He bowed toward Connie. "So now, *paisano,* I can tell you the truth. You've earned the right to hear it: No matter what happens to you in your life from this moment on, good, bad, right, wrong, the woman who is standing beside you, if it's good, she'll make it better, and if it's bad, she'll make it good. If it's right, she'll make it perfect, and if it's wrong, she'll tell you that. She'll tell you that she loves you no matter what. And if you're a smart man, Rodriquez, which I know you to be, you'll thank her for choosing you, first thing every morning and last thing every night. 'Cause make no mistake, Rodriquez, it was her did the choosing, no matter what you think!"

This roar was even louder than the first, made so by whistles and cheers. Then Abby Horowitz grabbed his wife and started dancing, and they grabbed hands and in a moment everybody was in a circle, dancing and singing and laughing and crying on the roof of Jill Mason's building, the whole of Manhattan spread out before us. I'd never felt so good and couldn't imagine how it could ever get any better than this. I was fully recovered from Tank's ass whip, owing in no small part to my living up to my promise of daily gym visits. I was stronger and more fit than ever, though I truly didn't intend to need physical strength for additional rounds of hand-to-hand combat on East Village street corners. I'd made that promise to Connie, and to myself. Anyway, I had my gun back—and carry permits for the two new ones—both courtesy of Ace Spade, and to the dismay and disgust of Captain Bill Delaney, who forswore never to forgive me for going behind his back.

I didn't care what Bill Delaney thought about me. Nor did I care that the Kearneys and a good number of their relatives, including Tim McQueen, Pat Casey, and Willie-the-Tank, were looking at serious jail time. The *Daily News* reporter I'd fed the story to had, as I'd asked, taken a deep and hard look at how our government treats innocent people who've been slandered by anonymous voices on the telephone, then robbed of their livelihood and property. Good reporters, like good cops, often let the accused tell their own stories in their own words. It's called giving them sufficient rope to hang themselves and the Kearneys amassed yards of the stuff as they expressed their outrage that the people who had destroyed two of the city's fabled landmarks and killed their relative were allowed to own and operate businesses. Somebody had to do something about it! They hanged themselves with their words and they dangled, gasping and strangling, until the DA cut the rope and dropped the entire clan into a pool of watery shit.

The reporter did a special story on Mrs. Nehru's return to her homeland of choice following the Homeland Security Department's removal of her name from its Watch List. The Nehrus' gratitude could be seen on Connie's ring finger: An engagement ring of gold and jade that I could never have afforded without the steep (extremely steep!) discount they offered. Unfortunately our Sikh tenants decided to remain in India. Yolanda and I have wished too many times to count that we had paid more attention to them, that we had fostered stronger relations with them, so that when they were targeted as terrorists, they'd have felt comfortable confiding in us. But that didn't happen and we'd have to live with our regrets. We'd also have to find new second-floor tenants. And speaking of tenants, those in the Avenue B apartment building still live under Boris's thumb, though we've been given assurances that won't be the case for too much longer. I plan to be there the day Kallen and Boris get busted. I want to see them get their due, which I hope is a one-way ticket back to their homeland.

Yolanda and I met each other's eyes across the dancing circle and we blew loud smacky kisses at each other.

It was April in New York City and all was right with the world. With the little part of the world that I called mine.

ABOUT THE AUTHOR

Penny Mickelbury is the author of nine mystery novels in three successful series: The Phillip Rodriquez Mysteries, the Carol Ann Gibson Mysteries, and the Mimi Patterson/Gianna Maglione Mysteries. She also is an accomplished playwright, and her short stories have been included in several anthologies and collections, among them *Spooks, Spies and Private Eyes: Black Mystery, Crime and Suspense Fiction* (Paula Woods, editor), *The Mysterious Naiad* (Grier and Forrest, editor), and *Shades of Black: Original Mystery Fiction by African-American Writers* (Eleanor Taylor Bland, editors). She has contributed articles to several mystery magazines and publications. Mickelbury was a resident writer at Hedgebrook Women Writers Retreat, and she is the 2003 recipient of the Audre Lorde Estate Grant.